Praise f

"A great, lyrical portrait of a   recreation about a great time of history...and I enjoyed the sheer trip of it. Beautifully observed writing—the emotions in the story are true and moments of life are rendered with clarity."
> — Louis B. Jones, author of four *New York Times* Notable Books, including *Ordinary Money* and *Particles and Luck*

"The wonderful descriptions of Golden Gate Park and the Haight will delight anyone who loves San Francisco. The circus material is so very good, I kept wanting to come back to it. *Circus of the Sun* is rollicking good fun--a novel of a place and time beautifully illuminated by its own strangeness."
> —Michelle Richmond, author *New York Times* bestseller *The Marriage Pact, The Year of Fog, Golden State*

"More than a love story, this is a portrait of the city of San Francisco, from roller skaters and stoners in Golden Gate Park to an epic night of joy riding, culminating in a game of chicken as Jack drives the wrong way up Lombard Street. The prose leans towards the poetic, which results in gorgeous, Kerouac-ian vignettes...seeming like a movie played on fast forward... King does capture the late-1970s zeitgeist beautifully, though, weaving in references to gay rights, the Iran hostage crisis, racial tensions, and newfangled cordless phones and personal computers."
> —*Kirkus Reviews*

"Very profound... The first hundred pages reminded me of a cross between *Catcher in the Rye* and *Forgetting Elana*."
> —Patricia Morin, winner Playwrights Center of San Francisco's Best Short Play of 2019: "Hit List," Pushcart Nomination 2012: "Pa and the Pigeon Man"

"...King's novel is engagingly honest and sets forth a story-within-a-memoir so skillfully that you forget this is a work of fiction. ...Captures the ups and downs of an intense relationship deftly. ...Reminds me of Jack Kerouac's *The Subterraneans* with its poetry-leaning prose and rich dialogue."
> —Rick Dale, *The Daily Beat*

Circus of the Sun

Circus of the Sun

a Novel of San Francisco

by
J.Macon King

King Marketing Group

King Marketing Group

ISBN: 978-1-7343722-0-5

Circus of the Sun, while inspired by true experiences and personal impressions of the time and place, is a work of fiction. Incidents, dialogue and characters, with the exception of some known and public figures, are products of the author's imagination. When such figures appear, the situations, incidents, dialogues are fictional. The characters in this book are fictitious, and any resemblance to actual persons, living or dead, is purely coincidental.

NOTE: This story is set in 1978-1980 California. The attitudes and language of the narrator and characters regarding sex, race, culture, gender and drugs are contemporary to that pivotal shifting time and may be troubling to some.

Cover photo: J.Macon King

This book is dedicated to her

One Thousand Doves
Your rose-like kiss and gold embrace
The secret garden of your grace
beckons to your special place
The spiraling aura of heat and light
play a melody on lute and lyre
A scent of Shalimar in the night
After all is said then done
you and only you are the only one.

Boulevard of Broken Dreams
Miss your sharp smile,
your slooow red kiisss
Afraid I can't go on like this
Torn apart at the seams
on the Boulevard of Broken Dreams

My window's cracked, neon sign still glows
Morning traffic just started below
Love you more than I can fake,
Love you more than life it seems
The Boulevard of Broken Dreams

Jack Barnes

BOOK I

CHAPTER 1

Would she feel better knowing that it haunts me still? I didn't want to leave her. I had to. Yet, I betrayed her. Her final request to me, I refused.

From the Haight Ashbury, the vast green expanse of Golden Gate Park stretches to the endless Pacific. San Francisco's ultraviolet spectrum had beckoned dreamers like me who were eager for a new life. Free of restrictions, boundaries and repressions—free of the past. I lived in the Haight, birthplace of 1960's hippies and Flower Power, where Peter Pans and Tinkerbells preserved Neverland in a patchwork community.

It was 1979 and the time-warping revolutionary circus of the Summer of Love remained glowing. A vibrant mixture of creatives, hippies and newcomers still desired a piece of free love. My apartment was at the southeast corner of Golden Gate Park just four blocks away from Haight Street.

Throughout San Francisco, gay investors boldly gentrified bars, shops, cafés— entire neighborhoods. They created a mad non-stop nocturnal culture. Alchemy! Yet Dr. Caligari's somnambulant would soon arouse from his coffin to carry away the weak of flesh, and the weak of heart.

We were enticed yet repelled by excessive drugs, anything-goes sexuality, the charismatic radicals and cults that stirred our pot with dark arts. The War was over but peace would often only come to many as a final rest. The illusory halcyon daze of San Francisco's mad decade would later be called "The Season of the Witch."

\#

It's peculiar how my life changed in an instant with a rolling shiny ball, a ball that once in play, kept me moving to stay in the game, only partially under my control. Pinball. That's how it all started. That's how I encountered the blonde artist and her circus of an entourage. We would rebound, play, light up, *score*. Win a free game...or tilt.

#

I was twenty-three. My roommate had moved out as my girl-friend readied to take his place. Then Ariel left me. For good. After that, I couldn't deal with another roommate, another woman, or much of anything else.

Saturday. I arose early and looked out my Victorian apartment's window at the perfectly crappy foggy morning. Typical. Bummed that I would miss my Saturday morning karate class, I headed up the street at my long-legged brisk pace, past *Dirty Harry*-famed Kezar Stadium's high walls. It was the first day of my court-ordered atone-ment and I wanted to just get it over with.

The "New, planet-saving, Recycling Center of the Future," as my lawyer had called it, turned out to be just a number of rusty de-bris boxes and dumpsters in the potholed rear lot of the little-used Kezar stadium. Two older, ponytailed hippies, both in stained Osh-Kosh coveralls, stood at the entrance. I asked, "One of you Hank? I'm Jack Barnes..."

"Nobody here named Hank, man," replied the one with a clip-board.

"But the Judge ordered me to report to Hank for community ser-vice."

They grinned. "HANC's is Haight Ashbury Neighborhood Council—H A N C," one spelled out, making me feel like an idiot. "They organized and set this place up. I'm the supervisor."

"You must be one of the newcomers to the neighborhood," the other said.

I just stood there, so he let me know, "Well, we've both been here since the beginning—the Summer of Love in '67." Their eyes seemed to flashback on the good times. "You here then?"

"No, I wish. I've read *Ringolevio*."

"Emmett Grogan's book is true. But it doesn't mean it all hap-pened!" the supervisor said and they both laughed. "You missed out but I guess you're lucky."

"What? Why?"

"Cuz you'd be ten years older! And look all wrinkly like him," the supervisor said pointing to the other, who gave him the finger.

I immediately liked these Cheech and Chong characters.

"Haight District's still great," the assistant said. "Rents are still affordable, lots of cheap, good places to eat." He frowned. "Looks to be changing now, though. Gays' crystal-stairs money, their new bars—I-Beam, Deluxe, Traz..." He lowered his voice, "Hey, uh, Jack, what'r ya' in for?"

I hesitated, embarrassed. I did not tell them about my unreal courtroom appearance with the man who had maliciously brought assault and battery charges against me. I had wanted to fight the case but my lawyer acquaintance pled *nolo contendere* and requested community service. He knew of my background and had advised, "Forget it, Jack. Eat a Valium and act like you're goddamned Gandhi when you get in front of the judge."

"Hey." The supervisor's admonition snapped me back. "Ya' know you can't ask him that, man."

"But maybe he's the Zodiac Zebra Killer!" More guffaws.

The supervisor led me out to the bins for a rundown on the simplicities of the operation. "We do aluminum cans over there. You start here breaking down the cardboard and paper. Just throw the bottles in there."

"Throw?"

"Sure, break 'em up. No one cares what this stuff looks like at the other end 'cause it's all mulched or melted or mutated. 'Cept the deposit sody pop bottles, which you just stick in that burlap bag there and I'll, hee-hee, take care of personally."

A thin, worn hippie in an eye-watering, tie-dye shirt and three-point jester hat popped up out of a bin like a jack-in-the-box. "Hey, man, hey, man." He jumped down and adjusted the coat-hanger antenna on his boombox radio like a divining rod. He chanted, "KMEL, camel time."

"Any questions, be sure not to ask him."

"You mean Tie-dye?"

"Yep. Ha. That's a good name for him. That's about it. Got it, Jack?"

"Got it." I got the fact that I had been railroaded. The Judge had said, "Young man, I see your record is not exactly spotless; previous arrest for belligerence and brawling in Los Angeles, ... and, what's this? Disturbing the peace...at a funeral service!?" In addition to the community service the Judge had placed me on one-year probation. If I got busted getting into a fight, any trouble, I would go to jail. I couldn't even defend myself now. What bullshit.

Tie-dye munched trail mix while methodically unfolding cardboard boxes and stacking them neatly as if he believed Jose Cuervo, Mr. Clean, and Jolly Green Giant themselves would glue the boxes back together for reuse. Tie-dye appeared to be an "acid casualty"—someone who had "broke on through to the other side" so often that they never completely came down.

I relieved some anger at the kangaroo court system, and made up for my missed martial arts class, by axe kicking the bigger boxes open, stomping them and throwing them like opponents up into the big bin. Tie-dye gave the boxes a concerned look but wisely said nothing about mistreatment of the cardboard.

Recycling turned out to be more interesting than I thought. People handed over a mini-snapshot of their lives: what they read, bought, ate, drank, and how much. A goateed man recycled two thick North Star computer cartons. I told him that I had never seen a personal computer.

"Check one out. They are the future."

Around noon the grey fog lifted as if on cue with the arrival of a woman wearing a snug yellow summer dress and a goldenrod shawl. The supervisor said something to her, pointing my way. She glided toward me carrying tattered Macy's shopping bags in each hand and a Moroccan bag slung over her shoulder. She was a few years older than me, probably twenty-five or six, with long, fluffy, sun-blonde hair. She radiated voluptuous sensuality *and* innocence, a potent combination, making every man in the lot gawk. In me, she triggered a restless longing, which I tried to ignore, busying myself with a bin. I had not dated since the accident almost a year ago.

"Good morning, Hank. I have something for you."

"Aaah, those two were having fun with us. I'm not really Hank, but I can help you." I breathed in her scented mixture of paint and oils and when I stood, recognition slowly filled me as I realized how much she must tone down her looks for her job at Stanyan Street Supernatural Foods. I said, "Oh, it's you, Health Food Store girl."

She appraised me with uniquely colorful eyes and promptly gave a rejoinder. "Hello, recycle boy. I'm actually heading to work. After I change clothes." She giggled. "I wanted to check you out for the store. They should start recycling there." She set down her shopping bags, one overflowing with sheets of paper and the other containing a box of vitamin bottles mixed with expensive-looking wine and brandy bottles.

"Oh, I didn't drink all these." She seemed embarrassed. "They're from my salon."

"Good booze for a beauty salon."

"I didn't mean that kind of salon." She watched as I stomped on a box. "That looks like fun."

I motioned to her. "Share in the fun and we can bring your old box back to life."

She looked at me oddly. "I'd better not. I'm late for work."

She walked away. I realized my remarks could have been misinterpreted. When I lifted her cardboard box, the corner split and crumpled sheets of artwork scattered across the black asphalt. So, she was an artist. That explained the oil scent. Why would she throw these out? Her entire persona intrigued me.

The day eventually wrapped up. The great, smoking diesel trucks drove in and chugged off with the bins. Over by the tall stadium wall Tie-dye and the assistant motioned me to join them to smoke a fat joint, which I declined. One Saturday down, three to go.

I walked home through Golden Gate Park along JFK Drive. Seeing a number of joggers, I began to jog on a paved path. On the grass, a hippie with a guitar beseeched his pot-smoke-enwreathed, dandelion-haired girl to need "Somebody to Love." In quick counterpoint, Donna Summer's distorted "Bad Girls" boomed behind me. A group of women roller skaters whizzed past in colorful short shorts, butterfly antennae and suggestive kneepads. Their wheels were silent, unlike the pink tutu girl's blaring boombox. Skating had made a comeback, the old gravel-grabbing, knee-scabbing, screechy metal wheels replaced with smooth polyurethane. Golden Gate Park was becoming a freewheeling disco roller rink.

I stopped to stretch on a grassy knoll by The Children's Playground with the colorful old carousel. Happy young families, a mother and father holding their daughter on a giraffe, a man holding a wide-eyed kid on a horse, a brave redheaded boy alone on a lion... Round and round, up and down as the soothing calliope music played, a pony, an ostrich, a tiger, a brass pole, a pony, an ostrich... I drifted back, remembering how excited I had been to enter the Big Top that day, to see the costumed performers and their dangerous stunts. I imagined their exotic lives behind the scenes and beyond.

#

Uncle and Mother had taken me to the circus when I was thirteen. The circus perfume of cotton candy, corndogs, greasepaint, monkeys and musky big cats, intoxicated me. Calliope music floated through the humid air. I no longer felt like a child, although I wished to remain one.

The circus was the best entertainment for a Midwestern town and had traditionally been one of the special outings with just me and my father. All that had ended abruptly. Pop, pop, pop! On hustling arcade row, I wanted to try my aim in the shooting gallery but Uncle grabbed the rifle, popping three balloons and winning a small stuffed animal. He tossed the lion to me while I wasn't looking and it fell to the dirt.

At the sideshow "Freaks, Oddities and Human Curiosities," a creepy sign proclaimed, "See the Two-Headed Baby." Uncle was excited, insisted that we enter, while Mother was appalled and refused.

A fat man sat on a little stool at the entrance. "S'allright. I'll keep an eye on her."

As Uncle and I went up the steps, I turned to see the fat man's eyes walk all over the beauty of my waiting mother. In the booth's dim lights, intrigued yet repelled, I examined the macabre freaks of nature—the albino turtle, the Cyclops-eyed rattlesnake, the hideous vampire bat... There it was. The Two-Headed-Baby! The Two-Headed-Baby was tiny, shriveled, piteous. And very dead. Preserved in a murky three-gallon pickle jar grave. Strangely agitated, I peered closely. It looked like me. Suddenly the creature moved. The faces floated right to my face. I hollered and stumbled out the exit.

Uncle guffawed. "Got you, scaredy-cat." He poked his face out of the door. "I shoved the shelf with my shoulder."

CHAPTER 2

Monday, I fired up my old Honda CB750, wiped the foggy dew off the custom flame-painted gas tank, grabbed the high ape-hanger bars and timed the green lights on 19th Avenue out to my job. As jobs go, my management gig at the Student Bookstore on San Francisco State University campus was cool. Especially since there was a pinball arcade in the basement level.

I entered the Student Union building, which looked exactly like two sinking ships. I walked into the odd, below-ship-deck angled Book Store. Rumor had it that the architect drew inspiration from playing *Battleship* while on LSD. As the sleepy-eyed student workers moseyed in I directed them to tasks. I had started as a student part-timer myself and last fall had been promoted to full time assistant manager, based partly on my "returns" skills—convincing publishers to accept returns of unsold textbooks well past the ninety-day cutoff. Pallets of these "write-offs" had filled an entire storage room before I took the matter personally. I didn't like that the books were unwanted.

I worked all morning trying not to think. Yet I did think of her, I did think of pinball, and I did think of my uncle. Those last thoughts stabbed at the recesses of my brain. On my lunch break, I walked downstairs to the Union Arcade, aching for my pinball fix. My boss's words from a few weeks before, restrained me: "You want to keep your job, Jack? No more stupid pinball."

Two students were playing my favorite pinball machine. Jealousy filled me. *Superman* was "The One" that year, an oversized and powerful pinball game with striking artistic graphics. My boyhood hero seemed to fly out of the backglass. Superman could not be hurt and could feel no pain. The raucous bells and buzzes from a dozen pinball machines sang to me, the flashing lights and sounds—physically thrilling. The arcade reminded me of the circus midway. I had comforted myself with pinball since my girlfriend left me. But now I was hurting. Mr. Stone, the cigar-smoking man had ruined one of my life's joys.

I wandered out to the wide sunny quad where Ariel and I had shared many lunches and plans. I thought of her last September, running toward me across the grass in her crisp SFSU Volleyball uniform, yelling, "Jack, I got it. I got the job at City Hall."

With a high-cheekbone-lovely face, Ariel was a total fox with athletic animal energy and a Sagittarius's unabashed laugh. A few weeks before that she had pouted to me, "No one takes me seriously." She returned with her long, wavy, blonde hair bobbed and tinted brown, wearing a new white blouse and dark blazer. Apparently toning down her Neutrogena Norwegian looks to a more boyish appearance had helped her career path in San Francisco.

"Catch me quick!" She jumped at me in our private game to wrap her sleek legs around my waist as I spun her. We both had good news to share that day. I told her I had just been promoted to a manager position at the bookstore.

Now, morose in memories, I wandered back to the Book Store. In the book returns storage room I locked the door and hid away. I was lucky to have kept my "career" after the pinball incident so I renewed my dedication to my duties. I leaned back on the big stack of McGraw-Hill business textbooks. McGraw was tight on returns but they had the money. The company had just bought *Byte* magazine. I would call them again. As I munched my sandwich I metaphorically compared the drab-brown business books to the colorful literature and art departments volumes, a smaller stack, since they were easily returned.

On rainy days I had sometimes brought Ariel here. We'd share our lunches and dreams. She liked to describe how we first met, South of Market at Hamburger Mary's, as "a delectable merger of pheromones, testosterones and hormones." It had been almost a year since she was gone and our dreams were over. Why was I so melancholy today? My mind shot straight to where it had really been aching to go—the blonde artist.

I pulled the rolled-up papers from my backpack. I fanned out and smoothed the sheets. Her artwork. The figures and designs were metaphysical with a dark-edged reality of modernism. In one, the quixotic gold and black elongated, Picassoesque guitar-shape lovers amidst grape leaves were splattered with drops of red paint and as my nose confirmed, red wine. Another was a jazzy urban street scene of overhead wires as a musical staff, pigeons as the notes, canary-winged yellow taxis, and trumpet shaped traffic lights. The next sheet was a collage of torn current-event clippings obfuscated by antique typewriter's round keys and silhouettes. A fourth contained images of war machinery with legs and teeth, slanted eyeballs in tunnels, flames, and Daliesque dripping bullets. I was compelled by her strange dark drawings. Why had they all been dumped? Why would so much passion be rejected? Despite my intent to not go out with women, the artist intrigued and mystified me.

The storeroom doorknob rattled and a young woman's voice cajoled from outside the door. "Jack?" Rattle. "I know you're in there." Sigh. "It's me." A cute bookstore cashier. "Hey, what do you think the lyrics of *Hotel California* really mean?" A pause. "Jack, I want to invite you over for some din-din."

Why did my descents to the lone wolf state have the reverse effect of my intentions, rendering me more appealing? I opened my prescription bottle and ate a Valium. I ignored her as I had found a home-cooked dinner invitation, female or male, implied more. She was a sweet underclassman with a crush. How could she know what love is?

#

Under the Big Top, Mother, Uncle and I watched the tumbling clowns. A young uniformed boy had guided us to the best front row bench in the stands. Uncle was rich. We bit into perfect-looking caramel apples, which beneath their sweetness, belied a hard and sour taste.

A spotlight shone hot on the ringmaster in his red jacket and top hat. With his whip he directed our attention to a buxom lady garbed in sequins and fishnets. She flung sharp knives and hand axes to split melons and apples. The audience buzzed in shock when she revealed her final target—her male assistant, now bound and spinning vertically on a red-spiraled wheel. As her knife penetrated an inch from the man's crotch, Uncle jested, "That was a close shave."

In Ring Three, Rollo the Romanian Strongman was a barrel-chested giant, dressed in a blue and yellow bodysuit. With massive furry arms he lifted an impossibly heavy barbell overhead with two women dangling and spinning from the ends by their teeth. The crowd cheered Rollo as the women cartwheeled off and two large roustabouts shuffled in with a long steel rod. The Strongman took the rod, held it aloft, and with obvious effort slowly bent it in half. He tossed it clanging against the barbell, demonstrating that the rod was real. I would have given anything to be that strong. I bet nobody could hurt Rollo.

The Strongman lumbered up to the audience and flexed his muscles right in front of me. His huge bearded face was intimidating but his smile reassured me. Rollo formed a massive bicep and gestured that I stand up and do the same. I shyly held up my arm as he made a big show of measuring my boyish arm muscle with his finger and thumb. The crowd laughed. Surprisingly gentle for a man of such immense strength, his eyes lingered on my arm before glaring at my uncle. I tugged my sleeve down to hide the ugly purple bruises. Rollo displayed a spike-sized nail and bent it into a miniature horseshoe, mugging for the crowd. He held the nail in front of Uncle. Uncle reached for it but Rollo bestowed it on me instead. In a thick accent he spoke.

"For good luck, buddy."

#

The rest of the week crawled by at the Bookstore with late shipments and professor complaints. I found myself strangely anticipating my forced community service. Saturday morning, I was at the recycling center early.

"There's that mutt again," the supervisor yelled.

It took a moment to realize he didn't mean me. A collarless beagle mutt was sniffing around the bins. He peed on a stack of *San Francisco Examiners*. "Certainly gives new meaning to yellow journalism," I said.

Tie-dye sighed. "Poor dog. Poor lost, lost dog."

I whistled and called, "Beagle Boy, here boy."

"I wish we could recycle that dog," the supervisor said. "Every time he comes in here he just pees and howls."

On signal, Beagle Boy howled, *Arroo*. I took a handful of Tie-dye's trail mix and called, "Beagle Boy." The floppy-eared hound skeptically came near. "Hey, Buddy. Where you going?" I placed the food out and the skinny stray approached, sniffing. I scratched him on his neck as he nibbled.

"Well, look at that. Jack's the first person to be able to touch him." Beagle Boy glared at the supervisor.

I sang a few bars, an impromptu parody of Bette Midler. "They made him blow a beagle for his Uncle Sam. It really brought him down because he could not jam. A root, a toot, a toodlie-a-da-toot. He toots eight lines on the bar in boogie rhythm. The Boogie Woogie *Beagle* Boy of Company B."

"You have a great voice, man, a great voice!" Tie-dye exclaimed. "What band you with?"

"I'm not," I replied. Beagle Boy reminded me of my childhood dog and I immediately wanted the half-breed stray. Too bad I couldn't have a dog in my apartment. I spoke harshly to him. "Looks like your ma and pa were not very well matched, either. Fucking marriage made in hell!" At my angry tone he ran off.

When the early-afternoon slowdown arrived, I felt restless. I kept looking toward the entrance. The artist finally returned carrying bags of papers and bottles. She wore a dressy red top with gold lamé pants. Perhaps she had been out all night? Jealousy seeped into my heart like a chemical. Her looks and vibe reminded me of a performer—a memory from the circus. Her gold necklace and earrings glinted as she walked right up to me. This woman had dimensions well beyond my first impressions.

"Hello, Sunshine," I said.

"Volunteering to help save the earth is very admirable. You are at the forefront of the residential recycling movement."

I was touched that her compliment sounded rehearsed. She seemed so happy about my saving the earth that I couldn't tell her it was either this or jail. "Thanks. It's something I feel compelled to do." I took her box and asked her, "If you're recycling more of your art I have a special place for that."

"You peeked."

"Sorry, the box busted. Why'd you toss them? I thought they were suitable for framing."

"Thanks, but those were just some sketches I did to help me through... some difficult nights. Those projects are finished now. You should see my new work."

I nodded, not knowing how to respond.

"I really need to go." She turned but stayed. She switched to a lilting voice. "How does this recycling work, anyhow?" As I liberally elaborated on the simple program, she feigned interest before asking, "May I stomp mine this time?"

"Certainly." I respectfully emptied her papers and set the box down sideways, with some other small ones. She placed a black ankle boot on the box and hopped up and down. Inspired, Tie-dye twisted the radio dial, crackling to Santana's "Black Magic Woman." He cranked it up. With Carlos's evocative guitar gliding in, D minor over voodoo polyrhythmic percussion, her stomps quickly evolved into flamenco dance steps flourished by serpentine arms. Time slowed as I beheld her hypnotic dance. She tripped and I reached for her. Our hands clasped, our temperatures shot up, and she fell into me. She smelled of peaches and paint, and as we held each other and our eyes met, like, Did you feel that, too? I wanted to Rhett Butler her up into the big bin, hiding us away under all that cardboard. Applause sounded from around the lot and Tie-dye called, "10, 10, 10."

I looked at him, and he said, "*10*, like that new movie. She's 10 on a 10 scale."

We shrugged and laughed. Feelings that I had not experienced for the past year, since Ariel, welled from deep inside. The sensations were as disquieting as they were irresistible. I moved away from her, uneasy. "You are something special, aren't you?"

"You're something, too." Inhaling deeply, she asked, "Who are you really, recycle boy?"

"My name is Jack." She was flushed and glowing and I couldn't help but desire that look from her again.

"Jack. Ja-ack." Her open-mouthed pronunciation of my name made me tingle. "I'm Bretta."

Bretta, Bretta, Bretta.

A car beep-beeped in front of the entry to the potholed lot. A classic "Bathtub" Porsche. It could only be for her. "I'm so-o late for my friend's gallery preview. That was fun." She turned to leave. "Ciao."

"Bye."

After a few steps, she looked back. I still wasn't sure if I was ready for this. I resisted. She didn't. "What do you do, Jack?" Bretta wanted to know.

I gave my trademark smart-alecky answer. "Whatever I want, Bretta."

"Well, Jack, do you want to come to a party tonight?"

"To a party, or to a party with Bretta?"

She retrieved Magic Markers from her bag, chose yellow and blue and looked around. Bretta extended her hand once more, and I hesitated as if afraid of touching something hot. She gently pulled my hand close to her considerable bosom. I was right. She was.

Writing her number with a design, she signed my arm like a canvas. She squeezed my hand and soon the Porsche vroomed her off.

The crew thanked me for the floorshow. I complimented Tie-dye on his DJ-ing, and he told me, "You're smooth, man, you're smooth."

"You want to burn one after work with us?" the supervisor asked. I passed again.

Back at my apartment, I grabbed a beer and sat down at the round table in the bay window overlooking the street corner. I thought if I ran into damn liar Stone again, I should thank him for getting me my community service sentence. Perhaps that's how life works—that you have to get a bad in order to get a good. And if you have too much good, you get a bad to wake your ass up.

I picked up my Ibanez acoustic guitar and figured out the chords to "Take Me to the River." I about had it before miss-fingering the transition to the bridge. Discouraged, I laid my guitar down. I counted my cash. Twelve bucks. I hoped that was enough for tonight. My stare switched from my olive-green phone to my yellow-and-blue arm. The swirling numbers filled with portent. At that moment, my instinct signaled that this call would change everything. The well-known Haight Fates had conspired for me to meet the incandescent artist who might renew my life. Fittingly, at a recycling center. My throat constricted. I fished a pill out of its little brown bottle and chewed the harsh alkaline bitterness. Twisting the phone's curly cord around my finger I dialed, watching the clear plastic rotary slowly spiral back counterclockwise. I heard the pickup, Spanish guitar music, a muffled voice, something hitting the floor. I said, "Hello, hello, is Bretta…." I moved to hang up. A giggle and Bretta finally answered breathily.

"Oh, Jack? We must first absolutely meet for a drink. There's this no-name bar near my place. Jack, I can't wait to introduce you to my girlfriend."

CHAPTER 3

The "no name" bar really did display no discernible name. It was a fine night and I stood out front for a moment, watching it get dark, watching the few signs light up, the signals turn from yellow to red to green, chatty couples sauntering by, solitary figures wandering past, dog walkers rushing to the tiny nearby park, dogs straining from their masters' control, and a pair of cropped-haired women trying to keep their hands off each other until they made it down the block to the safety of Maud's bar. I went into the no-name and sat at the far end. All I had just witnessed mirrored my emotions—caution, stop, go. "Introduce you to my girlfriend" still worried me.

Bretta appeared—European elegant in a checked brown tweed fitted blazer, sunflower blouse, flowing hand-painted vermillion silk scarf and a dark beret. Her vivaciousness seemed to light up the dingy bar. She was alone.

Close up, her porcelain skin and upper lip mole drew me in. Shimmering makeup of pool-cue-chalk-blue highlighted golden eyes. I was mindful not to stare but not to look away. I ordered drinks from the unobtrusive, maybe Persian, bartender. She told me, "I like your enthusiasm—about recycling." In mid-sentence, Bretta would slip into a girlish voice and mannerisms, which would be appealing—rather than annoying.

"Yes, I am now passionately into recycling," I joked. "So, besides art, umm, what are you into?" I eyed the door, still half-expecting her girlfriend.

"I am into..." She flashed a smile."...passionate living."

I couldn't keep a straight face and we giggled and we looked deep into each other's eyes. She turned a little red so I changed the subject. "I have an idea, Sunshine," I said. "We could bring attention to the recycling movement by doing a performance art piece. We'll take all the boxes that come into the Center on a Saturday and you'll do extemporaneous art on them. My crew will build a big stack of the boxes like Hollywood stuntmen use, and at sunset, you'll light a match to them, and I'll somersault down on the burning boxes from the Kezar Stadium wall. We'll call it, let's see, *Circus of the Sun*."

She laughed. "You're crazy."

I nodded. "Yes."

We walked to the nearby party where Bretta briefly introduced me to the hostess and host and, the other shoe finally dropping, to "my best girlfriend Robin." Bretta put her arm around Robin. "Robin has sold much of my artwork at her marvelously perfect art gallery, Galleria Di Belle Arti."

Robin, husky and shy, gave an odd laugh-snort as her large brown eyes peered up at me through oversize dark-framed glasses. A curly-headed brunette, Robin wore knee-high boots and an earth-colored outfit, and she smelled of chocolate, and no—yes, she smelled faintly of hay. After the intro, without explaining why, Robin backed away from us and bobbed her head, saying, "I am leaving you now." Although she still looked at me she continued, "Bretta, I'll be back later to pick you up." She backed up all the way to the door, still bobbing.

"...Comes bob, bob, bobbin' aloong..." I sang. Bretta laughed.

While others passed a bong of "Here today, gone to Maui" in another room, Bretta and I sat on the couch in the living room by ourselves and drank the Korbel brandy and cream she brought but nobody else cared for. The party was small and boring; no wonder Robin left. The place was a standard-issue Victorian flat with narrow rooms over-decorated with incongruously large pieces of modern furniture and hanging art. Overwatered ferns grew yellow-tipped in macramé pot hangers above water-stained spots on the oak floor. A fluffy pumpkin colored cat dozed atop an overstuffed chair cum scratching post, blinking a rheumy eye at me. Dusty symphonic LPs dropped and skipped on a record changer. Bad stereo gear and record care irritated me. The modern paintings were embarrassingly suggestive—a floral stamen and pistil as near-human genitalia. Robin's gallery? As my initial bravado waned our date began to feel awkward.

I tried to break the silence with an insightful critique, "This place certainly is..."

Bretta bubbled, "Isn't it? You know, my friend Francine designed this interior." She lowered her voice. "When the hostess inherited money."

"Ah." I felt the familiar flair of anxiety. I confessed, "I like you, I do... so I should tell you... I split up with my girlfriend a while

back... and I'm not looking for a relationship." Such a dumb thing to
say. I half rose, ready to bail, but Bretta pulled me back down. Her
eyes sparkled gold. She told me, "That's all right. I have a lover."

Here it comes, I thought. I fingered a cigarette or joint burn hole
in the couch. She said, "His name is Benjamin."

I was oddly relieved on two counts that she had a boyfriend.
Bretta leaned toward me. "What happened with your girlfriend?"

"She left me. End of story."

"I just want to get to know you." Bretta placed a hand on my
arm. "What is the story, Jack?"

"I mean she's out of my life. She's gone. But she's not."

"Please. Tell me about her."

"Ariel was...I just don't talk about this." I started to get up and
again she pulled me back. She looked at me with those eyes and I
gave in. "Very smart, a good athlete. Double major, psych and bio-
chem. She didn't seem the pocket calculator type. So I asked her
why? She told me she wanted to discover—no, more than that, she
needed to know—our essence, what life means, where we could go.
Not philosophically or spiritually, but scientifically—what or where
was possible."

"I'm impressed. Go on."

"She wanted to get to the heart of change, so she scored a part-
time job at City Hall in Mayor Moscone's new environmental office." I paused while Bretta refreshed our drinks. "You remember,
November last year, there was the Jonestown massacre. Then, back
to back, only nine days later, Supervisor Dan White shot, murdered,
Moscone and Milk right in City Hall."

"It was terrible," she said, shaking her head. "I did some
sketches about that. Very dark. San Francisco went numb."

"Ariel knew the three men, spoke to them regularly, and she
saw the pair bleeding on the floor. She could have been killed."

"I can't imagine."

"Sure you want to hear this?" Bretta leaned closer so I continued. "Ariel was depressed, the stormy weather didn't help. I wanted
to take her to the movie, *Days of Heaven*."

"Beautiful. Richard Gere and Sam Shepard in love with the
same lucky woman."

"Yes. This day, the sky is dark, the rain is shooshing, the wind
is whooshing, and I'm driving her red Mustang through Golden Gate
Park. All at once the sun breaks through black sky and she changes

her mind and wants to do something to honor her dead associates. In a spiritual place she knows. She has me stop and we walk through the woods. In a glen, under these big oaks, is the Goddess Altar."

"I've never heard of this. Where is it?"

"Monarch Bear Grove. Not too far from where we met. It's a secret spot where this giant grizzly bear used to live, and there's all these old stone blocks from a Spanish abbey left over from William Randolph Hearst. Ariel tells me the grove was starting to be used as a sacred Druid shrine. I see the little tributes—flowers, shells, feathers. For a moment a sun ray probes the swaying treetop limbs to light up the Goddess Altar, and my Goddess Ariel...it is...enrapturing...magical." Bretta's artist eyes seem to picture the scene. "All at once the storm kicks back in with big gusts whistling like a mad teakettle. Eerie. Like a warning."

"A warning?"

I nod. "Ariel grabs my hand and says, 'The Circles turn, life and death dance together.' She says, 'I think the Goddess is saying, I'm beautiful, and this is my garden, but you still need to be aware.' I said, Then let's get out of here. In a tempest of rain, we run back to her Mustang and I'm a little weirded out and take off." I took a drink. "This truck...races through the stop sign, about to ram into *her* side of the car. I gun it, spin it to avoid a T-bone, miraculously avoid the truck, which takes off, but we run off the pavement and slide in mud. And *wham*, hit this big oak tree. The front fender is mashed up but we're OK."

"Thank goodness. That was lucky."

"That's what we thought. We're laughing now, that we're so lucky, and we...hug. Ariel says, 'You know that I love you desperately. But you hurt poor Seattle Slew.' That's what she called her Mustang. She says, 'Better let the Goddess drive now.' So I get out of the car... so she can scoot across and doesn't have to get any wetter." I took a big breath.

"Go on, Jack."

"As soon as I get out...hear this dreadful... groaning... sound. And this monstrous ugly thing, a giant grey, scaly foot...stomps down onto the car."

"No. What the...?"

"The roof of the car crushes down on Ariel. Glass flies. I reach for her to try to pull her, and I push her...but I can't. Ariel's pinned in...this red mangled metal, she's bleeding, her brown hair stained red...and her blood crawls all over me."

"What was it?"

"This huge, fucking dead tree limb. I try to move the limb. Of course, I can't. I'm not strong enough...I'm not like Ro...a circus strongman." We both took a drink of the Korbel. "She can barely breathe, she can scarcely speak, but she whispers something to me. I tell her I have to go for help. She grasps my hand but I pull away. I run through the mud, the bushes, looking up in swaying trees, fearing more falling limbs, running into things...my heart pumping, lungs burning, out to the main road. I'm madly in the middle of Lincoln Avenue, soaked, muddy, bloody, running up and down in the storm, and cars honk and swerve, a car almost creams me, and I have to jump out of the way. And no one stops. No one stops to help me! I'm frantic. I run back to the Mustang. And her brown eyes stare through me." I stared at Bretta, who clutches at the flowing scarf around her neck. "It's too late. Ariel's already...left me."

"Oh, my God, Jack."

I took a big breath. "I told her, I'm sorry... baby, I'm so sorry..." As Bretta placed an arm around me, I dropped my eyes. "It should have been me in there. It should have been me. I walked away without a scratch."

"No, Jack, it wasn't meant to be."

"I've heard all that from my shri...the counselor. Then why? Why? In silences of the night...I still can hear Ariel... whispering that to me."

"What? What did she whisper, Jack?"

I slumped down, breathing hard, and Bretta held me. "She said, 'I see it.' She said, 'I see it. Stay with me. Stay.'"

We sat silently for a few moments in contrast to the lively chatter and laughter from the other rooms. "But I didn't. Her final request... I betrayed her. I left her...just like I left my...I fucking left my Goddess...to die all alone."

Bretta looked in shock. The record stuck at that moment, click, click, click, click. I realized that this had been a mistake to pretend to be normal. I went over to click eject on the stereo to drop the next LP. A movie soundtrack played.

"Look, Bretta, I'm sorry to ruin your evening. I should have stuck with the first-date superficial bullshit."

"No, I pressed you. I'm glad you were able to be open with me." She tugged my hand to sit back next to her. "You had to make an impossible choice, Jack. A *Sophie's Choice*."

"Oh, that new novel. I haven't read it."

"You should. Written through the eyes of a writer. Your story...I was just flashing on my favorite dancer, Isadora Duncan. She fingered her scarf again. She was so free, so liberated, so unconventional, kind of like your girlfriend. She was born here in San Francisco, you know? Sadly, her scarf became tangled in the rear wheel of a sports car. It broke her neck."

"Jesus. Let's talk about something else. Tell me about your art."

"Art should be seen and not heard."

I forced a smile and determined to change my mood. Bretta deserved better. "O.K. Hey, I bet I can guess your sign."

"Bet what?" she asked.

"A kiss."

"An 'I'm not looking for a relationship' kiss?"

"Yes, exactly right. In three guesses," I said.

"All right."

"Yield?" She shook her head. "Curves Ahead." She laughed and shook again. "A Gemini."

"Wow. How did you know? Isadora Duncan was a Gemini. Is that how I gave it away?"

"Lucky guess."

"I guess so. How?" she asked. The LP's next track was a romantic tune.

"Hey, pay up first." She kissed me—a very nice kiss. I told her, "I have a confession." I waited for her to look concerned. "I used to be a professional guesser. I worked the 'Fool the Guesser' booth in a Circus."

"You're fooling me. Really? You were with a circus?"

"I was young. A roustabout laborer first. When I was a little older, I was promoted to 'A&S operator'—for guessing Age and Scale, meaning weight. I developed my own particular version called 'Guess Your Sign.' I'd make them laugh. Like I did with you. A guy with long hair was 'Stay off the Grass.'"

She laughed. "What sign are you?"

"I'm Leo the Lion-Hearted."

She stroked my thick dark hair. "I like your curly mane, not too long, not too short. And, I think you're very smart. How did you get so smart?"

"When I ran, uh, left home, I spent a lot of time in libraries."

"Hmm. How was your childhood?"

"Short."

She made a sad face. "I liked staying at home and drawing, and playing with dolls, being cozy. My brother and I would build forts and castles and things. It was fun." Her face lit up. "I know. Let's make your childhood longer. Let's play another circus game."

"I know how to erect a tent."

"Now, that's entertainment," she said. I grabbed some blankets and bedcovers the host had left out for overnight crashers and directed Bretta to help drape them from the sofa to a chair to the coffee table, to make a covered playhouse. She joked about needing a pole for our circus tent and we crawled in. Her eyes flashed, eyes that changed from hazel to dark gold seemingly dependent on her mood. We snuggled up and I rubbed my face into her long, sun-maiden hair. She turned her face to mine and we made out, experimentally, like junior high-schoolers. She reached down to me and her eyes widened. I moved her hand off. Why? she asked with her expression.

"Because we are playing kids. And kids shouldn't have sex." She appeared both surprised and impressed that I restrained myself.

"This can be our circus big top," she suggested, "or it can be our little fairytale magic castle."

"Yes. Any fantasy in a storm."

"I've been to the real one, in Hollywood, the Magic Castle, an elite restaurant for magicians. My dad took me." Her eyes drifted before focusing back to me.

After holding each other in our tent for a while, Bretta confided to me in her lilting voice, "I'll tell you my fairytale castle story. When I was a little princess, my father, who was away in L.A. working most of the time, gave me Barbie and Ken dolls for my birthday. I loved Ken the best. I soon talked Mother into buying me four more. I liked changing Ken's clothes and putting on their contractor and cowboy outfits. I really liked their little suits and ties, too. One time when my parents were both gone, I disrobed all my dolls and painted clothes on them with Magic Markers."

"Yeah?"

"I thought I was being artistic, but didn't realize that it would ruin them."

"What happened? You get in trouble?"

"I never told anyone this before. This is a secret, all right?"

"Yes. Our secret."

"I took them into my father's garden—where Mother lives now; she has all these peacocks out there—and found the perfect special spot, maybe like your Druid shrine."

She paused so long, I had to tease, "And what, they all married Barbie and had genital-less sex?"

Bretta looked at me like I was a dentist drilling into her nerve. "No. No. I buried them all in the garden."

"Whoa. Wait a minute. You buried your Ken dolls?"

"Well, along with my Barbie. I told my father that they ran away from home. I was going to dig them up later. I thought, I don't know, that they would be back to the way they were—you know, colors rubbed away... healed. But when I did...I dug, and dug, and could never...and I tried, really, I did...but I could never find them again." Bretta choked up and I kissed her eyelids.

"I don't know what happened to them, Jack!"

I gave Bretta tickling butterfly kisses until she was happy again. Despite a few partiers wandering in asking, "What's going on in there?" and "Are you guys tripping?" we continued talking and kissing for a long time without our magic castle being invaded. We heard an odd laugh-snort, followed by Robin's voice. "Oh, Bret—ta. I'm here to drive you to North Beach to meet Benjamin."

Bretta looked at me, looked away, looked back. She crept out while I stayed hiding in our play tent. I silently counted backwards from one hundred, waiting for my hardness to subside.

Having confessed to Bretta, I felt somehow at peace. I was ready for this. For her. Through the bedcovers, I asked, "Do you want to get together next week?"

"Oh, Jack. I can't."

Of course. Just my luck.

"I have to fly down to L.A."

I needed to persuade her. "Well, come to my party next Saturday night. I'll have something very special for you." I held my breath.

"Bret—ta," Robin called.

Bretta poked her head back in the tent. "In that case, yes. But I may have to bring my—Benjamin." Bretta poked her head back in the tent. "I have some time tomorrow. You simply *must* call me in the morning." Those pool-chalk eyes came at mine. She gave me a last lingering kiss, then she was gone.

What had I gotten myself into? I had to plan a non-existent party. I also had to start counting all over again before I could leave the fairytale warmth and walk out into the foggy night chill.

CHAPTER 4

On that day of My Pinball Mishap in the San Francisco State basement arcade, I had lost most of my balls on the first game. In the second game I became the "Pinball Wizard," riding a high, dancing with the *Superman* machine that felt alive and prescient, both of us struggling, vying for control. The silver ball raced up the spinner lanes "faster than a speeding bullet" and rolled across the colorful red playfield targets. Propelled by the flippers, active bumpers, slingshots, and nudges, my pinball rang bells, spun around, and scored points. My dance moves had to be subtle and nuanced enough to slow the ball down, to gently control the timing, to catch and hold the ball on one of my flippers, to pause and pick my best target before shooting the ball to new heights. After the flip, I would bring this adversary, this partner, this thing that consumed me, almost to the edge of tilt.

Although video games like *Asteroids* and *Space Invaders* were gaining digital domination, we diehards enjoyed pinball as a physical workout. My hands would clutch the machine as if speeding my motorcycle through hills and maneuvering sharp curves, until I was damp with sweat.

I jacked off the spring-tensioned plunger a couple of times and confidently hammered it with my fist. The whirling silver ball shot out of the shoot "more powerful than a locomotive." Hanging poised for a second, unsure which way to go, I dropped, barely in control, banging against bumpers, rails, and targets. With red lights flashing and a rush similar to a circus clamor and fireworks, my senses launched into overdrive. Keeping everything in motion with split-second instinctual decisions I fought to postpone the inevitable—when the silver ball, like a live mercurial thing, would lose momentum, and plummet down, down, down.

Finally, I ascended into the zone. The *Superman* game was primed to absolutely light up and I skillfully trapped the escaping ball with my flipper, juggling it over to the other flipper. My adrenaline was racing, anticipating the explosions and shock-like rush of the BANG indicating the high score and free game. My trigger fingers were ready for more. I aimed at the last drop target on the extra ball and shot. Suddenly, smoke wafted across *Superman's* glass top.

Right next to me, an older balding man played the *Evel Knievel* machine. He had lit up a huge cigar. The man spoke to me right in the middle of my shot. "In my student days at Princeton, we still played pachinko machines." He had an anxious sexual vibe. I didn't really care that he was hitting on me. I'd been hit on plenty. What rankled me was...he reminded me of my uncle. Whom I detested. And feared. I struggled to stop my ball from dropping down the drain.

"You're an engaging young man. What's your name? My name is Ralston Stone. What's your major?"

I glanced at him. Stone was solidly built, a chimney of a man. I blew him off. "There really ought to be a law against smoking cigars in places like this." I knew very well laws often don't protect the victims.

Stone gave a lascivious grin. "Right. Well, perhaps we should go elsewhere?" He brushed against my rear as he stepped to my other side. "I have something really nice, to brighten your day, if you know what I mean." He pulled a corner of a baggie from his pants pocket.

"No, thanks."

Undeterred, he pulled out some folded bills, wagging them next to his unzipped fly. Stone's smoke clouded over my game like Kryptonite.

Not only was he ruining my game, he was offering me money like I was a Polk Street whore-boy. "Get out of here, will ya'?" I told him.

His demeanor contorted and he leaned over my back, rubbing into my ass, and blew smoke right in my face as I tried to turn. I felt like I was suffocating again. My ball went down the drain like a silver fish jumping off a hook. I lost my ball, I lost my high score game, and I lost my cool. I was amped up with power and abilities far beyond those of mortal men.

Before I knew it, I was back upstairs at the bookstore. Like a "jump to" in a dream. Surrounded by books once more. I felt safe. I calmed down. I was not even sure what happened down there.

The fall semester had just begun and Franciscan Shops University Bookstore was busy, which meant my boss, my employees, customers—everybody was there. The bust went down right in front of them. Within minutes two campus security cops appeared and told me, "We have a few questions." They escorted me away. At the new underground Campus Security office, a third officer informed me, "We have a citizen's complaint for assault and battery."

I wondered what student reported the man pestering me. "Right. But, look, I don't want to press charges or anything. Just a misunderstanding."

The three officers stared at me. "No. The man has filed the charges against you. This is a serious matter. Wait here."

Mr. Stone had covertly tailed me to the store, squealed to security, and lied about the severity of our altercation. I believe. I'm almost sure of it. The sure thing is my game went TILT.

\#

All week I had Friday on my mind. And my party Saturday night. I was anxious, as there was no party until Bretta had agreed to attend. Now I was hosting the party with my best friend Nick Adams. He had been trying to get me to throw a party "to pull you out of your funk," and was pleased that I had suddenly agreed. My reluctance had turned into anticipation since a special someone was coming. I was eager to show Bretta a real Haight party; compared to the sleeper she had brought me to.

Friday morning, I was a little early at State so I walked off the damp chill of my motorcycle ride, making the rounds by the School of Business as well-groomed, serious-faced students arrived. I hurried past the Science Department, Ariel's former school of studies, trying not to let the melancholy seep back into my soul. Two lab-assistants sat on a bench sharing the screen of the latest pocket calculator, HP's first LCD, the HP-41C, a nerd's dream, of which my bookstore had quickly sold a hundred units. Out on the rear grassy lawn of the Art Department the pungent odor of dope hung in the air, as usual, as couple of students tossed a Frisbee. The one with russet, rock-star-long hair, pointed to me like a quarterback and I raced near the art garden to catch his throw. I sailed it back in a long arc and checked out the new sculpture that had arisen over the weekend—a ten-foot tall, fat businessman figure of rebar, mortar, mirror slivers, broken tile and Blue Willow plates, holding a cracked green glass globe, leaking actual oil.

"That's ours," Rock Star called. "Haven't seen you much lately, man." He lowered his voice. "You need some killer weed?"

I waved him off.

\#

Saturday at the Kezar lot, Beagle Boy trotted right over to me and sat on my foot. I massaged his neck as I gave him some chicken pieces and gently put my loop of twine over him. He sensed something good was up so trusted me.

Soon an old Volvo wagon drove up with a sad-faced middle-aged couple. I helped them unload stacks of string-tied yellowed newspapers. I glanced at the old headlines: "SAIGON FALLS!" "DEATH TOLL RISES" "HANOI FREES LAST P.O.W." I mentioned, "Thank God, that's over with."

The woman looked at my eyes, held up a frail arm, and slowly spoke, "Not for everyone, I'm afraid. Our son is still MIA." They both wore the MIA copper bracelets, now green tarnished. "He was about your age when he...disappeared. He was a good son. Had blue eyes like you," she choked out.

"Come on, honey," her husband urged.

"He hasn't come back home. We kept those papers for years...you know, just in case. And now..." The woman teared up.

Her husband held her and finished her sentence for her. "Now, it's time to move on. I hope some good comes out of this." He pointed at their Vietnam-era newspapers in the recycling, although we both knew he meant more.

They were perfect. I told them I had something for them and trotted out Beagle Boy. They weren't sure of their present at first, but warmed to the dog when he sat in front of them and *Aroo'ed*. I said, "He seems to know that this is his chance for a new 'leash' on life." The woman gave me a hug and the two drove away with the tail-wagging Beagle Boy looking back at me. I had a familiar pang in my gut.

The rest of the day went slowly. I picked up the alternate press newspaper I had fished out of recycling, this week's *San Francisco Bay Guardian*. Thumbing to the cover article "Our Generation — Lost and Found?" by Benjamin Cohn, I read:

> As 1980 looms before us, one wonders, will we
> find the sense of purpose we lost when the war
> was over? Will we find true shepherds to lead

us? After the political and cultural revolution of the sixties, and the finale of the anti-war effort, some find their existence—meaning reality—aimless, meaningless and unfulfilled. Some feed readily into the burgeoning corporate lifestyle filled with expensive new toys and acceptable narcissisms.

Many of our friends act as if these days will never end. Others know that it is all too good to last, and we should get it while getting is good, and revel in the divine decadence of life's Cabaret. We are like Pinocchio on Pleasure Island. The San Francisco seventies innocent fun is eclipsing into the eighties. The sun is in our eyes. Will we keep staring?

I reflected on my own existence, seemingly on hold for the past year. What was to come? What would I become? What would I do? Right now, I had a lot to do. It felt like my shift would never end. I really was ready for a party.

Playing DJ had always given me a rush, as it was a physical art form. By moving fast with both hands, I could balance a combo of LPs and Maxell XL-II tapes, mixing songs to both control and respond to the flow of the party's energy and mood. My stereo rack in the hall closet boasted British Quad gear running huge Infinity speakers that I had bartered from the bass player of It's a Beautiful Day. The Teac was ready with my hi-energy mixtape including Devo, Elvis Costello, Talking Heads, Lene Lovich and another ready to mellow the mood with musicians like Peter Tosh and Bob Marley.

Party time. Georgia and some of her fellow SFSU nursing students showed up early. Georgia exuded sex in her dress and manner. I was one of the few on campus who knew her nocturnal clandestine activities. She handed Nick a big brown jug and me a yellow Tower Records bag. "You have to try these new pale ale suds from Sierra Nevada home brewery. It just turned legit—can't even get this in stores yet."

"Dynamite. I'll get some chilled mugs," I said. Coming back, I lingered in the hall near the front door, willing Bretta to appear.

Nick poured and Georgia toasted, "To Jack, finally having fun again."

If she shows, I thought.

Georgia flipped through my albums, some of them advance singles she had given me from her KFOG DJ friend, and held up The Pretenders with a grin. I said, "The American rock scene has been emasculated, but Chrissie Hynde has more balls than most dudes."

"Patti Smith, too," Nick said.

"Stick on your present. It's from the U.K.—it's ska, vinyl hot off the press."

I placed Madness *One Step Beyond* on my Technics turntable and lowered the Signet cartridge. We immediately started bopping to their Rasta-New Wave upbeat sound. I cranked it.

"Here we go!" Georgia squealed, and pulled us to her wriggling and shimmying nursing friends in the living room. Nick unfurled a bag of weed. Soon my place filled with partiers and pot smoke. No Bretta. Just as I was resigned that Bretta was not coming...

"Dónde está la fiesta!?" Bretta burst into the room making a stage entrance, waving her flowing scarlet silk scarf. Bretta's style for the evening was seductive—tight pink pants with a black stretch tube top with a peek-a-boo of her navel, and a pendant chain that invited one's eyes to her cleavage. I felt a thickness in my throat. The bad news—she was with not one, but two men. As I hugged her, Bretta's shampoo blended with bergamot, opopanax, iris, vanilla, jasmine.

Her exotic scent aroused me. "Ummm, nice, Shalimar?"

"You are good." She kissed my nose giving me a close-up of her quivering pool-chalk eyelids. "Was 'Guess Your Fragrance' part of your circus act?"

I showed off. "Shalimar was created to commemorate the undying love that erected the Taj Mahal."

The man in the suit joked, "And erect other objects, too." He pretended to aside in Bretta's ear, "Ooh, he *is* interesting."

"Allow me to introduce Zachary 'Zomething.' We call him Z.Z. and we adore him." His tailored suit looked sharp, although personally, I couldn't stand ties. He held a wine bottle.

Z.Z. straightened my collar. "Love the vintage vest. I'm a buyer for Macy's in the Financial District, so clothes I knows." His glance at my crotch confirmed his preferences.

Bretta's other escort was a wiry young man with intense eyes and dark-hair. He frowned at the attention Bretta and Z.Z gave me. She introduced him. "Jack, this is journalist extraordinaire Benjamin Cohn. He is the smartest man I know."

"Thank you, dear, but I'm better known as Bretta's boyfriend," Benjamin declared. "Hmm, you're athletic looking. Handball, tennis?"

"Frisbee." His name was familiar and he seemed a little toasted already.

He snickered and returned a lob. "I'm a ranked tennis player, so if you ever want to get beat some time…ha-ha." He leaned in as if to whisper, but spoke loudly, lifting a foot and his straightened his hands in a pose. "And I just got my black belt in kung fu."

"Your mother must be very proud," I backhanded, baiting him, trying to gauge him. When I made my move for Bretta tonight, would he play the jealous lover and come at me?

"Uh, yeah." He served, "So are you following what's going on in Iran?" Fortunately, a guest yelled, "Hey Benjamin, read your article." Benjamin immediately engaged him in a current event conversation.

"Don't mind him; he's very insecure about his modesty," Z.Z. said. He sniffed the air. "Well, Dorothy, I'm off to see the Wizard— of bud." Z.Z. winked at Bretta and sauntered off. I took her to the kitchen for a drink where I showed her my vintage cocktail shaker.

"Ah, Aladdin's lamp." Bretta stroked it. "My wish is for you to show me how the magic works."

I stood behind and placed my arms around her, with my large rough hands over Bretta's on the shaker; her hands delicate, nails paint-smeared. I guided her in mixing Martinis. I breathed in the Shalimar and asked, "Do you know the secret ingredient of a Martini?" She turned her face to mine. "Cold. So keep shaking." And she did, very close to me. "Slowly, not too hard." I brushed her full breasts. "Or you'll bruise my ice."

"Well, we mustn't do that." Bretta murmured, "You always seem to get me shaking and wiggling."

Georgia strutted in for a beer, scolded, "Hey, the dance floor is out there" and looked at me with a gamut of emotions—jealous, bemused, cautionary, Wow—and turned, tapping her stiletto heels out.

"To our fortuitous meeting." I kissed the beauty mark above Bretta's mouth and clinked our glasses. We sipped the ice-cold nectar. She licked her lips. "Delicious." Her eyes looked hungry and wanting. "This is all so sophisticated for a boy in the Haight."

"I studied sacred cocktail arts from my friend Bino who lived in this unit before me."

Z.Z., holding a joint, called from the doorway, "Where'd my tie go? Somebody took my tie." I poured him a Martini and he snuffed the jay and stuck it in his pocket for some reason.

I introduced Bretta to Nick, and, keeping with my environmental mirage, I bragged that he worked for a solar company, which was true. Nick gave me an appreciative nod for Bretta's charms. The revelry had amped up, so I went back to DJ-ing. Feeling guilty about ignoring Georgia, I put on "Lust for Life," turned up the volume, and told her, "This is for you." She danced with me, saying, "Bretta's so-called boyfriend has been handsy with my friends. He's a bit of ass." Nearby, Benjamin danced an odd Mick Jagger impersonation, before switching to Elvis-in-Vegas, kung-fu moves, I assumed for my benefit. Georgia spun us around wildly, purposely-bumping Benjamin.

"Wicked paaty!" The two hard-drinking Boston Boys who lived in the apartment below me had come back up to the party. Laughing, Jimmie and Obie shared their sentences, "The plasta'is crackin' off our ceiling…" "…like snow." "It's falling in our blow…" "…hey, a rhyme" "…and getting mixed in…" "…we lost our hit."

"Sorry, boys, I'll fix it up so our manager doesn't have to know about it." Jimmie slipped me a little folded paper bindle, saying, "A samplah. It's the real thing." He glanced to Bretta, now speaking with Benjamin, and said, "Love those boob tube tops."

"*Tha's* the real thing!" Obie said.

I wasn't into hard drugs so I palmed the bindle to Nick. As he tried to discretely round up Georgia and a select few, Benjamin butted in. He told Nick, "I have a blade," and pulling a thin box cutter from his rear pocket, he slid it open and closed. Benjamin looked to Bretta and when she shook her head no, he startled Georgia by wrapping an arm around her to follow Nick into the spare bedroom. He closed the door. I figured I should slow things down and put on "Jamming."

"This party is a trip!" a Bookstore worker called to me.

I reached for Bretta to dance, but she demurred, "I'm a bit shy sometimes, and not very good on the dance floor."

"Sure you are, you can repeat your command performance of the old box stomp."

A petite, almost-a-nurse gyrated between Bretta and I. "I will. Dance with me, Jack, pleeze?"

"Maybe later." I funneled Bretta through my kitchen, where I refreshed our Martinis, and out the back door, up the outside stairs to one of my special spots—the graveled flat roof. We stood silently looking across to the dark shadows of Golden Gate Park's trees.

"Tell me something exciting about yourself," Bretta said as she leaned into me. I held her close in the chilly night.

"I was in a few movies in L.A."

"From what you proposed, I bet you were a stuntman!" She pointed at the Kezar Stadium wall.

"I did stunts all right. Probably not your type of movies." I usually didn't tell people. I wasn't sure why I had even done them, besides the money. As a test for myself, I think. Or, to torment myself. That would have been a good question for my shrink to ask.

"Foreign films?" Bretta asked.

"Yes, very."

"You are so mysterious." We kissed. I picked her up and balanced her voluptuous body above my head. "Oh my God, Jack, don't drop me!" I slowly brought her back down. "How did you get so strong?"

"I was trained by Rollo, the circus strongman. Weight training was how I was able to get roles, you know, perform, in the movies."

"Are you going to perform for me?" Bretta rubbed a hand down my belly. "All those muscles..." My breathing tightened and my body tingled. I pressed my erection against her and kissed her deeply. She nibbled my lips. "No, not here..." whispering, "...not until you do something about this gravel." She held me. "And my poor needy Benjamin. I guess we'll just have to hold off..." She smiled and when she abruptly moved toward the stairs, I felt like I would explode. "...and I really should check on him."

The party continued. Z.Z. gave a brief, "Thanks, let me know if you find my tie. Really hope to see you later," and split. By two in the morning Benjamin hadn't taken Bretta's hints, and was still hanging around. Bretta had certainly imbibed Dorothy Parker's requisite four Martinis. Nick's City College friends were in all states of inebriation, one with Z.Z.'s necktie around her eyes, playing blind man's bluff. Going with the idea, I wrapped Bretta's red scarf around her eyes and led her into my bedroom.

With a "*ta-da*," I revealed my hanging Tibetan prayer rug. "Beautiful, Jack." I exposed the second surprise–the rug concealed my walk-in closet. Inside, under the little window, was my yellow cloth mandala. Framed by connected jungle animals, the spiraling labyrinth ascended to a central golden-threaded sun. "I can't believe it. My father had one like this," she said running her finger admiringly around the labyrinth.

"My photographer friend, Bill, brought both back from Tibet for me."

"Far out, man," she teased.

"Bretta, I have your present. The more you look, the more you see. Stay in here. I'll be right back."

Benjamin was prowling around looking for her, becoming more and more agitated. He front kicked a footstool sliding across the hardwood floor. I avoided lying by telling him she left with some dude—true, me. He said, "Probably Z.Z. Bretta, she's such a fag hag." I nodded to Georgia, my co-conspirator, who encouraged her nursing student nemesis to ask Benjamin for a ride home. We had seen her earlier listening to Benjamin's lecture on medical malpractice. I could then truthfully tell Bretta her "boyfriend" left with some chick. In my current state I figured it a win-win-win-win for everyone.

"Sure, babe, I'll give you a ride." Benjamin extended an arm and escorted her toward the door. Nick, with the petite nurse clamped to him, led a conga-line to the kitchen, bearing bottles, glasses, party detritus, and then ushered them out the door with passing words of, "night, thanks, great party." I gave Nick a thumbs-up and he grinned. I returned to my bedroom, glancing at my bed I had outfitted with fresh sheets. I smoothed the bedspread and plumped the pillows. I slipped back into my hidden closet and presented Bretta with my mixtape of romantic songs.

"Thank you." She indicated my guitar in the corner. "You play guitar. I love stringed instruments. Next Friday night, I'll be back from L.A. You should come to the Sav with me."

I nodded, assuming The Sav was another new band. There were a lot of new bands. I had no idea that Bretta's invitation to the Sav was to be an invitation into her solar system. She pulled off her tube top in a fluid move. I stared, and swept a pile of sweaters and jackets from a shelf to the closet floor. She kissed me and pulled me down to the pile as she pulled off my pants.

My bedroom door banged as someone barged in. "Jack!" Right outside the closet a slurred voice demanded, "Where'd that Jack go?"

Bretta looked frightened. I rose to a crouch. A woman murmured something.

"Yeah, yeah. Fuck him. All right, let's blow this pop stand." Trailing away, "You're a lucky girl. You get to ride in my Porsche."

Ah, that Porsche. It figured Benjamin would drive a Porsche. The front door slammed. We finished stripping and stretched out, touching as much skin as possible. Under the twin to her father's mandala I wrapped my body in her golden mermaid hair. I slid my hand below and twirled there. Bretta reached down for me with both of her hands and inhaled deeply. Roxy Music played softly and except for the stereo, all was quiet.

"My big boy! Go eea-sy, eea-sy," she urged. I was gentle and eased it. She gasped, "Wait!" and I waited, but, "It's Ok. Go ahead...go ahead...go ahead. Yes, yes, yessss." The live version of Bryan Ferry's "Out of the Blue" wove its aural enchantment. It was nothing, then it was something, then it was everything. I saw my girlfriend's face. Then it was over quickly.

This was my first time with a woman since Ariel. I sucked air in gasps.

I wanted to be more than next to her, more than on her, more than in her, more than with her, more than deep within her. The second time, at Chrissie Hynde's insistence, I was "gonna' use my arms...use my legs...use my style, gonna' use my fingers, gonna' use my, my, my imagination." So I did and we did, and I did, and we did feverishly, and I thanked God that he made Bretta, and thanked God he invented lovemaking and designed it so supremely, sublimely otherworldly pleasure, pleasure...plea...sure... pleas...pleasurable and we writhed on the floor.

"Did you feel that?" I asked and she laughed and asked, "Was it like we knew it would be when we held hands at the Recycling Center?" and I said, "Yes, we knew," kissing the globes of her breasts. "Love is the Drug" played as we joined again—slow, slower, slooo-weeer, slower, and it became giveittome, giveittome, giveittome-mazing.

Bretta's fingers stroked the tattoo on my inner bicep. The dagger's handle was shaped like clasping hands, and an eye was in the middle of the sun. She said, "Curious, a dagger going through the sun?"

"The circus Tattooed Man inked me when I was fourteen."

"So, you're a Tattooed Love Boy."

"More of a rite of passage."

After the fourth time, we lay damp. She sighed, "Oh, Jack." With an imaginary paintbrush she traced the lines of the mandala's labyrinth. "Now that, was a religious experience."

"I try to make love like it could be my very last time."

She trembled and began sobbing. Because I was so romantically tragic and poetic? So I thought.

CHAPTER 5

After Ariel's funeral debacle I had been assigned to a shrink. The office was above the Jack Tar Hotel on Van Ness, the hotel's "modernism" having been described as, "Texas' idea of what Los Angeles looks like." My shrink was a woman, and fittingly, one of those modern over-groomed types—too perfect. I had the sensation that I was shrinking in front of her.

She opened the file and opened conversationally, "Circus performers live outside the bounds and rules of society." She paused. "Do you continue to live that way, Jack?"

"Don't most people my age, here on the Coast?"

"Your performance at your girlfriend's funeral service? Her family thinks that was out of bounds. Do you?"

"Why should the truth out of bounds?"

"Jack, you're very lucky your "truth" didn't land you in the psych ward or, frankly, on suicide watch."

"I've been locked up before—darker places than those. It wouldn't have mattered."

"Your life does matter, Jack. I want to help you if you'll let me."

I considered: could a perfectly-coiffed woman who smelled of sour apple Tic Tacs masking Virginia Slims help me? "I don't need anybody's help."

"You know that's not your choice now, right?" She tapped the file. "I know you loved your girlfriend. And I know she would want you to move on." She watched me closely. "Jack. This dependence on women you have—have you considered you may still be longing for your mother?"

I scoffed. HA. Are you kidding me?

"Let's start with the troubles your family had. Do you often think about that?"

"You seem more interested in my past than helping me deal with my dead girlfriend. I'm already over my goddamn uncle and all that."

She jotted down "god-damn uncle." "This is helpful, Jack. Let's talk about your parents' relationship."

My muscles tensed, my body craving to bolt. I looked at the lines in my palm. "My mother and her older brother moved to Illinois from Nashville. My Scottish, Catholic father fell in love with her dark Italian looks. Despite her Italian roots, she was Baptist, not Catholic—she and her brother disdained Catholicism. Father renounced his faith and they married right away."

"Interesting. That must have been challenging."

"No, that was the easy part." I laughed bitterly.

She made a note when I hesitated. "We're finally getting somewhere. Jack, it would be so helpful, to me, if you continued."

"So...she was only eighteen. Obviously, they had me too young. Things were all right for twelve years, but, who knows, I was a kid."

She pretended to look nonchalant, and casually asked. "What was it, Jack, that changed then?"

"My father, my father bought me a shotgun. I killed more game than I could count with that shotgun. You ever eat fresh killed game?"

"Ah, no, I'm—I don't think I could stomach that. Why do you bring up the gun, Jack?"

"We were poor and needed the meat."

"Oh. Did your parents get along?"

I pictured my mother sitting at the kitchen table with her child's box of watercolors. Or that time she was in her yellow sun dress on the porch. It was so hot and I saw the perspiration start at the top of her breasts and trickle down. She dipped her brush in the milky, multi-colored water in a Mason jar. I asked if I could drink the colors. Mother said, Sure sugar. I sipped the jar, made a face but it wasn't bad. Then she drank some. She told me, Jus' don't tell your daddy, he's such a fuddy-duddy sometimes.

I said, "When my mother water colored it made her happy."

"And when she wasn't happy?"

Mother would wear short-shorts and flirt. Men would 'let their eyes travel clear up her legs,' as Daddy put it. He would clench and unclench his fists.

I said, "Daddy was a little jealous. Her being a waitress didn't help. But she made really good tips..."

"Was his jealousy justified?"

Of course not. Men only fantasize that neighbors covet their wives. I said, "He suspected her of being sweet on a customer, the local Phillips 66 owner."

"Go on."

"It's a June afternoon. Daddy follows Mama and watches as she met the man by the park. She and the man both have VW Bugs, he a yellow one and she a green one. After the fact, it made their relationship seem so visible. In his Bug, the two drive out the white gravel country road to lover's lane. They are on the blanket in the cornfield when Daddy creeps up on them through the cornrows. My father is a good hunter; he's very silent. They are uncovered, naked, exposed. He pumps the shotgun so they will jump." I looked her dead in the eye. "When you are not expecting it, that slide is the most frightening sound."

Her eyes widened. "You mean when *one* is not expecting it, right?"

"Their bodies jerk, and then they are still."

"What? He...what happened?"

"They are petrified with fear. He aims at them. Mama screams. Daddy shoots."

"Your father shoots...I mean shot them?"

"They thought he did. Corn, cornstalks splatter all over them. He pulled it. He couldn't...shoot her."

"Oh my, thank goodness." Another scribble. "So, what do you think about that, Jack?"

"I imagine I might feel the same way too, if I saw the mother of my child cheat on me."

"You know those kinds of violent feelings can have serious consequences. What were the consequences for your father and your family?"

"My father. He left...he had to leave. And mother and I moved in with Uncle." I thought this would be enough, but she knew she had me. She probed and she probed. "So, you and your mother ended up living with, not the other man, the Phillips 66 owner, but her brother?"

"I remember. I remember—very sharply, it is a sunny bright day. Mama and I are driving in her blue Bug. She tells me, Now

Jack, I'm sorry, honey, but he helped us with a lot of things we couldn't afford on Daddy's salary at Olin. He gave us extra fuel oil for the heater last winter; remember when it was such a cold spell. He discounted gasoline, and truth be told, even financed my Bug. And you know this car is my baby. She wants me to say something, but all I can do was watch this green bottle fly trapped in the car and it buzzes again and again against the windshield. We pull up the circular drive to my uncle's mansions. We are here to stay. My uncle is in his white suit waiting on the veranda, leaning against one of the Dorian columns. I try to shoo the fly out of the car but it still buzzes against the glass. Uncle waves us in with his big cigar. Inside is the sweeping staircase with massive oak newel posts and balustrades. Mama always loved his grand house and is thrilled. She says, Finally. She rubbed my hair and says, It will be good for you to have such a masculine mentor as Uncle."

I swallowed. Shrinks love sexual subtext, with Freudian knots and slips and lingerie and Jungian hijinks. I heard her nylons rub as she crossed her legs. "And?"

An angry voice from the reception area penetrated her inner sanctum. A bell chimed. Her perfect exterior wavered. She scribbled a prescription and handed it to me. "This should help you, Jack."

"No. I may smoke pot once in a while, but I don't do drugs."

"It's only Valium. It's not really a drug like you young people think of." She finished writing on my form. "I'll be right back."

On her leather chair she'd forgotten my file. Inside was a copy of my psych eval from L.A. By the time she returned to dismiss me, I had it memorized. I never went back. She kept re-upping my scripts anyway.

#

I backed my bike in between the parked cars until my tire kissed the curb. Helmetless, I pulled off my bandana headband and smoothed down my hair in my mirror. I tugged my Bogart-style fedora from under my coffee-brown bomber jacket. Bretta had invited me for a date. All week I had Friday on my mind. "The Sav" was the Savoy Tivoli bar, in the heart of North Beach. The exterior was painted sunflower yellow with burnt sienna trim. Colors Van Gogh would have approved. I was drawn between the divided, tabled booth area and the inviting old-fashioned dark wood bar, which ran the entire length on the right.

I couldn't miss Bretta at the far end of the bar. She was Sav-synchronized, wearing a snow-white, cowl neck, cashmere sweater, midnight-blue skirt and matching beret, with a sunflower-colored scarf. There was one little problem. This was not the private date I thought it would be. She was with a group of a half a dozen. I ate a Valium.

Bretta forwent my expected hug or kiss, immediately introducing me to her friends, "This! is my Jack!" In her inflected voice, she continued, "He is marvelously masculine." I blushed as the group looked me over. "You remember Z.Z. Don't you just adore Z.Z.?" Bretta demanded. Bretta seemed to have a thing for him. I thought about Benjamin's comment. She continued, "Z.Z. is very organized; he's so good at keeping my life together."

"Darling, at least with me, you don't have to worry about keeping your legs together!" Z.Z. replied. Everyone laughed but me. Clearly it was Bretta whom the entourage "just adored." They gravitated to her and lit up in her presence.

Benjamin, to my dismay, was still included in this entourage. I assumed she had told him she needed some space, because he glared at me from a table in the back, as he engaged in political debate with two men. "Meet Craddock, my housemate," Bretta said, introducing me to a short, slender man wearing round wire rim glasses. "Craddock is the most brilliant classical guitar student at USF."

He shook my hand delicately. He certainly needed to loosen up, so I said, "What's up, Doc." Others agreed with glee, "Doc, yeah, that's him, exactly." So "Doc" he became. It was not, as some thought, my abbreviation for his name, nor because he was wearing a white shirt—always, it turned out—but because, with his glasses, he resembled Snow White's dwarf. That was perfect, because the creamy-skinned, fairest-in-the-land Bretta would be his Snow White. I thought, If he's Doc, there must be six more. Later I would determine, excluding the charming Prince—me—that I was right.

Mismatched translucent-white deco light fixtures on the uppermost shelf of the back bar glowed a mystic light, mesmerizing to thirsty moths. And God, I know, I was one. I gave the bartender a one-more sign—for Bretta, a Brandy Alexander, and a tequila grapefruit for me.

"How about a drink for Bretta's friend." The raven-black-pixie-hair-styled woman asked with no question mark. "Jack; my *new* best friend, Francine." The decorator, Bretta had mentioned. I bought her sangria. Francine was as tanned—considering San Francisco fog—as Bretta fair, and turned out to be as supercilious as Bretta was considerate. Francine's bitchiness was still effective sex appeal, albeit aided by her tennis-player body, long R. Crumb-defined legs, and short designer sheath dress. I soon found Francine to be provocative in every sense of the word—sexually, frustrating, baiting, rousing, and argument provoking.

Robin sidled up in her tall boots. "So, we meet again." She still gave off an odor of hay and chocolate.

Z.Z. pointed. "This is our spot. We always take over the left-of-center barstools; never sit at tables, and heaven forbid, not the middle room. George the barman affords us, Bretta and company that is, the star treatment." I nodded. Z.Z. motioned me to follow him to the back. To the restrooms, I thought. At the dim corridor he continued past the restrooms to a green "No" stenciled above the glowing absinthe-green EXIT sign. A red sign hung on the heavy door, "Emergency Exit Only." Z.Z. looked expectantly at me. "This is the perfect setting for us regulars to catch a buzz."

"That sign's glowing like Kryptonite," I pointed out.

Z.Z. considered it and croak-sang, "'Superman or Green Lantern ain't got, nothin' on me.' Speaking of which, uh Jack, do you?" He reached into his sport jacket. "I have the money if you have..."

"Sorry, no." His disappointed face indicated that I was not measuring up to the Haight's reputation. Although in 1978 San Francisco had approved Prop W directing city law enforcement to disregard low-level pot "crimes," the new mayor, Feinstein, disregarded it and the cops recently kicked down doors of couple of people I knew in the Haight and dragged them away. People were in prison for years for selling a few ounces. Z.Z. was an odd one. Even if I had some grass, I barely knew him and his business look made me a little nervous. He was not a classifiable gay–Castro, South of Market, or Polk, not flamboyant, but projected a gay affectation off and on. I figured he balanced a corporate vs. lifestyle dichotomy.

He looked me up and down which could have been sexual or narc-like. "I guess we'll have to drink," he said. As we walked back, I noticed that the Sav retained an Italian flavor despite a Persian interior—the pointed arched windows and doorways were highlighted by a monkey and mosque-domed mural. The spacious two-room bar, plus sidewalk patio, had a solid feel with its box-beam, midnight blue ceiling. Bretta took my arm, "Oh Jack, here's Monty. Isn't he dashing?"

I shook hands with the reserved, appraising Monty, a tall man in his early thirties, with a broad nose, possibly flattened in a fight, and silver-grey already flecking much of his hair. In his cardigan, he reminded me of a mean professor, whose appearance would be replete by smoking a pipe, yet was juxtaposed by his dark beret. A beret like Bretta's. I sensed that he was as straight as he looked, meaning he didn't get high, rather than the more recent sexual definition. Bretta said, "Monty owns a Big Yellow Taxi." I knew this meant he also owned an expensive taxi medallion.

Monty announced, "I had a hundred-dollar day today, so drinks are on me," We cheered him while we ordered beers and wines, another Brandy Alexander for Bretta, and Coke for Doc. Doc was mostly straight, too. As I learned, he also rarely drank.

Benjamin popped up like a Whac-A-Mole between Bretta and I at "on me." He asked, "George, do you have fresh lemons?"

"I picked them myself out back in our garden," George responded sarcastically.

"Splendid. A Top Shelf Long Island Iced Tea." Benjamin eyed me.

George glanced at Monty, because it was an expensive drink, who rolled his eyes but nodded yes, pulled out a wad of cash, and asked, "How about you, Francine?"

"I'm a self-supporting feminist. There's no need to buy me a drink."

"I'm not buying a feminist a drink." Monty replied unflustered. "I'm buying my friend Francine a drink."

Francine's politics established, she ordered champagne. The young New Wavers, Edith, with short blonde hair, and Robert in his skinny tie and black hat ambled over to get in on the free drinks. Bretta toasted, "To Monty, *Cin cin.*"

"Bretta," Monty said, "you should've come with me to the tenth anniversary celebration of Kerouac's death the other night."

"Seems a rather odd thing to celebrate," she said.

"At the Old Spaghetti Factory. Ferlinghetti, Herb Caen, a bunch you know from Enrico's were there. Hey, I even met Jack's daughter, Jan Kerouac. 'The Princess of the Beats.'"

Bretta shrugged but I asked in excitement, "Daughter? I've read most of Kerouac fan and I had no idea he had a kid. What's she like?"

Bretta crinkled her nose, so Monty motioned me to the Wurlitzer jukebox. "Like Jack. Like standing next to the mythic source of the... sacred flame. I mean...she has this...she has It." He eyed the little printed selection cards. The Sav's jukebox collection of Jazz and Big Band 45s subtly imparted the classy charm of those eras. "You enjoy jazz, Jack?"

I eyed his unfamiliar selections on the tabs as he pushed the buttons: Brubeck, Davis, Coltrane, Monk, Mingus, and their intriguing song titles. I was feeling a little rough around the edges amongst Bretta's entourage. They were an older-than-me, sophisticated, wealthy, artsy group, far different than the rock-and-roll, anything-goes, Haight Ashbury types I knew, or even the diverse SFSU students. I said, "I'm a rocker but I like any music that makes my blood sing."

"Good answer. Check this out." Monty snapped all four of his fingers to the beat. I was impressed. "Dave Brubeck Quartet. A local cat. I've met him. 'Take Five,' man."

The piano danced, the saxophone teased. At the bar, Bretta undulated, taking five on her barstool. She had been jealous, it seemed. She glanced at Monty before she pulled me into her arms, writhing as she announced over my shoulder to the entourage, "I'm just mad about jazz. Those unusual time signatures, and superimposing contrasting rhythms, meters, tonalities." I grew hard. Bretta's golden eyes captured mine.

Francine said, "Isn't that a bit bombastic, Bretta?" Bretta ignored her and watched me.

I swivel to the stool adjacent to Bretta, order a glass of ice water, trying to stay cool, tapping time on my thigh. Francine teases one of my curls. "Jack, jazzy-snazzy San Francisco must have seemed a Garden of Eden to you when you arrived from Po-duuunk." She pronounced Podunk with the Southern drawl that Coasters confuse with Midwest accents. Francine motions to our group and challenges me with a smile. "Tell us, Jack. What do you think of San Francisco?"

I think...San Francisco? The jukebox jazz beats like a live thing...

I think, The City of Saint Francis, this cool, foggy, breezy, chilly, hilly metropolis. Restless by the pulsing sea.

San Francisco… Surrounded by saltwater embrace…The Golden Gate—radiates her sun-kissed span, Golden Gate Park— transcendent over shifting sand. **Foggy horns forlornly sighing, jangling cable car bells crying, Cow Hollow, Bermuda Triangle singles opportunely trying.**

Over a HILL: Hot & cold running colors, aromas, climates. Climb! Natives know… their hills make San Francisco women's legs so curve-aceous.

San Francisco, I thought…

Twin peaks …p e e k i n g…Palm-treed parks, green-knolled, square oases' Seven hills a-laying, **Islands of Alcatraz, Treasure, and Yerba Buena floating, Crabs cocktailing, seals rocking, The Lady from Shaing Hai … Hai-ing, Maltese Falcons hiding, Writers and Poets HOWLing. Jacks, KEROUAC and LONDON CALLING, from vertiginous Hitchcockian streets, through Dark Passage alleyways…**

…to Ladies of the night —Minna, Natoma, Clara, Clementina… and their tenderloins...

Lipsticked enchanted Victorians. Pretty little made-up maidens all in a row...

I think…

Francine places a hot hand on my palm and presses her nail in. "Well, Jack? Say something." She curls her full lips to reveal perfect porcelain-white teeth that glow invitingly, like the lights at Carol Doda's Condor Club. "Don't be shy. I may bite but I won't bark. Not very loud anyway."

Men at the bar eye her, this leggy, mean, Hill-Climbing Queen, the Mistress of Mixed Signals. "Jack? What do you think?"

It's my turn to smile. "I think…I LOVE this City."

"To San Francisco!" Z.Z toasted. Everyone toasted.

"You're right to love us, country boy," Francine said.

"Watch it, Francine, I'm from La Crosse, Wisconsin," Z.Z. said.

"That's raaht, ya'all, too," she retorted.

"The point is," Z.Z. teased, "what do you know about Garden of Eden? You're an interior designer, not a landscape architect."

Benjamin chimed in, "I know that a ribbon of verse from Dante's "Paradiso" is inscribed on Saints Peter and Paul cathedral here on Washington Square. Something about, God…" he smiled hopefully at Bretta, "'…glows throughout the universe.'"

Francine answered, "I know the colossal bronze doors on Grace Cathedral are called Gates of Paradise. One of the panels depicts Adam and Eve,"

I mounted a comeback. "Wait a minute, Francine. I'm not sure I want to see San Francisco that way. Remember, Eden is the garden man must lose."

"Paradise lost, Paradise regained," said Z.Z. "But you may have to die first."

"You are so wrong," Benjamin said. "The 'regain' poem is about resisting temptation, as in the Temptation of Christ."

Z.Z. asked with sarcasm, "So now you're a Jewish Jesus expert, too?"

Benjamin was about to spout off when Francine put an arm around Bretta and jiggled them both, exclaiming, "Well, here's to temptation!" We laughed and raised our glasses. The two beauties caught the attention of some male patrons.

Robin told me, "My favorite painting of Bretta's was inspired by this one." She pointed to a painting behind the bar. "Hieronymus Bosch's *The Garden of Earthly Delights*."

A man on a neighboring bar stool raised his shot glass and leered at Bretta, "*You* certainly glow like an Earthly delight. Here's to you." No one toasted back.

Bretta spoke in her storybook voice. "I believe San Francisco is a Garden—of Earthly Delights. Once you have been here, wherever you go, you always yearn to return to the Garden."

The man tried again, slurring, "I'll return to the garden with you, blondie."

I moved toward him but Robin held my shoulder. George gave the man a "watch it or be cut off" signal. Robin whispered to me, "See, dealt with, Jack. Men go crazy over Bretta, they really do. She receives marriage proposals from men she has only met for two minutes. One time we were at Union Square and after a man stopped addressing her breasts, he looked up and proposed!"

Robin announced to everyone, "I believe San Francisco is a Garden of Eating. It is our very own Boschian Buffet of life. All you can eat." Francine's eyes widened. Robin's speaking up seemed to surprise everyone.

"Just don't overindulge." Bretta said.

"Ha, too late for this group," Francine said.

I quietly asked Robin, "What about Francine? She claims she's a feminist, yet still she flaunts it. Her sex."

Robin frowned. "She feels that she—I mean *we*, because Bretta and I are feminists, too, and as feminists—we may use our bodies however we want. Francine—I mean *we women*, desire to be able to express our sexuality, but not be objectified sexually."

I was right about the mixed signals. I managed an, "Oh. Is that what *you* want?"

Robin's big-browns eyed me through her glasses. "I like horses." This was Robin's out-in-left-field manner, which I would grow to appreciate. I noticed Z.Z. listening in and suppressing a laugh. She continued, "Horses are gorgeous creatures and I am in love with them."

"You mean you relate to them better than men?" I asked.

"I'm relating to you, right now, Jack!" She retrieved a roll of candy from her feedbag-size purse and offered one to Z.Z and I. They were Rolo chocolate caramels.

"Ha. Rollo is my friend's name."

"That's delightful. Bosco is my horse's name." Robin and I ate Rolos together. Encouraged, she told me more. "Bosco, lives at Miwok Stables in Mill Valley. I ride there two or three times a week."

Now I understood Robin's hay flavoring. "You own a horse? I like horses. I have a steel horse."

"You own a train?"

"No, that's an iron horse. I ride a motorcycle."

"Oh, I see. That explains your *élan*."

I thought, It does? Bosco chocolate syrup. Perfect. I nicked a couple of cherries by the stems from the waitress station and offered her one. "Cherry with your chocolate, Baskin' Robin?"

She laugh-snorted, and I dropped it into her mouth and ate the other. She blushed. I meant "Baskin' Robin" as a backhanded compliment, which she interpreted as flirting. I looked for Bretta and saw her talking to George the bartender and some other men. I was about to go to her when I overheard Z.Z., Monty, Francine and Robert speaking rapidly in low tones behind me. Not as low as they thought.

"So, what do we think about Bretta's new toy?" "A stud, but a little rough around the edges." "Yeah, I saw him roar in on a motorcycle." "A biker?" "It's not like he's a Hell's Angel." "Still, I can't wait to see him in all leather." "Ha. I suppose Bretta is back to bad boys now." A few snickers.

I felt my anger welling up. I sat my drink down and studied the palm of my hand. My L.A. shrink taught me the technique to help with the anger.

The conversation continued. "It's not that funny." "He's surprisingly sharp, though." "Good sense of humor; I mean 'Doc,' how good is that?!" "Great." "...our best chance to displace Benjamin." "She'll be able to polish the kid up..." "...break him in." More snickers. "And crazy Winston?" "He's supposed to be doing good." "Maybe he won't come back." "I hear he is." "I wonder how Jack will handle him?"

My ears perked up at the rest: "Is she done with him, or not?" (unintelligible whispering) "So...?" "Time for our little talk with Illinois." "Yes." "Me, too." "I'm good." "Ready?"

I let out a hissing breath and finished my drink. Francine joined Bretta at the bar. Z.Z. and Robert approached me, and I allowed myself to be pulled over to Monty. I was surrounded and became anxious. Tall, impassive Monty just stood in the background. Robert prefaced, "We think you and Bretta are cute together." Z.Z. said, "We all worship her, so be nice to her."

"We don't want to have to hurt you," Robert said with mustered sternness. I considered his slight frame, and his skinny tie, knowing that I could have him on the floor in one punch. Z.Z. was zero threat. Long reach Monty was the wild card. But this was apparently a business conference. Robert laughed nervously so I smiled and said, "Even bad boys know when they meet someone special."

The three looked at each other with a question, followed by a look of approval. "Jack, I have to tell you, about Benjamin..." Z.Z. warned. "...karate, tennis..." "He's a little insecure and uses his knowledge of world affairs as a kind of weapon to feel superior..." "He doesn't seem to understand that Bretta's friends are creative, not realists." Z.Z. touched his cheek. "Oh, that's right. At your party, he told you."

Robert confided, "Benjamin is brilliant, he's just *ob-knockt-shus*. I mean, Long Island Iced Tea. Just be careful. He really does have a black belt in karate fu or something and he says he's kicked a couple of guys ass over Bretta." I looked at Monty. He nodded affirmative. I nodded. Robert nodded. We all were nodding. I supposed we were now bonding. I relaxed. I had missed this camaraderie, a closeness and protectiveness which was reminiscent of my former circus friends. Robert asked in a low voice, indicating Bretta, "Do you know who she is, man?"

"Yeah, she's the Supernatural food girl," I replied cleverly.

"Right, but you don't know who her father is, huh? She just visited him in L.A."

"What, her father owns the store?" The pair laughed, and even Monty cracked a smile. "I hate to say, Robert is it? I don't even know Bretta's last name. All I know she is cool and a hell of a lot of fun."

Bretta heard my comment and walked over to slip an arm around me. She threw her other arm to her forehead, to declare theatrically, "Jack, take me away from all this. Please escort me home." She waved bye saying "Ciao, ciao," to her friends. "Jack, you simply must see my art."

On the street, I walked her to my fog-damp motorcycle. "Ready for a ride?"

"Oh, my, no." She clutched her scarf around her throat. "Isadora. I can't. Let's take a cab."

I looked at my bike and I looked at Bretta. "Taxi!" I called.

Bretta's top-floor flat was a periwinkle Victorian with gold trim above a corner café, a few blocks from Haight Street. She turned on the lights with the old-fashioned push-button switch. The hall was filled with artwork; large pieces on top and smaller below. "Home is where the art is, darling."

I paused to look but she said, "Those are not mine. Look later, they're not going anywhere. I want to show you my work. But first some brandy." She pointed to a closed door. "That's Doc's room." She led me to the living room. The flat was dark, with hardwood floors, oak beams and panels, wainscoting and large bay windows. She said in tour-guide voice, "Three bedrooms with a street view, with kitchen, bath, living room, and lovely dining room on the left."

In the living room, a large hand-painted vase of orange and yellow sunflowers towered above a small, unopened gift box. Bretta said, "The sunflower head is composed of many individual flowers joined together." As she put a cassette in the sleek white B&O stereo, I noted the accompanying card, "Happy Autumn. You are my love, Benjamin." Classical guitar played. Bretta said, "This is Doc playing. Isn't he fabulous?"

I answered, "Really? Powerful and passionate. He's very good."

As she emptied the brandy bottle into crystal goblets, I covertly checked the mixtape case label: "With love, Winston." Winston. What? Not mild-mannered Doc. Her mistake, or mislead? She said, "Jack, you made an impression tonight. You even stimulated Robin out of her shyness. She made a joke! What did you think of my friends?"

"I enjoyed meeting them. You have an interesting entourage."

She stood close to me. "Is that what you call them? Hmm, I like that."

"Hollywood term, right? Close friends, better than family."

"To our entourage." She clinked her glass to mine. "Follow me," she urged.

I followed Bretta to her studio room—oily scents of linseed and turpentine. She switched on the light and an artist's world leapt to life. On easels, paper, canvas and walls, were colors, brushstrokes, bold lines and fine. Musical notes danced through whimsical figures. Other work was on racks—abstract to Modernism. She watched my intense expression of wonder carefully.

"I'm experimenting," she said in a giggly voice. I met her gaze and she pulled me in for a sustained kiss. "Be right back."

I was overwhelmed as I took in the art and the artist. Bretta *was* art. I was in the presence of a truly creative person and I could feel her raw creative energy like a physical force in the room, something beyond mortal, mundane endeavors. I wondered if some science-fiction meter could measure this radiant aura. Her being an artist made her even more fascinating and desirable, like an exotic, sexy sprite.

One canvas caught my eye—a hand reached for a peacock-feather-winged butterfly as it crossed a sunflower sun. Yes, Bretta was a bright, beautiful gossamer-winged butterfly flying high through the rarified air—and I desired to catch her, and her creative vitality, tapping into the exquisite beauty of her imaginative world. I shook my head, and cautioned myself, Jesus, Jack, reel it in here. Down boy.

Bretta glided in front of her painting wearing a revealing gold silk robe. My resolve waning, my idolization rising, I said, "You, look so...delicious."

"How blue your eyes are." Bretta stared, inches from me. "I really do love the startling blue of your eyes."

"I love your work."

"I would love to paint you sometime." We were using the L-word. She kissed my eyes and breathed, "Jack, come with me."

There amidst her art, on her white daybed, with her new lover, Bretta took charge. The mystery guitarist's licks played, Bretta maneuvered me to the bottom and sucked on me. She cooed, "Oh, you're the one who is delicious."

She climbed on top and eased herself down, paused, testing. She slid the rest of the way home. She settled in and rode me slow and gentle at first, with a rhythm of her own, which, to my rock-and-roll sensibilities, were unfamiliar, and I was off her beat, so I yielded, I yielded to her. I fantasized her riding me as a carousel horse, as she rose and fell faster, then teasingly slower, then faster and stronger, and pausing again and waiting for me to settle down, and she was off to the races riding, riding, riding, reaching, reaching, reaching, as she almost reached, but missed and tried again, and finally reached that brass ring, and she fell on me in a gloriously blissful and satisfied heap. Alcohol-seduced sex, lust fulfilled, is Pagan's Garden of Earthly Delights.

I must have fallen asleep, as my mind drifted back. To childhood. To making what my mother called the "Lantern of Summer." Screened porch, guitar licks drift from park, hot evening darkens, cicadas chant soothing rhythms, buzz buzz buzzing in sweeping weeping willow. Lightning bugs we collect in a Mason jar. "Don't take too many," she warns. "You might get burned." Flashing supernatural lightning of living gold. Later, bare toes pushing willow's rope swing, with mystic lantern we float in glowing arcs. Soon I would be a child no more. Magic is fleeting. A firefly not set free, the glow will fade, fade, fade away.

CHAPTER 6

In Bretta's bed, in the middle of the night, my memories of childhood restlessly roamed...

#

On the way home from the circus, lying across the back seat of Uncle's new black Buick LeSabre, I gazed up at the clouds. The sticky sunny summers and blue skies were frequently interrupted by what my father had called "God clouds"—gigantic white puffs concealing animal shapes, often transforming into dark thunderheads.

After Rollo had given me the bent nail I tried to get Mother's attention to show her my joy. I was happy for the first time since my father left us. But these days my mother was so distant. Snapshots of Daddy slid in and out of my mind like changing the images on his old stereoscope View-Master. Oh, how I wished that he were here.

When the car slowed, I sat up to see the old brick and wood buildings of the familiar town square with its Civil War cannon we boys loved climbing, then the Dairy Bar, and Day's Café where Mother used to work. After a few blocks I looked beyond the railroad tracks, toward my old house. To Daddy's dismay, Uncle always called it "the ole' shithole."

Uncle's palatial white home sat on the edge of our town with spreading maple trees in the front and green cornfields right up to the backyard. My new home. Now that I was no longer one of the poor kids, I had expected to no longer be teased and picked on. It hadn't been so simple. I held the stuffed lion in my lap, making Leo valiantly battle the bent nail sword.

Uncle broke the silence when he turned and eyed me over the seat. "You nailed it, kid. For today."

"Thanks, Uncle."

"Be quiet, Jack," Mother warned.

Uncle's mansion. Uncle's "masculine Dorian columns, just like a Southern plantation" stood sentry—both ways. In the foyer, we passed the life-size sightless Italian marble statues. My aunt originally forced Uncle to keep them in the back garden. After her accident, they "moved in" and now lived with us. In the great Hall were Uncle's acquisitions from recent travels. Gilt-framed European paintings hung from every wall. Strewn throughout the mansion were pine crates filled with more paintings. Mother glared at the crates. "When are you going to do something with all these?"

"I like them that way." Uncle waved his arm. "I can do whatever I want with them. Maybe I should just throw them right out into the street." His eyes bore into her.

My mother nudged me toward the grand wooden staircase, turned and wordlessly walked away from Uncle.

In my third-floor dormer room the fading light from the window fell across my bookshelf and bed. I flung myself on the bed with an open book but my thoughts wandered with colors and sounds. The sun ground westward for a night of indefinite secrets. The circus made me optimistic that my family's losses and misfortunes could turn around. My proof was Uncle's kindness today, the lucky nail that Rollo had bent for me, and my stuffed lion. Even though I really liked the lion, the nail was special. I decided to award the lion prize to my mother for persevering through her own bad fortune.

That evening I came down the staircase and heard chopping sounds. I hoped for dinner. As I approached the cigar-smoky dining room I overheard voices and realized Uncle was using his hard laugh with Mother. The laugh I knew so well. I crept closer and placed my eye to the crack between the closed mahogany doors. Uncle chopped kindling at the fireplace with a hatchet. Mother sat at the long table. He was pressing his point and I heard my name.

"You have become too comfortable, sister. You know good and well, the arrangement about Jack is final." He smirked and said in his fake British accent, "Right between the eyes, where your beauty...lies." He raised the hatchet to Mother's face.

I slid open the doors and screamed, holding my nail up, prepared to defend my mother. Almost. In my mind—at that time, and again in ceaseless re-imaginings for years. Uncle leaned in closer. Through the crack, I saw her shiver. The hatchet was not the most alarming. What chilled me to the bone was what my mother said. I helplessly tried to unbend the big nail until my hands bled. That was the night I grew up. That night I found out the truth about my mother.

#

My relationship with Bretta intensified. I spent more time at her flat than at my place. We spent the most time at the Sav. Bretta had coined that nickname which was used exclusively by her entourage. The Sav quickly became my favorite bar ever, and Italian North Beach my favorite neighborhood—Italian blood ran in my veins. North Beach was now only part Italian with Chinatown encroaching, along with tawdry strip clubs. The wealthy owned Telegraph Hill with its landmark Coit Tower, middle-class apartments spread throughout the rest, and towards Ghirardelli Square and Fisherman's Wharf were housing projects.

The North Beach scene was swinging, with many live-music venues along Grant Avenue. I soon appreciated why North Beach had been a haunt of beatnik godfather Kerouac and his lost Beat Generation. Jack with Ginsberg, Ferlinghetti, Corso and other poets, were, by ten years, the precursors to the Haight's Hippies. North Beach retained that bohemian feel.

The twin ornate spires of Saints Peter and Paul Church towered nearly two hundred feet above Washington Square Park, once commanding—now seemingly less of a force, yet still watching over—the neighborhood. A classic, majestic cathedral, I was unsure why they called it simply a church. I was half Catholic, but not raised as one per se, and had not attended church in years. At one point in my life, I felt that I had been forsaken. All the same, I took to furtively crossing myself when passing by the cathedral, which may have been a breach of Catholic protocol. I figured it was better than nothing.

At the Sav, Bretta, Francine, Robin and George the bartender listened to Robert describing his audition at A.C.T. theater company. Z.Z. and I talked separately. "Jack, how do you like Bretta's artwork?"

I smiled. "It turns me on."

"Too bad you missed Bretta's opening last month at the gallery Robin manages, Galleria Di Belle Arti. She combined newsprint collages with Underwood and Hermes typewriter images—all black and white except for some accented color splashes. The gray scales were a little washed out. I don't know, perhaps it lacked passion."

"Oh, I think I did see one of those."

"The opening was still a success, except Bretta always gets so nervous at her openings, and then the comedown after the rush.

Benjamin hasn't adjusted so well to that, and to you of course. Have you talked to him?"

Benjamin was not over Bretta and he still hung around. I had gained some respect for him when Francine informed me that he wrote for the *Bay Guardian*. And that he was the author of the "Our Generation" article I had enjoyed. Since he was the sensitive writer type, I tried not to be a dick. I decided to use my experience with counseling to encourage him to move on. I found Benjamin in the middle room stumping for the re-election of President Carter. Motioning Benjamin away, I invited him out to the Sav's sidewalk patio table for a beer, a.k.a. a man-to-man chat. "So, Benjamin, how you doing with the whole Bretta thing?"

He floored me. "Bretta and I are getting back together."

"Benjamin, look, that's not happening any time soon. You know how fickle artists are."

"Artists? I'm so sick of artists getting the slack. From their first brush stroke on the canvas, or whatever, everyone can see their work, and say, 'Oh, it's so magnificent.' That's such bullshit! I'm a writer, and alone at night with my typewriter, trying to make my deadline and no one hovers around me, telling me how brilliant my first damn line is. I could type, 'In the beginning...' and no one would tell me how God-like it is. Or they think, 'It's just writing. I've been writing since second grade. It's not that hard.' Artists like to believe they're the only ones that suffer. Well, I suffer."

So much for our reconciliatory chat. Letting him rant would have to do: "Rock singers strut and sing, 'If I could stick a knife in my heart, suicide right on stage' pouring their hearts out about some misplaced love, and the chicks think they're so dreamy and studly and throw panties at them. But me? Where's my groupies? Where's my matron of the arts? I write an article or column that I edit and re-edit and polish, and the piece is artistic and sensitive and beautiful and, OK, maybe a little flowery...and everyone thinks I'm a flaming faggot! What's up with that?"

"I hear you man. I like your writing."

"But I tell you what." He lowered his voice. "I'm writing a "novel" that is going to blow some minds, man. I'm going to lay it out there. No holds barred, or no bars hold in this case, ya' know what I mean?" He finally paused for breath here, before amping up again. "But what really gets me, I try to talk to these people about what's going on in the world, and the world is going to hell, believe me, they act like it's below their artistic integrity or something. I mean the Mideast, Russia, right here even." His anger shifted to me in a verbal sucker punch. "Like assholes stealing other men's girl-friends. I've been nothing but supportive and faithful to her. She's a bitch." Benjamin panned his challenging glare from me to the motor-cycle encroaching in the red zone at the curb. "And look at that grubby piece of shit. Motorcycle riders are all dumbass...assholes. And they're getting laid."

And I was trying to let him down easy. "Dumbass assholes? Isn't that what a writer calls hyperbole? I'm the asshole who owns that bike." He didn't look ruffled, so I knew he knew. He shrugged.

I changed tack. "My party was fun, huh? Boy, that sexy little nursing student with the big lips, wow." He let a reminiscing smile slip. "And then you took her back to your place..."

Benjamin fidgeted in alarm. "How did you..."

"I'm sure she was worth cheating on Bretta."

"What...it's not like I...She ..."

I got to it: "Hey, everybody at some point gets dumped. When the music's over, turn out the light."

"You are a fucking fling. I'm going to marry Bretta."

"Benjamin, from what I hear, everybody wants to marry her. Maybe she's not the marrying kind."

He raised his voice. "You don't know her! You don't know Winston. You come out of nowhere, literally, I mean, like hop out of the fucking briar patch. And you think you're the man who was meant to tame her?" He slammed his beer down. "You, the circus clown?"

He was baiting me and he was coiled like a rattler, expecting me to blindly strike first so he could justifiably nail me. I held my tem-per in check. I had to. Since he begun agitating, I had surreptitiously positioned my right foot behind the front leg of his chair. Knowing he was a lefty, I placed my right hand gently on his left wrist on the table, and said, "Benjamin. I'm trying to play nice. You want to keep it that way, or get to it right here?"

As I anticipated, he tried to scoot his chair back to jump up. My foot stopped it and he fell back into the chair. He tried to pull his hand away but I held it fast, trapping him. He squirmed with sur-prise. I held my flat left hand up between our heads, ready as a karate chop for defense or a strike. He recognized it, yet unlike a fist, it would look casual to an observer.

"Brer' Fox," I drawled, "y'all appears to be stuck in this here clown's briar patch."

I glowered with my best alpha-male vibe. His eyes widened in fear before he relaxed in submission. Benjamin stammered, "I...I'm clearly up-s-set. S-s-cuse my manners, Jack. Thanks for the d-drink." I let him stand up. "I have to go write."

He stumbled away down the sidewalk wiping his eyes. I fished a Valium from my pants and washed the bitterness down with a slurp of beer. Benjamin was right about one thing. I felt badly. I should wash my grubby bike.

Unlike Benjamin, I didn't brag about my martial arts. I preferred the element of surprise. I was only a brown belt in Shotokan Karate and Tae Kwon Do. I liked the discipline and had been going three to five times a week. The Saturday morning sparring class was the toughest. No matter how much partying the night before, I still went. Despite what that damn Judge had ordered, I was prepared to protect myself. I had sworn that nothing like what I had once been through was going to happen again. I finished my beer and walked over to the butt-strewn gutter to check my bike. Bretta had never been on a motorcycle and refused to ride on mine. She confided that she was afraid of the spinning spokes and chain. I bent down to look at the leak. A tall figure loomed behind me and I swung around.

Monty took a step back. "What the hell did you do to Benjamin?"

"Et tu, Professor'"

"Ha. I'm just messing with you." Monty circled around me.

I unclipped my key ring from my belt loop. "Your buddy's not taking Bretta dumping him very well."

"Good, he can join the club." Interesting, but I didn't pursue it. He said, "Nice bike. What's with the big bent nail on your key ring? A weapon?"

"Maybe. A gift. My good luck charm."

"I had a 1970 Norton Commando 750 for years," Monty said.

"Those bikes rock. Everybody wanted one. Still do."

"Well, I hope the guy who wanted one enough to steal mine crashed and burned alive on it."

Something about Monty put me off balance. His vibe of being out of place, not making others, or even himself, comfortable. I should know. My life for the past year. Like he would never live up to expectations he had set for himself, or worse, assumed people had for him. It would take me a long time to discover what his troubles were about.

"You know that Dave Brubeck song we listened here to the other night?" he asked.

His question made me wonder if had seen my reaction. "'Take Five'. Smokin'."

"The hell of it was, it was his only big hit song, and the one track he didn't write. His sax player Paul Desmond did."

"Hmm. Like Jim Morrison. Supposed to be the writer, the poet. And the Doors first big hit was by the guitarist Robby Krieger. 'Light My Fire'."

Monty nodded and patted my bike's seat. "Motorcycles really separate the men from the boys."

"Yes, they do."

"Come on, Jack, I'll buy you a drink."

I clipped my nail back on my belt loop.

#

I was thirteen again. I ran across the field. My entire realm was Illinois prairie flat, which I thought to be the lay of the land in all places. An incongruent brown hill stood before me, the sun just risen, glowing to reveal the hill was the circus big top. Suddenly, the tent flattened straight to the ground as if an elephant had stepped on it. The rugged roustabouts rolled canvas and loaded up semis. Through the chilly dawn I saw light emanating from one of the little round-backed trailers. A giant figure loomed in the doorway. I gingerly walked toward it.

I held up the bent nail in my punctured hands and Rollo the Strongman looked down at me and smiled. "Hey, buddy," he said in his thick Eastern European accent, somehow tinged with a Southern drawl. He frowned. "Still having a rough time at home, eh? You need more muscle, buddy. Come in. Have bowl of oatmeal and fisheyes vith me." The trailer swayed under his weight. I limped up the stairs. He pointed to a chair before his tiny drop-down tabletop. "Here, sit."

"I—I better not. Fisheyes?"

"You know, ze cooked raisins."

Rollo placed two large bowls, serving bowls really, on the table. He was right. The raisins did look like cooked fisheyes. We ate in silence, his giant jaw working up and down. I finished and hinted, "Thanks. I guess maybe I should get going now?"

"Vhere you go?"

"I dunno. Can't go home."

"Vhy not?"

"No family anymore."

"Oh." The big man thought for a minute, like thinking was difficult for him. "Well, ve are like family. Zat's vhy I stick around. Bunch of characters, zat is for certain. Ho-ho."

"Could I...join your family?"

"Sorry, buddy. I cannot ask you to, you know, run away vith us."

Crestfallen, I turned away.

"But," he scratched his head, "if a feller climb in ze back of that blue trailer truck over zere," he pointed, "under some of zat canvas, and no one saw him, vell, ve'all are heading south to Paducah. Very nice in the Soud. And once zere, Mr. Skeeter, you know, the boss-man, vould maybe have to put a feller to vork as, you know, as vater boy, or animal feeder, or such, to earn his keep."

"Oh."

"So, you eat another bowl of z'oatmeal before you head out–to vherever you are going." One of his big eyes winked at me.

Just like that, I left my old world behind and entered the world of illusion. Ten years later a man called The Joker would reveal how similar those worlds truly were.

#

Robin was right. Bretta was the type of woman whom most men desired, and for whom some men went gaga. I needed to play it cool. I was not going to wind up like Benjamin. Bretta was catnip for men. "Brettnip" had the Gemini's dichotomy, the duality of the twins. She flipped from the effervescent light of a girl to the irrepressible sexuality of a woman. She was unlike other women I had known. My late girlfriend was "the girl next door" type. The women I had worked with in L.A. were liberated, but still tools for men with power and money. I could understand their hollow coldness. To us, it was a job, a well-paying job. After the shoots were over I kept to myself, often watching classic films at revival house cinemas like the Nuart.

One evening after her shift, Bretta complained, "It's irksome that the customers at the store keep asking me out."

"Well, look at you. You're irresistible."

"All those customers flirting with me does make me horny." She swayed her body. "Don't I have fascinating problems?" Bretta immediately waltzed me up the hall, disrobing me along the way, past guitar-scales-practicing Doc, and into her bedroom. We playfully struggled for dominance before she surrendered.

After all the covers were in shambles, I rolled over, sucking air for a moment, listening to her roommate's guitar. She nibbled on my nipples. "Ow. I'll show you," I told her. "I am King Dong! and you my captive, Fay Wray." In a ringmaster voice, I continued, "Ladies and gentlemen, announcing, for the exciting climax of their performance…I am going to make you scream, my queen, by driving you ape-shit!"

We made love once more, with the classical guitar as a soundtrack, until Bretta's moans intensified to a loud release. A few moments later, she breathed, "Now, my turn." She crawled under the covers. Later, I would consider the significance of Doc's guitar halting mid-phrase and the front door slamming.

Eventually resurfacing at the foot of the bed, Bretta, in damp repose, attempted the intimate post-coital conversation males dread, lilting, "Jack, my lover, what brought you to our Golden State? The circus?"

"A fortuneteller told me to—" I switched to a crone's voice. "—'Head west where you will meet a short, light and handsome—artiste. And she will pull you in like the *moon* to the *sun*.'"

She laughed. "Come on, really."

"Not with the circus. I hated leaving my circus friends behind. My circus friends were like your entourage. A real cast of characters."

Bretta stroked my tattoo and kissed my bicep as I continued. "In between circus seasons we spun off in different directions to return in the spring. When the circus toured through the South I met a woman in Savannah. She was in town for a photo shoot on Southern artists. She invited me to visit her in Colorado where she now lived. Later I hitched to her home in Boulder and met her son Bill. Bill was a little jealous of my relationship with her at first, but soon was cool with it and we became good friends. She was a surrealist landscape oil painter, very hip, and turned me on to Beat poetry and Kerouac. She encouraged Bill and I to road trip together. So Bill and I got *On the Road* ha-ha and headed West. Bill's mom was not really a crone, at all, as you probably figured. Not at all."

Bretta wrinkled her nose.

"We followed Route 66 to L.A. Bill launched his photography career with a volunteer gig at the underground Freep…"

"*The L.A. Free Press.*"

"Right. Bukowski's drunken poetic column, "Notes From a Dirty Old Man," blew my mind. Anyway I needed the bread, so I became involved in the, umm, erotic film scene there. Like I said, I wanted to see the Golden Gate Bridge and San Francisco, so I moved up here."

"So you were just a normal teenager." We laughed. "My years growing up in upstate New York were almost normal."

"Is that where you took your art training?"

"I went to NYU's Gallatin Art School for awhile. I traveled in Turkey, Afghanistan, hitched around Europe, for a year or so with a friend…"

"Oh. No wonder you can blend in the Haight. I figured you for first class all the way."

"No, that's not me. I returned to New York but, you know, it's New York. My mother and I soon followed my father out to California."

"Good thing for me." I reached for her again, but she sat up and opened her Little Blue Journal ("LBJ") with silver stars and a tiny lock. She wrote in it, what I hoped was romantic things about me. Bretta locked it, kissed me, and went to take a shower.

I stared at the mysterious LBJ. I got up and looked in Bretta's closet searching for my missing favorite vest. I parted hanging formal gowns I had never seen, and lacy slips, with interest, and there it was. I grabbed my vest off a worn guitar case and knapsack. The case was covered with peeling travel stickers: Roma, Barcelona, München, Madrid, Marrakesh, and other exotic locales. The nametag stopped me cold, "Winston." Winston, again. I wondered, who is this Winston? Why was my jacket there? A Freudian slip? Why did I have a weird feeling about this unknown man more than Benjamin or Supernatural's customers? The jealousy wormed around my insides.

#

Events broke quickly after that. Bretta quit her job. "Time for my next phase. I've flying down to L.A. for a meeting about a possible art project. This could be a big break for me. While I'm there I'll spend some time with my father."

Just before she left she sat with me on her sofa and she told me about her parents. As Robert had implied, Bretta's father was somebody. As was her mother. In fact, Bretta was American royalty. Her father was a big Hollywood star in film and television. Her mother had been an actress, magazine cover girl, and a world-renowned dancer sought for her risqué Egyptian belly dancing technique. I was embarrassed that I had tried to impress Bretta with my cheesy roles.

We kissed lingering goodbyes in front of her flat, like only new lovers can, and Monty took her tugging heart away in his Yellow Cab. That week, I was appreciative and surprised that she frequently called just to talk. From the City of Angels—where dudes partied harder, faster, richer and prettier than Baghdad-by-the-Bay, "Brettnip" was phoning me. Jack. I accepted this as a good omen that my sunshine girl had more than a fleeting crush on me.

I finished my stint at recycling, received my "Certificate of Completion," and bade farewells to the recycling crew. Bretta returned, hopeful that the art project would come through in a few months. Despite the elation I felt with our passionate relationship, a sense of unease began to build like atmospheric pressure. It was difficult to ascertain whether the feeling was just mine, or everyone's. As it turned out, the pressure was from below. The rolling jolt hit on a Monday morning before noon.

CHAPTER 7

At work I was researching Bretta's dad in the bookstore's film section. On a campy TV series in the sixties that everyone saw. Just a few years back he had a big comeback in a Best Picture movie and only this summer the hit sequel had come out. Nominations for Oscar, Golden Globe, Tony, BFTA awards. Won several Emmys, and a star on Hollywood Boulevard! Man, Bretta was *so* out of my league. Last year he was in a movie with the slinky Goldie Hawn, whom I once bumped into in LA and said hello to her lovely lip mole. Come to think of it, Bretta resembled the headshot of Goldie, with the same mole and...

Rumble CRASH! Bookshelves collapsed. Stacks of books hurtled to the floor in tumbling clatters. I stagger-stepped, dropped my clipboard, ran through the store, not quite knowing what to do. So I froze, wondering if I should run out an alarmed exit door. Then all was still again. I had felt a couple of smaller quakes before, but this rumbler was freaky. Apparently just freaky for non-natives like my co-worker Montesha and me. Now, everyone else went on with their business like the quake had been a passing cloud.

Montesha was an older heavyset woman and our only black employee. From her plush office chair, she ran the Bookstore helpdesk like a director on a movie set. She had covered my butt often and now she needed a return favor. During the quake, she had partially squeezed under her desk.

"Jackie! I'm stuck. Don't you let folks see my ass this way," Montesha called in a muffled voice. "Pull me out, pull!" As I helped her back into her seat, she declared, "Gotta duck and cover, baby!"

The earthquake was a 5.8. Native Californians had an attitude of "Relax, Ex-Lax, no big deal," acting like they had personal immunity built up from the '06 quake that had leveled and burned the City.

Something else would rock my world that day. Bretta called me for the very first time at work. My immediate thought was that the trembler dashed her art collection from the walls or broke the big bay window. No such luck. Bretta's fabled shadowy friend, Winston, had inexorably returned from Scotland. She announced with excitement, "I can't wait for you to meet him. I've invited the entire entourage and friends over tonight for 'Winston's Welcome Back Soirée.'"

The day continued off kilter. That evening, getting ready in my apartment. I heard another rumble: an aftershock! I eyed the space between the milk crates holding up my bed, ready to dive, until I realized that the *bumm, bum, bum, bummm* was a rolling bass line. It sounded like the Clash and I knew the riotous notes must be from the Boston Boys below. The music was visceral, pummeling a number of emotions out of me— sexuality, excitement, anxiety, yearning, rebellion, more sexuality. My entire body seemed to vibrate as the song called to me.

I grabbed the six-pack of Michelob I was bringing to the fucking "soirée" and trotted down the stairs and into their open door. The Boston Boys were jumping up and down in the kitchen with big grins. "Brand new!" Jimmie yelled. "*London Calling*. Wicked good!"

"So good," Obie yelled, "we just bought this pissa 200-watt RMS system at Pacific Stereo."

Jimmie restarted the album. Obie spied my paper bag and pulled out a "key" opener as encouragement. With beers in hand, we sang along as Joe Strummer wailed, "…The ICE AGE IS COMING, the SUN is zooming in… …'n I... LIVE BY THE RIV-ER…" We all jumped up and down like kids, bottles spewing beer foam on the linoleum. I was blown away—the "oh-oh-oh-oh," the charging bass, the echo. It was as if we knew we were jumping into an entirely different world.

Exhilarated, I marched down the street. I couldn't wait to see Bretta! Of her current entourage, apparently many of us were meeting Winston for the first time. My elation melted. Jimmie had mentioned that "London Calling" was about the Three Mile Island nuclear meltdown just a few months back. Why did there have to be an earthquake today? Churning jealousy returned.

Outside Bretta's flat, I reflexively fished a Valium from my vest pocket to my mouth. The place was swinging when I arrived. Pot smoke and guitar music filled the air. This was, for the Haight, an upscale crowd. It was conspicuous that even during the recession, money came easily to these people. I furtively crammed my contribution, a ripped bag with two remaining beers, into the fridge. A group in the kitchen talked politics, including Benjamin. I nodded to him as he lowered his head.

Bretta appeared. Brilliant in her long burgundy skirt with matching fitted short-waist jacket over a gold midriff top. Her trademark pool-chalk liner made her golden eyes pop. She touched my cheek, and greeted "Welcome, Jack, and all my wondrous friends!"

The New Wavers squealed hellos with Robert blurting to Bretta, "My acting classes are going fabulously. I'd love you to come watch my next workshop performance."

"My first time at Bretta's salon!" Edith gushed. She thrust a portfolio case at Bretta. "Please look at these and tell me what you think. I mean, when you have a chance."

Bretta breezed through them. On one painting she suggested, "Adore your steely blues but why don't you try a palette knife instead of a brush in an area like this. Come listen to Doc." Bretta ushered us into the crowded oak-paneled living room. Doc sat in a curve-back chair in his customary white shirt, fingering classical pieces on one of his two exquisite Martin guitars, worth thousands of dollars each. What a culture Clash. I could play decent rock guitar, though I still felt shy about performing in public. Doc was a superb technical guitarist, yet, something was lacking in his performance. Music is not just about technique.

Bretta clipped Edith's charcoal cityscape over a beautiful painting, announcing, "My good friend Edith's latest work." Edith was delighted as polite applause sounded. Francine, in red capris and a tight, striped French sweater, moved in to look, followed by several men with eyes on her rather than the drawing. One passed Francine a joint, which Z.Z. got in on. Edith cornered Robin to ask her opinion.

"Oh. Um. It's very much Woody Allen's *Manhattan*," Robin offered.

Z.Z. grinned. "Loved the movie; with Hemingway's granddaughter."

"And with Gershwin," a long-sideburned man intoned.

"Well, hello, handsome," Z.Z. greeted me. In an aside, said, "Robin means it looks like Bretta's work from last year."

Bretta gleamed as hostess, giving everyone a measure of exclusive attention. Doc launched a ragtime, Betty Boop cartoon-sounding tune.

"What's that Doc's playing?" I asked Mr. Sideburns.

He looked at me appraisingly and said, "Jangle."

"Jangle?" I repeated.

"No. Django. D-j-a-n-g-o, as in Reinhardt." He walked away smirking, I assumed to share the humor of my ignorance.

Bretta, who made theatrical gestures seem natural, held Robert's hand up and announced, "Robert is an apprentice actor at the American Conservatory Theater. His class performs a scene from *Streetcar* next Wednesday afternoon. See him now before Hollywood snatches him up." Robert brandished flyers and made a move to pass them out before Bretta guided him to a side table.

A glass of wine hovered in front of my face, with Robin attached. I shook my head no. "Thanks, but wine's usually too sweet for me. I'll stick to beer."

"Jack, that's him—Winston." Robin indicated with the glass.

I looked across the room for Winston, saying, "Not really looking forward to him," before realizing Robin meant the man standing right damn next to us. Winston smiled and waved a big hand with slender fingers to me before resuming his conversation with Bretta. He had a similar tall build and look as Monty, who was notably absent from this affair. Winston was maybe thirty, had trimmed, premature Steve-Martin-silvery hair, a scar on his face and walked with a limp. He wore a loud teal and pink Hawaiian shirt and seemed a little too cool and comfortable with himself, as if he was unconcerned how others might regard him. Bretta's hand poised on his waist with an undercurrent of more than friendship. Perhaps a rip current more.

Restless, I confided to Robin, "This seems like a cocktail party for our parents rather than for us."

"Bretta's soirée is really more of a salon."

"Edith said that, but what does that mean?"

Robin recited, "French: an inspiring host's open house for refining, avant-garde cultural, social, philosophical gatherings, and of course, mutual amusement."

"Well, I'm not amused."

"But you are..." she laugh-snorted "...a muse."

I looked at her quizzically and excused myself. I moseyed by some conversations. "The quake damaged Lawrence Livermore Lab in the East Bay." "Scary." "Nuclear materials are stored there." "It will be OK," Z.Z. said. "No, it could be another Three Mile Island!" Benjamin insisted. Benjamin and Sideburns' political disagreement heated up. Benjamin said, "...plus, you're disregarding the nice

Christmas present the Russians are giving to Afghanistan —an invasion."

Bretta diffused the serious talk in a Chinese accent, "Confucius say, 'War does not determine who is right; War determines who is left.'" People laughed but pedantic Sideburns protested. "Now, Hagel, in *Philosophy of Right...*"

Bretta held up a napkin-covered platter to the man and posed a riddle. "What is the only fruit with its seeds on the outside?"

"Uh, the pomegranate," Sideburns guessed. A moment passed and Francine impatiently called, "We give up."

Bretta pulled the napkin off, announcing, "Strawberries!" The group *oohed* and *aahed*. She passed the platter with brown sugar and crème fraîche to Doc, which was his cue to stop playing. Bretta beamed him a smile. "That was splendid, Doc."

Her friends pattered applause and murmured in agreement. Bretta continued the floorshow by bringing out the tattered and travel-stickered guitar case I had spotted in her closet. She handed it to Winston.

"Bretta, my dear, I must beg off, I apologize—I am very rusty. I have not played for months while ensconced in my Scottish castle. Perhaps...if you have a set of bagpipes?"

We didn't know if he was kidding or merely being odd. Bretta laughed, though insisted. "Please Winston, please! For old time's sake?" He nodded acquiescence. He unlatched the case, retrieved a pedestrian-looking Harmony guitar, and slowly strummed discordant chords. Some rolled their eyes while Francine twittered. I wondered why he had not tuned it first. Bretta patted his back in encouragement. He tuned and strummed again. He was rusty. Guests resumed chatting and partying. I wondered why Bretta would embarrass him this way, although it gave me some satisfaction.

Robert and Edith joined me. Edith said, "That Winston, what a character." Robert whispered, "Some of the entourage are surprised he actually came back."

Francine did not whisper. "I heard he was a little prick."

Winston pulled a Sucrets box out of the case, took out five long fingernails, and carefully glued them over his own right-hand nails. Still a little jealous, I insulted him, saying, "I haven't seen a dude wear fake nails outside of Hollywood Boulevard."

"Or Finocchio's," Francine joked, referring to San Francisco's well-known female impersonator show. The group's attention resumed.

As Bretta lit some candles, Winston casually explained, "These are not fake. In fact, they were given to me by an old gypsy. These are the actual fingernails of a Spanish guitarist, long dead." He paused, to continue in a low voice, "Are you aware, one's nails continue to grow in the grave?"

The group stared with rapt attention. Some snickered. Francine murmured, "Creepy."

The lights went out and some jumped. I saw Bretta's finger on the button.

Winston continued. "The gypsy told me that he had traded two burros and a chicken for them. Legend was they would allow the owner to play guitar as no other. He was dismayed that they were not right for him. In fact, the nails were very wrong." The candlelight flickered across his scarred face. "He told me he could sense gypsy blood in me and that I should have them. I too, thought it unbelievable, macabre. Nonetheless, I found with these..." he blew and waved the nails. "...I could play my instrument like a man *possessed*."

Winston opened with the guitar solo from "While My Guitar Gently Weeps" while fine-tuning and transposing into the bridge from "Here Comes the Sun." Not bad. A cascading Spanish melody intro. Then he kicked into a heart-wrenching series of notes that gave me chills.

Doc sighed, "Al Di Meola's 'Mediterranean Sundance.'"

Winston's fingerpicking, strumming, and syncopated tapping on the soundboard of the guitar body gave the aural sensation of a *trio* — two guitars plus percussion. Winston's performance wove together like a rich tapestry. Many of us sank to the floor, enthralled.

Bretta dramatically removed her jacket and with a wink, placed it across my lap. She swayed sensuously, slowly at first, easing into a dance. She was captivating, juxtaposing an erect, upright carriage with serpentine hand and arm movements. Willowy evocative Mid-Eastern belly dance moves, and melds back to flamenco. She must have trained with her mother. Her handclaps and body movements maintained perfect sync with Winston's music.

The intensity built, with Winston's guitar and Bretta's stomping dance steps reverberating on the hardwood floor and through the flat. Eyes followed from Winston's flying fingers to Bretta's exotic performance. Bretta plucked Francine's scarf and changed styles, flowing, undulating through the room like a Greek goddess, beckoning and beguiling her guests. Z.Z. murmured, "She's channeling Isadora Duncan." Right in front of me, Bretta performed a backbend while shaking her hips. I became sexually aroused. Embarrassed, I clutched her jacket in front of my lap, suspecting that was why she gave it to me.

Winston's lush sound valleyed and peaked, volleyed and paled, only to rise again to reach little sustains, Bretta holding her poses during the sustains. After more guitar riffs and Bretta's twirls around the room, Winston leapt from his chair and squeezed out the longest sustain I had ever heard on an acoustic guitar. Bretta caressed the guitar body and held her pose. Winston's crescendo to a soul-wrenching, flourishing, resonant climax was mind-blowing, and Bretta fell onto the sofa close to Winston, "spent" for perfect theatric effect.

I about fell over, too. Everyone *ole'd*, cheered, applauded enthusiastically. Francine exclaimed, "That! was the next best thing to sex." Laughter erupted. I felt jealous of this magnificent guitar man and suddenly inadequate.

Even Sideburns was impressed. "You sound like Al Di Meola and Paco de Lucia at the same time!" Doc proclaimed, "You are the Paganini of guitar."

Winston held up his fingernails. "Flamenco is really Gypsy blues."

I must have appeared noticeably concerned about the now coolestguyintheroom, for Baskin' Robin whispered to me in her sometimes-robotic way of speaking, "It's COOL, don't be jealous. Winston is just her best man-friend. Kind of like a horse."

Semi-encouraged, I moved over to the heaving-bosomed Bretta with her jacket. "Not much of a dancer, eh?"

Bretta caught Winston's eyes before she whipped Francine's scarf around me and pulled me down next to her, radiating sultry energy. I possessively kissed her. Francine watched with an envious look, perhaps because her scarf was getting more action than she. Doc looked embarrassed, which I thought at the time was because he had been upstaged on the guitar. Doc bowed to Winston and went to his room, where scales soon emanated.

The party was reinvigorated. Sideburns put an electro-pop LP on the stereo. He announced, "I feel that *zeitgeist* is shifting."

I listened. "Zeitgeist sounds just like Kraftwerk."

"No, it's not a band. Hmm, it should be. Don't you read? Hegel. Zeitgeist! The spirit of the times. We are precariously entering the new decade. The quake was a presaging. Gird your loins, young man. Gird your loins."

The entire day had racked me with disorienting moods. When Bretta introduced me to Winston, I briefly complimented his skill but avoided a conversation.

In the wee hours, when all guests had gone, even Z.Z., Bretta and I retired to her bedroom.

"At last," she sighed to the ceiling. She placed a hand on *my* waist. I let my gird down from my loins.

"Now my Jack, my patient lover, we must consummate the pent-up passion of my performance in a rapturous dance of our own."

Watching Bretta that evening, I realized how much I loved her, although I had tried not to. Loving her seemed—not dangerous, for that is too strong of a word, yet with such a woman—risky. Now that she had fallen for me, my love was rendered safer. I knew that as I was letting myself go, I might go all the way.

> One does not have to be
> so careful who they love
> but how they love.

CHAPTER 8

Bretta preferred we sleep at her flat as she liked to paint when inspiration struck. Fortunately for me, wanting Bretta for myself, Doc was determined to be as good as Winston, his new guitar god, and kept to his room, practicing. Winston dropped by a couple of times. When he was around, Doc hounded him about guitar technique which Winston tired of. I discovered that the sophisticated voice and manner which I was intimidated by that first night was a put-on. Speaking of acts, Winston made a disappearing act as quickly as he had arrived. Bretta dismissed this as normal.

For a blissful week it felt like a honeymoon. We ate out and came back to her place. Her entourage somehow survived at the Sav without her. We spent a good portion of time having sex. I couldn't get enough of that Sugar Crisp. Our accompaniment was often with Doc's grimly determined, endless guitar practice. Bretta and I practiced *our* technique—fulfilling each other's wants, needs and desires.

Somehow, although we lived mere blocks away, Bretta's flat received more sun. Of course. I loved waking up late on weekends in the bedroom of her flat with the big corner bay window facing easterly. The morning sun would break through the fog, giving her yellow bedroom a beautiful luminosity, and we would have wake-up sex.

I knew that women easily could fake climaxes to boost the partner's ego. I sought the real thing. I ascertained that when Bretta and I were having sex and kissing, her tongue and mouth would rise slightly in temperature. When she climaxed her temperature noticeably dropped. Temperature doesn't lie. I used that indicator as my signal for me to go ahead and orgasm in the Holy Grail of relationship sex—the coveted simulgasm. She was impressed with my timing, although I never revealed my "tongue test" trick.

One morning she resurfaced from at the opposite end of her bed, saying, "Jack, you're so hard to describe."

"Why?"

Speaking in Jack-be-nimble rhyme, she said, "Jack my sensitive warrior, if we hadn't met, I'd be sorrier."

I laughed. "Actually, I would feel better with a sword in my hands."

"What do you mean?"

"The fortuneteller—I'm serious this time—told me that I was reincarnated from William Wallace."

"I don't know who he is."

"He was a Scotsman who became a leader for Scotland's independence. He led the Scotts in battle. My father was named after him."

"Ahh, so you are a natural born leader."

"No, I'm more of a private person than you. I don't like being the center of attention. When I am, I get into trouble."

"Do you think I like it?" she teased.

"You love it. You can handle it. When people expect me—want me to be something, do something…"

"You don't have to."

"Sometimes we have no choice. Sometimes it's their choice, or our—I don't know—non-choice…nature. Like we are destined or compelled to react in certain ways. Like pinball."

"I've never played. With those balls." She caressed mine. "Everyone simply must love you at the Bookstore. You're King of the Books."

"Sure. But I have always considered myself more of a lone wolf."

"You think that others know what they are doing, but have you ever considered they are winging it, too? Or maybe reacting to you? You cause things to happen, people to react, more than you think. Weren't you under tutelage of a ring master? You have potential to be even more of a leader. At some point you will take charge."

"William Wallace took charge because he wanted freedom for Scotland, but he was betrayed by his own goddamn people."

"Jesus, Jack, somebody really hurt you, didn't they? I'm so sorry." She became teary eyed.

"No, Bretta, I'm all right. Don't cry. I survived."

#

I survived because I had run away. After I realized my mother's complicity. And betrayal. By dawn's light I walked to the dark cattailed pond in which the boy had drowned. I peered into the peaceful murky water and startled when a bluegill jumped. I almost fell in. I wondered if my classmate had lulled himself into a premature sleep. After what my Dad had done, it seemed so inviting, so easy.

I opened the trash bag with the pillowcase inside, and filled it with rocks. I tied, swung the pillowcase around my head and threw the whole nasty business of my uncle out into the water to watch it sink. I had my revenge.

I walked across the fields to the circus and never went back. My mother? At first, I had wondered how much she knew. She was clearly afraid of him—under Uncle's spell. My innocence was just the cost of doing business. Me paying her rent. Damage of a collateral nature. That morning, I had discovered the final ugly truth.

#

I returned to my Willard Street apartment for the first time in several days. I took my mail upstairs and relaxed, feeling good about being in my own space again. Sitting on the sofa I sorted through my overdue bills and student loan late notices and was pleased to discover a letter. The envelope had no return address and a Las Vegas postmark. I opened it and read the ornamental writing on stock blank stationary.

Dear Jack,

This will come as a surprise after all this time, but I feel I owe it to you to reach out. Hard to believe it has been 10 years. I hope you are in good health and spirits. Sadly, I am not. My new abode has not done much for me. Pretty much everything you have heard about a place like this is true.

You know that I have always, and will always consider you my son, and much more. You know the way I feel about you. I have missed you. I hated it when you ran off like you did. Without even saying goodbye. But now that we have finally tracked you down, I look forward to resuming our relationship. You are in San Francisco, after all. Ha ha.

You're probably wondering how I got out here. Not long after I became Mayor, that bitch accused me of embezzling the money. She shut up pretty quick, but I guess not quick enough. You know how things can go when they turn on you. Then the Feds had to get involved and it all went to shit. Anyway, I've about served my time now. So, I'll be hoping to see you real soon, Jackie. You understand that this has to be our little secret. But I know you can keep a secret.

P.S. Keep your back door open for me!

Yours, aka XRAY

Ray is my uncle's name. I sucked in air. How did he find me? I hoped this was a psychological threat and not a real one. I swore bitterly and tore the letter into pieces. There was nothing I could do but wait and see. I had no idea that I would be preoccupied with unexpected danger close to home.

#

Our honeymoon over, Bretta's desire for the Sav and her entourage not only resumed, but amplified. Bretta remained adamant against riding on my bike. Like many young people in the city, neither Bretta nor I wanted the expense of a car and the hassle of parking. We could get cross-town to North Beach by jumping on the streetcar and a couple of bus transfers. Francine had a BMW, but also varying excuses for her to never drive us.

Baskin' Robin always offered her vehicle, a *Deux Chevaux,* a Citroën model which I had not known existed. Sporting a cheap Earl Scheib two-tone paint job, Robin bragged, "The *Deux Chevaux* was France's answer to the VW bug."

"Yes, and the answer was given by a mime," Francine quipped.

Robin adored that weird little underpowered car, calling the red and off-red vehicle "Mon Chéri" and saying, " Je t'adore, Mon Chéri!" I called it simply "Cherry."

Robin used the car for Bosco-the-horse activities, so Cherry also smelled hazily of stable. Z.Z. nicknamed the car *"Eau de Chevaux."* Weather permitting, I would pull the strange curved canvas top back for fresh air. The half-eaten Ghirardelli and Guittard chocolate bars in the glove box, and the wrappers fluttering underfoot, did help mask *Eau de Chevaux.* I suspected that Robin's cherubic figure was chocolate based.

As a motorcyclist, I understood the sentiment for temperamental machinery. Owners of vehicles of a certain breed and age needed a personal relationship—"Com'on Betsy, please start." Robin always let me drive because she was an easily distracted driver, and I was a nervous passenger. A cassette tape of Piaf hissed nonstop through the bolted-on Radio Shack player. Bretta, Robin, Francine and Z.Z. frequently sang along with perfect dialect.

At the Sav, members of the entourage were always present. Benjamin still frequented the Sav but kept more of a distance. Now that Winston was back, more-or-less, Monty's appearances were less frequent, I understood from some past dynamics I was not privy to. Still adjusting to "group dating," I asked, "Bretta, can't we just go somewhere, anywhere, alone?"

She replied with that innocent lilt, "Oh, Jack, isn't it more festive with everyone?"

Her lilt made it difficult to disagree. However, I did. Festive, to me, meant the barkers and the colored balloons, fire-eaters, monkey-shines, roars of the crowd, and a sword swallower. At least I had my own sword swallower now.

That evening Doc looked perturbed. Later in the week, the flat, usually filled with music, seemed strangely quiet. Doc acted more detached, but again, he was never Mr. Ebullient. I passed by his room one Saturday afternoon and saw him just sitting on his bed, staring at his guitar lying before him. I was about to joke if he wanted a cigarette for his "girlfriend," but restrained myself, and just said, "What's up, Doc?" He gave no response.

I asked Bretta about him, and she said he had skipped his music classes all week. I suggested that perhaps he received a bad grade. Late that night as I was drifting off with Bretta in my arms, I heard Doc's guitar music. I was relieved he was playing again. It struck me that it was the first non-classical tune I had heard him play. A Dylan tune I couldn't quite place. Early the next morning I awoke and saw a red-eyed Doc standing next to our disheveled bed, observing Bretta sleeping. He was holding a barely-visible guitar string stretched between his clenched fists. I nudged her awake and Doc just stared at her.

I raised the covers, prepared to flip them over his face and the string and leap from the bed.

"Good morning, roomie," Bretta mumbled sleepily.

He wordlessly marched out of the flat. That whole deal was weird, but got weirder. I reminded Bretta that I was part Italian and I had seen *The Godfather*. I know what can be done with a wire.

#

There was no word from Doc for days and we worried. A neighbor had just told us what just happened to the son from *Zen and the Art of Motorcycle Maintenance*. Chris Pirsig had been stabbed to death just up Haight Street near the Zen Center. He was not quite 23. Horrible. I loved motorcycling, and that beautifully metaphysical book, and was quite shaken. Doc sometimes meditated at the Center and it made us both worry...murderer, or about to be murdered? It seemed that anything could happen.

The doorbell buzzed and we both jumped. Bretta and I both ran for the door. I pushed her behind me and peered out the little brass peephole. It was not Doc. I opened the door.

Standing there was an older couple. They could only be Doc's parents. The father was a spitting be-spectacled image of Doc, wearing a white shirt, only bald. The Craddocks entered cautiously glancing around at the mish-mosh of hanging art. Doc must have told them something about us.

Mr. and Mrs. Craddock curtly explained that they had received an odd call from Doc and that they had quickly flown in from Dallas. They had rescued their son from some seedy Tenderloin hotel and immediately admitted Doc to a hospital.

"For what?" Bretta asked in dread.

The Craddocks looked at one another and announced in unison, "Exhaustion."

Mrs. Craddock qualified, "The poor boy simply wore himself out. All that practicing. We are here to collect his things." We assumed she meant Doc's personal items for his hospital stay and offered a bag.

"ALL his things!" Mr. Craddock clarified.

The Craddocks seemed afraid to touch anything in Doc's room, and actually put on gloves. We watched through the door, which they shut. We sat in the living room and heard little phrases of disgust and alarm. They finally exited, having retrieved Doc's three Martin guitars and sparse belongings. They now looked at us with wide eyes like we were fiends from *Reefer Madness*. Mrs. Craddock held a pile of brown spiral bound notebooks. I had seen them and thought they were his schoolwork, notes and so forth. She held an open one up. At the top of the page it read, "MY DIARY III."

Oh shit. I thought. Later Bretta told me she had thought the same thing.

"This! Is a den of iniquity," Mama Doc remarked tersely.

That night at the Sav, the entourage helped us piece it together. Doc was in love with Bretta. Z.Z. and Francine had suspected this, but since everybody was in love with Bretta, no one paid adequate attention. Z.Z. agreed with our suspicions.

"'Exhaustion' means nervous exhaustion, which means nervous breakdown, which means Doc lost it."

We were unaware and perhaps uncaring that Doc, while trying to concentrate on his music theory and classical guitar lessons, considered our frequent sexual escapades extremely noticeable, and perhaps offensive. He had perfect pitch, so certainly perfect hearing from his musically trained ear.

"I should have been more compassionate to the poor man," Bretta moaned.

"Would have only encouraged him," Francine said, coolly sipping her cocktail. "Men don't want a woman's compassion, only passion."

I recollected to our friends, that after one of our particularly exuberant lovemaking sessions, in the still of the night I thought I had heard him crying. I said I wondered if the gloves had something to do with fingerprints, and what we had suspected Doc might have done to someone with his guitar string.

"I think that his parents were more concerned with particulate from ejaculate," Francine suggested with all her finesse.

A few nights later we found out it was worse. Mr. Craddock phoned Bretta while I listened in. They were withdrawing him from school, and he confirmed that the hospital caring for Doc was UCSF Langley Porter. The psych ward.

He reported icily, "If our son doesn't improve in the next week or so we'll have to send him to the Mayo to receive electric shock treatments, for God's sake. I hope you hippies are happy."

Bretta, in tears, offered to visit Doc. Mr. Craddock hung up on her. It was admittedly a bad idea. Doc just got hit with that flipper one too many times and flipped. Bretta and I felt terrible of course, but it was Bretta's place, and even with his bedroom just on the other side of the wall, what were we to do? Doc flew east, west, and over the Cuckoo's Nest. For some reason, Bretta thought Winston could help Doc. However, Winston disappeared again right at this time.

Saturday night, our entourage organized to meet at the Sav for a special Doc tribute. Bretta, Francine, Robin, Z.Z. and I squeezed into the *Deux Chevaux*, running late as usual.

I ground a gear, and Robin cried, "Sacre bleu!" The car's four-speed shifter oddly stuck horizontally from the dash and I double clutched to make it shift smoother. With that many passengers I kept on the flat streets, and still had to keep it floored to maintain speed. On fast corners, the body would rise up on the soft suspension as in a Mickey and Goofy cartoon, giving the feeling that the passenger compartment was about to simply fall over. When this or other quirky car events occurred, Robin exclaimed, "Sacre bleu!" and we all started singing out as a chorus, "Sacre bleu!"

The Dolby-less hissy, stuck tape played and the girls and Z.Z. sang. I hummed, as I did not know French and my Mid-western mouth struggled to form lippy French.

Des nuits d'amour à plus finir, Un grand bonheur qui prend sa place, Les ennuis, les chagrins s'effacen, Heureux, heureux à en mourir...

"We can't sing Piaf!" Robin cried. "Not this song. Not now." The singing faltered.

"You're absolutely right, Robin," I agreed. "Uh, why?"

"We're meeting up to honor Doc. 'Endless nights of love, pains and bothers to be banished...'" Robin choked up.

"'Happy, happy to die of love,'" Bretta finished.

Everyone was quiet for a minute. I yelled, "Sacre Bleu!" and everyone perked back up.

Parking in dense North Beach was very challenging. I became frustrated. "Time for some creative parking" I searched for a dark middle-of-the-block hill and found a half of a parking space between two parallel-parked cars. Z.Z. screamed as I cut in at ninety degrees, straight into the curb. The soft suspension and high ground clearance helped as I eased the front tires over the curb and onto the sidewalk. With fudged French I said, "A la motour-cyclette."

"C'est magnifique!" Francine proclaimed. We walked to the Sav. Bretta kissed me on both cheeks, "You are superb, Jack!" Robin vacillated between giggling and glancing back in concern. Z.Z. was pale and quiet and when I hung back for him, he told me, "Jack, I need to talk to you about something later."

Bretta and our entourage made a big entrance into the Sav. Bretta, with her slipover jersey, sweater, scarf, and tweed skirt, was the Sav's center of attention as usual. Bretta and I led the entourage in toasting to Doc. George sat a glass on the bar to represent Doc, but Francine complained, "It's not like he's dead," so he took it back.

Bretta spoke, "As the extraordinary Isadora Duncan said, 'Perhaps he was a bit different from other people, but what truly sympathetic person is not a little mad?'"

We all lifted our glasses, including George. "To Doc!"

"There but for the grace of God go we," I toasted.

"It's *oui*," Robin incorrectly corrected.

"Here, here." We drank. After a moment of silence, we were all still a little down. Monty—The Professor, I nicknamed him—put on some fast jazz. "Chick Corea. Better than coffee to perk you up." No one mentioned the absent Winston. Robin suggested to Bretta, "Perhaps this would be a good time to tell us how you met Doc?"

Bretta pantomimed her story. "I met Doc through an index card placed on Supernatural's bulletin board. 'Creative Roommate Wanted.' My doorbell buzzes, and when I open the door, Doc's on the landing. He is holding his gorgeous guitar and plays me a lovely song. He was so cute. He auditioned to be my roommate." She laughed. "Now, I am *c'est fini* for roommates."

George bought the entourage a round of drinks. Z.Z. invited me to smoke a J with him back by the EXIT sign. After an appropriate number of drags, the reason for this meeting was revealed. "My dad wants to come out from Wisconsin for his first visit."

"Oh, good."

"He doesn't know I'm gay."

"Right."

"I'm so nervous. Where can I take him? Should I tell him?"

I exhaled and thought for a moment. I wondered if Z.Z. heard that I had gone to therapy, which would somehow make me an expert on family problems. No, nobody knew. I felt like telling him, your dad would be like a visit from the Easter Bunny compared to my uncle. "I don't know, Z.Z. What is he like, what does he like?"

"He's a total straitlaced businessman—so, insurance, the Packers, of course, and I guess, fishing."

"And what do you normally do with an out-of-town guest?"

"Umm, make them comfortable and show them around."

"So, make this about your guest, who just happens to be your Dad."

"What do you mean?"

"Take him to your job at Macy's and show him around. Let him see how well you're doing, and he'll be proud of you."

"You think?"

"Of course. Let him see other men like you at Macy's and other places. Just not in the Castro. Charter him a fishing trip from Fisherman's Wharf. Just don't go yourself. I don't think your stomach can handle it."

"That's a great idea, Jack. But shouldn't I tell him?"

"Later, if it feels right. But, maybe better to bond now as father and son and tell him next time. Just remember, it's not about you."

"It's about my guest."

"There you go."

"You must have a great relationship with your Dad."

"Not after he killed himself."

"Oh."

#

A few days later, Bretta was still blue about Doc. I told her, "Well, we knew he was sexually repressed, but he'll be OK." I lied. "I am sure it was not just about us." Bretta looked toward Doc's old room and sighed. I continued, "Maybe he lost it when he realized he couldn't match Winston—who never practices—just picks up his guitar and plays, and knocks Doc's frets off. Or, you know, the only other time I had heard of anything like this, it was from a bad acid trip."

Bretta dismissed it. "Doc didn't do drugs."

That night Bretta received a phone call from Langley Porter. Doc had escaped. The doctor suggested that she call immediately if she spotted him but not to engage. In fact, she should be actually be on alert and always lock her door.

"He has a key," she protested.

I moved Bretta to my place. The next morning, while watching my back, I changed her locks.

#

We heard nothing else for a few days, and when Bretta called the hospital, Doc was still on the loose. He was possibly spotted back in Texas.

When Bretta moved back, I suggested, "Your art studio is tiny. Why don't you switch your bedroom to Doc's because it has less street noise, and use the master bedroom for your art? It has the big bay window and better light."

She reluctantly agreed. I pulled on Winston's Playtex dish gloves and scrubbed the room clean. I had figured out the elusive Bob Dylan tune that Doc had played that night. "She Belongs to Me." The verse includes something about a "hypnotist collector" and "She's an artist, she don't look back. But you will wind up peeking through her keyhole, down upon your knees."

Months would go by before Bretta was informed what became of her poor broken-hearted casualty of a roommate.

My entourage analogy of *Snow White and the Seven Dwarfs* had exhausted its "heigh-hos" with Doc falling down the "mind shaft." I conceived a superior version. Since Bretta was the sun, the entourage was her solar system of orbiting planets. Mercury was the mercurial Winston, Venus was Francine, and of course, Earth was the Earthy Earth-toned Robin. Mars was the god of war Jack, Jupiter was Benjamin, Saturn—Monty, Uranus—snicker, snicker—Z.Z....Farther out, Neptune—Edith, Pluto—Robert.

Soon, I would discover, on the farthest reaches—Nero—the distant, burnt-out, fiddling Finn.

CHAPTER 9

On an unseasonably warm evening Winston showed back up at Bretta's with both acting as if it had been hours, not weeks. Winston brought a pack of Bicycle playing cards. We three played Hearts on the coffee table. Winston seemed distracted and out of sorts, which I assumed was the weather, or that Bretta was beating us. I had spent a lot of time playing cards with my circus friends, so Bretta's luck, as well as Winston's increasing presence, bothered me. Winston probably thought I was the one distracted and out of sorts. I was, off and on, especially after my uncle's letter.

"All right, let's bring out the Bitch," Winston said assuming Bretta had the fearsome Queen of Spades. I actually did. Bretta was getting stuck with hearts, so finally losing. He asked for the second time, "So nobody has even a little pot to roll a joint?"

Bretta jumped up and danced around the table, "Rolling! When I was a girl I loved rolling down the grassy hills." Receiving no response from the cranks, she elaborated as she downed her wine. "I'd roll over and over and get dizzy-high, grass stain my dress, and my mother would get mad, but not for long. One time a weed stem became stuck in my ear, and I didn't know it until that night when I got an earache and started bleeding from my ear."

"Huh." We kept playing. I said, "I rode all the amusement rides with the circus. Over and over. Free; why not? Now those could make you high. But my favorite high as a kid was spinning in my rope swing."

"Me, too!" She interjected, winning the hand.

I continued, "The playground chain swings were not as good. I'd wind around so tight in my rope swing that I could barely touch the ground. I kept my head ducked under the twisted ropes. It was better if someone wound you up. I'd start spinning with my legs out, then pull them in as I spun faster, until I could lean back and my legs would fly, and I'd struggle to pull them back in, almost spinning out of the swing. Oh my god, I got so dizzy, I'd get out and stumble around—my first high!"

She played a spade. Feeling safe I discarded the Bitch. Bretta grabbed the hand and tossed her King of hearts down. Then the ace of hearts. "Ha," Bretta cried. Winston and I realized that while she conducted story time, she had taken all the hearts. She truncated the game, throwing in her remaining hearts and sing-songed, "I shot the mo-oon."

She flipped over her perfectly played tricks. Winston groaned and threw down his cards. Winston scolded me. "Jack!"

"I didn't want to be stuck with it," I whined.

As I recorded the points Winston picked up the cards for his shuffle and took his turn at remembrances. "When I was a kid, I loved putting together Revell model cars. Up in my bedroom. Just me, the plastic car parts, and the Testor's enamel paints…and their glue. It came in that orange tube, you know."

Bretta and I looked at each other. Winston continued. "I realized, hey, I could get light-headed and dizzy on the glue. And I liked it."

Bretta and I were silent on that one, until Bretta disagreed. "It's not the glue, not the paint, it is the creative process. Art makes us high! You know that, Winston."

"The strings gimme blisters on my fingers. I'm just trying to re-create that creative, artsy feeling. My substitute is getting a buzz."

Buzz. As if a theatrical cue, the door buzzed sharply. Winston and I jumped and laughed. Bretta was expecting someone. The staginess of our scene heightened with Baskin' Robin entrance—in tight breeches, jacket, and dusty tall boots with spurs intact. Unchanged from riding.

This was the first time I'd seen her in full equestrian mode. I asked with British exaggeration, "And how was the hunt, darling?" No response. I tried a compliment. "You look fetching, all horsey like that." Her only response was to blush. I tried again. "Baskin' Robin, how is Bosco?"

"He's a swell horse," was Robin's old-fashioned answer.

Winston took his turn at teasing."We were just talking about what we liked to do to get high as children. You know, like roll down hills 'til we bled, spin circles until we threw up, sniff glue, things like that. What did you do, Robin?"

"I liked looking at people's auras and trying to figure out things about them."

Winston and I glanced at each other.

"What do you mean, Robin?" Bretta asked.

"Like, feel their energy?" I asked.

"You know, auras are just what shows, but they are really the emissions of the body's chemistry, like pH, alkaline. The physiological transformed into the metaphysical manifestations." Robin explained.

"Like the exhaust from an engine?" I asked.

"Yes. So *you* know," she answered.

Winston scratched his head, "OK, but these manifestations made you, what—dizzy, high, sleepy, a Jedi knight, what?"

"Right!" Robin answered. "You get that way, too?"

"This is a fascinating awkward social interaction," Bretta lilted.

Winston said, "I thought auras were a good thing, now they sound like farts."

We all laughed, except for Robin. Robin was sweet, but her clutch was not always fully engaged. Like her car, she slipped a little. But, God bless her, I think she was happier for it. I couldn't help but continue the tease. "All right, we're making good progress here, Robin. So, we'll see you same time tomorrow."

Bretta gave me a warning look which cracked into a smile.

Robin said, "I know you guys think I'm weird. That's so ironic. OK. I will tell you something that makes me high. Chocolate! I loved chocolate when I was young. I would eat as much as I could and hide the rest. It made me feel, I don't know, yummy and excited and dreamy and creamy in my mouth all at the same time."

Bretta looked embarrassed for her. I watched Robin moisten her lips as she continued. "It is like eating artwork. I wish chocolate came in tubes, like paints."

We laughed again, and Bretta exclaimed, "Sounds delicious to me. Come on Robin, let's go get high on chocolate!" She kissed me bye, saying, "We're off to Robin's Galleria Di Belle Arti." She looked at Winston and me. "You two can have a little male-bonding time now."

Bretta took Robin by the hand and led her down the hall to the door. Robin kept looking back at me. She waved. As soon as the door shut, Winston mocked me. "Now Robin thinks she has a date with you tomorrow, Jack. 'Same time.'"

I shook my head. I felt a little guilty for being mean to her. Now I was stuck. I was unsure what Winston's motives were for hanging around. I wasn't comfortable spending the evening alone with him.

"Wow. After all that, I need to do something. Excuse me," Winston said heading toward the bathroom while I shuffled the cards and began playing Solitaire. After a while, he zipped back out.

I remarked listlessly, "Well, here we are—boys night. You want to play poker?" I looked up at him. Winston had an unexpected restless energy and his eyes were dilated.

Winston spoke rapid-fire. "Did you know that Kerouac, Neal Cassady, Hunter Thompson, Philip K. Dick, and the Nazis were aficionados? It put the blitz in the krieg, man! Did you know that hyper people like us can medicate ourselves into managed multiple focus? I'm surprised no doctor ever prescribed it for you. It is clinically proven."

"What are you talking about, Winston?"

"Try snorting a match head of this and see for yourself." His pant leg was slightly rolled up. I figured what he had just done, and told him, "I'm not really into that hard stuff."

Winston looked upset and retorted, "I don't know why the powdered drug has such a stigma. You and your college friends ever do white crosses to cram for exams?"

"A couple of times, sure. A lot of students do."

"Maybe some did black beauties, bennies, dexedrine spansules, or Christmas trees?"

"Yeah, I guess."

"Your mother or a girlfriend ever take weight loss pills?"

"Probably."

Winston held up one of those little glass-vial-and-spoon-chained-to-cap deals. "Same thing, really, Jack. Pixie Dust. It will make you fly. Used to call it 'fairy dust,' too, but that word has been pre-empted! Would you be surprised to know that Neil Young worked in a bookstore for a while and he did diet pills?"

"Yes, no."

He spooned a hit out and waved it in front of my nose tempting me. "Just try this, OK?"

"The night owl powder? I don't know." The spoon waved closer. I was feeling weird and depressed after my Uncle's letter, so for medicinal purposes…fuck it. I snorted and the burn hit my nostrils and smelled like ammonia. I thought, This is a mistake. I still snorted the other heaping spoonful he held out.

The warm, rushing, time-compressing-expanding powder coursed first through my head, upper body, then all through me. I flashed on a hatchet being held in front of a face with no eyes or mouth, only a nose. Now I was energized like I had drank ten cups of coffee. Only better. I was glad I didn't have an addictive personality because this was great. Really, really great. I felt like the super-speedy comic book superhero, The Flash, only with strange sexual undercurrents. Oh my God! I was a sprung pinball—wow!

Winston looked at me closely. "Nice, huh, Jack?"

I glanced around the flat and felt confined. I urged, "Hey, Boys night out! Let's get out of here and go do something."

Winston grinned. "Sure, like what?"

"Like something crazy wild."

"I'm sure from what we're taking, we can let the night take care of itself."

We scrammed down the stairs to the streetlamp-lit street. I looked around. "What a rare balmy San Francisco evening. No damp foggy wind." I knew Winston was equipped for it, because despite any weather, he always wore a Hawaiian shirt. Tonight, his choice was blue with gardenias, which electrically brightened, through my enhanced vision. "Winston, why do you always wear a Hawaiian shirt?"

"Because it makes me feel like I'm on vacation."

Great answer. Now I felt like I was on vacation. Elixirific, I took in the normally mundane street scene. People strolled by, seemingly in slow motion. The fastest moving thing I saw was an old-fashioned, green slug-looking, N-Judah electric streetcar lumbering by, heading west. The timeworn Muni streetcars were still mixed with the brand-new double cars. I heard a new one coming, heading to Sunset Tunnel for Market and Church Street.

Winston said, "Let's jump on the streetcar. I've got an idea. I want to pick something up."

"I think I'm too buzzed to be cooped up in that claustrophobic streetcar."

"It's a short ride, Jack."

"Wait, I have an idea. Not in—*on* the back of one. Never done that. Come on." I led him toward the modern sienna and white car.

The cars were designed to drive both ways, like Doolittle's Pushmi-pullus. It stopped, a few people got on and off.

"Follow me. We'll jump on the back and grab hold of that wiper blade knob," I said.

"You're serious? You sure about this?"

"Sure. I used to hop freight trains and ride the rails." My brain was at cruising speed now. "If the nuts on the wheels are blurry, it's going too fast, or we're too messed up, and we'll skip it."

"I don't see any nuts. Just us."

"Follow me. Don't fall off."

"No. We could get hurt."

"That's the point! You've been hurt before, right?" I indicated his leg.

"More than you know."

"Well so have I. More than you know. We both made it, Winston. As unlucky as we were, we are still lucky to have made it, right?" He had sold me on the meth and now I was selling him on the ride.

The streetcar took off slowly across the intersection. "Right. Right. Right! Let's do it!"

I ran along the tracks, and as the car sped up, I hoped Winston could make it in time with his bum leg. We caught up to the back of the departing streetcar and jumped onto the small, narrow connector linkage. Holding tight to the long, single wiper blade, we had to stand very close together. I looked back to a couple of guys who had seen our jump, and waved goodbye to them. The streetcar picked up more speed on the curve to head through the portal.

Winston cried out and swung precariously as the wiper lifted. He had held on the end instead of close to the base. He started to fall. I grabbed the sleeve of his shirt and pulled him in until he was able to get a grip. He looked at me with grateful eyes, and said, "Good thing this is an Aloha shirt and not from Penny's."

We felt the swoosh of the tunnel and saw graffiti as we entered. The tunnel was dark and the only light emanated from the streetcar's interior lights and the occasional blue with yellow electrical sparks of the cable overhead. We ducked down under the window when a passenger looked back. The ride was noisy, cold and clammy and the wind rushed by. It smelled like old damp dirt and stone and of burnt electricity arcing and crackling. I was thrilled and frightened and I loved it. This brought me right back to hopping trains as a teen. Winston and I had big grins on our faces.

Pushmi-pullu, back and forth in the tunnel, in and out of the tunnel. Pushmi-pullu, my Streetcar Named Desire through The Tunnel of Love to the Flamin' Castro District. What a song title. I should write that song! How perfect was that? Everything was so perfect.

After about three quarters of a mile, the car emerged at the Duboce Triangle. We waited until it stopped close to the Safeway.

We jumped down onto the track and casually walked to the side. He said, "Wow, that tunnel ride was out there. Good to know if I'm out of quarters I can still get a ride."

"Made me thirsty; let's grab a beer." We walked up Market to the funky hip Café Flore. I had spent many a sunny Sunday there with my previous girlfriend. It was one of those superior San Francisco spots that are blessed with good sun exposure. I paid my respects to Prince Kar-Mi. In a large framed vintage poster, the smiling hypnotic visage of the turbaned Kar-Mi guarded the register with "Occult Powers, Astounding Feats." I loved the poster, but knew little about the magician, other than the additional framed flyers. In the hallway to the heads, the promotions for he and his lovely assistant Selma extolled, "Kar-Mi buried alive for 32 days!" and, "Swallows a loaded gun barrel and shoots while it's down his throat."

Kar-Mi's Eastern Indian eyes bore into me with his power from beyond the grave. We waited in the enclosed garden patio, decorated all-year-long by strings of clear Christmas lights. Café Flore made superb cappuccinos although I certainly didn't need one. I still felt super. I scanned the mixed, attractive group. Many of them looked distinctively sexy. I looked coyly at Winston. Was he sexy? Did Bretta find him sexy? I wouldn't consider him so, but he had something attractive, something different. He caught me looking and grinned, and I looked away feeling perverse.

I felt a little weird and a thought pooled like a clot in my mind—what if Uncle was here? Right here in the crowd. Would I recognize him? Would he recognize me? I frantically scanned the faces again.

"Looking for someone?" Winston asked.

"Hoping I don't run into somebody," I replied.

"I know the feeling. Like somebody I owe money to."

I didn't think he was joking. I stood impatiently waiting to snag a patio table as soon as a party was ready to stand. Some sporty-looking guys got up, talking about "kicking Commie ass" and "miracle on ice." I nabbed their spot and we sat, pushing dirty dishes aside. We ordered some drinks to celebrate our adventure—a Corona for me, and a Calistoga with lime for the teetotaler. I tapped my foot and glanced around restlessly until finally focusing on Winston again. "How did you meet Bretta?"

"I was in Sonoma for the formal Harvest party, mostly older folks, and I'm bored, and take a smoke on the veranda. This dazzling creature says to me, "'Rather a labored affair. Whatever shall we do?'"

"What ever did you do?"

"She said she'd always wanted to stomp grapes. I thought she was kidding. Playing along I took bunches of grapes from the display and put them on the tiles. I'll be damned if she didn't flamenco on them right there. Didn't even bother to remove her high heels. The Sonoma society thought it *scandalous*."

"I would have loved to see that," I said as the drinks came.

"Bretta was there with her father. That was a few years ago. You met her father?"

"No."

"Oh, he enjoys his wine. Has an extensive cellar in his home. Interesting man, tough character, though. Turned out Bretta and I knew some people in common. Like Monty. She was still living in Grass Valley, and we arranged to meet there when I played a gig in Nevada City."

"So, you became...friends?"

"Yeah. I moved to the city on business and we became great friends. I like her friends. I absolutely love her—artwork. She was, you could say, my muse. I have played my finest guitar inspired by that woman."

"Yeah. Well, I really like her. You know what I mean, right?" I stared Winston down.

He looked away. "Oh, sure I can see that. And she adores you, too. But, it's not that way with us. We're just good friends."

I could almost see the parenthetical (now) hanging in the air. "All right. We can be, too."

"Sure. You are way cool, Jack. I can see why she has a thing for you."

"I think you're cool, too." With intense, drug heightened affection, I viewed Winston's masculine jaw line and engaging green eyes. The speed made everything real and important, and somehow all good. I was already considered a bit hyper, but Winston was right—after I got in tune with it, it became a calm hyper. Hard to explain. We drank and people watched—the mix of gays, couples, and regulars—mostly neighborhood folks. Winston surprised me when he said, "I have a confession."

Here it comes. "Yeah?"

"The Harmony I played that night? Not a Harmony. It was a classic old Martin."

"What? Come to think of it, the tone did sound awfully rich."

"I just stuck a Harmony decal on it. You know some guitarists are such egotists, so I mess with their minds. They think it's my skill, not just the guitar. Plus, nobody will steal it."

"Tricky. But you have plenty of skill."

"And...those nails I put on."

"Yes..."

"They're just fake nails. I bought them at Long's Drugs."

"Come on!"

"Hey, it's show biz."

"Well, it sure worked. You about knocked me over. You sounded so rusty at first."

"The magic of vulnerability. Pretend to fall and when you rise, the audience is with you."

"Like a circus high-wire act," I said.

"That's the idea. Here's a bit of trivia for you. George Harrison's famous guitar solo on 'Gently Weeps'?"

"Yes. His best."

"George didn't play it."

"What?"

"He asked Eric Clapton to play it on the record."

"I did not know that. Hmm, it does sound "Layla"-esque."

"Exactly. Clapton's Les Paul."

I kept glancing around until Winston finally stood up. "Let's go pick that thing up." We chugged our drinks. He handed me a stick of Wrigley's. "This will help relax your jaw."

As we headed up the sidewalk the gum was a good thing. Within a few blocks he stopped at an older apartment building's lower unit and rang the bell a few times. After no answer he lifted out a loose board on the side and retrieved a key. Unlocking the garage door, he heaved it up, on its rusty rattrap springs. What was inside, I did not expect.

In the back of the two-deep garage was a mint 1967 Camaro SS blue convertible. The classic had fat chrome wheels, white striping around the front grill, and the little crossed-checkered-flag medallion.

"Wow, V-8 396 cubic inch, what three speed—four speed!" I exclaimed.

"Any speed you want. Including what we have."

"Ha! We're going to, uh, just take this?"

"The owner and I have an understanding. This used to be my car and he still owes me money, so this will help pay the interest." While I admired the car, he fished the keys out from under the mat, tore off a piece of an automotive girlie calendar from the wall, and jotted a note. With his well-chewed gum, he stuck it to the wall.

"When I was a kid, this was the car the cool older guys drove," I said.

"That's me, the cool older guy." We jumped into the inviting black leather seats. He fondled the custom, small chrome steering wheel. "After I got this, I bought a model kit version. Never did put it together."

Winston showed me how a small section of carpet pulled up, to the right of the 8-ball stick shift. There was a little plastic bag with two neatly rolled jays. "Cool," he said.

Under that carpet, he slid over a piece of tin to reveal a pint bottle-sized hole. He said, "We get pulled over, anything we got—booze, dope or whatever, stick it in one of these black socks and it drops down to the pavement."

"Sneaky. Got it."

"Let's do another hit of that stuff." We snorted a little bit more. The nose-burn was not so bad this time.

"I better see if she starts." He fired up the Camaro, letting it warm up to a resonant rumble. He pulled a fake alligator skin box from the rear floorboard and handed it to me. It was full of old rock and roll 8-track tape cartridges.

"You? Mr. Classical Gas," I teased.

"I used to rock and roll."

I stuck in Cream's *Goodbye*; clicked to "I'm So Glad." Winston carefully backed out. I closed the garage, asking, "This is kind of high profile. You sure it's OK?"

"Mostly."

"Winston revs the Camaro SS and the reverberated power of the muscle car surges through my body. He tests the brakes, pumping and bumping to the stop sign. Vroom-vra vroom-va vroom, and in the first two gears he burns rubber—B.F. Goodrich's, with the white-wall thin accent ring and raised white logo letters. The exhaust sounds so damn good. It brings back Muscle Memory. Man. Wow, I am really buzzed..."

CHAPTER 10

"This Camaro SS is a leashed animal, straining to run wild and free, to tear up some pavement, eat fucking Jap cars, and prowl around Mel's Drive-In, radio rockin', to pick up some slinky chicks in cutoff-shorts for the backseat, and in the rearview mirror watch them *titillated*, their silky hair blowing back squeally-squirming in thrilled fright at the raw horsepower of testosterone-fueled machinery—with a driver named Winston or Jack or Neal—who is ALLRIGHT with just going, moving, rolling—being ALIVE."

I was on a roll but Winston put me down with, "Sure, we could get all Kerouac and Cassady, or you know, just drive around."

I scowled at the buzz kill and stuck in *John Barleycorn Must Die*, and "Glad" sounded terrific, so I turned it up until the aftermarket Jensen speakers rattled in the poorly cut door panel holes, and I laughed. The Castro was always kinetic and on this warm night the fairies were swarming and cruising. It was a memorable night to be in a convertible, but the wrong neighborhood to pick up chicks. The parade of cars slowly inched forward, the two of us high in the growling, gleaming blue convertible, with Winston in his blue Hawaiian shirt, me in my black T, with a huge, teeth-clenched, gum-chewing grin.

Next to the glass-fronted Twin Peaks corner bar was the late Harvey Milk's old camera store, and the Double Rainbow ice cream parlor, the first in California to sell frozen yogurt. We passed slowly by the enormous, phallus-vertical, red neon "CASTRO" marquee of the classic Castro Theatre. The lights and colors now reminded me of the backglass of a pinball machine.

An Alfred Hitchcock's double noir bill of *Notorious* and *Vertigo* was showing. The stunning, Swedish Ingrid Bergman smiled at me from the billboard and her notorious role reminded me of Bretta. I thought, Bretta is a cross of Ingrid's face and demeanor with Kim Novak's body, and became titillated. I snapped out of my internalized amusement and pronounced, "Bretta could play that." Winston gave me a funny look, and I wasn't sure if he got it or kind of got it, or maybe hadn't seen it, so I extrapolated, "More notorious Ingrid, not dead Kim." My thoughts were all running together like a vertiginous movie montage.

"OK, I do feel like Steve McQueen now," he conceded.

"And I'll be Hunter Thompson."

"Perfect."

I snapped my jaws on the gum and made another movie reference joke. "We're going to need a bigger gum."

He laughed and handed over another stick. A gay man diagonally crossing the street, probably from the open-windowed Toad Hall, who seemed higher than we were, lunged up to my side and sing-songed to me, "Hey, gorgeous, nice wheels! How about a ride?"

I waved him off and grinned to Winston. A little further down, after some more guys checked us out, I joked, "Instead of Steve McQueen, more like Steve PromQueen in a parade!" and we both laughed. At the hot spot of Castro and 18th we hit the red light, which seemed like it took forever. A couple of blocks to the left, by Moby Dick Bar, was where Ariel lived when we first met. Our car was in the midst of kinetic, buffed, mustached, cropped-haired Castro Clones, in their denim cut-offs, or 501 jeans, tight Tees and leather vests, or unbuttoned plaid flannel shirts, baseball caps, and work boots. Musk scent, Old Spice, and cologne wafted over us.

One clone called out like a gas station attendant, "Sir, would you like me to fluff up your tires, and check those butch things under your hood?"

Winston yelled, "Chinese Fire Drill!" I froze because of that car thing that happened with me, but he'd already jumped over the door, so I stood on the seat and jumped out. We ran around the car, I took a big breath, looked overhead, and we both jumped back in the opposite seat. "Emergency brake, down there, take it off."

I did, put it in gear and with a small squeal, drove off just as the light changed. The crowd cheered. One man teased, "Where you going, butch boys in your muscle car? Can we cuuum with you?"

We passed the tinted windows of Elephant Walk and I told Winston, "That's the bar the cops raided a few months ago. They broke those windows and rousted people to the street as payback after the White Night riots."

He gazed at the bar and said, "Yes, I heard."

"Now that was out of control. Twelve cop cars got torched that night, so the cops were pissed." I realized I had been talking more, and he less. Was I talking too much? When I get nervous, it seems like all I can do is make little jokes. But that was all right, right? I looked over my shoulder again. "The fire drill made me a little paranoid."

"That's all right, we have something that will help if you find a quiet spot."

I drove over to the generally unknown Seward mini-Playground. We stood at the top of the super-long, winding, smoothed-concrete double slides built into the hillside. He fired up one of the secreted joints, and after we smoked I did feel better. After we raced down the slides a couple of times I felt even better, and when I beat him to the bottom I felt better yet, like a supersized pinball.

We rested, panting, on the end of the slides. Winston said, "What a rush, huh? Like Bretta's swinging." He looked intensely at me. "You know my glue deal? When I did it, I felt so close to getting to the answer. To finding it."

"What?"

"You know, man! It! Behind the veil. Realizing the unknowable. I would get right to it and almost touch it and then I'd come down. And I'd try it again. So close each time...like the brass ring." Pulling out his vial, he said, "Go ahead and finish this stuff."

I snorted the last of it. "Let's go over the hill to Noe Valley and go to Bud's ice cream."

"I thought you would like Baskin' Robins better," he teased.

"Funny. She is funny, huh? Bud's line is always too long, anyway."

"Yeah, but everyone's stoned, so it's fun."

"Let's keep drivin', drivin', drivin'."

With Winston at the wheel, I stuck in Rod Stewart with the tape beginning in the ending of "(I Know) I'm Losing You." We twisted up to towering Twin Peaks. Winston did a quick racing shift down and scooted up the hill. *Vroom-voom!* On the curves he bragged, "Bilstein shocks, sway bars, leaf springs, Muncie trannie."

"This Camaro is like a big blue pinball springing up the entry lane!" I said.

"Cool analogy."

Under the ginormous red and white Sutro tower, the Twin Peaks parking lot was breezy and crowded with smooching couples. We leaned against the hood enjoying the sparkling-diamonds city lights view. He asked, "Wouldn't it be nice if the way we're feeling now were normal?" and I thought, yes it would, but I said, "Yes, we would be paranormal."

"And we would be parabolic."

A couple of short, shaved-headed, bandana'd cholos wearing wife-beater Tees and black Catholic-cross tattoos stared at us from their group of hairnet-wearing buddies and kandy-kolorful, metal-flaked, hydraulic-hopping Chevy lowriders.

"You ready to rumble?" I asked Winston.

Everyone knew many of these cholos were hotheaded, unpredictable and dangerous. I was too high to remember if the ones with hairnets or the shaved heads were the baddest. Winston turned his back to the cholos and lifted up his Hawaiian shirt to show me his quick open holster with a big folding knife on his belt. The knife was placed in, partially open and when he pulled it out across the nylon roller, it would open fully. It was a big knife. He said, "I'd rather not, but I'm geared up."

"That's cooler than the one in my boot," I said. Two approached in their little exaggerated steps to admire our Camaro and asked mechanical questions in wheedling Spanglish. "Let's check out, you know, Ese, under the hood." Winston politely declined, to which one took exaggerated offense. When one asked, "Which 'hood you live in, Ese?" I interpreted that as, "Tell us where you park this cherry ride at night," so I gave him the most ridiculous answer I could think of—"Chinatown"—and put on my badass face and stared him down.

Winston played along, "We have to go meet up with the China-man now, you know what I mean?" They considered the meaning of this, and one finally grinned, showing a gold-capped tooth. They walked away. We got back in the car, deciding to go somewhere less busy, and peeled out, smoke puffing from the wide tires, to the approving calls of the car cult crowd. He said, "We escaped."

"I could have taken them both, easy."

"What, leaving me to take the rest of their gang? I'm a guitar-ist—can't hurt my hands, man," he said.

"I don't punch much, myself. I can teach you to use your feet."

Our pinball game continued as the Camaro descended squealing on corners. I was glad he was driving because I got turned around. He found the cut across 17th, passing the planetary named streets—Saturn, Uranus, Mars, the Vulcan Steps!—and on through the Haight and West. He stuck in a tape and Clapton's exquisite longing for George Harrison's wife, "Layla," roused us and we were feeling it. We cruised through the dog-legged golf course of Lincoln Park. He made a stop in front of Rodin's *The Thinker* at the Legion of Honor, whose twin building, I remembered, stands in Paris. I flashed, and finally got the connection—the continuation of the lookalike theme for Hitchcock's *Vertigo*. I remarked cryptically, "The beautiful Carlotta, the sad Carlotta, viewed her painting in this gallery."

Winston segued from my film fixation, asking, "You remember *The Many Loves of Dobie Gillis*?"

"Vaguely."

"You were pretty young, I guess. TV comedy show, twenty years ago. Dobie would sit in front of *The Thinker* and ponder his girlfriend problems to the TV audience. A young Gilligan was his stoned-acting, beatnik bongo-playing sidekick, Maynard G. Krebs."

"Oh yeah, somebody told me he's how Shaggy from *Scooby-Doo* got his shtick."

On to Ocean Beach. As "Reason to Believe" played, I sang along and Winston told me, "Sounds good, you can really sing. Look, Seal Rock Inn. Where *Rolling Stone* put up Hunter Thompson."

And there—the luminous white Cliff House restaurant. Behind it was Musée Mécanique, crammed with vintage arcade machines that visitors could actually drop coins in and play. I treasured the circus-reminiscent atmosphere enhanced by mechanical music-playing devices. The predecessors to pinball and the crazy steam-powered motorcycle were my favorites. Adjacent to the museum was the odd Giant Camera Obscura attraction.

"The camera obscura was probably the cheat for the artist Caravaggio," Winston said.

"What?"

"Caravaggio! You know, the father of modern art?" After my shrug, he continued, "Beautiful painter. His realism was so unreal, some speculate that he projected his subject through a lens onto his canvas. Caravaggio was a 16th-century, hot-tempered, fighting man on the lam. A bad-boy artist, and the only one I would want on a boys' night out."

Other than Bretta, I thought. I turned toward the small back seat. "I don't think his casket would fit."

The salty ocean air held a portent of an outlying fog bank and was refreshing as we stopped to overlook the bird-shit stained Seal Rock and the indistinct, mysterious ruins of Sutro Baths. They had been modeled after Roman baths. I reflected, "Adolf Sutro really got around. Wonder if he had some Pixie Dust, too?"

"Maybe just drank Coke when it still had real cocaine in it," Winston said. "Down there, imagine thousands of bathers in their floppy grey one-piece suits, cavorting at his Bath House during its heyday."

"I would love to time travel back to the turn of the century—the Golden Age of San Francisco—color, excitement, power."

"I took some windowpane and went down there one stormy afternoon," Winston said. "I walked among the ruins. There's this tunnel-like cavern; it's pitch-black. I dared myself to crawl all the way in. After ten feet, I had to crawl by feel, and at about twenty feet I got the weirdest sensation that I had gone too far. Somebody or something was in there that was going to kill me. It was terrifying; I became chilled and my heart pounded and I thought I was going to die. But, I forced myself to keep crawling to the very end. I think that's what I really wanted." He paused. "To be scared to death, you know?"

I thought about what had scared me to death. My uncle. I thought about how I would tell Winston about my Uncle. Italian handsome, tall, with a black shock of hair, he had "finally" married when I was six. She was a genteel woman in town, with, as he described, delicate bones and a mansion. She was heir to a grain elevator fortune. My new aunt would often invite me to their home for a "continental-style" dinner. My parents were not often extended this hospitality. My aunt's hope was to develop my sophistication. Uncle had a commanding presence and a persuasive manner, and had always been exceedingly pleasant to me, almost saccharine.

Now, sitting in the blue Camaro with my new unexpected pal, Winston, my grey brain channels and furrows dilated, it all came flooding back to me. Uncle began wearing ties, smoking cigars and dressing dapper, which my father called, "Putting on airs." Three years after my uncle's marriage, my new Aunt fell down their sweeping staircase and broke most of her delicate bones, including the ones in her neck. She lingered for a few days in critical care, with Uncle so worried, he absolutely refused to leave her bedside. She lay there staring at him until she passed. The nurses thought him "so romantic." Following my Aunt's death, I had no appetite for weeks. Uncle, after the funeral, smiled and told me, "Jackie, everything's going to work out just fine." He immediately took a long European trip. I remember my father raised his eyebrows at his sudden departure, but my mother gave Daddy her look and fiercely shook her head.

Uncle returned months later with crated European art of debatable taste. Uncle affected a British accent and mannerisms, spent my late Aunt's genteel money freely, and became quite the gentleman about town. He bought rounds of drinks at the taverns, installed a billiard room in the mansion, expanded his art collection , and his collection of female admirers. He remained an eligible widower. He commissioned and donated a statue of Aunt's beloved grandfather to the town.

Everyone turned out in the town square, opposite the Civil War cannon, to view the bronze legend, clasping a model of one of his many grain silos. The ladies thought my uncle noble and selfless. I though it odd the plaque's inscription "Donated by" was larger than "Dedicated to." I overheard my father's opinion: "Looks like he's holding his own cock!"

#

I was about to tell Winston all this, when Winston clicked the button and cranked up the volume to play "Evil Ways"—*when I come home, baby, my house is dark and my pots are cold*— and I was about to tell Winston, Hey, *my Evil Uncle* is threatening to come get me, when Winston exclaimed, "God, I love drugs! I don't care what they say; I think they're good for me."

I looked at him, realizing he was dead serious. He was an aficionado. I said, "We are Jack the Kerowacked and Neal the Cassadee now, doncha' know?"

He yelled above the music, "Right. We should race out and sneak into to Fleishhacker Pool." Fleishacker was the abandoned ocean-water swimming pool, once the largest in the world, now drained. "Go, go, go! Hold on."

Winston stomped on it and wound it out on the wide, sandy Great Highway, the City's long-favored midnight drag strip. We roared past the late Playland amusement park, still aching like a pulled public tooth, now condo-ized, but he backed off well before the pool, to turn into The Beach Chalet lot. He parked next to a red classic El Camino with a chromed engine peeking through the hood scoop. Surfboards leaned in the truck bed. Winston killed the motor and music, and whispered, "Just in case. I have a feeling."

I knew what he meant. When one has lived outside the law, one learns to trust primitive animal instinct. We got out and I helped him quietly put the black vinyl top up to make the car look different.

The seedy Beach Chalet was a VFW bar where you could drink boilermakers or brawl with veterans, bikers, surfers, or old hippies; or you could play pinball next to beautiful WPA murals, which is what I had done in the past. The Beach Chalet was where the only other *Superman* pinball game lived, that I knew of. The bar was a hideout, like Superman's Fortress of Solitude—away from the milieu, on the outlands of San Francisco's civilization. I was tempted to stop and play the silver ball with Winston. I knew bar pinball machines were often shabby with overuse—springs worn, rubber bouncers weak. I reconsidered; the Camaro was better than pinball. Had pinball really been ruined for me? Maybe so. I hadn't played in many weeks. Winston an I looked at each other, both of us shrugging. No desire to go in.

We admired the El Camino, and sat waiting a few minutes for another car to leave first—safety in numbers. A loud rough-looking threesome exited the bar, weaving to their El Camino, and one called out, "Hey, you two faggots making out in there, or what?" I snapped at the bait, with my hand on the door handle, responding, "Why don't you bend over and find out, asshole?" The asshole hesitated, cogitating in an alcohol haze, so I opened my door but Winston grabbed my arm and urged, "No, Jack!" I reeled in my jangling adrenaline as Winston taunted them, "Hey, our car will beat up your car out on the Highway."

They jeered and roared their El Camino to life. Winston motioned, After you, and the truck peeled out of the lot. Winston eased the Camaro out. Good thing he did. Our instincts were right. The police cruiser, a great black and white shark, grill-like teeth gleaming, lay in wait between cars in the middle parking area of the wide roadway The El Camino burned rubber again and the cop flashed his cherries. Their boys' night out was over, just like that.

Winston, without moving his upper body, reached down to the floorboard, just in case. The cop glared at us, but was happy with his catch. With an eye in his mirror, Winston took it easy through the avenues where we had a chance to outmaneuver or hide, rather than be a shark's seal meal on the wide-open beach road.

He soon wound among palatial mansions on manicured ocean-view parcels. We were in Sea Cliff. I wondered, "Where the hell does all their money come from?" and Winston replied, "Old money, Jack."

I laughed. "I can see it now: old money—musty British banknotes and gold piled up in basements and dumbwaiters. Like a Scrooge McDuck comic."

Winston pointed out a stately mansion on El Camino del Mar. "That was Houdini's home." We parked across the street and sat staring at the stained glassed brick manor as if Houdini's muscular, strait-jacketed and chain-bound apparition might appear on the balcony to shake free his bonds. But Houdini declined to entertain us.

We rolled down toward the Bay where The Palace of Fine Arts dome glowed like a giant mushroom, summoning us. Our footsteps echoed on the walkways under the massive sand-colored arches and columns of the open structures. We hesitated as our eyes adjusted to the dimness. Above us the colossal statues of ample-reared women peered over the edges of vast vaults—of what? Were they weeping mothers, sisters, lovers of the Great War, gazing into the crypts of dark voids, needing to know but petrified from the truth of their losses, longing, praying for their men to return? And for golden years *to come?* At ground level stood giant urns, each with lines of virgins shouldering a shared long, scaly-serpent garland. I felt a disturbing empathy to the virgins, pinned to the urns for eternity. Passing by bas-reliefs and carvings, we were drawn to stand dead center under the immense rotunda dome to behold the eight figures with wings high above. Winston's voice sounded amplified. "This place is a trip." The dome echoed back—(trip!) He added, "I have to —'Pick up—my guitar and play...'" (n' play.)

We laughed at the spooky acoustics and I had to echo, "'Get on my knees and pray...'" (n' pray), Winston joining in, "'We don't get fooled AGANE!'" (fooled agane!)

Winston and I jumped up to the long-unused stone planter boxes, utilizing them as giant steps toward that magic dome, *high* above the past and present worlds. On a ledge *we* got high, overlooking the lagoon, with the statues of Herculean men and Amazonian women towering above us. The paranoid thought occurred to me, that one little shove, and Winston would have Bretta to himself. I distracted him. "Did you know? This was built for the World's Fair during the Great War."

"Past or present, does war bring peace?" He took the jay. "Hmm, beauty and art in the midst of war. Must have been a world-class affair." He blew out smoke. "Tell me, Jack, is that what you consider Bretta?"

So, he *was* thinking about her, and me. "Well, Winston, Bretta does have a lot of class, and life's not fair."

"You should know," he retorted. I wondered, What did he know?

"Jack, just don't hurt...each other." Winston looked at me. "Like we did." He took the last hit and threw the glowing roach downward.

We gazed at the fancy Marina District apartment building windows across the way. Most lights off, some on, boob tubes flickering in others. I mused, "A lot of those people have it made, and there's, like, no struggle now."

"Don't kid yourself. There's always a struggle."

I waved my hand over the Marina District. "I mean, is this all there is when you make it? A nicer house, a new car?"

Winston scolded, "Rich or poor, you either live with passion or you don't." His tone softened. "Hey, you know what I like about getting all jacked up?"

"What? More passion?"

"Ha. That, too. Even with no money, a night like tonight, man, we own this fuckin' town!"

We laughed. "Yeah we do. I know, let's go down under 'our' Bridge," I suggested.

"Sound's good."

I teased him politely, "After you." We cautiously lowered ourselves back to earth where Winston tossed me the keys. "Thanks, man." I fired up his Camaro and revved it until I was satisfied with the throbbing growl. Winston and I grinned at one another. I drove us down to the eerie and almost-vacant Fort Point, right under the octave sets of harp strings that levitated the Golden Gate Bridge like Apollo's instrument—that god of music, poetry, light and sun. The temperature was noticeably cooling here. The phantom fog was crawling towards the Bay like apocryphal, giant radioactive sponges from the Farallon Islands, reminding us not to get used to the balmy weather, as San Francisco's famous natural air conditioner was returning.

At Fort Point, the rogue waves could soar up the jetty and over you if you weren't careful. We parked and stood just out of range of the saltwater spray, and looked past the rusty big chain into the swirling Bay. I imagined myself as Hitchcock's obsessive James Stewart rescuing spellbinding Kim Novak (played by my dead girlfriend) from the dark churning water. Unlike me, he was able to save his love—that time.

"Cool. I wish Bretta was here," I said.

"Instead of me?"

I shrugged. Chilled by the misty breeze and by our silence, we jumped back into the leather and steel cocoon of the Camaro. At shotgun, Winston sorted through the 8-track tapes and stuck in another oldie, Country Joe and the Fish. We sang along and our moods brightened with the pretend-to-feel-good, anti-war anthem. I piloted into the dark, labyrinthine, oily-odored Eucalyptus trees of the Presidio military base.

"...Next stop is Vietnam...five, six, seven, open up the Pearly Gates...ain't no time to wonder why, Whoopee! we're all gonna' die."

Closed white gates loomed. I slammed on the brakes, and we slid a bit on the damp, Eucalyptus-oiled road. I had become disoriented, which was easy to do in the expansive Presidio, even if one were not high and it was daylight. We were lost and dead-ended. I had a déjà vu of Ariel's last moments.

"What's that?" he asked.

The headlights shone on the brass plaque. I read, "'Veterans'... shit, it's the veterans' cemetery." A foggy finger crept in over the graveyard, beckoning. I uttered softly, "Perfect. Let's check it out."

Winston looked at me, to make sure I was serious, and I killed the Camaro's engine. The driveway's large, ornamental iron gates were shut, but we found a small side gate unlocked. I left the headlight high beams shining. The Monterey Cypress loomed overhead as we walked along the slippery, sloping grass in need of a mower. A stone wall ran the length below where the Doyle Drive bridge traffic hissed by. Darkly stretched out before us were thousands of uniform white marble headstones mixed with old stones, crosses, large monuments and a statue or two. Indian Wars, Civil War, World Wars, Korean War, Vietnam War. War, war, war.

"Vietnam was a dirty war. You know, the hell of it was, we could have won," Winston said.

"What?"

"We were betrayed by our own people. Our government, military commanders, the fucking CIA and Air America."

"What were we fighting for?" I asked.

Winston answered, "Always something—for the government and money-men."

"Yes. Did you go?"

"I would have been drafted, so I volunteered for the Air Force. Got a year at Travis, and, then I was sent... here to the Presidio for a while. They released me on a Section Eight."

"What the hell is that?"

"Uh, a kind of medical discharge. How about you?"

"I was lucky. I got a high lottery number. Bastards missed me. But I missed being *Apocalypse Now*."

"Great movie." He sang, "'This is the Ennnd.'" He continued in Dennis Hopper impersonation, "And man, like, Dennis Hopper, man. I got really loaded, man, and sat through it twice when it came out on New Year's Day."

Oooo-oooo. The foghorn called its forlorn warning. An obscuring, ethereal sand storm of water particles hung above the cemetery. The Golden Gate Bridge's brave glow dimmed. We sobered and stood silently, reflecting on the reality of it all. Where each of us will inescapably end. Winston's demeanor changed. He gazed at the fog, urging, "Let's get out of here. Split before "A-deathfog-gets-us *Now*."

The fog did appear to be a-coming to a-win us. He turned, and I crossed myself, murmuring a quick prayer for our dead brothers— only six feet below, the mortal remains of souls from mostly sudden, cruel, and violent deaths. Winston waited, and put his arm on my shoulder to comfort me. It spooked me so I brushed it off. "Sorry," I muttered.

"Hurry," Winston whispered, and I knew his arm was really to comfort himself. He was the paranoid one now.

I told him, "We can outrun it, Winston. I always have." I held out the keys.

He looked at me, "I'm not so sure I can, Jack." Winston pressed the keys back into my hand.

Maneuvering the hills of San Francisco with a clutch-tricky thoroughbred, you nearly need three feet for brake, clutch, and gas. Hovering at the precipice of Lombard Street on Russian Hill we gazed across to the glowing giant fire hose nozzle cum phallus of Coit Tower perched atop Telegraph Hill. "From Castro to Coit," I said. I waited for an empty Hyde-Powell cable car to pass—then nudged the Camaro pinballing down the be-bricked, yet surprisingly smooth, bip-bip-bip-on-the-tires, crooked Lombard Street. "Where there lived a crooked man," I joked.

At the bottom, Winston ordered, "Pull over for a minute, over there."

I wanted to check out Scottie's house for my personal tour of *Vertigo* sites, just a block down, but I double-parked across Leavenworth Street. The scary, worn-brake smell always lingered around the incredibly vertical, eight-hairpins-in-one-block Lombard Street.

"Kill the lights. Pull up a little more, so we can see."

"What're you up to?"

"Waiting to make sure the coast is clear. Are you game?"

"Sure, I guess."

"When I give the word, you're going to drive us up Lombard."

"What? Up the wrong way on the one-way, one-lane, 'Crooked-est Street in the World?'"

"Yeah, something even Bullitt never did. Look, if a car comes down, we may be in trouble. Remember you can always pull into a driveway."

"Or play chicken."

"Right. Whatever you do, just don't stall the fucking car."

I looked up the hill, mentally running the curves. Winston took another look around. "Go, man, go!" I turned out my headlights and eased out the clutch and darted across Leavenworth, held my breath, pulled the spring back on my giant pinball machine, and with a *vroom, vroom* headed up the steeep, steeeep bricks. I left it in first gear and did well on the hairy, hairpin curves, clutching and revving to keep the RPMs up.

About three quarters of the way up, a big confident Buick turned down Lombard. We both said, "Oohh shit!" "Keep your speed up," Winston urged.

I kept going. I did not want to have to stop and do a possible rollback or a re-start as I would have to engage and disengage the emergency brake. Our cars crept closer and closer. The other car must not have seen us without our headlights. Was our pinball adventure going to hit Game Over, with me shooting back down the drain?

With one curve left, the Buick turned into a driveway of one of the mansions. The garage door opened. He was going home. We cheered. We kept going.

Off the top at Hyde I hooted, "I am fucking Superman!"

"You are the Lombard Wizard!" Winston slapped me on the back.

"Yeah, yeah, yeah," I raved.

Deciding that was sufficient tempting of fate for one evening, Winston nixed Coit Tower. "I'm done. Wow, Jack, you really get jacked up."

After a few blocks away, I pulled over to let Winston take back the wheel. I said, "Monty really has a cool job. I could do that—drivin' a cab."

"I think after this they should give you an honorary license."

Winston said he had to get the car back and dropped me off at Bretta's street corner. I waved goodbye to my new friend. I felt horny in a kinky, strange way, and woke the soft, cozy, warm Bretta up, who knew I was high, and, cool chick that she was, did not ask for details. We had sex in rolled-around, unusual, topsy-turvy positions, and I couldn't sleep until I took the downer Winston had fortunately provided me earlier.

I felt like shit the next day, which Winston had warned me about. My brain had dried up and shrunk. Bretta suspected what we had been up to, but when I told her, she did freak out. "Oh god, Jack, what have you done? I know you two were male-bonding, but don't get him going."

I didn't see Winston for three days and I was worried, but Bretta assured me that it was normal under the circumstances. She, however, did not look very assured. When Winston did show up, he looked dragged out. Bretta gave him the cold shoulder and he left. I walked him down the street. Winston didn't tell me where he'd been. I didn't tell Winston that I had just read in the Chronicle. A young man had attempted our streetcar stunt through West Portal Tunnel. He fell off and was run over by the big steel wheels of a streetcar going the other way. It was a gnarly accident, severing his lower legs. He bled to death. I hoped he wasn't one of the guys that I had waved to.

I did ask him why Bretta was so upset. He merely said, "Those who live in glass bottles should not throw stones."

Winston took off again, and we didn't see him for a while. In retrospect our San Francisco noir tour was more like *The Streetcar Named Denial.* Winston's dark secrets would continue to reveal themselves in the most unexpected fashions. At the Bookstore, I looked up "Section 8." The term means a discharge from the military for being mentally unfit.

CHAPTER 11

At Bretta's flat, the salons resumed, with Winston's re-reappearance providing increasingly intense streams of lush music. Friends, art pieces and wines would come and go. Bretta entertained with her stylistic dance, humor, and snatches of verse from her "three R's"—Rimbaud, Rumi and Rexroth. I was a fan of Winston's musicianship but felt outclassed by his, and formerly Doc's, guitar skills, I never played for Bretta.

Winston still told people he did not drink—the (anymore) unstated. I was impressed he could refrain around our entourage. Bretta and her troupe, like many in the creative world, were night owls. It was harder on me, as I did not have the pleasure of sleeping in. I had to get up early. Winston was really a night owl, and when he was around, the late nights become later and more frequent. Occasionally, entourage members needed to crash over.

I got up one Saturday morning for my sparring class and went into the living room, looking for my wallet. Z.Z. was sacked out on the couch. I bent over looking around. I didn't have much on, and he sat up and sleepily remarked, "Lord, look at your bubble butt!"

"I don't even know what that means, man."

"And those abs! You're really muscular for being so lean. Honey, how can you stay in such good shape when you party, uh, so hard?"

"Under this muscle I'm really fat."

Z.Z. snickered. He spoke in a sultry voice, "Love the dagger tattoo. I didn't know you had one. Did you get that in prison?"

"I wasn't in prison." Self-conscious, I tossed back as I left the room, "Jail."

I headed down the hall. After a few moments in the bathroom, I heard a couple of moans. Soon they were followed by an exaggerated sneeze. Z.Z. called in a husky voice, "Uh, Jack, be a sweetie and bring me a big wad of toilet paper. I, uh, kind of sneezed on myself."

I wound some around my fingers and returned to him, lying there under the blanket with his knees up and legs splayed. He looked embarrassed, avoiding my eyes and did not reach for the tissue. "Just drop it there on the blanket. Thanks, Jack."

I suppose I could have attempted to pull Bretta away more into my world and circle of friends. But the opposite gravitational force occurred. All the same, I enjoyed her entourage. It seemed to me like family. But like visiting relatives that outstay their welcome, they were getting on my nerves. Little did I know that the relatives, and more relationships, would appear.

One day I noticed a partially-opened package postmarked from Nevada City, CA. Inside was a Sony cordless phone and the first I had seen. Bretta told me, "My mother sent it to me, so I would be sure to pick up whenever she calls, even in the bathroom." I set up the rectangular handset with a car antenna that telescoped out, for signals going through the separate base box antennae.

Bretta enjoyed prancing around the house chatting without trailing a long, trip-prone cord. The technology was the latest, even though it was a little static-y and had an electronic chiming ring. When the new phone rang for the fifth time, Bretta still answered cheerily. "Hi. Welcome back." She roamed into the kitchen. I thought, Not another ex, please. She spoke sweetly and tenderly and I became a little jealous, so I followed her in "to get a glass of water" and listened—a woman's voice. Bretta smiled at me and mouthed, Mother.

"No, don't worry. I don't really see Winston much at all." Pause. "No, not him either. It's Jack, his name is Jack. No, not like that. Though he is very vivid." Bretta moved close to kiss both my eyelids. She pushed me back to the counter and unbuckled and dropped my pants with one hand. "Mother! Of course I am, mother." Bretta patted the counter, and I hopped to sit on it. "He's soo attractive." She caressed my thigh. "I will. I'll see if I can get him to *come up* some time. Yes, he's ever-ready to do something fun." Bretta suggestively slid the telescoping antenna out and in a few times. The line filled with static and without hanging up she slid the phone into the sink. She gripped the counter on both sides of my thighs and with a mischievous, bad-girl grin, said, "I need my Eveready battery." The apparent controlling mommy issues made me uneasy, but Bretta went for me with unanticipated aggressiveness. I counted backwards and managed.

While Bretta had plenty of curves, Francine's taut, fit body reminded me of Ariel, fostering my sexual tension around her. Francine, for better and worse, added a different dimension and spark to the entourage. She was the only woman any of us knew who went to a gymnasium. We thought only gay men and Jack LaLanne medicine-ball types went. In fact, Francine worked out at a gay men's gym at Market and Castro. Why was I thinking about Francine, and Ariel, while Bretta was blowing me? "Men!" as Ariel used to exclaim in her faux-exasperated voice.

Like Francine read my mind, she presently showed up, wearing such tight-ass jeans I could see the outline and indent of her muff. For some reason, she excitedly talked us into a foray to Maud's just for fun, one of the City's two known all-lesbian bars. It was right down the street from the no-name. Bretta slipped into her pink, which she called salmon, super-tight brushed denims. I wasn't so sure I'd be welcome, but Francine told me to just not be so butch and if anything happened, pretend to be queer.

At diffusely-lit Maud's, Joan Armatrading crooned and pleaded from the juke. I was the only man there, and maybe the only man ever to brave the interior, for all I knew. I quietly ordered us some Buds from the shaved-head dyke bartender who stared me down, before her eyes settled on Bretta's and Francine's figures. She pulled three bottles out by Braille, I suppose. A wolf-whistle sounded and a mannish woman in boots marched over to compliment the girls. "Honeys, you have some looks. In abundance."

Bretta laughed in the woman's face. I tensed. Bretta thought the word was so funny, she repeated, "Abundance, abundance, A Bun Dance." I wondered if the dyke might smack her. Or me. Bretta swayed rhythmically. "We should do a Bun Dance!" The Runaways began rocking on the juke and Bretta shook her buns in earnest and yelled, "A Bun Dance!" She took Francine by the arm to get her shaking.

Bretta took the dyke by the arm and they all shook buns. Bretta led the three singing, "Everybody, let's do A Bun Dance!"

Almost everybody in the bar, except for the pool players began shaking their booty. I nervously joined in. At least I had my first bar dance with Bretta. Encouraged, I started to put a quarter on the pool table for a game but the bad vibes made me withdraw. Apparently, men playing pool was verboten. I soon chugged my beer and suggested, "Let's high*tail* it out of here for a cock*tail* at Bretta's."

Bretta agreed and Francine reluctantly conceded. On the short walk back at her flat, Bretta said, "That woman asked us to ditch you and scoot to Peg's Place with her."

"I heard that Peg's doesn't even let queer men in," Francine said.

"Whew, that was 'Los Lesbos' enough for me," Bretta said.

"Hmm, Español puts me in the mood for margaritas." Back at the ranch I put on some Latin music and scrounged up enough ingredients for close-enough margaritas.

Francine suggested, "Bretta, you have all those sexy clothes you never wear. Ooh, let's play dress up!" The pair disappeared into the closet while I mixed and waited in the living room. Bretta's current style was not the hot fashions and high heels that Francine strutted. She would have attracted even more wolves.

Bretta cried, "Dónde está la fiesta?" and the pair came out in strapless red and black see-through disco outfits.

"Je-sus' Cristo, you look good. Where did these come from?"

"I did live in Hollywood and New York, Jack," Bretta responded.

My pulse rose, watching the private showing by the two gorgeous women. After the third pitcher of margies and numerous costume changes, the women danced, spinning in and out of each other's arms, spilling drinks and laughing. Francine grabbed my shirt to pull me up and into the dance, and when I resisted, the shirt slipped off my back. We all laughed and as we gyrated, my mind screened my old "acting" scenes which three could re-enact.

The front door banged open and Winston energetically strode in with two grocery bags. Winston saw two overdressed women and an underdressed man and nonplussed, announced, "I'm going to rustle up some grub. Who's hungry?" The mood was over but I was always hungry.

Stoned at four o'clock in the morning, long-legged Francine was long gone, and Winston, Bretta and I were still cooking in her kitchen. Until Winston had made his come-back, that room was sadly underutilized. Winston played CSN&Y's "Woodstock" on the tape player, urging us to "get ourselves back to the Garden." Winston told me, "I grew up on a farm and discovered the magic of fresh ingredients. I eschew Julia Child's 'butter makes everything taste better.'" He pulled out the gallon-gas-can-sized olive oil he purchased for Bretta's kitchen. He demonstrated. "Olive oil and garlic make the true Sorcerer's Stone. Behold, I will now transmute the only food in Bretta's refrigerator, a crust of stale bread, into a something—wondrous! Crostini."

He did and it was. "Jack, it's crucial for you to balance your partying with a healthy diet. Watch, I will give you a speedy nutrition demonstration." He pulled fruit out of a bag, and lined up a red apple, green grapes, a banana, and blueberries.

"I don't like apples."

"That's unfortunate. See these primary colors? God made them colorful so you would want to eat them." So we did. Except, I didn't eat the apple.

Winston had sharpened the knives and Bretta was chopping vegetables. She looked up to say, "We should throw another big dinner party like—ohh!"

Blood dripped from her finger. I took her hand. "It's just a nick."

But Winston knew. "She's a bleeder." Sure enough she bled like a stuck pig. I held her hand above her head and wrapped it with an ice cube in a dishtowel. Winston said, "It's her blue-blood hemophilia."

"Or from wrapping too many men around her finger," I half-joked.

Winston came and went on his own erratic schedule. I couldn't quite figure out his relationship with Bretta, but since it was not sexual, it was all right. When he was around he would sometimes crash in the spare bedroom, Bretta's old studio, without announcing his arrival. But when bouquets of flower arrangements or groceries appeared, we knew he was around. I knew he didn't have much money, so I imagined they were midnight garden supply deals from who knew where. When Winston was not around to cook, we dined at the neighborhood French restaurant, Bretta called "Le Comme ci Comme ça." I thought it was only so-so. An eight-inch wheel of cheese sat on a side board and I impulsively and tipsily nicked it on the way out, hiding it under my jacket. Back at Bretta's I revealed the cheese as a parlor trick and spread a thick chunk on bread for her, stating, "Our finest French cheese."

She tasted it and made a face. "Silly. That's not cheese. It's butter."

One early evening at the Sav, Z.Z. invited me away from the entourage back to NO EXIT and sparked a joint, and gave me a joint.

"Here, I wanted to thank you for the advice about my dad. His visit was a success. He caught a thirty-two-pound salmon and took it back to La Crosse happy."

"I'm glad. And?"

"You're right. I think he knows. He's not stupid. I'll talk about it with him next time."

#

My dad was a thorough man. After he caught Mother and the Philips 66 man, and almost shot him and maybe her too, he went back to our house. He dressed up in the dark suit he wore to their wedding. In the Baptist church where he had married Mother, he climbed to the bell tower. He still had the shotgun. It was my shotgun. Mine. A used Remington 870 pump, 16-gauge, vented rib. Too bad it was cursed. The man who sold it to us was the father of the boy who drowned in the pond. He was my friend and we were young—maybe ten. I found out only later the Remington had been his.

Daddy placed his wedding ring in his mouth. Followed by the barrel of my shotgun. That one. He shot himself so that he would fall—fall down in front of the church steps.

To kill himself, my daddy must have loved my mama very much. So very, very much. More than he loved me. To leave me. The pain. Pain that is hard to imagine.

#

The New Wavers interrupted Z.Z. and I. Robert indicated the glowing NO EXIT sign through the haze if smoke, and said, "I'm auditioning for that play."   Z.Z. asked, "What? Oh, I get it. What about all those other plays you auditioned for?"   "I never seem to get a callback."   I indicated the sign, pondering for the first time, "Has anybody ever left this way?"

Z.Z. protested, "No way man, that's illegal," and blew a smoke ring. I left the three giggling, finishing the joint.

Oddly depressed, I went to the bar, only to see Bretta talking to a stranger with a sax case at his feet. I complained to Robin, "She always has people around. What happened to quiet evenings in?"

"I know. Sometimes, I would rather go to the library and pick up a book and bring it home. I'm reading *The Right Stuff;* it just came out. It's soo good."

"I love libraries. In fact, when I was a teen, I'd spend the night in them."

"Wait. You camped out in libraries?"

"Better than KOA Kampgrounds or barn lofts. Libraries are very convenient for bedtime reading."

"I would do that with you! We could build a castle from stacks of books, like the little private place you and…" She trailed off awkwardly.

"Doesn't Bretta ever want any privacy?" I helped her out.

"We all need her! She is full of light; she makes us feel good."

I looked up at the Sav's bar light fixtures. "Are we a bunch of moths?"

"Bretta needs us, too. Don't you see that?"

"I only see the same places with her. I'd like to go someplace new, somehow, get out of town, or somewhere."

"She used to go everywhere with Winston. Sorry, I shouldn't have said that. Running around that hard sucked her artistic energy. Bretta had to change."

Monty put his selections in the jukebox. A woman's voice, fluid as wine and divine, glided through the Sav. Monty called over to us. "Listen! Ella and Louis are 'Stompin' at the Savoy.'" Ella's singing turned to energetic scat, followed by wild drums and trumpet.

I sat down next to Bretta, ready to talk. Edith and Robert swept back in and Edith began peppering Bretta for painting advice. Obviously high, Edith rambled. "Which color palette best portrays angst? Hunter green, oh like your beret, and cool gray, maybe a slate gray? I like the look of oils, but acrylics just have a better feel. What do you think?"

Bretta pulled off her beret for a look, and responded, "I like oils, but…"

Edith stopped rubbing her head and jumped in before Bretta could finish and asked two more questions, "The brush strokes show up more, right? Do you use sable or synthetic? Bretta, you're such an inspiration to fellow artistes!"

Bretta began, "When I was in New York, at the Factory, I told Andy Warhol, the same thing, and…" Monty, Z.Z., Edith and I gathered in fascination around Bretta.

Francine had listened restlessly to Bretta fielding the entourage's attention. Francine shrieked, "Ohhh no! I've mis-laid my earring," with the accent on "laid."

Francine wore a tight white cashmere sweater and short navy-blue skirt. She lifted her dark tomboy hair back from her Audrey-

Hepburn neck to demonstrate, showing that the earring was a dangly gold design. Everyone commenced looking around the dim bar. Most men spent more time looking at Francine than at the floor. Questions and quiet snickering jokes, as to how and where the Miss misLAID her earring, went back and forth.

Francine lifted her hair again with both hands, raising her smallish but up-pointed chest, as Benjamin helped her look around her neck and back. He asked, "MISS (could you have) LAID it down here?" He patted and rubbed her sweater. "How soft your, umm, cashmere is."

"Now, now, you keep rubbing me like that, I might puuuuur," Francine purred. Benjamin pulled his hands away, not knowing which way she meant it, as one never did with Francine. She pulled the top of her sweater and looked down her bosom. "I wonder if it fell in here, somewhere?" she asked coyly. All the men nearby were paying rapt attention. She reached out to Monty for balance as she lifted first one shapely leg up on a chair and then the other leg to see if the earring got caught on her mules. Throwing all modesty to the wind, she moaned, "That was such a favorite earring. I simply must find it!" and proceeded to pull the band on her skirt and looked down there. A couple of men's jaws opened and Robert couldn't resist asking what every man was thinking, "You need some help looking there?"

People chuckled and she gave an innocent, open-mouth laugh, and stuck her tongue out at him. Men were practically drooling. It was quite the spectacle. I had been looking and saw her earring under a table where I had previously seen her surreptitiously bend down. I fetched her earring. "Oh, Fran-ci-ine."

Francine rushed to give me a big kiss and lingering hug, effusing, "Oh, Jack, I am so thrilled you recovered it."

A few of the men glared at me, disappointed I had put a stop to the show. Francine was quite the cock tease and her jealousy-fueled performance succeeded; Bretta had been upstaged. I wished I could just get Bretta away.

Monty asked me, "You and Francine are the hard bodies of the group. You two ever think about getting together?"

Bretta overheard this, and already miffed at Francine, took my hand and led me out without a word. I had finally broken Bretta away from her entourage. She escorted me hurriedly across the street and down to the Lost and Found. Lynyrd Skynyrd's "Free Bird" enveloped us as we stepped in the downhome saloon.

CHAPTER 12

Lost and Found was a part-time biker bar and could be badass. The joint was mostly empty as it was still early, and the band would not show until after ten. I had only been there one late night when the joint was jammin'. By natural light, with few people, the Lost and Found looked more lost—worn and threadbare, with a spilled-booze odor I found uninviting. The bearded bartender and a long-blond-haired man leaned in across the bar. They were toasting a shot of Jack Daniels to that late-brawling, whiskey-infused band, not Charlie Daniels, but Lynyrd Skynyrd, which literally crashed and burned two years earlier.

Alone at last with Bretta, I thought. Of course, Bretta went right over to the wiry, dishwater-blond-long haired man on the stool, who greeted her with a too-friendly hug. Just great. He had the pale, too-much-time-in-bars pallor, yet retained Tom-Petty good looks, even in his well-out-of-fashion, faded, green Army jacket.

"Bretta. What are you up to, baby?" he asked.

"Shhh! We're getting away from our usual crowd. Don't tell anybody." Bretta mock whispered.

Exhaling a Camel straight, he said, "I am with my usual crowd on my usual barstool." He was alone except for the bartender.

"Finn takes his drinking very seriously," Bretta assided to me with a smile.

She introduced us and coming out of obvious suppressed verve, Finn vigorously clasped my hand soul style, hands angled up and thumbs overlapped. Finn turned out to be a former entourage member. There was no getting away. And the hits just kept coming.

A woman had entered the bar just behind us—Georgia from my party. She spotted me and tap-tapped over in high-heeled white cowboy boots and a clingy blue dress.

"Well, well." I said. We're just getting away from our usual crowd." She was looking damn good, and she gave me a damn-good-feeling hug, which *quid pro quo*-ed for Finn's. Bretta gave Georgia and her dress a sharp, appraising look, and Georgia appraised Bretta back, in her tight jeans and black crushed-velvet jacket with the half-dollar-sized silver buttons.

"Me, too," she said.

"You two met at my party."

"I remember," Georgia said.

"Funny, I don't," Bretta said pointedly.

I sensed that Finn had leftover feelings for Bretta, so I subtly maneuvered us so that Georgia was closer to him than Bretta. It worked. As Georgia bummed a smoke from Finn, he sniffed her perfume. Willie Nelson's, "Whiskey River," played as he told her, "I'd like to buy you a drink." Georgia smiled until Finn continued, "Sadly, I am currently out of happiness coupons."

Georgia inhaled from his light, pulled back and exhaled, "What?"

"That's all right, Finn," I answered. "I'll buy." I pointed to the others as we ordered drinks from the burly bartender. "What are you doing around these parts?" I asked Georgia.

"I ply the hotel circuit now, if you know what I mean."

Bretta didn't quite get it and responded, "I may be doing some work at a big hotel chain."

Georgia ignored Bretta and said, "My original spot was El Matador. You know? It's the bar up on Broadway that has bullfighter decor from the ex-owner's big collection."

Bretta and I looked at each other, nodding no. Finn nodded yes.

"Anyway, I just happened to notice all the men coming out from Carol Doda's and the other strip clubs, with their britches bulging, and their wallets! I thought, 'that's an opportunity,' and one thing led to another and another. That's how I am putting myself through nursing school at SF State."

Bretta's eyes widened. "Oh. I meant I'm doing artwork for a hotel chain. You are a liberated woman!"

"Thanks. My ass is mine, as COYOTE says," Georgia answered.

I explained to Bretta, "Call Off Your Old Tired Ethics."

Finn snuffed out his Camel. "Right, Margo St. James' prostitution lib group. She comes in here sometimes."

Bretta recalled, "Oh, those huge parties, the Hooker's Ball!"

"Right," Georgia and I said together. The music died with an awkward silence, so I handed Georgia some quarters.

"Oh, Jack, *you* don't have to pay me," Georgia joked.

"That's nice of you," I retorted, "but honey, that there money is a contribution for Willie Nelson, ZZ Top, and Allman Brothers to continue their Southern Rock mix."

While Georgia sauntered off, Bretta gave her swaying ass a frown and turned her attention to Finn, asking, "How's your sculpting going?"

Finn shook his head. "My last project was too monumental. I lost my inspiration."

"Finn welds scrap metal art for huge installations. They're fantastic. Finn also plays bluegrass fiddle."

"If You Got the Money Honey I Got the Time" played and from across the room Georgia winked. Finn and I snickered. I said, "Another musician in Bretta's entourage."

"Not lately. Not either." Finn shrugged. "I still have the blues, I just don't play them."

Bretta kept trying for whatever reason. "Finn, we've missed you. How about skiing?" Then said to me, "Finn was a competitive ski racer."

And a sports star! Bretta's friends were tough to compete with. Poor Benjamin. No wonder he tried to excel at everything, or at least say he did. I said, "I went a few times in Colorado and liked the rush, but I get my kicks on a motorcycle."

Finn perked up. "Far out! I used to have a flat-head chopper. What do you ride?"

"A chopped Honda 750." Finn and I kind of hit it off from there.

Ray Charles' version of "Georgia on My Mind" played and Georgia danced slowly in front of the jukebox. I said, "All right, Georgia!" Georgia saluted us and exclaimed, "This year my song became the official state anthem of Georgia. Isn't that cool? They should give me a key to the state!" Bretta rolled her eyes.

I teased Finn, "Used to race, huh? You've heard that tune?" and sang the chorus, "'Now, I'm the best skier in the barrr-roooom!'"

Finn declared, "Yes I have, but I am now the best drinker in the barroom. A professional drinker."

Georgia joined back in, laughed and declared, "I'm a professional fucker!"

The men smiled. Bretta interjected, "Yes, but you may not be the best fucker in the barroom."

Georgia teased Bretta, "If you hired me, I guess we would find out." Bretta blushed. "Or, we could ask around." She turned to me. "What do you think, Jack?"

Now I was embarrassed, even though, contrary to appearances, I had not had sex with her. I covered by bragging. "I think I'm the best fucker in the barroom!"

Finn protested, "Wait a minute, I'm..."

The bartender interjected, "Fuck all of y'all." We all laughed and toasted. Bretta bought a round. I gazed at the bar mirror seeing our reflection. I reflected morosely, Could my and Bretta's lives decline into the next Georgia and Finn?

Georgia asked, "You hear about these weird diseases some gay men got in New York? A doctor client warned me: lung infections like pneumonia, and strange blotchy skin cancers, like their immune system had messed up."

We shook our heads. "Never heard that." "From what, too much back-door sex?" "A couple of them died!"

The bartender interjected, "Good."

"That's depressing," Finn said. "Let's talk about drinking. When you go out drinking, you only have to worry about one thing, right?"

"Running out of money," I said.

"Or running out of friends' money!" Georgia offered.

He tried again. "OK, when you go out drinking you only have to worry about two things: running out of happiness coupons, and closing time."

"I loathe closing time!" Bretta exclaimed.

Finn continued in a conspiratorial voice, "I'm not talking about expensive private clubs or anything, but what if I told you...a way to get around closing time?"

We all nodded, Please do. Finn checked for eavesdroppers over his shoulder and revealed, "This little club's on Union and Cadell Alley, Silhouettes, which, it's new management maybe hasn't been cited yet, serves a little later than California's lame two A.M. cut off. Kind of New Wavey now, with dancing. On a good night, if the Liquor Lord is with you, you can time closing time right. You get last call at your regular bar, like this fine establishment, then run over to that new club and hit late last call there for a couple of quick ones. Finally, you hit the Stockton Street liquor store in Chinatown, which must pay off the cops, because that Chinaman has always pushed closing time, and you get a bottle to go!" He proudly settled back on his barstool as if he had just announced his discovery of a gold mine.

The seductive guitar riff eased in from Elvin Bishop's "Fooled Around and Fell in Love." I saw Finn search and find Bretta's eyes for a brief moment.

"Hey, let's play pinball," I said pointedly to Bretta. I ignored the expressions of, why would you leave our little fun group, grabbed Bretta and led her to the back. There, all alone, beckoning was a *Lost World* machine. Dragons airbrushed on the cabinet. A winged muscular man and gorgeous female with hair like Bretta on the back-glass. Maybe a year old. The familiar rush of anticipation surged.

"Beautiful artwork." Of course, she would appraise pinball on that alone.

"This is the first time I've pulled the plunger in months." I put a quarter in the slot.

Bretta caressed the machine with a silky hand. "Jack, you mentioned that you absolutely loved playing pinball. Why did you stop?"

Pop! Ching, ching. Ring! As I played the game, Bretta put her hands around my waist, rubbing against my rear in rhythm to the song. The visceral memory made me jump away like hit with an electric current. My balls went straight down the drain.

"Jack? Jack!"

Next I knew, I found myself back on the street, gulping in air like a blue gill on the bank of suicide pond. Alone. Maybe being alone, dying alone, was what I deserved.

CHAPTER 13

Bretta's mother invited us to her country home near Nevada City. Nevada City is a former gold mining town nestled in the California foothills of the Sierras, midway between Sacramento and Lake Tahoe. I was finally getting away with Bretta and this felt like a real vacation. As I had not spoken to my family in years, I enjoyed meeting mothers and siblings of friends. Dads or uncles, not so much. We boarded at Berkeley station as the coaches filled with dozens of chatty Catholic schoolgirls. Bretta and I shared my suitcase because hers had gone phantom. I was in a wonderfully fine mood.

I lifted two Coke cups from the concessionaire. In the head, I filled them with Bass beers I had smuggled on board. As I exited the restroom two of the matching schoolgirls stood waiting and stared in big-eyed innocence at my foaming cups. I felt a pang of guilt, a holdover from my father disseminating Catholic doctrine when Mother was absent. Catholics know their guilt trips. The good Catholics have one true path. I once thought I did—before my mother and I moved in with Uncle. I soon learned there were other paths, and some disturbingly dark alleys.

We rode through peaceful rolling hills of browned and yellowed grass, and the cattle grazing in the valleys of open ranch land. Bretta idly drew in her sketchbook. The Bass and the choo-chooing and swaying of the train made me delightfully drowsy and giddy. One beer to the wind, I dispensed with caution and poured another Bass. Of course, two nuns chose this moment to hover down the aisle, so I promptly turned to the window to conceal the beer, causing it to foam over. I stuck my finger in the bottle's neck, reminded of Sam's "Adventures..."

"Jesus," I remarked, "Are they a sign we are on the wrong train? Maybe we should be on the 'Hellbound Train.'" Bretta looked puzzled, so I expanded, "A song by Savoy Brown."

"Kind of like the Savoy Tivoli."

"Right. We've been on that train a few times!"

"Do you believe in Hell?" Bretta asked.

"Hell, yes. My father was Catholic and my mother was Baptist, so yes, I unquestionably believe in Hell and Heaven. They were married in the Baptist church, though."

"When one gets to Heaven, is that it?"

"It's kind of a secret, but there are levels of heaven. Most people enter on the ground floor, the clergy go up a floor where they have quality Swiss-made harps and choirs with perfect pitch. Bonified holy folks are on the top levels with a grand piano and billiard table in each suite."

"Come on!"

"God lives in the Penthouse suite with a *simply fabulous view*."

"You are so full of it!" I shrugged. I was a little buzzed. I was sounding like my friend, Wild Bill. "But Heaven is for all eternity?" she asked.

"No, eternity is not endfinite. Endfinite means there is an ending to infinite."

She laughed. I was getting silly now. "I'm rambling."

"No, Jack, I like to hear you talk. I can't help but chatter so much when I'm around everyone, so it's nice to be quiet and listen to you. It's soothing." She was right, she put out a lot of energy. She looked soothed.

So I kept rolling. "So, eternity does end. However, after e-ternity there is an f-ternity, followed by a g-ternity. So it goes."

"Ha. What does your Baptist mother think?"

"My mother, may she rest in peace."

"Rest in peace? I thought she was still alive."

"She is, I believe, but she should rest in peace, anyway."

She nudged me. "Why do you hate your mother?"

"I don't hate my mother. I loved her. That's the problem. She hated me."

"No! Of course, she loved you. You're so lovable!"

"If she loved me why would she do that to my father, make him do what he did? Why would she let what happened to me happen?"

"I'm not sure what happened. Why don't you tell me? Sometimes it helps..."

"Nothing could help now. She betrayed my father. My father betrayed me. Uncle betrayed everybody. I betrayed my mother. I left. I appreciate your—I just can't talk about it. I don't even want to think about it."

"All right, it's all right, Jack. Sometimes people, like your mother, if they're not strong, just feel helpless, and do what's the easiest."

I mulled this over. A man walked by carrying a radio broadcasting a static-filled Giants baseball game. A nun floated close behind. The radio announcer spoke something about "the Yankees and the great Joe DiMaggio would have…" The man looked and smelled like a compulsive gambler, with the twitchy nervousness, the cigarettes, the vacant expression of wasted wages and dreams. Probably on his way to Reno. The nun appeared serene and stern. She smelled of bleach and starch. Two beings in diametrically opposed worlds, sharing one. From behind, a woman yelled to the gambler, "Wilson Harris, turn down that radio, you're bothering the passengers."

I changed the subject. "Did you know DiMaggio and Marilyn Monroe lived in North Beach? My favorite cathedral, Saints Peter and Paul, didn't let them get married there." She shook her head. "Because he sinned by divorcing. Joe got a civil marriage and posed with Marilyn for photos on the cathedral steps anyway. All the papers covered it. He faked their church wedding. It was an illusion."

"How do you know these things? You should go on Jeopardy."

"You should play Marilyn Monroe in a TV miniseries. You look like her."

Bretta beamed. "My parents divorced long ago. In fact, my father is thrice divorced. I guess he's really going to Hell! He kept marrying younger and younger women. But Heaven and Hell, that's it?"

I reverted to my humor. "No. You, and God of course, have some choices. One. Purgatory—in between. Two. Horizontal, with no shoes, if you know what I mean? No, not that. I mean, just dead and cold in the ground, hopefully in a box. Three. Heaven. Four. Hell. Five. You can come back as a spirit—or a poultry-ghost or a poultry-heist, you know a chicken thief, or a poltergeist or whatever."

"Ha-ha-ha-ha, I don't think I'd like that."

"Oh, yes, door number six.—if you're Hindu, your "everlasting life" is coming back reincarnated as a better or worse entity."

"I like that one."

"Yes, but you take your chances. You may not materialize." A nun patrolled by again. I teased Bretta. "You could come back as a nun."

"I don't know about that."

"Yeah, with a body like yours, that would be such a waste." I kissed her. "You do have the Marilyn look, you know? You have a body built for bed."

"So do you. I have a bed waiting for us at my mother's. If you can't wait, I could take care of you in the cuarto de baño."

"Not with these schoolgirls around." We snuggled together. I admired her sketches of animalistic trains, tunnels, and horned flames and angelic winged clouds.

The landscape quickly flattened into the Central Valley. We drowsed and eventually pulled into Sacramento. Passengers came and went. Some farm workers came. The schoolgirls and nuns went. We climbed in elevation, rocky hilltops adding dimensions to the landscape. After passing through a pine forest, both sides opened onto a sudden green valley and we rounded a curve into a town.

Duzinella was waiting at the Colfax Station and picked us up in her vintage, pine-green Jaguar. Bretta's mother welcomed me warmly with a double-cheek kiss. She exuded European refinement, speaking with sing-song Scandinavian inflections. She was still in fine shape and lovely. The conversation was mostly small talk about our train ride, her recent trip to Paris, British luxury cars, and life in the Sierra foothills.

Her hilltop ranchita resembled a spiritual retreat, replete with meandering peacocks. The serenity made me meditative that staying here would be soothing after the hyper-activity of my new relationship.

The long train ride made us both hot and bothered and Bretta was ready for some loving. With the excuse of a nap, we retired. Duzinella had prepared Bretta's upstairs childhood bedroom for us, next to the master bedroom. In the upstairs hall, I perused the set of framed black-and-white photos along the wall: young Duzinella in revealing belly dance costumes and poses; Duzinella in fishnets, mink, and peacock feathers. She exhibited a dancer's body with the full yet muscularly sub-surfaced belly that only belly dancers attain. One shot showed sword balancing on a dagger clenched in her jaws. The photos gave me goose bumps as Duzinella reminded me of the exotic, sexy trapeze artists and tightrope walkers I had worked with. I thought, I should be able to easily relate to this performer.

Bretta told me, "My mother was considered for the role of the TV genie in *I Dream of Jeannie*. She didn't get the role but was a body double when Barbara Eden became pregnant."

In one photograph, Duzinella appeared to be dancing on the set for a *Sinbad* adventure film. In other photos she posed with Ed Sullivan and other TV hosts. Bretta pointed out some candid shots of her mother dancing at parties. A young blonde girl was in the background.

"Is that you?" The young Bretta, rather than looking at her mother, was studying the *mesmerized men* who were lustily ogling Duzinella. Mother had clearly imparted sensuality, charisma, dance moves and more, to her daughter.

In bed Bretta became particularly vivacious. Bretta and I did a half-and-half of exceptionally randy sex. I paused, hearing odd rustling on the other side of a wall, but Bretta was too passionate to be concerned.

Bretta took a real nap while I dressed in mountain style—Levis, yellow three-button undershirt and oversized denim snap-button shirt with tails out, jacket style. I descended to visit with Duzinella. I found her in the cozy kitchen.

"Jack dear, I trust your nap was...refreshing? We shall have a bite when Bretta comes down. Here are some berries to start." She poured white wine as we sat at the golden oak table in the nook and chatted—casually enough at first—while she elaborated on proper care and feeding of peacocks. I nibbled from the dish of small, somewhat bitter berries.

"The angle of incident light and the structure of the feathering allow the peacock colors to transform in front of one's eyes. The peacock is quite the remarkable artist, really. But of course, they are not the only creatures with that attribute. Do you understand, Jack?"

I nodded vaguely. Her tone shifted. "Peacocks enjoy colorful berries, also. Some say that it is the vibrant berries that give them their radiance." She sat back. "Especially the poisonous ones that would kill most other animals."

I resisted the urge to spit out my mouthful. I stared at the unusual berries.

"The peacock's plumage is a living illustration of transforming poison into beauty. It is symbolic of how suffering and pain can yield strength and beauty. Into a work of art, really. You understand what I am saying?"

Finally realizing the game, I looked directly at her. I felt flushed. "Yes, I understand that we are playing Hearts."

Duzinella's feathers looked momentarily ruffled, before she narrowed her eyes at me. "You are a clever one." She returned to her fetching intonation. "What is it that your family does back in Iowa?"

I didn't bother to correct her. "Commodities. Grain. Pork bellies. Sod and clod futures." I couldn't help but enhance.

"Oh yes, farmers."

"Not exactly." I knew it didn't matter. She had already formed her opinion.

"And as a rural boy, what do you think of Bretta's artwork?"

I thought, Bretta's art is much like herself, seemingly naive and guileless on the surface, yet with complexities that seduce the more-than-casual observer into her world. I detected her impatience while I thought, so I replied with alacrity, "Bretta is very talented. I'm a big fan of her art."

Duzinella sipped, looked at me with nonchalance. "And she tells me you have had numerous and sundry, um, *aptitudes* in your short life."

"I left home at an early age so I got by the best I could."

"Well, you know what they say about a jack of all trades?"

I forced a half smile.

"All right. Shall we dispense with small talk? Tell me Jack, what *do* you think about my daughter and Winston's rather peculiar relationship?"

By the end of her question, her insouciant green eyes transformed to high beams, as if she were critically appraising a piece of art, or a piece of meat. "I suspect Winston is asexual, maybe closet homosexual."

"No. Worse." She sipped her wine and let me ponder this. I came up blank.

"He and Bretta were madly in love. They engaged to be married."

"Oh."

"Do you know his background?"

"He grew up in a rural California. Central Valley? He said his family was in the produce business."

"A fellow farmer you suppose? Ha. Do you know his surname?"

"No. In the Haight we often don't use last names—for, uh, legal reasons."

Duzinella arched a brow. "*Last Tango in Paris* influence, perhaps." She spun the Chardonnay in her glass, and continued. "This is his family's wine. Lovely, isn't it?" She displayed the bottle's wine label, a fine brand even I knew of. "Winston was very successful in the business. He was the only heir to his family fortune."

"Was?" I asked. She finished her wine. So did I. It was fine but the wine didn't matter to me. Duzinella's lips were accented by the same beauty mark as Bretta's.

"Tragically, although he was quite jealous of Bretta, he was not faithful. He had a love affair." I kept sipping. This was fascinating.

"Winston's love affair was with drugs. Drugs he loved more than my beautiful Bretta."

"What happened?"

She sighed. "Winston dissipated with drink and drugs, lost two very important winery clients, squandered his money, and was disinherited by his family. 'The Grapes of Wrath,' as one reporter put it. Winston became a bankrupt. We, I mean Bretta, called the marriage off. Begging for a chance at redemption, Winston admitted himself into rehab at a well-known Hawaiian clinic. You don't know *any* of this, Jack?"

"No."

"Doesn't your generation speak of your lives?"

"Not really. We don't talk much about our past; we prefer to live in the moment."

"You children really are the nouveau 'Lost Generation.'" She crinkled her nose. "Jack, surely you must know that Bretta still loves Winston desperately." I tried to remain emotionless and shrugged.

"You think it was coincidence my Bretta acquired *another* guitarist?"

"Doc? Craddock? Yeah, uh, no."

"Oh yes, the unfortunate young Craddock. Actually, Jack, I was speaking of you."

"I'm nothing like those two." She had flustered me. "Not classical. She's never even heard me play."

That did not appear pertinent to her. "This is delicious. My daughter has added yet another musician to her collection."

Before the hook could fully set, she reeled in the line with, "Don't be modest, I know you have other...'attributes.'" She let the lead sinker settle before reeling again. "Tell me, is Winston still on the meth-amphetamines?" She scrutinized carefully for my reaction.

"I couldn't tell you." My blinking eyes gave us away.

She smiled. "Time for red. She reached a nearby bottle, displayed the similar label, and poured deep red tannic scents of chocolate and figs. Lovely. She swirled so I followed suit—of the Queen. "Poor Winston returned from rehab clean, and still Bretta could not take him back. Winston struck my dear Bretta."

"No. Really? Winston?"

"Yes. Devastated, Winston fell from the wagon, and succumbed to his terrible habits once more. And, even…" she took a deep breath, "…commenced running with common whores." She looked hard into my eyes as I looked away. Had Bretta mentioned Georgia?

"Winston took a room at the Sir Francis Drake Hotel on Union Square. He consumed drugs and drink and drugs and drink consumed him. He became wasted, as you call it. At five in the morning he fell off his balcony. Miraculously, his plunge was cushioned by the Drake's large canopy awning above the entrance." She looked into her goblet, pausing for effect, which worked.

The wine did not seem so lovely now. As I looked at mine, the liquid appeared blood-dark, ugly. She had no idea how much this upset me. Because of my father. I took a breath.

Yet she had more. "The miracle came with a terrible cost. The awning broke his fall, and he landed on the luggage on one of the Beefeater doorman's carts, which further saved him from the impact." I drained my wine. "Winston was nude."

This was unreal; like a scene from a movie. I repressed a snort of disbelief.

"I know this may sound rather humorous, Jack, although it was anything but." Duzinella dropped the bombshell for her story's climax. "On the cart, the bindings on a pair of skis caught and maimed Winston's man parts. The doctors could not save his—well, his penis."

"You mean…"

"Yes, gone."

I looked away from her burning intensity, once again. My mind reeled. The searing pain. The haunting loss of blood. The terrible, terrible suffering. Permanent suffering.

"Unfortunately, for Winston, he is as over-sexed as you apparently are." She twisted the knife. "Only now, he cannot do a damned thing about it."

Winston was fucked. More to the point, he still had the horny desire to fuck, but his fucking was fucked. I couldn't imagine the tension, the frustration. No wonder he put so much passion into his music.

Duzinella seemed to clinically examine me, assessing her impact. "The whole affair was such a pity." This was too much information. I felt nauseated. She sipped her wine, observing her handiwork, and admonished, "Please refrain from questioning Bretta. She has had quite enough of this matter."

Speak of the devil; Bretta strolled in, looking sleepy, wearing a slightly wrinkled flower-print dress I had never seen, I assumed from her old wardrobe. She exclaimed, "I'm ready for some wine and then we'll go tear up the town!"

Duzinella frowned and suggested, "Honey, I think we can do better than that." She poured Bretta a glass and took her by the hand. Bretta looked back at my still-stunned face, before trailing Duzinella upstairs, reluctant yet compelled.

I walked out the Dutch door, to the cobblestone path winding through the flower gardens, to her pond. I stuck my finger down my throat, coughed and heaved. Just in case. I breathed in the lush scents and watched the opulent peacocks on the sloping green lawn with a new perspective. The garden was highlighted with a freestanding, wooden double-bench swing. The peacocks strutted and fanned their plumage—iridescent bronze, green, and royal blue, indeed changing with the angle of the light.

I realized that when Francine and I met Winston, how cruel but on-the-mark were our sex jibes, such as the Finocchio's crack. Now, Duzinella had dredged up from the depths, my own sexual nightmare. But Winston's nightmare? The whole time Winston had been sitting next to me in the Camaro he had no cock. At least mine still worked. I tried to put the bizarre, graphic story out of my mind. A screaming cry pierced the garden's serenity.

I jumped, terrified. My body shuddered, in a physical flashback, half expecting my uncle enveloping me. Of course not. Maybe it was Bretta—Duzinella psychologically torturing her now. A shriek. I realized it was only a peacock. They must have a big tongue to be that loud. Maybe that's why people ate the tongue as a delicacy. What does a peacock cock look like? What could make a man beat a woman like Bretta? Somewhere here in the garden were the unmarked graves of Bretta's long-lost Barbie and Kens—their blank abandoned faces and semi-anatomically correct naked bodies—with nothing but Magic Marker tattoos between them and the dirty underworld.

The sun took her final costumed bow and opposite, the pale moon peeked with no make-up from behind Earth's stage. I contemplated my planetary analogy of Bretta and her entourage. Where was Duzinella in this? Of course, Duzinella was the waning moon! The moon, diminished and eclipsed by the dazzling sun, yet an influential force and source of illumination. The sun watches her movements in the moon like a reflection through Alice's looking glass.

Hearing voices, I re-entered the house and put on a sunny face. Bretta was now dressed in white Tony Lama cowboy boots, colorful knee-high socks, laced-bottomed short white skirt, and a denim vest. The vest revealed her bare shoulders, the sloping of her fine breasts and her bellybutton. Duzinella had braided Bretta's tresses over one shoulder. I had to hand it to Duzinella, Bretta looked gorgeous. I kissed Bretta. Bretta clicked her toes together. "Look, I found my old boots. I'm so happy!"

Duzinella patted her approvingly and was again the gracious hostess as she laid out a prepared platter with cheeses, baguette, apple slices and hardboiled eggs. She asked me to open another bottle of wine. I noted that the top button of Bretta's vest trailed a thread, but Duzinella declared it fine. We all became a little toasted and everything seemed grand again. Then, despite earlier conversation, and my preference for her old Dodge pickup, Duzinella insisted on loaning me her fine Jag for our drive into town.

Driving the purring big-cat-of-a-car was a pleasure after the horror Duzinella had forced upon me. Contrasting with my somber mood, Bretta was bubbly and excited. I wondered why her mother had made such a surgical strike. Europeans are sophisticated in their weaponized charm. Bretta directed me on a quick tour of Nevada City for me to see the layout for my first visit. The rustic, old-time foothill town retained the feel of the Wild West. We walked on the holdover plank boardwalks passing the brick saloons and honkytonk bars. Bretta asked, "Isn't my little town the most marvelous place?"

A man in tooled boots tipped his hat at Bretta. I said, "Looks like a Western movie lot."

"What's wrong, my darling? You are awfully moody considering we had such a superlative nap."

"Nothing," I lied. "I should've brought my cowboy boots and hat,"

She looked down at my worn motorcycle boots. "Let's see if we can fix your costuming, and your mood." Just past the hundred-year-old wooden National Hotel, we entered the Fur, Leather & Feather Shop. Bretta insisted on buying me a straw Stetson Durango cowboy hat and a leather vest. No boots were available in my size. Her honey-eyed generosity diverted my dark thoughts. I was intrigued by a poster on the store's cash register for "Mark Twain Redivivus: Twain Returns in order to * lend a hand out of this mess * recall the divinity of laughter * give us what for * accompanied by the Bay Area Troubadour on harmonica and guitar." The act was playing at the Old Nevada Theatre for a Sunday matinee the next day.

"I love that theatre. We have to go!" Bretta declared. "I'm thirsty." She did an Irish Jig in the street and mock-sang the "I'm Henry the Eighth" tune, "I'yam part Mick, I'yam, I'yam!"

I snorted. "In that get-up, your Jig is more of an Irish Jiggle."

I couldn't count how many bars were in the tiny town but it was a good town to be thirsty in. Many were authentic saloons, with country or bluegrass playing, and some featured live bands. I looked through one honkytonk's door to see the western-garbed band, Lucky Lu's Gamblers. The attractive female lead singer belted out "When Will I be Loved."

"She's good. Let's check them out," I said.

"Later. I'd rather just talk for a while." We passed on by. She pointed out one saloon with a sign boasting, "McGee's—Since 1980." It was 1980. "This one," she said.

I uncovered Bretta's secret system. The saloons with live music we hit before the band started, and the one's without bands, we went to later. By evening's end we had hit most of the watering holes. Some bartenders and townies knew Bretta and considered her a local celebrity. My smooth face stood out among the rough, bearded, flannel-shirted mountain men, who looked like they knew their way around a bar fight. I could visualize a Wild West character like Marshall Dillon pacing in with spurs jingle-jangling. Instead, I had Bretta with breasts bursting into each establishment as if making a stage entrance, with her trademarked demand. "Dónde está la fiesta?"

Some men replied variations of, "Esta aqui, ahora, chiquita bonita!" When Bretta was lit up she was the life of the party, at a salon or a saloon. Her unique spontaneity simultaneously charmed all men and even most of the women, instead of making them envious. She inquired of a handsome handlebar-mustached stranger, "Sir, can you tell me? Is it legal in California for a man to marry his widow's sister?"

The man stalled wondering why this gorgeous woman was asking him marriage advice, and proclaimed, "Sure! Of course."

She batted her lashes and exclaimed, "Really? Even though he's dead?" The bar crowd crowed.

"Now, wait, you said…" the man protested.

She cut him off and used a western drawl. "There are two theories on arguing with a woman." She paused. "Neither works." The group howled. "One argument fer'sure don't work." Everyone waited. "Never slap a woman…" She puffed up her cheek like it was full of chaw and spit, while still looking sexy. "…who's chewing tobacco!" She tapped her cheeks, making an exaggerated spoinking, spitting sound.

Great. What's her next trick, spin the bottle? Tonight, Bretta's glow was attracting even more than usual attention, especially with the outfit her mother had chosen for her. I made the choice to give Bretta a little rope since it was old home week. At the various bars I made sure to enter with my arm around her, and stay that way through the introductions and howdys. With a kiss or ass-patting intimacy, I'd stake my claim that this here Bretta was my gold mine. Then, I sat at the bar and concentrated on my drinking while Bretta entertained. What was I supposed to do—compete with her, tell better jokes, shoot the shit better, juggle shot glasses? I was too shy to consider myself an entertainer, notwithstanding my circus life. Perhaps I should make her go stand in a corner quietly? Or, should I cause a scene, smack her around and drag her by the hair back to her mama's?

I realized why she typically passed on live entertainment; Bretta *was* the show. Of course, she'd avoid the competition for attention from a band, especially featuring a female. I kept my jealousy under my new hat and tried to enjoy the country and western music of The Band, Allman Brothers, Kris Kristofferson, Waylon, and kin. Late that evening, Bretta really loosened up, and the men's circling wagons drew tighter.

While a man enjoys a certain amount of appreciation for his lady's charms, he must be on watch and prepared to defend her honor, or his if needed. Knowing where this invisible fence line stands, partner, that's the rub. My father made his choice and it had ended badly. What was I to do? Bretta was a man-magnet. I looked pessimistically into my glass of Jim Beam. I thought of poor Winston, well not so poor in that sense, and Benjamin, probably Finn, and who knew how many other men? I wondered how they handled Bretta? Not very well. What was it Benjamin had asked? Did I think I was the man to tame her?

Bretta gesticulated wildly, and the strained button popped off the top of her vest and actually splash-landed in a man's beer. Cheers and much acclaim. Her bosom was out of the corral, the filly was out of the barn, and all three were more than a handful.

Near the door, a bristly-bearded cowpoke observed the proceedings. He was a head taller than me and with his ten-gallon hat he looked seven feet tall. I noted that he had no drink in his hand. He was talking to some other flannel-men who would occasionally look my way. Hopefully, like him, with my Stetson I appeared taller and more intimidating to the circle of wolves. I didn't mind fighting if I needed to make a Bretta intervention. It was the damn Judge that minded. If the Judge were in my boots, what would he do? He would just bang his gavel on the bar, and order "restraining orders for everyone, and a sarsaparilla for the lady!"

I held in my rising belligerence. I would have visualized peaceful peacocks, but not after today. A fight would rush adrenaline through my veins like a drug. I felt the most alive in a fight. That and sex, I reckoned. I smiled. Fighting was a real man's version of spinning in a swing, but certainly not as bad as sniffing glue. To clear all these conflicting thoughts, I needed a breath of air. Once outside, I made my way through a group on the boardwalk. A cute, dark-haired, pig-tailed girl, with jeans camel-toe-tight, brushed against me with an invitational smile. I stood against the rail, the Ponderosa Pine scent refreshing me, and looked up at the night sky. Was that one Saturn? Ha, like Monty watching. Pigtails edged closer. And closer. Until the same tall, barbwire-of-a-man with the bristly beard pushed into me, a Swisher Sweet cigar clinched between his teeth. Through the smoke, his sly trickster scent impinged my nostrils. This cowpoke was a coyote rather than a wolf.

"Good evening, brother," Coyote said in a deep voice.

I nodded. Pigtails appeared frightened and backed away. He drawled out, "That big-mouthed blonde sure is built like a brick shithouse." A pause for effect. "With every-fuckin' brick in place."

I took a breath and formed my response carefully. "I'd appreciate you restraining your colloquial admiration, as that blonde is my girlfriend."

"Huh? Oh. You sure? Seems to me she's flirting with every man in there." His vibe which had registered with me at the bar was accurate, and I recollected his two sidekicks. Sure enough, Slim and Jim were hanging back in the shadows, ready to enjoy the show, or volunteer to help if needed. The smell of acrid testosterone settled around us. What was it about cigar smokers and me?

"I suggest you mosey back home and let me and the boys look out for her. We'll take real good care of her."

I set him up with misdirection. "I suggest that you might want to back off before I kick you in the nuts."

He gave a disarming grin before setting his body for the attack he was baiting me for. "Whoa, partner. I know she's your mama, city-slicker. I'm just fuckin' with you." Exhaling smoke toward me he landed his punch line. "I'd rather be fuckin' *her*, though!"

With him expecting a kick, I pulled the cigar out of his teeth before he could make his delayed flinching reaction. I gave him a grin back, flipped the cigar, and drove the glowing tip toward his face. He brought both fists in front of his face, giving me the opening between his elbows that I wanted, because my cigar move was just a fake. I reverse-punched him with my right, shifting my full weight forward and driving my knuckles deep up into his gut, with a final flesh twisting motion of my fist under his sternum. He doubled over.

His posse was caught off-guard when their back-up was needed, but raised their fists to come after me, so I surprised them by charging into them first. I dropped the fastest looking one with a rib-cracking front-kick, and as the biggest, bearish man rushed his grab for me, I held up my arm for him to grasp, and used his momentum to push and trip him. As he stumbled, I swung him face-first into the rough wall behind me with a nose-breaking crack. I elbowed him backwards into his fat-encased kidney for good measure, just as bristles caught his breath and rose up. I grabbed his beard with both hands and spun him around in a circle with his head still down, to send banging against the railing post. He reached for the hunting knife in his boot so I jerked him around and snap-kicked him in the coccyx, not hard enough to break it, just bruise it, so he would not want to hobble back in the bar after me. With a yelp, he tumbled down the wooden steps into the street.

So, this was the Wild, Wild West. Maybe I should have challenged them to a shootout at high noon in the street. I looked at the small group who witnessed this with astonished expressions, some with grins.

Pigtails handed me my hat, excitedly asking, "You know who that is?"

I shook my head no. A man whispered, "That's Stamper, the town bully and his pals. Everybody's afraid of him."

I shrugged. "Lucky for his asshole, I'm not wearing my pointy cowboy ass-kickin' boots." As I passed by them, they scooted out of my way. The man patted me congratulations on the back. I tipped my new Stetson to Pigtails, drawling, "Nice evening."

Damn. I almost didn't get into a fight. That should account for something. A fight is damned if you do, because you didn't hold your temper and somebody got hurt or arrested, and damned if you don't, because you feel like a chicken. If I'm backed into a corner, I'll be damned if I don't come out swinging. I would be damned if this was all as I suspected—Duzinella's plan.

...IN THE SALOON, Bretta still chats away to a throng of admirers, her sexual glow radiating from twenty feet away. Unaware of my fistfight, she waves her fingers at me, and I slide onto my jacket-covered stool. I become almost cross-eyed with keeping an eye on her, and an eye on the door, although I doubt anyone would come after me. Typically, after a fight, I leave the scene to avoid pigs possibly called in by the bartender, or an escalated reprisal. Right now, I just don't give a shit. I hope the Hole in the Flannel Gang comes in after me. That way I can break body parts as justifiable defense, with witnesses. I pull a partially empty longneck Bud within my reach. A longneck Bud gives a satisfying crack against a head.

...IN THE SALOON, I sit on my stool, catch the bartender's eye, A shot of Jack. I hold my ochre drink up to the back bar lights. Swallow it *burning down.* (slam glass down) I regard the variously-shaped crystal bottles—The amber, clear and tinted alcoholic **Spirits**—captured within. Displayed like pharmaceuticals in an apothecary. Each row of elixirs inviting—tranquil remedies for our discontents. Each bottle, entices with a forbidden fruit—crooked, hooked liquid medicated fingers beckoning us, to induuulge, im-meeerse, suuub-meeeergge. **The Keeper** of the bottles mixing, stirring,

conjuring his potions (flourish of hands) *Behold*! Summoning us
from life *mundane*———to the **mir-Ac -Culous**.

In each magical bottle indeed dwells a **Spirit**——a **GENIE!**

I Dream of Genie… in a Bottle, awaiting to be uncorked, in-
voked, *caressed*, and from each Genie—a *wiisshh*. A wish rife with
poss--aBility! A wish for renewed courage, anewfriend, astory,
aonenightstand, acelebration.   A night's *Adventure! Desire!* Perhaps, PERHAPS even (soft) TrueRomance. (pause, hold heart) But
for some, the mere craving, God willing, to forget—forget a misera-
blefailure, a brokenrelationship   sufferingandsorrow (loud) **and
slippingintoblessedoblivion**—(soft and slow) for
just…One…More…NIGHT.

Pigtails hovered close to me and I raised fingers for two drinks.
I startled as I felt hands reach up under my hanging shirttails and caress my abs. Bretta, bless her, had returned. She finger-walked my
belly. "Hey, cowboy."

Her thumbs went under my belt and her fingers clasped my belt
buckle as she tugged up gently. "Let's head back to the barn for a
ride."

"This bronco is already bucking."

"Good. I can't wait to tame him."

"How many marriage proposals tonight."

"Only two," she pretend-pouted. "Your confidently-quiet background drinking, and stink-eye, made would-be suitors very-wary."

Miraculously, I made it back to the barn with Hag's Jag and
Mustang Sally in one piece. With me wearing only my new Stetson
and a leather belt, Bretta in her boots and neckerchief, and her calling, "Getty-up," our sex that night topped the afternoon. I wanted. I
wanted to make any past lover recede from her memory. I wanted. I
wanted to make any future lover pale by comparison. Ride, Sally,
ride. I wanted. I wanted to make her not want any other lover. I
wanted. I wanted to drive the wayward desire out of her. I wanted. I
wanted to love her until I was hollow and she was filled. Filled,
filled, filly, filly, frilly filly. Ride, Sally, ride. I wanted. I wanted to
fill back up with the desire for her. Ride, Sally, ride. All I wanted…I
wanted her, I wanted her, I wanted her. I wanted her—to want only
me.

My persistent feeling that we were being watched was sur-
mounted by our passion.

CHAPTER 14

I awoke to a scream. I sometimes suffered with bad dreams. Unfortunately, my nightmares were real. As were the peacocks. As we drifted off to sleep, Bretta had warned me of the cries. This nightmare had been reliving a funeral.

I attempted to forget the details of my father's funeral for a very long time. My mind went back to that dark time—the smell of the grave. I stared vacantly as in a bad dream within a nightmare, half-hearing the Biblical passages and kind words. Perhaps that was the origin of my olfactory acuity. The night crawlers cut in half by shovels, the rendered roots of grass, the damp but drying mound of earth that I thought might be scooped from Hell. The deep, cold rectangle summoning my father, flower wreaths mingled with women's perfume, suits retrieved from mothballs. And inevitably, my tobacco-scented uncle.

A well-wisher told me, "Your father lives on in you." Those words, meant to be kind, made me feel both proud and ashamed. And anxious.

Mama told me, "We're going to move in with your uncle, just for a while. It's such a beautiful big house, and he's there all alone. He's giving you your own room with a big four-poster bed. Isn't that nice of him? I'm afraid we can't bring your dog, Mootsie. Uncle's place is too well kept for a dog. He said he'd make it up to you. You know how my brother loves you."

Uncle escorted me from the grave after the service, his arm around me, consoling, patting. My mama's own brother—him. He limped from his artificial lower leg; the leg he said he lost in Korea.

I had overheard Daddy suggest to a friend that the leg had really been shot off by a shotgun blast in Tennessee. "And not a hunting accident, either."

Uncle told me, "Son, your daddy felt he had to shoot someone. Of course, it is a sin to shoot someone." Uncle warned, "You can get sent to some hellhole of a prison, and you're going to burn in Hell anyway. Better this way. Instead of your poor mama being shot dead."

I kept looking back toward the grave where Mama followed us alone, until the minister caught up to her. Relatives and friends struggled awkwardly with the arrangements. Most, finding no good advice in Ann Lander's for an affair as sordid as this, simply stayed away. The former Catholic's suicide with the service by a Baptist minister, wasn't a big draw, either.

In my vulnerable state, my uncle made his move. "You'll be all right, Jackie, I'm going to make you my special friend." He leaned over, his tie falling down my chest, and he stroked his hand up and down and up and down his necktie. His hand slipped around to rub my nipple. He whispered, "Jackie, I know a secret way to make you feel better."

My uncle's secret way. Mama said, "Sure my brother has some odd ways, but you'll get used to him. His house is much better for us." We moved into his big mansion. Mama settled in. I remained unsettled. Up in the dormer, away from everybody, I had my own private room, with the solid door and four-poster bed with high, double-fist-size sturdy posts. I felt scared in my stomach. Uncle did have some odd ways, and he had a plan to make me feel better—but I didn't feel better and I didn't get used to his odd ways.

#

I laid awake in Bretta's old bed since the scream, in trepidation to face Duzinella alone. Late morning, when Bretta finally awoke, we groggily trudged downstairs. Duzinella gave no indication of surprise that I was not a bloody pulp. She pleasantly served us rewarmed bacon, biscuits and gravy. "Specially made for our..." she arched an eyebrow "...growing Southern boy." Again, Duzinella performed her wiser, loving, caring mother charade.

We were supposed to visit Bretta's older brother but had slept in, Bretta being epically hung over. Donovan offered to pick us up for a visit, go to the play with us, and take us to the train station.

Duzinella said pointedly, "Donovan chose very well. His wife graduated magna cum laude from Vassar. She's a prominent attorney."

Bretta showed me photos on the fridge and said, "Yes, Donovan lives in a wonderful world with his perky wife and three flawless young children who adore their Nana." Duzinella chose to smile at the face value, ignoring the undercurrent. I mused if someday Bretta and I could be like them. Or if I even deserved to.

Her brother pulled up in his vintage Jeep. He had Bretta's blond good looks with a bodybuilder's physique. He greeted us, and gave me the requisite brotherly once-over. Bretta mentioned that he played the villain's non-speaking henchman in a few movies and was now a contractor. Donovan fluidly flicked out his knife and efficiently hacked a wayward Camilla branch as we came out. He waved to Duzinella as she bade Bretta goodbye. I noticed the quick-open knife holster on his belt. It was odd that it was a duplicate of Winston's. Other than a steely glint to his eyes, he seemed a regular guy. He drove us into town in his rattling, open-top Jeep.

The old brick Nevada Theatre had large metal shutters surrounding the windows and doors like a stockade or a calaboose. As we bought the three-dollar tickets for the Mark Twain impersonator, I noticed a sign on the wall stating, "All firearms and projectiles to be checked at the door." Were they serious? An announcement was made that the scheduled show was starting late. An unadvertised short act had been added, a sneak preview of another one-man show, "Hemingway's Fifty Stories in Five Minutes." I liked Hemingway, the man and the legend.

We settled back in the worn and faded, burgundy velvet, springy theatre seats. Bretta leaned against my shoulder. The thick maroon curtain parted with a whooshy squeal. The stage was set with a wingback chair, an end table with wine bottle and typewriter, and on the sides were a fireplace mantel and coatrack with scarlet bullfighter's cape, fishing and hunting caps. The floor was strewn with stacks of books and crumpled papers.

A heavy-set, gray-haired, bearded man entered, spotlighted, striding from stage right, wearing a grey tweed jacket, dark sweater and tie. Hemingway stood before us. He regarded the audience, held up his goblet and spoke in a resonate voice, "This is a very short story, a simple enquiry into the nature of a writer." The actor drank from his goblet. "One time up in Michigan, my old man, a real battler, and I set out for Indian Camp, on the two parts of the Big Two-Hearted River. It was a real fathers and sons thing. We said goodbye to Mr. and Mrs. Elliot, the doctor and the doctor's wife, saying, 'Che ti dice la patria?'"

Hemingway paced across the stage, holding up the glass and looking through the claret liquid highlighted by a narrowed spotlight.

"It was almost winter, out of season for camping, so we had to do a day's wait, after the storm, wait for the three-day blow, almost like we were in another country, perhaps Canada. We finally headed out in the cross-country snow for a real alpine idyll—an homage to Switzerland." He stroked his beard. "You may think this a banal story, but it was a way you'll never be." He stood behind the wingback chair and suddenly SCRAPED the heavy chair downstage, startling the audience. "We passed the old man at the bridge, and with the snow—the hills looked like white elephants, almost as good as the snow of Kilimanjaro. That country—should be the capital of the world. You could not hire the Indians or killers there for fifty grand."

He sat and settled back in the wingback chair and refilled his glass. He drank. "Now I lay me, with this—the wine of Wyoming..." he downed his wine "...the natural history of the dead in a pursuit race to a soldier's home as the sea changes." He shot from his chair and threw the goblet CRASHING into the fireplace as a red spotlight beamed as embers. The audience gasped. Hemingway raised his voice. "The mother of a queen is the revolutionist. The cat in the rain, ate a canary for one. Today is Friday, and the Gambler, the nun, and the radio, are all on the quay at Smyrna!"

I nudged Bretta, and whispered, "Wow, that's exactly what we saw on the train."

Hemingway purposely strode downstage and leaned out, making the front row recoil, and paced back to center. He grasped a book and raised it. He became loud and vehement. "Now this is the end of something. As one reader writes: May the light of the world shine..." another spotlight hit him "... in a clean well-lighted place." With a BANG, Hemingway slammed the book flat down to the boards. He ran to leap off the stage. "May you have short happy lives. May God rest you, merry gentlemen. May you remain undefeated." He bowed, saluted. Lights down. Hemingway was gone.

A long, appreciative applause and some calls rose for the surprisingly powerful, yet short performance. I was not expecting anything like this. Murmuring and scattered calls continued. Hemingway did not return for a curtain call. A couple behind us talked, "There's only forty-nine original short stories." "That was forty-nine stories." "Right. What's the fiftieth?" I knew the answer. It seemed evident, so I said nothing.

In the lobby we ran into Donovan's city councilman friend who said our train schedule was out of date. He urged us to leave the

Twain act early as we might miss our train. Donovan and I waited for Bretta to dash to the lounge. I uneasily broached the subject of Winston.

"Donovan, your mother told me about Winston's accident."

"What about it?" he asked curtly.

"He must have really been fucked up—your mother said he fell off a balcony."

"Balcony? There are no balconies at the Sir Frances Drake. Well, one on the 16th floor. You mean a window. Anyway, yes, he was fucked up. And a fuck-up."

"Maybe," I conceded.

"Maybe? Well, maybe he didn't fall. Some figured it for a botched suicide attempt. Winston's family just spun it into a fall to protect the winery's name."

Just as I was absorbing this, Donovan reversed himself. "Maybe I'm wrong. If Mother told you, she knows more about it than I do. Drop it, Jack. You have to promise me—don't bug my sister about it, all right She's suffered enough."

BOOK II

CHAPTER 15

Back to San Francisco, back to work, back to reality. My Colorado friend, Wild Bill, was flying into SFO, for a long-talked-about fishing trip that weekend. I made use of this opportunity to break out of the all-consuming galaxy around Bretta, and deliberate the ramifications of our little family excursion. I was distressed about the Winston revelations. I was disquieted that I had broken the court order against fighting. More tormenting was Bretta's lurid sexual symphonies, and that she and her mother were the conductors.

And, there was still the matter hanging over me like a noose. I pulled my uncle's letter from under a stack of books on the floor and sat on the couch. The pieces were taped back together. I had examined it upon occasion for any clue I might have missed. I reread the damn thing. So much like my uncle—manipulatively dosing honey and vinegar, or more like antacid and acid. I just didn't know. Maybe he wasn't even in prison. I assumed the letter had been forwarded to Nevada to conceal his, and my address. Maybe he was still in Illinois. Maybe he had been executed, and a prison pal sent it so Uncle could torture me from beyond the grave. Yeah, right.

My doorbell rang. I jumped like the wires were attached to me. Shit, what if it was him? I ran to peek down from my bedroom window. I was surprised to see Robin at the gate, I buzzed her up. She darted in, all smiles and odd energy. "I haven't seen you in a while and I heard you were going to motorcycle up north for some fishing."

"Yes?"

"And I brought you something." She did not hand me anything. She looked at my books on my mantle, where I kept my collection of recently published and ARC books: *The World According to Garp, The Hitchhiker's Guide to the Galaxy* (Brit edition), *The Right Stuff, The Executioner's Song, Pinball, 1973* (translated from the Japanese), *The Funhouse, No One Gets Out of Here Alive.* Robin caressed her hand along the spines of the books, stopping at *Forgetting Elena*.

"Hmm. *Forgetting Bretta*?" Her eyes twinkled. "I didn't know you were such a reader." She looked at me, wide eyed. "I thought you just raced your motorcycle around to cafés and clubs with gorgeous clinging women." She turned pink at her own jibe. She pantomimed giving my books a wide hug. "I lo-ove books."

"I do work at a bookstore. Employee discount. Too bad we don't sell vinyl."

"That's an odd knife." She indicated the small red leather-sheath on the mantel.

"A throwing knife. A circus performer gave it to me." A modified dartboard hung on a wall in the spare bedroom. I took a step and threw the knife spinning two-and-a-half times to stick the bullseye.

"Impressive. So macho."

"The knife thrower was a woman. Very...um, self-determined."

"I'm sure that was...very appealing." She plopped down on the couch. "Are you and Bretta breaking up?"

"No. Why?" She had honed in on the mangled letter. I opened *Catch Me if You Can* and slammed it on the letter. "From my uncle. I hate him and he wants to come visit."

Robin looked closely at me and said simply, "He's the one, isn't he?"

"The one?"

"The one who hurt you."

I closed my eyes. "How do you know that?"

"I've been hurt, too."

I slumped back in the couch. "No, Robin. Not you."

"Even Bretta doesn't know. So don't tell anyone else." Robin retrieved a bag of Hershey Kisses from her feedbag-size purse, and offered it to me. My present? I declined and she opened the bag, carefully unwrapped the foil and into her mouth the Kiss went. "When I was eight, two older neighborhood boys held me down, and, well, you know." She gazed out my window.

"Jesus. What happened after that?"

"I became really good at seeing people. For who they are."

"That's it?"

"Yes. It happened for a reason. Like all things. It protected me later from things much worse."

"Worse?"

"Yes, Jack. I know people think I'm peculiar. That's all right. Bad people feel my strange energy and they don't bother me. Good people like me."

"I like you." She went through the ritual of offering me a chocolate before eating one. I took it this time. Her whole body seemed to lift and brighten. "And I can help people now. Help them be…feel good about themselves."

I felt uncomfortable and looked down. "I wish I could."

"You're a very strong man now, Jack. He can't hurt you. He can only hurt your spirit. You mustn't allow that. This fishing trip will be good for you. Put it out of your mind. I should go now Jack." With that, she pulled a little wrapped box from her purse, laid it on the table, gave me an awkward hug and arose. "Be safe."

And she left. Just like that. I stared at the present.

I had been neglecting my friend Nick, who was doing a solar installation and couldn't make the trip. He was kind enough to loan me his black Yamaha TX 650 for Bill. I prepped our bikes for the trip and took Friday off. Wild Bill's father had been a bush pilot in 'Nam. He was killed when his chopper was shot down picking up wounded comrades after a firefight. To paraphrase the song, we both "sometimes feel like a fatherless child." Bill was a freelance photojournalist, and had just traveled for a "From Budapest to Bangkok" piece that *Rolling Stone* picked up. He regaled me of his adventures abroad as we strapped and bungeed our camping and fishing gear onto the sissy bars. We zipped up our leather jackets over sweatshirts, and although there was no helmet law in California, we wore our brain-buckets for the high-speed run way up the coast. The weather forecast looked clear.

We rode under the spectacular cabled vertebrae spanning the Golden Gate Bridge and through the Rainbow Tunnel, with its enormous rainbow arcs around the opening. Years back the inspired transportation department head, named Hart, appropriately enough, had big-heartedly and boldly got away with the paint job just before he retired. Popular adoration kept them from being covered. The rainbows had been recently repainted and still looked freshly wet. I chuckled at my vision of Bretta up on a ladder painting the stripes with a broad brush.

California is a picture puzzle of myriad landscapes. To rephrase Mark Twain's line about the weather, "If you don't like California's scenery, just wait a few miles." The juxtapositions were quick and sometimes strange. Only a few miles from the bustling skyscraped City, rose the Sleeping Lady profile of Mount Tam, with giants hiding in the valley—the redwoods of Muir Woods. Soon we entered increasingly rural land with gentle hills, cattle, horses, and fencing, all reminiscent of my Midwest upbringing. We passed a cornfield oddly bordered by palm trees; an old barn with a new black limo parked in front. As we approached the old country town of Petaluma we saw chickens and strange llamas. I thought Pet-a-lama!

We pulled over so Bill could snap a picture of the fog bank over the Petaluma River. A few vineyard signs appeared as we were near Sonoma and Napa wine country. In front of one fancy winery was a hitchhiker—maybe *the* Fabulously Furry Freak hitchhiker. He looked so much like the comix—slouched against a pole, his black lab slouched against him, and, slouched against the dog, a cardboard sign picturing a crudely drawn thumb requesting "Ore." After Santa Rosa we passed through only small sleepy towns.

On the open road, I realized that my city nightlife had become so absorbing that my outdoor adventuring had ceased. My bike felt strong after blowing it out on the highway. I loved my steel horse, how it could take me away, always ready for me to make an escape. Bill and I were aficionados of motorcycling and shared a passion for outdoor life. Bretta had shunned both. Wild Bill had gone on previous excursions, including abalone diving, skiing, and mushroom hunting. Once, while we were searching for chanterelles and the hard-to-spot black trumpets deep in the coastal forest, Bill told me, "Jack, mushrooms are like women. You pick the wrong one, and it's all over."

We stopped at a weather-beaten general store for gas and beer. Bill examined a casting rod as I picked out some extra fishing line. An old man, gaunt, wrinkled and sun-darkened, sat on a stool behind the counter. As we paid, we admired the enormous lavender-and-purple-striped marlin mounted overhead on the wall. The old man examined us from under his straw hat, with cheerful eyes the color of the sea, and he smiled a missing-toothed smile. Bill took a photo of man and fish. The old man said, "*Qué va.* You should have seen the one that got away."

Under a giant spreading oak in back of the store, we sat at a splintery hand-hewn-log picnic table. Bill had not changed, with his tanned good looks, aquiline nose, and wide-eyed grin, appearing that he had just pulled a fast one, or was about to. Bill brought olives, cheese and San Francisco sourdough bread, which we ate with our cold Buds. I brought "dessert." I lit up a fat one and inquired about his mother, still in Colorado, who had opened her home to me.

Bill told me of her quirky life and asked, "How you doing with Wild Thing, you know, Bretta?"

After I filled him in, Bill remarked, "I'm glad she pulled you out of the dumps." He exhaled the smoke through his Cheshire-Cat smile. "But it sounds like hopeless romantic meets out-of-your-league, high-maintenance artiste."

I enjoyed his sense of humor and immediately called him out. "Oh, you're chick-cynical."

"Touché," he replied, "However, despite what the Beatles say, you do need more than love. You need *doob-ois*!" He held up the jay.

"Yes. And motorcycles. No one ever lives their life all the way up, except for motorcycle racers."

"You got that right, Jack! You know what somebody said, 'There are only three sports— motor racing, bullfighting, and moun-taineering—all the rest are merely games.'"

We strapped our helmets to our bikes, now that we were on the back roads, and slung our legs over. Flipping petcocks on, we grasped our handlebars like horns of a bull and kicked the engines to life. I warned Bill, "Try to keep up, but remember, it's your hand on the throttle!"

Bill revved his bike and retorted, "He who hesitates is lunch!" Bill spun out with me close behind, spraying dirt and gravel, pur-posely revving, weaving and feinting at each other to the highway. We rode the rest of the way with renewed recklessness and hairy abandon like we were teenagers again. There is a thrill knowing, playing, gambling with the edge of life. There are those who know this place, and those who do not. Those who do not know this place, but seek only the safe life, do not understand.

After a short time, came the turnoff to a little blacktop road. A few more miles and we were into the trees and across the brownish-green river on an old bridge. A church bell tolled in the village. I steered close to the bridge rail and superstitiously spit over the side. Bill gave me a quizzical look. Since it was not Sunday I wondered for whom or what it tolled.

Slowing through town we passed by the beautiful old church with the bell tower with the mountain in the background, and a cemetery where a funeral had just ended. A lovely, slim young woman, maybe eighteen or nineteen, with short, cropped golden-coffee hair and sad eyes walked out. Our eyes met briefly before I looked back to the road. It was a surreal and haunting moment. I thought, That could be her. Her at my funeral. If I had been the one to die under that tree in Golden Gate Park. The girl, framed that way, was a striking image that I knew Bill would have loved to capture. Bill and I each gave her a polite nod and drove on with more reserve.

The sun was precisely at high noon when we pulled our dusty motorcycles into an appealing Navaro River site. I turned my face up to the glorious gold. Under the dappling branches we made camp. We tied the beer in the cold river water and became excited as we spotted some of the chrome-colored Steelhead trout. Bill pulled out a baggie filled with dried dark plant pieces, which I thought was some kind of bait. He smiled. "This will help." I said no, but he persuaded me into taking some of the psilocybin mushrooms with him.

Bill was a fine fisherman and he shared his art of casting, accounting for undercurrents, finessing the fish. He continued his lecture on the art of hand tying flies, although he would be using Roe and I kicked over logs for local 'hopper bait. My stomach felt upset from the mushrooms but it passed. We prepped our gear and walked down the gravelly, rocky shores and chose to wade into a protected section of the cold cold flowing silvery-snake-of-a-river. One had to be wary of the strong spring currents. Bill explained, "Rainbow and Steelhead are really the same trout, and are often called salmon trout, but are actually salmon."

I found that extraordinarily ridiculous and I laughed out a retort, "That is clear as mud" and at first he looked offended as a sportsman, then laughed, too.

I asked, "Who comes up with this stuff?"   "I don't know," he mused.   I gazed at the wisping blue clouds in the white sky, or was it white clouds in a blue sky? I thought, Whoa, and realized I got off. I grinned at Bill and he gave me a huge grin back, and he said, "Oh boy, here we go!"

Our little world   transformed into   an intense   cartoon.

The fishing was a joke as we got caught up in the shimmering water, and discussed philosophical meanings of pebbles and ripple effects, if water was a sentient being, which we decided it was, and grains of sand on the beach, and if fish were smart or just instinctual, and we wondered the same for ourselves, and we snared our lines in the trees and tulies, and soon into each other's lines. Bill looked toward the mountains. He slowly spoke, or was I slowly listening? "I was in New Mexico last fall, and a friend took me to an Indian ceremony. At a sweat lodge. Whoa. We did peyote buttons that make these 'shrooms appetizers. You have to do that with me sometime."

A commotion, and he proclaimed, "I got first strike!" He reeled, dragged and reeled in—an old fishing hat, replete with hooks and flies. He put it on his head as the water dripped and he shivered and we both sat down on stones in the water in a laughing fit.

"Bill! Bill. The Sentient Water Being used that hat for a lure, and, and… ha…it caught you!"

He sputtered, "I'm sitting on the Water Being's arm so she can't grab me!" We howled.

We both simultaneously determined to catch some fish, which we did, with more laughs here and there. Steelhead are a challenging, fighting fish which dig into the water, and they jump, making us lose some, and breaking my line, but Bill, a better fisherman, caught more, and Bill had me, with some reluctance, release all but one, which is all we could eat.

"Jack," Bill looked at me with a straight face. "Even if you love them, sometimes you have to let them go."

I lifted my grinning face to the sky, where white frosted cupcakes floated—white frosting with little peaks and tufts, applied with an artist's palette knife. The cupcake clouds made me hungry. "Let's make dinner."

As we prepared for dinner, I threw dead branches together to make a fire, but Bill insisted in precisely lining up all the little sticks, big sticks, and bigger sticks, and logs, before I could make the actual fire. E-vent-ual-ly it was made per-fect-ly.

I made coffee for us. I handed him a cup and he sang, eventually recognizable as his altered, off-key tune from *Cabaret:*

"Coffee makes the world go 'round, the world go 'round, the world go 'round. A late, au lait, a dark roast pound. A late, au lait, a dark roast pound. Is all that makes the world go around, that perking, steaming sound—can make the world go 'rooo-u-n-d."

He performed a quick diagonal jitter-dance toward me with a mug in both hands, singing more rapidly:

"Coffee, coffee, coffee, coffee—Coffee, coffee, coffee, coffee—Coffee, coffee, coffee, coffee, *coffee!*"

We cooked the big trout for dinner, along with fresh miner's lettuce and blackberries we had picked, and drank from our bota bags of cheap wine. Bill told me, in his nasal faux-French accent, "Hau-hau-hau-hau! Most of ze poor fools, they will nev-aire enjoy ze wild *poisson*, straight to ze pan, which is *nonpareil!* Hau-hau-hau, more for us! The French, they say Hau-hau-hau-hau, because, with their mouths full, they can communicate, still!" Bill jammed bread into his mouth took a big swig and demonstrated, "Hau-hau-hau, you see?"

It was a very good meal, indeed better than Le Comme ci Comme ca. The night grew colder and I was thankful for my thermal long underwear. While Bill put on more wood I rolled a joint in a white Zig-Zag and we were having a perfect time and it felt so fine to be out in God's real world. It was a damn fine time, and Bangkok, from what Bill remembered, sounded damn fine, too. "Jack, we have to go. You can still be free over there, do whatever you want." He reflected, "Even do bad stuff. They gave me some herbal-animal horn, bear-gall-bladder concoction that was supposed to increase my virility, which it did. But before I could hire a girl, my eyes went all blood shot, and I went fuckin' blind for hours. Couldn't even see my own hard-on!"

We laughed and later Wild Bill rolled a perfectly round, tight spliff mixed with Drum tobacco in a Bugle Boy paper—ha, Beagle Boy—and a makeshift cardboard filter. "Amsterdam style," he explained. I told him about Beagle Boy. He told me more about Amsterdam. "You must take care what you smoke over there, because sometimes they mix in opium or even heroin. Very easy to get in over your head in Amsterdam, and you end up stuck in Limbo Land."

We drank to our fishing. We drank to motorcycling. We drank to friendship. We drank to our trip to Bangkok. Bill gave me some flies that he had tied himself and we felt close. We wormed into our sleeping bags and looked up at the quarter moon and all the stars, like lightning bugs, in the cold crisp sky. In cityscapes, it is difficult to feel part of the earth. I caressed the ground. A hundred years ago, we were all so much more connected to the earth, to nature, the heavens. Heaven, too. I flashed on the image of the cropped-haired girl from the cemetery. I mused to Bill, "The moon is like God's nightlight. You know, for his children. Yet, it is only reflection of the sun. Two lights from one source. Very ingenious, that God."

Bill yawned, "With the stars to guide our way."

"One thing about living in the city, especially a foggy city like San Francisco, we can't see the stars. It's like they're not there, and we just forget about them. Nonetheless, they're up there whether we believe in them or not."

"Heavy, man," Bill sleepily intoned.

I hummed, before singing with increasing emotion, volume and Elvis twang. The song was an old Ray Price country song that my daddy sang. "Don't let the stars get in your eyes, don't let the moon break your heart."

Bill admired, "You still have a really good voice, Jack. I keep telling you, you should join a band, man."

I sang some more, "If I'm gone too long, don't forget where you belong. When the stars come out, remember you are mine..." I hoped that Bretta would remember she was mine. I started to miss Bretta very much.

CHAPTER 16

Bretta was not home when I returned and her phone rang and rang. The next morning, a notecard appeared under my door. My heart thumped, assuming the worst. Several tiny canary yellow papers were magically stuck to a notecard. My manager's handwriting layered the squares, like a cartoon flipbook—

"Brand new
    Post-its!
        Very cool!
            Investing in 3M!
                Welcome back!
                    Oops forgot!
                        This Dropped
                    off while
                you're gone!
She's gorgeous!"

I tore open the note. "In L.A. for my art project. Please visit next weekend. Bretta." A 213 number and an address were enclosed, along with two crisp Ben Franklins. She knew I was low on funds. A round-trip airfare was only fifty-five dollars. A trip to Los Angeles would also provide the opportunity to see my good friend Deo, whom I had not seen since my girlfriend's disastrously dramatic funeral. I called the number. My Jack, Bretta answered and excitedly told me about her designing for the "not supposed to say" big hotel chain.

On the hour flight to LAX I thought about my friend. Deo Popapolis was one of the most upbeat people I had ever met, with a stratospheric IQ and magical powers. I had seen him create parking spaces on demand, receive comp tickets to sold out Dead concerts, transform cloudy days into sunshine, turn a get-together into a party, and a party into a remarkable celebration just by walking into the room—all through his joyous nature and positive thinking. He and Bretta shared some similarities and I naturally assumed they would hit it off. Time would tell.

Deo had arranged my "acting" in the films. Sympathetic to my persistent fear of Uncle, Deo had fabricated papers for my new identity, different from the fake surname I had assumed when I ran away. Deo's mother was Greek and was related to the Greek Royal Family. He retained Greek mannerisms and accent as an American citizen. Deo served in the Vietnam War as a Naval Lieutenant on a destroyer and his military experience had been different than most. Deo, ever inventive, had parlayed his service into a Thai stick smuggling enterprise. Deo was one of the "chosen ones." Despite numerous enemy engagements, he never got a scratch. Ironically, he was injured in a training exercise. A Thai-stick-stoned idiot dropped an ordnance shell on Deo's foot, sending him home. Unlike everyone else Deo did not want to be sent home. It was bad for business. Deo currently owned a cancer research equipment company, among other legit and illegit enterprises. Business was booming in all.

Deo, in his forties, dark salt-and-pepper haired, bearded and dwarfishly-small, met me at the gate. We hugged, then he looked into my eyes, and said, "Jack, my friend, I am so delighted life for you is good again." In the parking structure we climbed into his new silver with onyx interior, Mercedes convertible.

"Nice wheels," I told him. "I can't wait to introduce you to Bretta. She'll love you."

"We shall drive directly to your lady in waiting. First, a welcoming toot for my friend."

"No, I'm good."

As usual, Deo had coke. Everyone of any importance in Los Angeles had coke. Coke had been fueling the film and music industry long before the drug became popular in San Francisco. I had refrained, as tempting as it had been during my stint in L.A. "Jack, you are the only one I have ever met to decline free cocaine." He pulled out a clear spice jar, labeled "Arrowroot Spice." "However, consider my friend: Peruvian flake. Better than pharmaceutical grade, better than Christmas." As Deo shook the jar, white crystals tumbled invitingly like a snow globe.

He held up a sniffer bullet, a vial with a turn-and-snort top. I hesitated. I looked around the parking structure—concrete columns, rows of cars, low ceilings—inducing my claustrophobia. I slowly accepted the bullet and pressed it to my nose. Deo looked pleased as I appreciated the sugary powder, with no nostril effect, which reminded me of light Colorado dusting. I turned it and snorted in the other nostril and I flashed on Bill's mother in a fur muff on a feather comforter bed in a Colorado snowfall. I looked at Deo. My mind elevated to the penthouse suite. I wondered if what I had just said was what I wanted to say or if I had even said it. I was two people at once, one outside doing and one inside thinking.

Deo did a toot with relish. "Yes! Did I not tell you?" He started up the Mercedes and "Love is the Drug" crooned as he pulled out and aimed toward the exit. I reflected how Winston's speed was more of a body high but coke is cerebral—an impressive ego boost. On the highway, he handed me a little inlaid wood pipe with a twist-out wooden lid over the prefilled bowl. Deo had the best paraphernalia. "Fire this up. Oaxacan bud. Keep the pipe as a present."

Deo had been a godsend. He, and his friends, attempted to instruct me in civilities as an underground finishing school for wayward boys. I had lacked such etiquette training since my Aunt broke her neck.

We smoked. An ambiguous mumbing-and-aware, care-and-don't-care, everything's-groovy, and-whatever, seeped into my brain. This was good shit. I was stoned. Stoned was the perfect word. I wondered where the word came from. Oh, I had forgotten to pay attention to what Deo was saying. He talked right over my head sometimes. It was hard to concentrate on his intellectual plane when my intellectual plane was still taxiing on the runway. I grinned. He smiled back, knowing I could be a space cadet, and kept talking anyway. "...with Venice Beach, Santa Monica, Hollywood, Rodeo Drive, this city combines the cream of Miami and New York. I love L.A.!"

Deo could really talk. In cutesy Santa Monica, we made a quick stop for presents before dropping down to the PCH to travel the short scenic route north to Bretta's. Deo joked, "Next floor, lingerie." I had spoken out loud about the penthouse suite. We were flying along the blue Pacific and I felt like Superman. I was smart and lucky and on top of the world—Deo was even more so, except I could never be so cool and as amazing as he. Unless I had another snort.

Just past Pacific Palisades we turned up the hill to the apartments. Bretta's rep had offered her entire apartment, while she

courteously stayed at her ex's. Bretta threw back the door to modern
unit, looking radiant in a revealing, strapped green flowered sun-
dress. I ached for her as if I had not seen her in a month, although it
had only been ten days. Seeing her made my blood pump and my
heart lurch. Bretta was similarly elated and jumped into my arms and
held my hair and kissed me all over my face. I felt like metal to a
magnet, and we would have fallen onto the couch right on the spot if
not for...

"Deo, may I present Lady Bretta. Bretta, Deo the Magnificent."
Always the consummate guest, Deo gave Bretta the lilies "to com-
plement your dress," a cold bottle of Mumms, "to match what Jack
calls your 'effervescent personality.'" Deo loved being the showman
for life's little productions and had a flair for presentation. Deo made
every *thing* and every *day* extraordinary, every *event* a singular experience. For Deo, life was a magic carpet ride.

I opened and poured the champagne. He toasted, "To Bretta's
artistic enterprise!" On the oversized glass coffee table, next to the
oversized backgammon set, Deo rubbed a spot with his pocket
square. "Now." From his larger vial he tapped the powdery delicate
crystalline flakes. "Frosty the Snowman in summer."

Bretta's eyes lit up as Deo continued. "This Peruvian Flake is
simply some of the finest coke I have encountered since Hong Kong,
1975." He chopped it with his American Express Gold Card. "That is
why I must make the lines so small." He laid out sets of white lines.
"After you, my dear, Bretta." He held out a pre-rolled Franklin—
Eden's green snake for Eve's albino apple.

Bretta leaned down to the perfect parallel sets of lines and
snorted two lines, as did we. Coke seemed to make me less talkative,
but Deo, like most, more so. Deo was loquacious regardless. He continued chopping and asked, "Do you two know the secret to living?"
He gave us time for reflective thought. "The secret to living is getting to know the right values. And I am always in love because my
value is love."

I knew he meant more than with people. Bretta, however, got a
little bitchy, as I had told her Deo was a bachelor. She asked, "If you
are so in love with love, why aren't you married?"

Within me, a rising chemical-change-producing heat and the excitement, in a flash, turned to nervousness. I was paradoxically pow-
erless to stop staring at the powder on the mirror.

Deo replied, "Women have proposed to me many times, but never the right one." He smiled. "I prefer to keep my license to be licentious." Deo winked. "The pair of you, on the other hand, are perfect together. Why not get married and make a genetically perfect baby, you two?"

We looked at him, and each other, totally embarrassed. Satisfied with his work, Deo excused himself for a moment. Bretta and I kissed longingly, until she almost bit my tongue asking, "Did he wink at me because he wants me?" and I laughed as I poured more champagne, "No, he winked at me because he wants me. His preference is the masculine persuasion."

Bretta's face showed the distress that I desired. I explained, "Yes, it's true, and women have proposed to him." My mind on overdrive, I added, "If I was queer, I would friggin' marry him."

She gave me a look. I thought I was funny although it was apparently the wrong thing to say. Bretta became so upset, she snorted the rest of the lines on the glass coffee table. Perhaps because Bretta was expecting some alone time with me, or the stress of her project, she was not warming up to Deo. Deo came back in time to observe his coke disappear. "Bretta, honey, as charming as you are when you are high as a kite, sip the coke slowly—savor the incremental mood elevation."

Bretta became jacked-up and scurried about, picking up the house, and looking for small, perpetually mislaid personal items, chanting, "My brush, my purse, keys, lipstick, oh my!"

There was something else going on with her that I couldn't place. Deo and I began a game of backgammon with his coaching, despite him knowing that I knew how to play. He asked, "What are you up to now?"

"Still doing books. Sometimes, I feel that I am just wasting my time."

"We are all wasting our time to some extent. What do you desire to do, save the world?"

"No. Just do something meaningful." Bretta squeezed past my knees, jamming her fingers under seat cushions. Only finding a barrette, which was not on her list, she crawled over me to search under the other cushion. She eyed Deo with suspicion and darted away.

"Jack, my friend, even though you have had many experiences for a young age, like that one," he indicated Bretta, "I appreciate that you have retained your wonder and innocence." I looked at him.

"The important thing is to keep active, thoroughly enjoy what God has given us." He rolled a double six. "Like perhaps an opportunity in South America."

"South America?"

"Yes, come with me. We will catch the big fish in Cabo Blanco. We shall see the bullfighting in Peru or, say Columbia. Perhaps see a few other things." He grinned as he expertly chopped more lines. "You have seen bullfighting?"

Clearly this was a trip that I could not afford on my own. I responded, "Deo, yes, I went once in Mexico. But, bullfighting doesn't seem fair, because of the bloodletting to weaken the bull."

Deo explained, "If it were fair, all the toreros would be gored to death quickly, and the bullfighting would not be much of a fight." Deo continued like a tour guide, "The matadors in their *trajes de luces*—the slinky, sequined suit of lights—the picadors, the *banderilleros*, sword pages..."

"Sounds like a circus."

"True, very costumed and festive; the Spanish *Greatest Show on Earth*. And the matador is as nimble as any circus performer. Like an aerialist, his very life depends on it. Anyway, that group is the core of the *cuadrilla*, or entourage."

"That's what I call Bretta's circle of friends."

He laughed. "Therefore, there must be a steer, and a ration of bull."

"That is truer than you think."

"But remember, the stronger bull can be easily corralled by the steer."

That was truer that I thought. I was excited with the possibility of a trip to South America, and was about to ask...Bretta returned with a stack of textile squares. She displayed her kinetic designs to be imprinted on bed linens, comforters and covers for select hotel suites, which I found appropriately titillating. Some were faces with brilliant blue eyes. Me?

"What hotel?" Deo inquired.

"I'm not supposed to tell you."

"I assure you, your non-disclosure is secure with us. So what is it that you are not supposed to tell us?"

"I'm not supposed to tell you that it's the Hiltons."

"Wonderful! Your designs are going into the Hilton Hotels?"

Bretta shook her head no while nodding yes, making her blonde mane bounce, and smiled, "Yes, absolutely not!" At that moment the phone rang with the kind of ring that psychically projects weird energy, especially when one is really b-b-buzzed. Bretta startled. I teased, "Oh god, this place is bugged. The Hiltons heard you!"

Bretta gave me a blazing look and ran to answer in a bedroom as Deo and I looked at each other and both yelled to her, "Don't pick up!"

Though her conversation was muffled, we could tell that she should not have picked up. I heard her say, "I am but I'm running late," and then, "Yes," and, "Yes he is!" and, "He's coming or I'm not!" She charged back in and slowed with attempted self-composure, to calmly announce, "Good news, Jack. He invited us for dinner."

"Who invited?"

"My father."

Oh, kind of invited. I had mixed emotions about meeting her father. I knew meeting the famous daddy of daddy's little girl would pose a challenge for a guy like me. I was far from being a sophisticate. However, Deo was.

I insisted, "Only if Deo comes."   She said, "Sorry, my father said no other guests."

I gamed her and told her, "In that case I don't want to meet him." Even though I did, just so she would talk me into it, even though I did think it was not a good idea, except her convincing me would give me an edge when our dinner went south, which it would, so cajole me she did.

"Jack, I promise, it will be just a quick visit."

Little did I know that visit would change everything.

"Well," Deo said, "one more toot for the road."

Deo, ever the good sport, offered us a lift up the coast. Since Bretta had finally pre-found everything, we left the apartment in short order. Bretta declared Deo's auto "a work of art," and we scrambled into the two-seater with Bretta squeezed in the middle partially on my lap.

We hit PCH once more. This narrow section of land was premium real estate for good reason. On our right rose the series of beautiful chaparral-covered canyons, with the perfect winding roads that I had loved to motorcycle, amidst thousands of acres of wild lands. We passed musicians, artists, and Charles Manson canyons—

Topanga, Tuna, Latigo. On the left rolled the perpetual Pacific, bathing the glorious beaches along that stretch—Zuma, El Pescador, Point Dume, even El Matador Beach, fitting to Deo's conversation. So many beaches, so little time.

"This whole L.A. scene is so picaresque," I said.

"You mean picturesque," Deo and Bretta both corrected.

"That, too." Since I had landed, I felt as if I were in a movie. Ocean. Seafood. I was hungry from all the coke and told them, "Let's go on up to the Trancas Market to get something to munch on, or an appetizer to bring." I was outvoted by them—"It's too far up," and "We'll have dinner there," and "I bought an extra Mumms, take that for your father."

This was my first visit to the world-famous Malibu Colony and it was as lovely as it had sounded, once you got past the security gate and the guards—and all the money. The homes, mostly ranch style, were built right on the sand, with no seawall blocking the dazzling view. This was the exclusive enclave of the wealthiest film, television and music industry people. I remembered the locale from movies like *California Split*. Why did the musicians choose to live up in the canyons and the movie moguls down on the beach? Was it cosmic convergence or earthly economics?

Deo dropped us at Bretta's father's expansive spread. Deo and I exchanged fond farewells, and off he drove—with Bretta's Moroccan bag with the Mumms Deo had just given us. I considered this a bad omen and my mood was fouled.

Now this was an actor I had seen playing macho, ornery roles in movies, TV, and commercials, and I looked up expecting the big star. The massive manly door swung open. There he was. I lowered my head. He was a lot smaller in stature that he looked in the movies. However, even in his seventies he looked good and remained a tough and intimidating character. And I was empty handed.

"I'm bigger than I look," he growled to me before clasping Bretta to his side to give her a kiss on the cheek. "It's about damn time."

Bretta's father seemed a little toasted, for which, in his star-studded galaxy, he had a reputation. Of course, so were we, and I suppose, in our little solar system, we had that reputation, as well. I was more nervous than I expected, but I knew being coked to the gills was a contributing factor. I hoped it wasn't too obvious.

After our fairly curt greetings we followed him in. He wore a red velvet smoking jacket. I saw absolutely nothing that looked remotely like dinner. He saw me glancing around the kitchen and said gruffly, "I'll get dinner going soon. Let's have a drink first."

Bretta disappeared. I didn't have much to say and the coke still rendered me less talkative. We were on different wavelengths. He growled, "I'll show you my wine cellar."

He always spoke in a growl, making me feel like I was in one of his movies. If so, the question was, did one of have to play the bad guy? He led me away. Perhaps he didn't have to act because all he had to do like the Beatles, "act naturally." He was a consummate character actor. I tried not to watch him like he was up on the screen. I tried not to be star-struck and told myself he was just another talented famous, rich guy who put his pants on both legs at a time, like me. Only I did it after I slept with his daughter.

The home's interior was a bone white, with dark-wood trim and bachelor-masculine feel. We went through an antiqued door and down three steps. Tucked away in an alcove I noticed a display case of his WWII service officer ribbons and memorabilia, which reaffirmed that veteran Deo should have been here. Through the glass door, the redwood-paneled wine cellar was temperature controlled and extensive—hundreds of sideways bottles and stacked cases. I had no idea any home could be this well stocked. Winston was right, this man liked his wine.

"Reds—French here, California there, others up there." He pointed out the sections. "Whites in this section, champagnes here, and the rare vintages back there, and, hard to miss, the Biblical Kings—Jeroboams, Nebuchadnezzars, and a Melchizedek right there."

He indicated a Champagne bottle that was the largest bottle I had ever seen—like it could hold eight gallons. We would waste no time making a dent in his cellar. He thrust a corkscrew and green bottle at me, so I could uncork one right on the spot, on top of a large, standing wine cask. Decorative or filled? He watched, in what I deduced was a test. I was not much of wine man, so I went through the motions I had seen in upscale restaurants, pretending to admire the French label, which I read as Chattanooga du Pop, and hoping to god the bottle was not borderline bad. Would I be forced to pass a sophisticated manly-mettle test to boldly send back a host's own wine?

Father pulled three sizable goblets dangling from the rack and sat them on the barrel. The cork smelled strong and musty, not sweet, so I hedged my bets by first pouring a ruby-colored taster for him first. He looked at me and gruffly commanded, "Don't skimp me, kid. It's my wine." I saw a familiar twinkle in his eyes, and I realized his humor was as dry as his fine wine and where Bretta got her charisma and humor. "It really should breathe, but screw it, I'd rather drink it while I still am."

I laughed. Then I worried if he had cancer or something and he wasn't joking. I poured the three glasses fully. We sniffed, we gently swirled and we sipped. He saw my glint of concern. He chuckled and asked, "What do you think?"

It tasted awful so I replied, "Umm, it's fine, sir."

He looked at me expectantly, and I couldn't think of a single thing to say. The silence was awkward. I knew to avoid a novice's mistake of gushing about a famous person's work; instead finally coming up with, "Too bad you couldn't have my friend Deo over, he is a vet, and you two would get along famously." He grimaced and I thought, oops, I should not have used that word.

"What? But I told my daughter that your friend was welcome."

I realized Bretta had gamed me, dammit. Women. We both realized she was not coming down, and he chose another bottle, sticking it precariously into the pocket of his smoking jacket. He abruptly took the open bottle in one hand, and glass in the other, and toddled up the stairs as I followed. I found myself trailing him with a brimming wine glass in each of my hands as he meandered throughout his house. The goblets were spilling so I kept sipping out of both goblets. The intense flavors were developing.

We went through rooms decorated with huge modern art pieces which I didn't recognize. Oddly, I saw none of Bretta's work. At first, I suspected that he was searching for the absent Bretta. But as we continued I thought perhaps we were seeking his misplaced glasses. Further on, I feared he was somehow disoriented and now lost in his own rambling home. However, since he occasionally pointed at random objects with the neck of the open bottle, I could only assume he was giving me a half-hearted tour. It was hard to say, as he did not verbalize the tour, so I did not comment, until in a bedroom, possibly the master, I spied a photo of motorcyclist hero and actor Steve McQueen posed next to my tour guide. Bill and I were in awe of McQueen. Included in the collection on the bureau were several gilded framed photographs of Bretta's father with a different glamorous actress in each. A larger shot caught my attention—a very slim Bretta, stunning in a risqué gold lamé camisole. "Uh, is that Bretta?"

He glanced at it, glared at me, and retorted crossly, "Don't be ridiculous, that's Ursula, my third wife."

I was embarrassed. for me, but more so for him.

Then he took another look at the photo and said, "I think."

I thought, Jesus. Finally making to a room with sweeping ocean views, he pointed the bottle to the white sofas. Our tour of the extensive, well-appointed house appeared to be at an end. We settled into the plush cushions and sipped what little was remaining of our wine. Between us was a broad cargo hatch coffee table of teak and brass. The requisite leather backgammon board was mammoth—twice as large as the board Deo and I had just played on. The checkers appeared to be jade and ivory and the board was hand-tooled like a saddle. I stared at the set and he cleared his throat as if he were about to challenge me to a game.

I joked, "That board's big enough to throw over a horse and ride down the beach."

He looked confused, then disturbed, and didn't ask me to play after all. He wordlessly drained his wine and I drained mine, and then Bretta's. He waved for me to hand them across the coffee table and he refilled all three.

Bretta thankfully reappeared. I impulsively leaped to my feet. She looked pale and damp around the edges so I supposed she had either taken a shower, or thrown up, or both. She rustled her father's white hair and he rejuvenated as he patted her arm and I knew that he truly loved his daughter, despite his persistent absenteeism. She walked to my side of the backgammon board. Father deflated, appearing tired and old, and, I read, filled with some regret. He knew he had traded his opportunities with her for his career and that his little girl had slipped away.

I gave Bretta "her" wine glass and she sat an appropriate distance away from me. She lifted her goblet and toasted, "May the hinges of our friendship never grow rusty. And our ale never turn musty."

We all toasted. He nodded approvingly and she giggled. His moment passed, he snapped back to me and, as he opened the second bottle before we finished the first bottle, began. "My daughter tells me you were in the industry, too."

At first, I thought he meant wine industry, like Winston. No. Right. "Just some extra roles, body double, stunts—it was a while back." Of course, she had told him, even though I told her not too, and of course....

He asked, "Anything I might have heard of?"

I didn't think he would appreciate films like *Bonnie & Clydesdale, Cocktasia, Pussy in Boots*. On the other hand, considering "Ursula," maybe he would. Bretta saw me squirm with indecision and redeemed herself by intentionally spilling some of her fine French wine, which also made me not feel so bad about my secret spills. Her diversion worked and she winked at me. Even after she cleaned it up, she continued standing and occasionally pacing.

Bretta's old man made another expedition to the cellar, and we drank, and dinner never came, which probably put me in a pissier mood with my level of intensity, and we drank, and given the snow blizzard Bretta and I had come through, I should have eaten.

Father remained hard to read. Next, he became personal and protective of Daddy's Little Girl. Followed by him turning surly and everything going downhill. We tried to make the most of it but I knew it was coming, he knew it was coming, and she knew it was coming—there would be an ugly scene. Maybe it was the drugs but I felt like I was in a sitcom. Yes, the absurd scene was unavoidable as if it was scripted for a:

```
                    TV SITCOM
FADE IN:
EXT. MALIBU BEACH HOUSE  - ESTABLISHING  -
LATE DAY
A wave crashes on the beach. Seagulls fly and
squawk.

INT. MALIBU BEACH HOUSE -  LIVING ROOM  -
LATE DAY

Somewhere, a grandfather clock faintly ticks.
BRETTA, JACK, and Bretta's FATHER sit. It is
evident that everyone has been drinking. Eve-
ryone is still drinking. Three red wine bot-
tles are on the big coffee table. There is a
```

red stain on the carpet. Father is stern, with
a token smile. He serves more wine.

                    FATHER
            (leading the witness)
    Tell me, how are you two doing, living
    together?

                    BRETTA
    We're not.

Jack shakes head no with exaggeration.

                    FATHER
    Living together is not working?

                    BRETTA
    Not living together.

                    FATHER
    Your mother told me…

                    BRETTA
    No. Dad, no.

                    FATHER
            (reverses psychological attack)
    Bretta, you know, your brother was mar-
    ried by your age?

The Ticking grows Louder.
                    JACK
    I met Donovan. Uh, nice family. I   loved
    his…

                    FATHER
    Jack, what are your plans now since
    you've graduated—what a year ago? More?

                    JACK
            (Jack turns red)

I thought I'd open a combo liquor and firearms store. Maybe sell fireworks and condoms under the counter to kids, too.

LAUGH TRACK of awkward laughs.
The Ticking   Grows   Louder,
and   slower.

                    FATHER
          WHAT?

                    BRETTA
          Father, you're interrogating us.

                    JACK
                 (to camera)
          I wish again to god that Deo were here.
          I know that he and Father would get
          along famously, and Bretta and I could
          just enjoy these beautiful digs.

                    FATHER
          You know, despite how things with your
          mother sometimes… I have always…

FATHER'S VOICE FADES AS:
FLASH TO:
B&W SHOT

EXT. PARK — STATUE OF RODIN'S *THE THINKER* -
LATE DAY

Jack (as Dobie Gillis) sits on park bench,
posed like *The Thinker*. In B.G. is San Francisco's Legion of Honor, with an obviously
painted backdrop of a too-close Golden Gate
Bridge.

                    JACK
                 (to camera)
          Girls! The problem with girls is that
          they have Daddies. I wish Deo was here—

and his snow. I could use one more little snort. Who knows? Maybe Pops would
like some, too.

The   TICKING   GROWS   LOUDER   and
faster.

BACK TO SCENE:
BACK TO COLOR:

INT. MALIBU BEACH HOUSE - LIVING ROOM -
LATE DAY

> FATHER
> I'm just trying to get to know your boy-
> friend. There's no need to get defen-
> sive. Bretta, it's just that after Win-
> ston, I'm…

> BRETTA
> (standing)
> Father, don't be a big baboon!

FLASH TO:
B&W SHOT

EXT. PARK — STATUE OF RODIN'S *THE THINKER* -
LATE DAY

Jack sits on park bench, posed like *The
Thinker*.

> JACK
> (to camera)
> I can tell he is truly trying to be nice
> to me, although it sometimes isn't in
> his nature, and I am trying not to be an
> asshole, but sometimes it isn't in my
> nature.

Jack pauses, gazes up at statue.

                    JACK
                (continues)
    There really is a generation gap. It is
    so difficult for young men like me and
    older men to relate. They don't under-
    stand or trust us, or our tastes. And we
    view them as authoritative, jealous of
    our youth, and out of touch. The real
    absurdity is, if he was fifty years
    younger, he could be acting the exact
    same way, and I would probably think he
    was so cool!

In B.G. Maynard G. Krebs, a goateed beatnik in
a beret, ambles by. He is Winston as Scooby-
Doo's Shaggy. He holds a bongo drum under an
arm.

CLOSE UP: Bongo

The bongo has an open top brimming with smoldering Thai weed. A long pipe stem extrudes
from the bongo. Maynard G. sucks heartily,
puffing out smoke-squares, instead of rings.
He accidentally bo-ngggs the drum into Jack's
head, making a:

SOUND FX: BO-NGGG!
LAUGH TRACK
BACK TO SCENE:
BACK TO COLOR:

INT. MALIBU BEACH HOUSE — LIVING ROOM -
LATE DAY

The TICKING GROWS LOUDER   and   FASTER.

Jack rubs his head and stands up.

                    FATHER
You'll see when you… …have children of
your own.

Bretta and Jack stare at Father.

                    FATHER
          (continues, changing tack)
Jack, what do you think of this '73
Stag's Leap Cellars Cabernet we're
drinking now?

                    JACK
Like I said, I don't really know wines.
Oh, maybe I didn't say that. Anyway, I
don't. Umm, it's
flavorful. Better than Mateus or Lan-
cers.

                    FATHER
Some just don't have the palate. As
someone said, Fine wine is a waste if
you have no taste. Oh, I said that.

                    BRETTA
Jack, what my father is trying to ask is
what flavors does your palate perceive
in the wine? Use your nose, Jack.

                    JACK
          (sniffing, glass, ogling Bretta)
The palette of the palate. My nose? Nobody ever told me that. Umm, a scent of
delicious fruit Starbursts, mixing with
oils, rather mouthwatering.
          (Jack licks lips at Bretta)
SEDUCTIVE accents; velvety SOFT yet very
FULL BODIED. Glowing with life with good
LEGS, perhaps but a bit of a TART—maybe
raisin…

                    FATHER
Currant.

                     JACK
Full—rich—taste—fills the entire mouth.
Good— LONG—satisfying—finish.   Yumm.

                    BRETTA
                  (grinning)
Any hint of Shalimar, Jack?

Jack smiles, shakes head no.
                    FATHER
You're just spouting words, you couldn't
know. How about this first bottle we
drank.

Father picks up the Chateauneuf du Pape bottle. Bretta gives encouraging look.

                     JACK
Oh, the Chattanooga Pop? You were right—
it did grow on me. The complex rasp-
berry, violets and lavender tastes came
out, along with the, umm, fruitiness.
Initially it came across as ornery,
fierce, intense, and confusing with a
little dirt from the past. I find it
challenging and stubborn, and past its
prime, but I could grow to like him.

                    FATHER
Very funny. I see what you're doing now.

                    BRETTA
Well, Dad?
                    FATHER
You're an asshole but… you some kind of
wine shark?

                    BRETTA

                    (in her child-like voice)
        Father, no, Jack just has very cute, I
        mean acute, senses.

                         JACK
                    (restraining)
        No, but I am better at pool. Sir, would
        it be all right if Bretta and I take a
        walk on the beach?

                        FATHER
            Please do.

    The ticking stops.
    Jack grabs Bretta's hand and wastes no time
    to:
    EXIT STAGE LEFT

    CUT

    I yelled, "Jailbreak!" Right off the back deck I made a flying
somersault over the steps to land upright on the fine sand of the luminous beach.
    Bretta gasped, "Oh, my god, Jack," and applauded. Hand in
hand we ran across the beach while Bretta sustained a giggle fit. I
half-expected to discover gigantic backgammon board and dice, like
those life-size chess sets—with such large checkers that servants had
to move them for you. I spotted J.R. from *Dallas* across the little
fence windbreak on the sand and he waved. He looked good. They
all looked good. I guessed that's why they're actors.
    We stripped off our shoes and ran into the refreshing surf. I did
a handstand and hand-walked beside her for a few feet.
    "Show off. I love it," Bretta said. She tickled my armpits until I
fell over. We strolled along the ever-changing shore, admiring the
Point Dume bluffs. Up in the northern hills we saw remnants of the
big Agoura fire of the year previous. Bretta said, "The Santa Ana
wind fueled the fire and evaporated almost two hundred houses into
ash."
    "Right. The fiery wind was so sizzling hot, Joan Didion wrote
the amazing line, "'Horses caught fire and were shot on the beach,
birds exploded in the air.'"

"That is horribly powerful."

I said, "If you try not to imagine exploding birds, I will try not to imagine conflagrating horses."

We both shuddered and laughed. "Agreed." We sat close on the warm sand. I lit up Deo's pipe. Bretta generally eschewed pot, but was happy for the effect at this moment. We watched the sunset. Sunsets in L.A. are sexy, Panavisioned, Koda-chromatic affairs— more so than San Francisco's. Unfortunately, L.A. sunsets are often as artificial as their movies; smog induced—smog's one benefit.

"You should have let Deo come to save us." After a short solar flare of jealousy from Bretta, I asked what she didn't like about him.

"He is just too, too..." She sputtered, "Insouciant."

I giggled and she joined in and settled down. Her new-found jealousy was appropriately satisfying. She cozied up to me and said, "But, I think you're utterly, marvelously superb." She brushed her sun-drenched tresses across my face before kissing me fully.

Unquestionably, Bretta was in love with me. This was a good as time as any to say, "God, I love you, Bretta!"

She murmured, "I love you, too, Jack." We kissed and dug our toes into the sand, listened to the lapping waves and watched the sunlight sparkle on the water. We rolled on our sides and kissed deeply.

"Sorry about my dad."

"No," I replied, "he's all right. I know I'd feel protective if we had a daughter as special as you."

"What?"

"If *I* had a daughter like you, I'd be protective."

"Oh, that's sweet. I thought you said something else." She abruptly rolled to her knees. "You know, none of this is real."

"The sunset? What do you mean?"

Bretta gestured. "This town, this place, houses on the beach, my father's life. It is all fantasy; a celluloid dream. This is a created world, an attempt to simulate perfection." She paused. "Like my artwork. Like me, Jack."

"Jesus, Bretta you must be crashing." I held her. "We're real. What we feel for each other is real. It's OK if everything else is bullshit."

She kissed my nose, arose and brushed off the sand. I followed her back to the deck. As I slid open the door, she said loudly, "Jack, do you honestly mean to suggest that if I'd kept my clothes on, those poor sailors would not have drowned?"

Her father gave us a look, and accustomed to his daughter's humor, laughed. I complimented him, "I like that plexiglass on your deck rails—blocks the wind but not the view."

"Thanks, Jack. I just had it installed, and it's the best money I've spent here lately. Except for the wine." He patted me on the back and we began again on a better note. He used a W.C. voice, whom he already sounded like. "Ah, that reminds me. W.C. Fields comes into the bar and asks: 'Was I in here last night, and did I spend a twenty-dollar bill?' Bartender: 'Yeah.' Fields sighs and says: 'Oh boy, what a load that is off my mind—I thought I'd *lost* it.'"

I laughed, and he continued on a more philosophical note as he led us to the kitchen. He poured us fresh glasses of wine. "You know, each new generation discovers alcohol and embraces it as if they were the first to truly enjoy it, as if it were their own; as if the Greeks and Romans knew nothing of Bacchanalian pleasure." He sat on a barstool and held his glass up. Bretta rolled her eyes and left the room. "Then there's war." He banged on the counter tiles. "After my war, we were the ones who added drugs. Hell, I smoked reefer with Bob Mitchum at what they called "tea parties," before he got busted in '48! Bob took it like a man, served his time without ratting anyone out." Did this have hidden meaning? He sounded like a James Cagney movie, but he was sincere. "In the last ten years, your generation added more and more drugs to the mix... And each new generation, when they discover sex and romance and love... they feel as only they truly know those pleasures. That their parents couldn't possibly... You know how many times I've been crazy in love enough to marry?"

I shook my head even though I knew the answer. Four. One committed suicide after he divorced her.

He held up four fingers. "Romance is easy. Romance is fleeting. Sex? Even fish can fuck. Love? Relationship? Family? That takes sacrifice. It takes work. It means you have to work and support your god damn family."

Her father gazed through the extended aquarium-like window, above the avocado-green sink—the wavy ocean disappearing in the night. "Dangerous waters out there—you can be quickly taken by the strong currents and undertows. But it's pollution that is the greatest tragedy." He tapped his head and looked straight at me. "You know what I mean?" He got up. "Well Jack, you must be getting hungry."

No shit. He opened the Frigidaire, which contained only re-corked bottles of white wine and a six-pack of Tab. He growled. My stomach growled. He banged the door shut. He went to the pantry and returned empty-handed. "My damn housekeeper. She neglected to go shopping for us." Bretta reappeared at the noise, took her cue and scrounged up some appetizers of stale crackers, canned oysters, a jar of artichoke hearts, and an inky jar of expired caviar.

"Dad really is a fine chef. As long as he has the proper ingredients," she said.

He made up for dinner in his own way. We made another trip to the cellar where he gave me a bottle of expensive looking-wine and a little card of wine terminology. He insisted, "You two should spend the night instead of calling a cab."

Later, he poured us all Courvoisier Imperial cognac for a night-cap, which Bretta mixed with Carnation condensed milk. He was cool enough to let us share her old room—a spacious room with shelves of stuffed animals, seashells, and jewelry boxes, Murano blown glass swans, a miniature Eiffel Tower, and other travel souve-nirs. We fell into her small bed and went after each other. We were filled with ten days of wanting, longing and needing, not thinking of anything else, although the naughtiness of us fucking in Daddy's house enhanced our eroticism. Blissful pleasure, the soft smooth skin, intense, deep, as the senses, follicles, pores, epidermis—alive with the rhythm of the ocean. Mind blank, not thinking, only pleas-ure, floating, hovering, the lightness, synchronicity, delicacy, deliri-ously working as close together as such disparate incompatible crea-tures as a man and woman can be, for the common goal, sweating, submitting, dominating, seducing, love, love, loving in bed, bed, bed.

Hot hot, too hot, slow down, hold back, easy, the frantic irrevo-cable rush to the finish that we desperately need but perversely desire to last forever and ever, and evermore—the throes of ecstasy, an as-tral plane of moaning and gasping, and the I love you, I love you, I love you, I loooove yoooou...

The waves crashed and I dreamt of horses on the beach. Wild Horses running, running, running...

Once in the night I woke up and heard the wind blow.

CHAPTER 17

The fog settled in San Francisco like a grey ghost. The following weekend Bretta and the sun returned. Her designs were complete and now in the hands, and hopefully beds, of the Hiltons. Bretta was homesick for her entourage and was disappointed that Z.Z. "chose the absolute worst time to abandon me." Z.Z. had escaped the fog and traveled to Guerneville, on the Russian River, for his vacation.

Bretta picked up Z.Z.'s three-piece suit from the cleaners and dressed up her new wooden manikin model, adding a hat and tie. She said, "Now he looks like a real boy!" She called Z.Z. with the cordless phone next to the dummy and made him appear to talk. On speakerphone, Bretta proclaimed, "How handsome Z.Z. is, don't you think so, Jack?"

"Oh yes, very handsome. Hey, let's smoke a joint together."

Z.Z. said, "Yes. Let's," and we both fired up a joint across the wire and simul-inhaled. Z.Z. confided, "'Queernville' may be the Gay Riviera, but I don't know if I quite fit in."

I asked, "I always wondered why, since you're gay, uh, you hang out with Bretta and all her straight boys."

He teased me, "You just answered your own question, stud."

I teased him, "You're, a, a fag-hag antonym."

He responded, "You mean a hag fag?"

"You sound dyslexic. Wait, I know you're not dyslexic, you're dick, dixlickxic!" I choke-laughed smoke.

"You mean I have to lick a dick?"

Bretta turned red and poked me. I kept it up. "So what the hell are you doing in your room on the phone with us breeders? You're just an empty suit here, so you'd better be *au natural* there. Go out and go get buggered or whatever your predil-dick–tion is."

He used a Chinese accent. "But it a pre-erection year!"

I said, "Not at that Polk Street leather shop that answers the phone, 'Hard-on! Please hold!'" It was great fun, although Bretta gave me a double look like, how did you know that, and you went too far, which I probably did.

#

One lazy Saturday afternoon, tired from a week of work, and having spent the night at my house alone, I dropped by Bretta's hoping for some afternoon delight. Unfortunately, Bretta and Francine were leaving for Daljeets store on Haight to buy Bretta a new dress for the night at the Sav. I declined the offer to go shopping and said I'd wait there for them. Francine sighed that she was tired, too, and would rather hang out and make some chamomile tea. Bretta grabbed her Moroccan bag and left. Francine looked attractive in her white sheer silk blouse, short denim skirt, and white socks with black high-heeled Mary Janes. I dreamily read:

The Rambling Wreck

FRANCINE brought the *San Francisco Chronicle* ...
and rolled up some herb ... and I joked ... now
I'm ready to read some Herb ... and I really got
into Herb Caen's column ... with the C of CAEN in
the heading, bending the flaccid pointed head of
the Pyramid building he reviled ... as we lounged
on the sofa ... in Bretta's flat in Baghdad-by-the-
Bay... sipping our Rolling Thunder tea ...

SOOTHING and dreamy is Herb Caen's writing ...
particularly in the morning ... hung-over ... He is
Mr. San Francisco, and is ... shhh ... San Francisco's Hangover Helper ... Caen's dot, dot, dots
... are the filling of his daily columns, and his
prose, icing on the seven-tiered layer cake that is
San Francisco ...

... his style transports the reader with gentlemanly
wit and charm through Caen's loving, fog-colored
glasses ... a view of bygone classier, halcyon San
Francisco daze ...

FRANCINE sure is a Chatty Cathy though ... I
didn't even think she liked me ... but I sure like

those legs as she kept chatting ... as I resumed my reading about glitterati Enrico Bandooch, Slick Willie Brown, and Wilkes the Bashford ... Chico's Velveeta is like Crisco but Don't Call it Frisco ... and Strange de Jim liked his Slim Jims which made it namephreakisim ...

ADD INFINITEMS: I idly noticed Francine's section's HEADLINE articles "Russian Invasion of Afghanistan," "Escaped Killer Found Dead" and "England's First Female P.M. Margaret Thatcher – The Iron Lady" ... Francine could qualify... I had to stop staring at Francine's legs ... except she brought those legs up under her, so I looked back at Herb Caen but fixated on the sexy MACY'S LINGERIE model (legs) next door in the ad ... while Francine chatted about what Benjamin's been up to ... and chatted about ... this (legs) party I attended in Pacific Heights ... and she chatted about ... (legs) and I are doing this Victorian interior on Alamo Square ... Francine turned toward me, and lifted her LEG with her three-inch heeled Mary Jane to my thigh and shook me gently with it. JACK!

ARE you LISTENING, Jack? ... I looked all the way up her long leg as she rocked my leg back and forth ... and she squealed, pointing to an ad in the paper, Have you ever been to *BEACH BLANKET BABYLON*? Uh, no ... The musical stage show about San Francisco? It's outrageous; the actors wear bigger and bigger hats until they are like ... (she opened her arms thrusting out her small breasts bigger and bigger) ... five feet across. The show actually started at the Sav! You want to come?

SHE kept shaking me, and my pants started feeling a little tight ... Come where? ... With a HISSS

turning to, SILLY! and one last kick, Francine finally stopped shaking. With her shoe still on my
thigh, Francine leaned in close again. Jack, you're
quiet. Everyone thinks you're so-o mysterious. We
never hear you brag, like that insufferable Benjamin ... Did you really run off at thirteen and join
the circus? What was that about your Uncle? Why
were you in jail? Were you really, like a porn star
in Hollywood? ... but Francine's legs were very
distracting ... she must really do a lot of hill walking ... although her breasts were small she
sported perfectly PERT pencil eraser NIPPLES ...

I gave up on Herb Caen to give Francine my undivided attention. I never read the papers much anyway. Francine crossed her
legs, facing me, revealing a goodly proportion of toned thigh. I
thought great; I guess I'm the only one keeping other's secrets. I protested with my usual lie, "It wasn't really porn, I was just doing
body-double gigs and extra work."

Francine kept going, "Tell me more. I can keep a secret! I'm
good at keeping secrets. I wouldn't tell Bretta. In fact, I wouldn't tell
her about..." She leaned back and gave this pouty, come-hither look,
and carried on in a slow, low tone, looking down at my jeans, "This
would just be between you...and...me."

"Nothing to brag about," I mumbled. What was in this woman's
tea?

"I grew up across the Bay in Tiburon. Do you know what that
means?"

"You grew up rich like the rest of the entourage," I replied.

"Not as rich as Bretta. She's the poor little rich girl."

"What do you mean?"

"Not enough attention from Daddy. It was challenging for
Bretta to grow up with two prima-donna parents."

"I know the feeling, only in the exact opposite way. I just wish
my uncle would have not given me so much attention, and spent all
of his time in the taverns instead of most of it."

"Taverns? How quaint. I prefer cocktail parties to taverns. Don't
you think being at Bretta's salons is like being at Gertrude Stein's?"

I played dumb. "Don't know. I've never been to Gertrude's.
Isn't she dead?"

"Well, yes. Anyway, I asked if you knew what Tiburon means."

"No."

"A shark." She showed a sexy shark smile. "Have you been there?"

"No."

"Jack, you poor lost boy!"

"Yes, I've led a deprived life in Neverland."

"Not deprived in some things, I hear!" Francine leaned over to look at me intently. "You should come with me sometime." She smiled. "You know, for dinner."

"I don't know which side of the plate the dessert spoon goes on."

She patted my face with a laugh. "That's what we girls love about you, Jack—your delightful lack of sophistication. It's a real turn-on. Bretta calls you, her 'diamond in the buff.' Isn't that funny?" She made poofy movements with her lips, which from inches away, were quite luscious. "That day we went to Maud's and we three came back here, that was fun. I was kind of hoping for more fun that night. Weren't you?" Her fingers stroked mine; she wanted me to kiss her. I wanted to kiss her. I didn't. She didn't stop. "I bet doing porno was incredibly sexy. Do tell me more. What were the girls like? Were they real nymphos? Did the girls have legs as nice as me?"

She leaned back and languidly held out and arched the other long shapely leg. I didn't blame Francine for dressing or even acting the way she did. She had to do something to get attention around Bretta.

"Jack, did you have to have a hard-on like all day long? I have some garters and stockings I could put on, you like those, right? Did they shave between their legs? I do."

This was all unexpected. Francine pulled a lacy garter belt from her purse and held it up, and I didn't want to give anything away with my face, so I stupidly looked down and I could see her matching lacy white see-through panties contrasting with golden-tanned thighs. She was shaved. Damn. Oh damn.

She looked down and saw my rising, poking out past the belt in my blue jeans and still growing. She mouthed, "Oh my. My, my." And then she said, "She's right, you're endowed. And are not just all this—but 'Eveready!' I think your battery's overcharged. We better discharge it before..." She reached over.

"Oh no, no, no," I protested, scooting away with her crawling toward me.

"Come on, Jackrabbit, it's just sex. It's not like we're getting married or anything."

The door rattled and creaked open. I scrambled to cover with the newspaper and pretended to laugh at the Herb Caen column as Bretta skipped in with a shopping bag. She declared, "I came across the perfect..." She saw us on the couch, and looked at us funny. "... dress right away."

Francine gave her a big, "Hello sweetie, let's see what you got," and jumped off the couch and made a commotion looking into the bag. Exclaiming, "Look at that!" she led Bretta away from my incriminating lap. Francine held up Bretta's just-purchased lacy garter belt, double ruining what was going to be a surprise for me.

I could not determine what was going on with Francine, whether it was real attraction, built up horniness, her normal cock teasing, a setup, or a weird jealousy thing. In spite of this, she was at least nicer to me after that, and I let it go. Francine was going to be the least of my worries.

Bretta was distracted with her gallery opening at Robin's. She madly sketched at any and every inspired moment. I would roll over in the middle of the night, and she'd be gone—her light emanating from her studio.

I would say, "I miss you."

She would say, "I just have to get the damn theme going." I was consoled that her work had a circus theme in my honor, with tents, clowns and wild animals. She alternately dismissed her sketches as "childish" or "more African than circus." Uninspired and frustrated, she sat at the bay window with a Bailey's and cream, writing in her Little Blue Journal.

Feeling shutout, I complained, "I thought you were an artist, not a writer."

"I have fascinating problems, Jack. My art is for everyone, my journal is for me."

My martial arts were for me. Sensei told our class we should look for the *Shogun* TV miniseries when it came out, that it should be very authentic. I informed Bretta, who declared, "I don't watch TV."

I said, "It's not TV. It will be like *Roots*. Orson Welles narrates.

"I've met him! My dad is friends with The Big O. He's larger than life."

"Richard Chamberlain stars."

Bretta swooned. "Oooh, I loved him in *The Last Wave*. All those bizarre dreams and cosmological premonitions." She paced about to finally gaze out the window. She looked expectantly up at the sky. She exclaimed, "I think I'm having one!" She kissed me and took the phone into the studio.

A few days later Bretta received a package from her father with five Beta videocassettes. They were Orson Welles' private copies of *Shogun*. I picked up a "hot" player from a connection in the Haight and dusted off the little Zenith TV in her bedroom. We decided to watch one a night as if broadcast. We played "Tape 1," the pre-release still with some rough edits and incomplete soundtrack, but we were enthralled. She adored Richard Chamberlain while I favored Toshiro Mifune.

The next day, Bretta went accessory shopping for the viewings. We watched in bed, heating *sake* on a new hot plate, with Bretta in a short red Japanese robe and chopstick hair barrette, and me in black silk boxers and headscarf. *Shogun* broke television taboos and we reveled in it. The third night Bretta appeared from behind a spinning parasol of varnished paper, costumed in geisha-white face paint with red bee-sting lips. "I am yours, my Samurai." We were so turned on we barely got the show turned on.

Through *Shogun*, Bretta thankfully discovered her new art theme. Bretta embodied *Shogun*, regularly fashioning silk Kimonos. Grunting fake Japanese during ritualized pillow fights, we practiced stern glares, bowed greetings, and used the word *"hai"* for every occasion. We attended the Cherry Blossom Festival in Japantown, followed by a hot tub spa. Sitting at a sushi bar, Bretta was amused that this was my first oral encounter with raw fish, called sashimi. I joked to the small Japanese sushi chef, "I need some fisheyes to go with this." By the time I told Bretta of Rollo's raisins in oatmeal, the chef had placed a bowl of glistening black eyes before us. Growing up on fried catfish, I first thought the burning wasabi had a better taste than raw fish. Bretta improved my appetite when she nibbled my ear and told me her theory. "Raw seafood is an aphrodisiac." I delighted her with immediate results. She took care of that in the base of the district's tall five-tiered Peace Pagoda, which we renamed, Piece

Pagoda. I quickly grew to savor the varieties of salty oceanic flavors while holding Bretta to her theory.

After showing zero interest in my martial arts, Bretta asked to visit a class. My dojo, Karate Do on Market Street, was small but topnotch, with red walls, the sensei in black gi and students in white gis, all fit black and white men. She intently watched my sparring class, aglow in the testosterone-fueled environment. Bretta loved the black, white, and red images, and made design sketches. She "interviewed" my sensei, and my fellow students enthusiastically volunteered demonstrations of their prowess.

Her new work for the opening became what she designated "Japanese influenced Minimalism." She called me "Jacko-san, my Samurai Warrior." For these glorious weeks, at long last, I had Bretta to myself. It was almost too good to be true.

On yet another grey afternoon, I accompanied Bretta to an art-supply outing. First to Mendel's Far Out Fabrics & Art Supplies on Haight, and next over to Project Artaud in the Mission. Bretta explained to me, "Project Artaud is a collection of large spaces developed by squatter artists in the old, abandoned tin can factory in the early '70s. The group's namesake, Antonin Artaud, was a crazy dramatist, radical even for the Surrealists. He used magic tricks and strange lighting with outrageous themes of torture, rape and murder, you know, to shock people."

"*Buried Child.*"

"What?" She looked appalled herself. "What do you mean by that?" Was she still sensitive about burying her Barbie and Kens?

"Sam Shepard's play. Artaud must have influenced him. Robert told me what an impact *Buried Child* made on audiences at the Magic Theatre. Shepard won the Pulitzer for it last year."

"Oh, right, Jack. Sam Shepard is amazing. And very cute."

Bretta knew an artist at Project Artaud who made rag paper, her preferred media. I found it soothing be in the universe of charcoals, pastels, camelhair brushes, tubes of oils and acrylics. Looking at the artwork in the studios, I remarked, "I wish I was an artist, or at least more creative."

"Jack, maybe you're not an artist, but you are a four-dimensional man."

"Thanks. I just need to find a fourth dimension where I can do something."

"You're welcome to use my materials to find out."

I said, "Still you have to have *it*—that raw emotion, that gut feeling, that desire. Who knows, maybe now that Doc went crazy, he has that. What a price to pay, with no guarantees."

"What would you give be one of the greatest artists or musicians of all time?"

"Not my soul, like Robert Johnson, at the crossroads."

Her next question floored me. "So, what would you give? An ear? *Something* else?"

Later that day Bretta attempted to capture the 4th dimension in me, which must have been especially challenging in a 2-D medium. I had told her about making friends with some of the performing circus monkeys, and she portrayed a monkey hanging by his tail in "my" drawing. The drawing was wild and kinetic with a vortex of vibrating lines surrounding the creature, which I assumed represented the fourth dimension. Thinking of monkeys, Scopes, and Darwin, I asked her out of the blue, "Do you ever think about the origin of life and where we're all going?"

She blazed a jealous glare. "You mean like *her*?"

I had forgotten I had told her of Ariel's quest.

#

Something happened. I didn't know what until it was over. Bretta got a little weird and called me on the phone. "I need to spend more time preparing pieces for the opening." She finished in a foreboding tone. "Jack, I must focus and stop partying for a while to do this. I hope you understand. I'm going up to Mother's for a few days."

The entourage didn't like her increasing absences but dismissed my worries. Winston said, "Bretta is Bretta." Robin said, "She's in art mode." I had my suspicions. Francine may have told her something happened between us. Perhaps Deo had let something slip when she retrieved her Moroccan bag.

Since I unexpectedly had free time, I decided to explore more of North Beach on my own. I launched my voyage at a burger restaurant where the Financial District, Chinatown, and North Beach trisected. The place was called Clown Alley. Monty had suggested it, saying, "Hey, Toby Tyler, you have to go see 'the Clown.'" I was surprised that some Chinese teenagers, speaking in dialect, were eating burgers there. The joint was cheerfully pink and blue colorful, with clown murals on the walls along with other fun circus-themed schlock. I now understood Bretta's challenge with a fine arts circus theme. Clown Alley was a grown-up child's nostalgic pastel mock circus, rather than the sweaty, gritty canvas-and-sawdust, rust-and-tumble reality of the real deal. However, the tasty burger and fries were the real deal and I walked up Columbus with a belch of satisfaction from the clowned ground beef.

I found it incredulous that Bretta had never been to a circus, and I fancied to taking her to the next one at the Cow Palace. A Yellow cab flew into the white zone in front of Enrico's Sidewalk Café. I laughed as I imagined all the doors opening like Dumbo's ears and a dozen Chinese clowns emerging to clamber around and over the cab, and tumble back, in a Chinese Clown fire drill. When the door opened, only jazz music emerged with the beret-clad driver.

"Professor!" I called and Monty steered me into the interior of spacious Enrico's café. He indicated the fellow beret-wearing owner, Enrico Banducci, standing at the bar. Enrico nodded in recognition to Monty, and continued sipping espresso with a couple of familiar-looking faces. The men were Jerry Garcia and the Starship's Paul Kantner. We listened through the jazzy background music.

Enrico spoke, "Back in the day, I booked the nineteen-year old Barbra Streisand. Barbra was so animated and just so full of moxie I told her agent, 'I'll give her $175 a week. If she sings, too, make it $200!'"

Monty looked tired, sleepy but edgy at the same time. He ordered cappuccinos from a waiter and we sat outside along the short iron fencing. He said, "Enrico is the unofficial 'Mayor of North Beach.' This place, Clown Alley, and the old 'hungry i' supper club were all owned by him."

"I went. Just had a great burger at Clown Alley. Thanks. You seem to know a lot, Professor."

"Not that I like that designation, but from you..." he raised a palm. "I used to teach history—Washington High—my old school. Early 70s were not good years to be in public education. Why? Stoners for one. Race tensions for two." Monty continued his history lesson. "In the 50s and 60s, the Beach was really swinging with live jazz everywhere. I know you like music, right?" I nodded. "Keystone Korner, over by the Central Police Station, in fact named for the Keystone Cops, is one of the few jazz joints left. I saw Art Blakey & the Jazz Messengers there the other night. Great set." He sipped his drink reflectively and spaced out for a moment. "Sorry, I'm tired.

Been double shifting. Drove last night." That explained why Monty
was so wired.

"This," he pointed down, "was the City's first-ever sidewalk
café. We used to meet here—it was our spot. Back then we had a
bigger entourage, as you've coined us." Monty tapped his foot to a
jazzy rhythm. "You should have been here—seventy-five to seventy-
six. I remember that night so well. You know how some memories
just fade away, and some stay with you, like…" He reached for his
pocket reflexively, but pulled back. "…I don't know, like a painting?

"Yeah, I've been there. At least I think was. Ha ha."

Monty painted his picture. "So, it's Friday night and Enrico's is
bopping. John McLauglin's "Follow Your Heart" swirls in the air
like cigarette smoke. This place has so much—atmosphere. The
North Beach literati are here. Most Friday nights, big Richard Brautigan holds court over in that corner with his own entourage. I'm feeling cool with my Italian leather jacket, goatee and beret. My hair's
longer, everybody's is. Finn and his harp player are with me. They
have a gig later at the Saloon. Finn could really make his fiddle cry
the blues."

#

Robin, yeah, our little Robin—cute as a button back then, slim,
mini-skirt, freckles walks in. Robin's companion is this super foxy
chick. All at once, this place lights up. A new heavenly body has
burst on the scene—Farah-Fawcett hair, tousled and flipped, full
makeup, heels, and Pucci fringed dress—she looks like a New York
doll. Everybody, I mean everybody's head turns. She tells her, "Here
we are. I told you we were going out on the town!" The lady scans
the room of casually-dressed regulars. "Yes, darling, but it appears I
dressed for the wrong town."

We all laugh, she is classy, but cool, you know? Robin intro-
duces her, "Now presenting! Miss Bretta—the absolutely divine artist." Bretta crosses her legs in a deep curtsy. Robin goes on, "After
her tour of mystic lands of Bosphorus, Agean, and Black Seas, she
managed to escape from New York, and is newly landed in San
Francisco to seek artistic fame and fortune."

Brautigan, already with two or three women (by sheer force of
personality he's somehow a lady's man), teases Bretta, "Hey New
York! I'm famous, come over here for some pointers. And these
guys," he toasted a couple of men nearby, "just made a fortune, because they have good fortune instead of talent." The men respond as

expected: "Fuck you." Brautigan continues, "They're writers, so don't believe a word they say." These guys were Don Carpenter, flush from his move script for *Payday*, and Curt Gentry who co-wrote the best-seller, *Helter Skelter*.

Gregory Corso stumbles in, the mad poet, with his hair wild, and dark eyes wilder. "A drink! a drink! my poemdom for a drink!" Bretta, so cool, raises a fiver. Corso cries, "Ciao, bella donna!" grasps her shoulders and looks straight into her eyes. Bretta warns him, "Look any deeper and you'll steal my soul." Corso spouts, "Love is an interplanetary evil! You want the pleasure, you've got to take the pain." The bearded man with him protests, "Corso, that's not your fucking poem." The bearded man is Allen Ginsberg. Corso re-buts, "I didn't say it was. I said poemdom." Ginsberg ignores Bretta and flirts with Finn. He admires Finn's blonde ponytail. Bretta ig-nores Ginsberg and she flirts with Finn's ponytail. Ginsberg glares at Bretta. Bretta tells Finn, "I like your leather pants." Finn, all so cool, tells her, "You're going to like my music better when you come see me play tonight at the Saloon."

Brautigan says, "Well, it's a regular New York invasion. Who's coming in next, the New York fucking Mets?" Ginsberg stands up. "I declare North Beach is the epicenter of creativity for both Left Coast and Right." Corso yells at Brautigan, "Yeah, Rich, thanks for fuckin' sharing. Speaking of which, I'd like to see your beautiful mother again." Wade the bartender keeps pouring, the night keeps roaring, and Enrico's is everything but boring.

#

A rude car horn pulled us back to the present. I said, "Wow. You guys hung out with Brautigan and Ginsberg?" I wasn't familiar with the others.

"Not really. Different circles—circles overlap. Bretta could have. Maybe she should have. But she chose our circle. Finn and me."

A group of tourists walked by, shivering in Bermuda shorts and "I Left My (heart symbol) in SF" tee-shirts. Tourists never seem to realize San Francisco is not part of sunny California. They gawked at us behind the little iron fencing like we were exhibits in a diorama. I grabbed the fence bars, bounced up and down, and called, ape-like, "Hoo-hoo-hooo." The tourists scurried away.

Monty continued. "Anyway, Bretta became one of our regulars, and we all loved her. Here at Enrico's, Bretta attracted too much attention from people like them." The tourists. "You know how she is. With the crazy writers *and* Bretta, it was a freaking sideshow! Hell, Enrico could have charged admission."

I laughed at Monty's rare humor. He was really on a roll today.

"He must have considered it because Enrico finally hired her as a hostess. She brought in more customers than Chris, the barker at the Condor! Enrico adored her. Still does." He looked away wistfully. "But then, everyone does. Anyway, the scene started to wear her down so I got her to quit and I moved the Bretta show over to the Sav. Just as a patron, that is. It was more relaxed there, and Bretta and I pretty much took over. She brought in her new confidante, Z.Z. Finn had some issues—we all knew that. His music helped, and Bretta had re-inspired his sculpting. Finn spun off pretty quickly from us after they...well...after a while. For me, those were the finest times. Everything was great. Then, she shows up with fucking Winston." He finished his cap and signaled for two more. I declined and ordered a draft. He asked, "So, how are you and our favorite artist doing?"

"She's in artist mode," I repeated Robin's line. He rolled his eyes. I thought, So Monty was the ringmaster at one time; influencing Bretta on the berets; his feelings turning to jealous animosity. This was a new version of the story. I changed the subject. "Why you working so much? You already own a cab and medallion, right?"

He noticed a beefy cop swagger down the sidewalk. He looked at Monty's empty cab in the white zone. Monty waved to him, and continued. "Two, actually. I'm saving money for a third. They make good money, Jack, all cash. Like last night." He looked around and lowered his voice. "A hundred and twenty-five bucks! I did the gay runs—big night, bar hopping from Polk Gulch to Castro to Folsom. After hours, I take them to the bathhouses. A little later I pick them up and take them to the Grubstake, Orphan Andy's or Pam Pam's for breakfast."

He spooned foam from his cup. "They're all such nice guys. They know how to tip— many being in the service industry themselves, bartending, waiting. The gays are a boon to the economy, for sure. I'm making a mint without deadheading airport runs."

"What's a bathhouse? Like there used to be out by the Cliff House?"

He chuckled. "Yeah, Jack, only they're about getting dirty, not bathing or swimming. A bunch of private sex rooms plus orgy rooms. There's Ritch Street Baths in the alley by Trocadero Transfer disco, the S&M one—the Barracks, and another out in the Mission. Nondescript places, one wouldn't know they were there. You should see what I see as a cabbie. There's the downside of their culture. It's unbelievable. The City is turning into a Greek orgy. Hedonists, weird kinky gear, cock rings, the nipple clamps, and the leather they strap up with in the back of my cab. They're obsessed with sex, like they're in heat or something. I can't believe anybody is that horny. Except for you, maybe."

I grinned. He continued, "Combine that with angel dust, amyl poppers, whatever— they're going to kill themselves. All that unprotected sex. Good Lord, if they could get pregnant! There'd be a lot of queer babies with cute little mustaches." Monty looked sharply at me.

I snorted at the image. This made me uncomfortable, so I thought I'd show off my city knowledge. I asked him, "You know about Houdini's mansion in Sea Cliff?"

"Where were you and where were you looking?"

"Parked past the white-scalloped-wall place. Saw Houdini's brick mansion across the divider on the Lake Street curve."

He laughed. "A trick. The magician's mansion was really the house behind the white wall next to you."

"You're kidding. Houdini was right next to us the whole time?"

Monty sprung the capper. "What's more, you were led to focus on one thing in order to distract your attention from another. A classic San Francisco myth—even the correct mansion was not Houdini's, but belonged to a fellow magician, the once-famous Carter the Great. Houdini performed in the City several times but never had a home here. You were doubly deceived by magician misdirection." Monty quoted, "How can you be in two places at once when you're not anywhere at all?"

"That from Lewis Carol?" I questioned. "No, wait, I know, *Monty Python's Flying Circus*?"

"Very funny. No, The Firesign Theatre."

"It is indeed," I intoned, "Harry Houdini's paramount trick— magic from beyond the grave. That's funny, because, that same night, we stopped at Café Flore and saw the picture of my other favorite mysterious magician, Kar-Mi."

"Kar-Mi, that powerful psychic from India?" Monty asked. "Ha. He was a white Midwesterner, like you, named Joe Hallworth. Joe was a carny whose whole shtick was an act. The dark secret of his sideshow? He dressed his son as a girl to be his lovely assistant, Selma."

Did Monty know something? Had he talked to someone? Like my Uncle? Did he have any idea how hurtful his remarks were? Hopefully not, he was just talking. My eyes darted around for an escape route. An old habit. "I gotta' get going."

"Sure, Jack," Monty said. "I have to gas up and get my cab back to the lot." He suggested a few more places to check out down the street and split with an, "It's been real."

At charming Vesuvio's, I had a whiskey over. Despite being tight-of-quarters as a double-decked wooden sailing ship, and its popularity with tourists, I loved it. That's why the Sav was our bar, plenty of room and fewer tourists. I ordered a Michelob and took it up the steep narrow stairs to Vesuvio's romantic balcony seats. I thought, I have to bring Bretta here. After my beer, lonely for some comfort, I wandered across the alley and into Lawrence Ferlinghetti's maze-like City Lights bookstore. The store had a stranger layout than my bookstore, but was old-fashioned comfy. Looking through books always soothed me. Renowned Ferlinghetti, the bearded poet-owner himself, sat at a desk, but I could think of nothing clever or poetic enough to say to interrupt his inward stare. I purchased *Men Without Women*. I strolled across Columbus past the odd and oddly-named Specs Twelve Adler Museum Café bar but kept going, and kept drinking.

#

Everybody's face looked like a mug shot. I felt like I walked inside of a flashbulb. The Chinese liquor store on Stockton Street was so bright with fluorescents, I put on my shades. It was 2:05 A.M. The store was the only one in North Beach which illegally stayed open till ten minutes after two A.M. The owner had to have "an arrangement" with the Central Station boys. It was Finn who had given me the tip and it was Finn I ran into.

Finn didn't recognize me but he was easy to spot. Wiry, same attire as when first introduced at The Lost and Found saloon—long-out-of-fashion, faded-green Army jacket, Camel straight in hand.

"Right. Right. How's it going with Bretta?" Finn asked, his eyes darting around for her.

"Great. Good. She's busy with another art project tonight."

I could tell that Finn tried not to roll his eyes, but he did. Finn invited me to join him. We bought a pint of Bacardi, a couple of cans of Coke, and two half-dead limes. On the way out, I asked if we were going to his place, which I remembered him saying was nearby, but he snorted, "No, not to that shithole."

I flinched at the term—the same derogatory my uncle had christened my childhood home. As a kid, I knew that my rich Uncle lived in a mansion, but my home was my home, which I really liked. Until Uncle said THAT. I flashed on Finn's place as my old tiny, clapboard house, AKA shithole, crazily crammed into a North Beach apartment building. Finn marched recklessly right into traffic to flag a Yellow cab. We jumped in and headed toward Fisherman's Wharf.

I mentioned, "Bretta's friend drives a Yellow cab. You know Monty, right?"

"Yeah, I know the son of a bitch. I was hoping it was him, so I could stiff him on the fare."

The driver shot a look of concern in his rearview.

"I thought Monty was all right. A little too serious most of the time. Did you have a problem with Monty?"

"Ask your girlfriend. And watch your back."

Just great, I thought. The plot thickens.

Finn jammed the Cokes and limes into one of his Army jacket's numerous lumpy pockets, making me wonder what all he had in there. But he held the bag of booze close to his chest, like a Bible. He saw my look. "Yes, I surely do love my liquor. Maybe too much, but fuck it."

"Come on, you don't drink that much, do you? You could stop, right?"

"Lemme' tell you a story. First roll down your window, you might need some air. You too, Bud."

The driver scoffed. I hesitated and cranked my window down. Finn said, "I have—upon a number of occasions—drunk through all my money. Every cent to my name. I have been out of money and booze and friends and out of the three, frankly would rather have the hooch. I have—swam from an anchored boat a quarter mile off shore, in the dark—drunk, to get one more drink. I have thrown up and still drank more. I have—pulled the t-shirt off my back, stretched it over a bucket, stuck my finger down my throat clear to my tonsils, to force myself to vomit. Why? To strain chunks out of my own spew—to raise that pukey bucket to my lips, and slurp one more half-digested, fucking drink."

Nauseated with each reveal, I coughed and sucked in the night air, thankful for Finn's open-window warning. The cabbie, a kid younger than me, made a gurgling noise and choked out, "What the fuck, man?" He slammed on the brakes and barfed through his window. Unfortunately, the driver's window was not rolled down. He coughed, burbled and swore some more. Finn dropped some bills over the seat and we both jumped out laughing.

We walked the last couple of blocks to Aquatic Park. We rambled down through the park, eerily silent without the regular afternoon conga drummers who gathered there, all the way to the misty, barely discernable, end of the long Muni Pier.

"Dark out here," I noticed.

"Yeah. Nice, isn't it?"

We sat in the breezy darkness, and he pulled a big pocketknife out of one of his pockets. He handed me the knife and the limes.

"Careful. It's sharp."

There we sat and drank some of the Coke so we could pour in the rum to make Cuba Libres. After yet another Camel straight, Finn squeezed an alligator clip on a fat roach and lit it up. I took a raspy hit and laughed some more about the driver but Finn did not. So, in silence we watched the Bay water and the flashing lighthouse beacon on Alcatraz go 'round and 'round like a crazy carrousel for convicts.

Finn eventually said, "Bretta tells me you're a stand-up guy, so I'm going to tell you something. A secret."

Bretta tells? Not told. "Finn, listen man, I'm not sure I want to know a secret."

"Right here, one night..." He paused and I held my breath. "...this dude with a gun held me up."

I was relieved it wasn't a Bretta story. "What happened?"

"I didn't have any money." Finn looked over his shoulder. "So, I shot the motherfucker."

"No shit? With his own gun?"

"I didn't need his gun." Finn took a drink and continued, "I looked through his wallet, he lived in the projects down the street there..." he nodded his head "...it was stuffed with all this wadded up bread, man. And his pockets? Tourist stuff; couple of watches, jewelry, a fat gold chain. Guess Vincent Garrone Washington the III already had his badassself a busy muthafuckin' night."

I sipped, looking nervously around at the few other stray souls on the pier. One looked suspicious, but it was so dark I couldn't even see what color he was. I again glanced at all the big pockets on Finn's Army jacket. I didn't know whether to hope he was still packing, or not.

"Shit. I guess he made one mistake," I said. Finn gave a snort-laugh in response. "What happened? What did you...do?"

After a long pause, he replied. "I pushed him off the edge of the pier—and he just—floated—away." He pointed out toward the Golden Gate Bridge. "After so many..." he looked at his Coke can. '...in country,' you know, 'Nam...'" Finn took a swig and looked into the water, "...he seemed like—just one more."

"Oh." My mind was blown. Ater an appreciative reflective pause, I changed the subject. I wanted to ask Finn about his fiddle playing but for some reason I said, "I was wondering, we had talked about your skiing..."

"Skiing? OK. I was priming in Vail for what was to be the ill-fated '72 Munich Olympics. You remember? The one where PLO hankie-heads kidnapped eleven Jew Olympic athletes?"

"Yeah that was heavy."

"What the news didn't report so much is just how much the Krauts FUBARed not only the "rescue," but the whole security. So badly, that there was suspicion of some collusion. They did manage to get all eleven Jews shot. And the Palestinians that they did manage to capture? Released a month later. Anyway, instead of representing the good ole' USA on skis I got sent to the tropics representing Dow Chemical. Napalm and Agent Orange."

"Right."

"You know, the fucking French were fighting in Vietnam first? The "frogs" started the goddamn clusterfuck and then cried oui, oui, oui all the way home."

"I didn't know that. Huh." A pause. I told him one of my secrets. "I'm glad I wasn't drafted, but sometimes feel that I missed out on something important, that I wasn't part of, I guess, history—like you were." I had to ask him, even though we all knew that most vets don't like speaking of their experiences. "I always thought the military, the band of brothers, getting some battle experience, would be a good thing for a real man to have. Did I miss out?"

Finn looked me dead in the eyes. He reached into a pocket. Fiddled with something that made a rattling sound, and yanked it out. I flinched.

The Bacardi. He had unscrewed the lid in his pocket with one hand so he could still hold his drink in his other hand. He took a long swig straight out of the bottle, passed it over to me. I drank.

"This is what you missed. This was toward what was to be the end of the endless war. My buddy Bobby and I are doing clean up with our platoon in one more cesspool of a gook village. Nam Poon Phuket Tang, or some such. Covert shit. Wasn't even in 'Nam." He hocked a loogie a good ten feet into the Bay. "Anyways, Bobby—is encouraging me—he tells me that I could still make the ski team for Montreal. He has a wife, baby daughter, ya' know, back in Texas. I spot this gook doll over by a smoking trash heap and I say, Hey, a souvenir for your girl. Bobby, he's seasoned, he looks for a wire, a booby-trap. Nothing. It's clean. Bobby bends over to pick it up— gives his grin, big as Texas."

Finn made a weird, choking laugh.

"This old rusty pipe pokes out from the bottom of the trash heap. It's a Stevens shotgun and the gook blasts at Bobby."

"Shotgun? Was he OK?"

Finn snorted. "No, he was not fucking OK. He was not fucking OK at all. He got shot in the face. And *civilian*, neither was I. He is bending over and I see his fucking brains just slide out of his skull and land on the goddammed doll. I got hit in a couple of places, too, before I could empty my mag on that trash."

Finn's head dropped. "That crippled me up. Too much for competitive skiing."

We sat on the dock of the Bay and things were suddenly very quiet. I was also familiar with the proximity of death's fingers. But, I did not did not tell him that we were somehow survivors or comrades in arms. I finally asked, "Where did you get hit?"

"In the gut." He took a swig. "Yeah, but more..." he pointed to his head, "and..." he pointed to his heart.

"I bet. I hear you."

"When they finally dug the slugs out of me—well, they weren't even lead."

"What was it?"

He passed the rum over to me. When I handed the bottle back he drained it. Finn tossed the bottle spinning into the Bay.

"They were Bobby's fuckin' teeth."

Finn gazed over the great gray Bay, almost as if seeing something inviting out there.

"Bobby still haunts me, ya'know? He haunts me like a fuckin' ghost."

CHAPTER 18

The Bookstore was frantic that day. There had been a mix-up in the Business Management textbooks, and the students were upset. Montesha whistled to me from the help desk. I indicated that I was busy, and she gave the signal for a personal call. Robin was on the line. She had never called me before. I feared bad news.

Robin told me Bretta was ill. I asked her, "Is it migraines, she cut herself or what?" Robin said she couldn't say, but it didn't seem serious, and she was sure that Bretta would be fine soon. Her other news was that Bretta's mother had driven down from the Sierras, and booked a suite at the swanky Fairmont Hotel. Bretta was going to rest there under Duzinella's care for a few days.

I called Bretta's flat with no answer. I tried calling the Fairmont, asking for several names, but Duzinella must have used a pseudonym, as the famous are wont to do, or to just keep me away. Why hadn't Bretta called me? I was persona non grata for less-than-clear reasons. With Montesha in my confidence, I feigned m own illness and left the Bookstore.

I drove by her flat and rang with no response. Unsure of what else to do, I went home. I wanted to talk to Winston, but there was never a way to reach him. Winston had not gone "back to the garden" but had been working in the "produce business" again—as a scab at the Marina Safeway during the retail clerks' strike. He had worked just long enough to buy a car, an ass-kickin' metal-flake green, old custom Chevy wagon. He had immediately quit Safeway and driven to parts unknown.

I looked in my cupboard for coffee but was out. I sat at the kitchen table. The table where Bretta and I had mixed Martini's before I loved her. This seemed as good a time as any to do some of the stuff Deo had given me. Maybe it would help me think clearly. Taking a paper bindle and a sniffer bullet out of the table drawer, I tapped the crystals onto a saucer. What was going on with her? I began to worry. Maybe she figured out something was wrong with me.

Which thing? Distracted, I minced them with a kitchen knife. I cut a few inches off a McDonald's straw and took a big snort. My nose burned. Crap. I mistakenly snorted powder from Winston instead of Deo. Oh, well. I hit the other nostril.

I had sneaked a peek at my psych eval from L.A. and filed it to memory. I recalled:

Subject's high IQ impaired by attention deficit enhances subject's predisposition to over-analytical cogitation and anxiety attacks. Intense need for independence conflicts with need for attention. Dependence disorder\abandonment issues\feelings of un-worth generate conflict with superiority complex. Repression of childhood trauma generates heightened defense mechanisms and passivity with resultant propensity to sudden risky behaviors, confrontations and violence. Subject's compensatory coping mechanisms of charm and bravura are very effective, as is passive-aggressive pretenses of obtuseness interspersed with exhibitions of intellect.

Recommendations: channel energy to positive hobbies or projects, enter committed relationship, bi-weekly visits to remediate long-term effects of extensive childhood trauma and resultant psychological damage. Initiate on-going anti-anxiety medications.

Ah-ha! Good idea. I darted into the living room to my mantel. I snatched my new secret astrological weapon. From under Kurt Vonnegut's new *Jailbird*, I pulled out another book. Direct from the publisher, I had received an advance copy of Judith Bennett's *Sex Signs*. The author had died tragically in a plane crash in Illinois just before publication, so there was already a buzz about the book. I thumbed to Gemini. The astrological traits included: "Scattered, High-strung, Nervous, Entertaining, Charming, Outgoing, Youthful, Freedom-loving, Footloose, Of Two Minds, Impractical, Dramatic, Neurotic Sex Drive." Neurotic sex drive. This turned me on. The book was written for women so I felt I was looking under the skirt. "...multiple personalities seeking to find a wholeness...wit and charm are legendary.

Her voice has a lilt to it, almost a melody (I caught a breath)...artistic flair...express herself...by painting...delights in the sun's rays and energy. She is just as much at home in a tavern as she is at...Windsor Castle...subscribes to the philosophy, Eat. drink, and make merry...loves to entertain...she herself is the main course...she will tease, excite and be the life of the party..." This description really turned me on.

"...outgoing nature always guarantees that a crowd will be around her...never expect...to be on an even keel... Her sudden and unreasonable changes will drive those around her wild." Yes, yes. I wanted Bretta. I became hard. "...could be a character out of Alice in Wonderland. Total immersion in people, projects, experiences, followed by boredom and disinterest."

Bretta was the Gemini poster child. I loved all of this about her. Was that bad? Was she bored with me and was this a way of breaking up? I phoned Bretta's again. Duzinella answered. "We're leaving for the doctor."

I asked Duzinella, "What's happening?"

"Bretta is getting a D and C," She replied.

I asked, "What is that?"

"Dusting and Cleaning." She hung up.

The understanding circled my mind and it seem as though time shifted, sifted, shifts...

I really need some music. I put on a record. Bowie cover of Easybeats. Cymbal crash. Ne-ne-ne-ne, ne-ne-ne-ne, ne-ne-ne-ne...Bass drum thumps. "Everybody seems to nag me." I feel hot. I struggle to yank up my front bay window. "Ba-ooom!" There is a CRASH. I think I broke the window but the noise is from down the street.

"I've got Friday on my mind." It hits me. Bretta had not prepared to spend that night at her father's. Or had she? Did Bretta intentionally become pregnant? I am sure that was when it happened. I'd had a feeling. Maybe it is Duzinella who is putting a stop to it. Maybe Bretta still wants the baby. My baby. Our baby. My blood thumps and races, or is it my mind? I sweep all my favorite books from my mantel. They tumble to the floor.

I do another couple of snorts. I zip on my motorcycle jacket "She is out of sight to me-ee" over my white tee and run downstairs. I hop on my Honda "Tonight, I lose my head, tonight..." I rev to shoot out my backyard gate, race down the hill and around the corner only to slam on my brakes. I see what the crash was—a stopped tourist bus and cars in an accident blocking the street. I got Bowie on my mind. I cut through the pedestrian-only opening in the chain-and-post fence surrounding Kezar Stadium's front lot and slalom between the parked cars. "Today I might be mad. Tomorrow I'll be glad." Behind the old stone Park Emergency Hospital building, vintage vehicles are being prepped for a parade. With a cloud of smoke, an Italian WWI wooden-spoke, Red Cross truck backs out in front of me. "Tonight! I'll lose my head…" I skid and swerve as workers yell. I have to see her. "(See my baby) (feel like fucking you)" Zoom zoom zoom zoom zoom.

I exit on Stanyan, and up Waller where a blue VW microbus putts. I pass, squeezing between it and an oncoming car. I gun it, flying by Tie-dye, driving. He waves a joint-filled hand, as he blasts a *Sticky Fingers* song—"Can't you hear me knockin'?"

Was seeing the ambulance a sign—a bad sign? She bled easily. What if she hemorrhaged? Bretta may not make it. I couldn't lose another one. Was I so cursed in love? If she died, too, I couldn't live with myself. I would jump off the bridge. I pray, Please don't let her die. I run the stop sign and wheel around the corner. In front of her flat, I look for a pine-green Jag but don't see any familiar vehicles. I pull up on the sidewalk by her steps. The whole thing has been left unsaid between us. Pregnancy is still somewhat of a mystery to me, as this is my first, and I don't quite know what is expected. Apparently, nothing. I run up the stairs to find the door locked, and I buzz. No answer. Why has Duzinella and Bretta kept it a secret? I knock and knock. Are they afraid I'll propose and demand to do the Christian thing and keep the baby? Maybe they are afraid that I will not propose, when that is what she wants, and it would be even more awkward?

Nobody answers so I bang on her door with my fist. "Can't you hear me knockin'?" I yell, "Bretta! Bretta!" A sarcastic voice shoots from behind a neighbor's door, "Stella's gone, Stanley. Go back to the bowling alley!"

I kick the guy's door and stomp back down dejected. I pace the sidewalk, restless. Another neighbor scrutinizes me from the window, pissed off at the racket. Deo's conversation foreshadowed the baby. I think of Donovan's kids and what a darling baby ours would be. It makes me sad, and I wonder where it would end up and if we were going to hell. Is this what people get for loving each other?

"Help me baby, I ain't no stranger," I sing. What am I going to do, anyway? I ride over to Van Ness Avenue. I thread my way up the steep, slippery California Street cable car tracks—clackety-clacking, hum-humming— with the cable cars' ding-dingling, and tourists and locals clinging on the rails of the car's sides until they predictably unpredictably jump on or off. At the top of Nob Hill, San Francisco's premier cathedral, the Notre-Dame-esque Grace Cathedral, rises on my left.

I gas the Honda only to screech to a stop, and roll back between two cars parked across from the Fairmont Hotel. I scan the entry and surrounding area for the distinctive pine-green Jaguar. Sitting on my bike, I look up at the masculine classic Fairmont. The multitude of many nations' flags flutter above the massive arched stone entry. No sign of the women or the Jag. I see a woman appear at a big third-floor window—Duzinella's red-lipsticked visage scrutinizes me, dour and unsympathetic. I feel like a dirty, naughty boy, worthless, insecure and outclassed. I drop my eyes and involuntarily shudder as the muscles of my rear tighten, anticipating punishment. She gazes across toward Grace Cathedral, then down at me. She moves away. Wait. Maybe it wasn't Duzinella. I am losing it. I get off my bike and stand on the sidewalk.

The twins of San Francisco stroll by arm in arm. The lovely Brown sisters are fixtures on Nob Hill and as famous as San Francisco's other twins—Twin Peaks. They are always identically dressed and coiffed. Today the beloved pair are sporting signature leopard-print coats over red Chinese dresses, topped with red cowboy hats. The twins bring a smile to my anxious face, and I greet them.

An *Alice-in-Wonderland*-falling-down-the-rabbit-hole sensation swirls around me like a dust devil...

Could Bretta be carrying twins? I had just seen the twins, Tweedledum and Tweedledee. The story reminded me that "Cheech and Chong's" mock introduction of Bretta at the Recycling center is what preambled this whole affair. That seemed so long ago. Was I the Mock turtle? Should I walk over to Huntington Park by to see the "mock" turtles and frolicking nymphs and at Tortoise Fountain?

I was feeling a little lost and vertiginous. The grand Brocklebank Apartment building was next door, and I walked past their palm-treed courtyard parking lot. No pine-green Jaguar there, either. Was I becoming obsessed? Was I turning into one of those boyfriends one reads about stalking their exes? Wait, that muscular man, was that Bretta's brother walking toward the hotel? I yelled, "Hey, Donovan." The young man glared at me before briskly walking away. I must have been mistaken. I needed to let my head clear, give up tracking her down. I had no idea what medical office to try. Close to the hotel on Bush Street was Planned Parenthood, a place Bretta could be taken for the procedure.

Something crept into my mind and took hold. The thought. I thought back to my original conversation with Duzinella, which now unnerved me. Her tale of Winston's transgressions had been a warning. A veiled threat of what could happen to me. The enigma of Winston and Bretta was a creeping fog across my relationship. We had some similarities. I had a hooker friend. And I knocked up Bretta. No, it couldn't be! Maybe it was coke paranoia. I didn't know, I mean a bunch of things had happened really fast, kind of like Winston's blitzkrieg and it was all difficult to discern the amount of concern, ha-ha, I should have. I couldn't even ask him because he had made one of his increasingly frequent disappearances to wherever Winston goes. I think I mentioned that. Now, I really didn't know what to think or do. And I usually did. Wait. I needed to see for myself.

I jumped on my motorcycle and cruised down Nob Hill toward Union Square along the Powell Street cable car line. As the street leveled, I hopped the white curb, nearly striking the wrought-iron poles for Sears' Fine Food awning. I looked across the street. There, the Sir Francis Drake Hotel rose at least twenty stories. Donovan was right; the rooms had no balconies. Something else was not right. The Drake's awning was solid stone—a cantilevered, Masonic-ornate faux-terrace. My throat went dry. There was no canvas canopy awning to break Winston's fall that fateful night. This art of deception was stroked from a blood-red palette.

I needed to go someplace to unwind. Unsteady, I veered through the Stockton tunnel, past Chinatown and into the heart of North Beach. I parked my bike between car bumpers. I had forgotten about Planned Parenthood. I wondered if I was getting the flu.

The sunlight traversed across Washington Square Park, one of the oldest in the city, and I followed, seeking solace of sun and grass. A few people relaxed in the park. Some walked their dogs. Everything appeared all so normal. The people were normal. I felt anything but. They had no idea what I was going through. It was all so fucking normal. Jack Kerouac and Alan Ginsberg had stood in this same spot probably feeling as abnormal as I. I said, "When Ginsberg howled, the Beat planets formed an orbit around their poetic sun."

My head was orbiting. I sprawled on the grass before I went spinning and fell down. As I massaged my temples I noticed the few cheerful yellow dandelions amidst the clover and bobbin' red-breasted robins and oily-concrete-colored pigeons. I closed my eyes and ran my fingers through the reassuring soft green blades. I returned to the backyard of my early childhood. I missed the crickets chirping, I missed the bullfrogs ribbiting, I missed the lightning storms, I missed the lightning bugs, I missed my childhood. Now I would miss my child. No one had protected me but shouldn't I protect the innocent?

Shade and sunlight dappled me. People walked by me, not knowing my struggles, as I have walked by them and theirs. At the sound of scattering pigeons, I blinked open my eyes. Stirred to connect to someone, I asked a man walking the pigeon-perky Jack Russell, "How's it going?" a little too earnestly.

He replied, "Fine, thanks," with a city slicker's suspicion. Of panhandling, I assumed. Did I look that desolate—a desolation angel or a dharma bum? I patted the dog. I felt a twinge for the beagle I was forced to give up as a kid. Mootsie loved me. We had spent many happy days out hunting. I wondered how Beagle Boy was doing. A dog would make me feel better. In fact, I did feel better. A Frisbee swooshed by invitingly, but I was older now, a parent—I had no time for games. Normal was not working for me. I needed a pick-me-up.

I paid my respects to the statue of Benjamin Franklin, sheltered by a stand of poplars in the middle of the park. Using Ben's granite base as cover I took a snort from my glass bullet. I liked the statue, although he seemed out of character for the neighborhood. Ben was the godfather of America's lending library so I was grateful. I circled Benjamin and thought of Richard Brautigan, who in his *Trout Fishing in America* had described this spot perfectly. Bretta and Monty actually hung out with Brautigan at Enrico's. Like Ginsberg and Neal Cassady, Brautigan was a link from Beat to Hippie. His book *The Abortion*, with the librarian and the sexy goddess would be more apropos to me. Plus, we had our own Benjamin.

After my father's funeral, after all the things that happened, in between circus stints, libraries had always been my refuge, my sanctuary. I'd find solace staying in libraries until they closed for the night. Later, I'd sneak back in through a window or back door I had unlocked. Security was just a couple of little-old-lady librarians. Who would break into a library? Besides me. Hiding in the stacks inside my sleeping bag, I would read by flashlight or candle with my Strongman-bent nail as both charm and defense. I treasured the scent of libraries and the books, particularly the old ones—the dry paper, leather, ink, bindings, dust, and the places they'd been. The new arrivals also intrigued me—no other eyes had seen inside the printed pages, and they had their own publishing-house odor. All held the promise of plot twists, denouements, vicarious loves, betrayals, sorrows and ecstasies.

Thanks to Ben I was able to follow the adventures of the Hardy Boys in their coffee-brown-covered books. Frank and Joe had thrilling adventures with Monty and chums, their boat the *Sleuth*, fast roadsters and even motorcycles. I had none of those. I would have put up with Aunt Gertrude to have their lives. The Hardy Boys and subsequently *Tarzan*, whetted my appetite for James Bond books, and from there I traced 007's British, promiscuous literary roots to *Alfie*, to *Tom Jones*, and to *Moll Flanders*.

Sleeping on the floor in libraries had other rewards—over time, I discovered items that had fallen under the tables and shelves—a ten-dollar bill, a silver dollar, a pocketknife, half a half-pint of sloe gin, a paperback non-library copy of Ray Bradbury's sinister *Something Wicked This Way Comes*, which I still possessed, a Duncan yo-yo with four embedded real diamonds, which I sold, and an onyx-and-gold graduation ring, which I pawned. I didn't feel bad about taking them, in fact, I felt that God was giving me gifts. I always treated the libraries with respect. I was always out early the next morning and never stole anything. Well, maybe some overdue fine change left out, and maybe a book or two, although that wasn't stealing, because I would return books at another library.

One stormy night I was at the climax of *Carrie* when the front doors rattled, scaring the shit out of me. I crawled behind the checkout desk and peered around to the glass doors. A policeman! I was sure he had spotted me, that I was busted. A clatter and bang. I ducked. A book dropped into the book-return bin and he moved on. A fellow booklover at four A.M. in the sleepy town. I went back to bed, but after a few minutes, I had to know. I crept out again. What was it, the name of the officer's book?

In the park, the sun reflected into my eyes. A woman sprawled on her blanket with a makeshift-tanning device—foil over an open album cover. I had an image of Bretta, on the table with her feet up in stirrups and my uncle in scrubs, spreading her and cramming stainless steel inside of her, and in the other hand, long forceps. *Cuckoo's Nest* Nurse Ratched inserts a clear, plastic vacuum D&C hose sucking bloody bits of baby out of Bretta's beautiful insides, and Bretta's bleeding but they keep sucking, and the blood keeps flowing, and they keep sucking, and Bretta becomes paler and whiter, and her blue veins stand out on her forehead, and her body shrinks, and at last a disembodied two-headed baby plops into the holding tank, and Bretta wakes up, mouth open but silent, shrieking NO!

I shouted, "NO!" and people moved away, and that was probably good, because I wanted to hurt someone, hurt everybody. I wandered down the street and entered Gino & Carlo. Monty had told me that in the '60s it had been a lesbian bar frequented by Janis Joplin. The joint was very blue collar now. Drinkers and bartender seemed quiet and depressed. Someone was muttering about the Iran hostages. I ordered a whiskey and a beer back and a handful of dimes. As I used the payphone by the men's room, I juggled the drinks and placed the beer on top of the phone. The smell of urine and urinal cake disinfectant almost gagged me. Someone had graffitied "Love Heals" on the phone cubby, under which someone had scrawled, "…herpes please!" Lovely.

There was no answer.

I pressed and held the receiver tab, pondering my next move. I tried calling Deo, who was good with sage advice. I was disappointed when his British roommate informed me in his clipped tone, "So sorry. Deo has absconded to South America."

I looked over my shoulder and covertly took another snort. I called Bill and he pronounced, "You knocked up that crazy artist chick you were banging like a screen door? That's a shocker. I told you we should've gone to Thailand. Just pack up and split right now. You've split before. Hey, instead of Thailand, we could be goin' to Jamaica, mon. We be smokin' the killer spliff there, mon."

I called Nick next. "Dude. Always use a rubber. If I was ballin' a chick as sexy as Bretta, I'd have to use two at a time. Be careful though, like the joke goes: 'Left nut goes *unh*, rubber goes *unh*, right nut goes POW!'"

"Ha ha."

"Look, I know you're in love with her, but…she's nymphonic, right? I mean how would you even know if it's…"

"That's a fucked-up thing to say. She loves me."

"Love is not a chastity belt, Jack. It is what it is now. Sorry. Hey, call me at midnight and I'll tell you where Scarlet Pimpernel's party is. He throws the most outrageous parties in town. I'm tending bar tonight, and I tell ya', a lot of pretty women there, and you're gonna' get you some."

I hung up the phone hard and my beer glass slipped off, crashing to shards on the dirty floor. I glanced around but no one paid the slightest attention.

"It's done. It's over with." Francine had picked up, business like.

"It's-It," I uttered.

"Yes." She rushed through telling me, "Bretta had a rough time, but she is fine."

"What do you mean?"

"Surprisingly enough, this was her first abortion. She is as naive as you, Jack. I know women who have had three or four, not to mention any name. Anyway, she started to hemorrhage, and the doctor had a difficult time controlling it, and they needed—never mind, she'll be fine."

"What? Oh my God. I wanted to be there for her. I should have been."

"Not a good idea. Robin and Duzinella are still with her. Jack, you can see her in a couple of days. After Duzinella leaves."

"Francine, you swear she's all right?"

"Yes, she…" She paused, speaking muffled to someone else. "I left…"

"Jesus, Francine," I interrupted.

"Yes. She'll be fine. Just take it easy, Jack."

"OK. Umm, is Donovan in town?"

"What? You want to take Bretta to see that Sunshine Superman musician?" She chuckled.

"What? No, no, her brother. Is Bretta's brother in town?"

"I'm kidding. No, haven't seen his hard body lately, but I'd sure like to. Why? Never mind, I have to go. I have a meeting for a design consult with that new Green's, vegetarian restaurant, you know, at Fort Mason. Bretta's fine. See you later."

As I walked out, a drunk fell off his barstool. No one seemed in a hurry to pick him up. I looked at my watch; it was only 3:00 in the afternoon.

Back on the sidewalk I felt angry and helpless and rolled my head back in exasperation. My eyes turned up to Saints Peter and Paul cathedral's twin spires against the azure sky. A wave of inspiration washed me toward the church like a hopeful drowning man to the shore. I sang a snatch of song, "Sunshine came softly…Could've tripped out easy, a-but I've-a changed my ways." After all this time, I guardedly went inside the church.

The interior cooled my flushed body. Gorgeous with ornate detail, the classic columned arches, alcoves, and stained glass created a peaceful timelessness. A handful of the faithful sat or kneeled among the polished pews. Candelabras flickered along with dozens of lit votive candles in the dim multi-hued refracted light, making it all slightly mysterious. The marble high altar was as smooth and white as if the Son of God was carved from ice cream. Doubling down, the demi-dome, far above, encircled a colorful painting of Christ. The powerful iconography was effective. I was brought me to my spiritual senses, then my knees.

\#

The last time I had been in a church was at my girlfriend's funeral service—the massive gray Gothic St. Dominic's on Bush. My girlfriend's passing was diminished by the celebrity deaths of Moscone and Milk, and, oh yes, that little jungle incident—920 lost souls of Peoples Temple Cult of death. My beloved Ariel's demise—not even an asterisk.

Ariel's bright mind had been full of ambition and vision. She relished working with the like-minded politicians, yet her moral compass pointed away from the back-stabbing, back-door deals at City Hall. She had an authentic no-nonsense manner. Her's was an uptight Wisconsin Norwegian family transplanted to Orange County. Her parents held the service in the City because other family lived here and the dad had been planning to transfer to UCSF. The mother had ridiculed my musical dreams as a monetary nightmare. The father, a UC Irvine surgeon of some note, had said that it would be best that I not speak with the eulogies.

Before the service, the family had glared at me in unison as if it were my entire fault, as if I did not feel guilty enough. My sweet Ariel Anne Vollan. Her poster-sized picture was propped on an easel next to the floral sprays and wreaths. Where was the simple casket we had discussed? There was only a wooden stand. Holding an urn. No! Her vivacious optimism and love and perfect legs now reduced to ashes in the silver-plated urn, which looked more like a sports trophy. Volleyball?

The family eulogies droned on. Ariel's large photo brought me swirling back to our picnic in the Park's Shakespeare Garden of Flowers. Masked by foliage and brick wall with plaques of stone and brass inscribed with floral Shakespearean quotes, the garden was a hidden gem. As I sat on the grass, Ariel, in a green woolen dress, had posed on a stone bench to recite literature's crowned prince. "*Quite over-canopied with luscious woodbine, With sweet musk-roses and with eglantine: There sleeps Titania sometime of the night, Lull'd in these flowers with dances and delight.*"

I remember that upon seeing her above me with sunrays behind her, like an erotic angel, my mind flashed an extraordinary image of my beautiful mother standing above me. I was a boy lying on the lawn in our yard, Mother singing to me in a crystalline voice...a love song, what tune? The déjà vu faded too quickly but had filled me with such—rapture. I blurted to Ariel, "I love you so. I love you more than life it seems."

She responded, "I love you desperately, you know." I captured her delight in a photo. "Catch me quick!" She jumped on me and wrapped her legs around my waist. "And I've decided, Jack, I will move in with you."

Then I recognized it. That was my photo of her, cropped and enlarged full-sized on the easel before me. At that moment, a eulogist (her lascivious cousin?) raised his voice, perpetuating the family fantasy of..."Ariel's aspirations of John Hopkins School of Medicine and becoming a surgeon... like her loving father."

This was such bullshit that I could no longer restrain myself. I stood up in the middle of the eulogy. I strode to her poster and spoke, "This young woman, this woman—has been my rock and inspiration. I am inspired now—for her to suffer no more—of this bullshit! Surgeon? Ariel didn't want to cut people up! She wanted to find out what made people real." Disgruntled sounds issued from the family. "Mayor Moscone and Harvey Milk were real. They were too real for some. They would be here for her today, if they could. If they were not dead, too." This received weird looks and a cough, but an appreciative, "Right on," from Nick. I kissed her giant lips on the poster.

"If I could only bring Ariel back to life and take her place, I truly would." I sobbed there. I grabbed her urn, heavier than I anticipated, hoisted it up in one hand. "This looks like a trophy. For what? Dying?" I choked out, "I would pull her right out of this urn like a genie from a lamp, and right here, right now, light fire to myself."

I rubbed the urn. With my other hand I lifted the lighted, heavy silver candelabra. I stood with my arms outstretched. Protest murmured from the pews, and her mother yelled, "Put my daughter down, for God's sake!"

I crossed the candles under my coat sleeve, close to the urn, for dramatic effect really, but my suit coat was more synthetic than I thought, and quickly smoldered. "Why? You knew she didn't want to be burned to a crisp. She was a goddess. She should have been buried."

The minister possessively snatched back his silverware. I impulsively yanked the lid from her urn, did a double finger karate strike through the thick plastic bag and grabbed a handful of ashes. Her sister screamed. I held up my fist and thrust the ashes in my coat pocket. Her Auntie fainted. Her father stormed up, swiped at me, which I leaned away from, so he mistakenly hit the minister, who dropped the candelabra, which crashed to the floor. Her father grabbed the urn, spilling ashes, and ripped the wrong pocket from my coat as I jumped over the flaming candlesticks and bolted down the aisle, trailing smoke from my sleve. Our friends rallied, stifling chuckles and tears, rising as one from their seats to follow. Nick and Wild Bill had my back, holding up the rear, blocking pursuing ushers, family members, and pastoral staff. I banged out the heavy cathedral doors into open air and daylight, and ran.

Deo, thankfully, organized our guerrilla group to hurry over a couple of streets and onto a passing Muni bus. After the safety of a few blocks we jumped off and walked into a bar. Deo bought a round of drinks for our huddled, puffy-eyed laughing and weeping friends, while I played her favorite band on the jukebox. A hatful of donated quarters ensured that the Stones' "Time Waits for No One" followed by "Sister Morphine" would play over and over for the appropriate melancholic mood. When a regular bitched, I played "Bitch" and Deo bought drinks for the bitch, the house, for us, and again for the house, and for us, until everyone in the place was drunk, and perfect strangers were making magnificent toasts, "To Ariel." Wild Bill riffed variations on, "Jack jump over the fucking candlestick," which proved difficult toasts without rendering them to dirty limericks, and we had our own goddamned wake right there.

After, my core group—my entourage I suppose—made stops at Liverpool Lil's and the Final Final. Late, that pitch-black night, Deo, Nick, Bill and I drove through Golden Gate Park and shone the headlights on the tree of doom. I attempted to get out of the car and kick the living shit out of the tree, but was forcibly restrained, most probably saving me the embarrassment of a broken foot. We stumbled into the Monarch Bear Grove. At the Goddess Altar, Deo lit a pilfered candle from the bar. I scattered a pocketful of my darling's ashes along with shreds of my tattered heart.

#

My mind segued to the now. A little alcove was to the right, a shrine to Madonna dela Guardia, whose statue held a baby. This was the place. I put a half-dollar in the box and lit a votive candle. I got down on my knees and, from a pocket, fished out my two charms— my lucky bent-nail key ring and a little purple cloth bag. From the bag, I retrieved Robin's gift—a silver crucifix on a chain. For the first time, I put the necklace around my neck. I placed the nail by the candle.

I crossed myself and warmed up with a prayer, the first one coming to mind. "Thank you, Lord, for my good looks and good luck. That's all I really have to work with, but as life goes, that is plenty for which to be grateful. A little more money would be nice..."

I was ready for the main event, the real reason I had returned to a House of God after all those years: I prayed for Bretta and her baby. "Dear God. Save Bretta." And the adorable baby. Bretta's and my adorable dead baby. "God rest its tiny little soul."

Would I be a better father than mine? What is fatherhood? Would I have ended up leaving my child, anyway? Was it a boy or a girl? You can't look at it that way now. It was an it. An "IT'S-IT— The San Francisco Experience." I gave a laugh at my own poor-tasting joke, which turned into a choking sob. Having strayed from my spiritual frame of mind, I decided I'd better leave. Low rumbling notes compressed into me. I jumped. The great organ of the cathedral played a magnificent lingering phrase.

The muscular man reappeared. The Donovan-looking guy from Nob Hill was on the other side of the church, in another alcove. I was unnerved to see him there. More so when I realized that Donovan was my child's uncle. I didn't want my kid to have a damn uncle. I held the thought away. A tourist probably. A coincidence. Or an evil villain's henchman tailing me? I entered into another shadowy alcove and pressed against the cool wall, peeking to watch the man seemingly admiring a figurine. I heard a cough. Another man observed me from a pew—a tall mustached man, Italian looking, dressed in a dark suit. Donovan's cohort? Plainclothes cop? A crony sent by my uncle? Uncle himself? Oh shit.

I walked briskly to another alcove, sniffing the air for trouble. All I detected was a garlic fart, stale Italian cologne, cold marble, charred punk sticks, candle wax and incense. I continued down the side of the cathedral past the wooden-doored, claustrophobic confessional booths, inhaling the perspirations from telling the priest the truths and the sweat from telling the lies, or vice versa. And more— the smell of the suffering Christ, whipped and shredded and bloodied, and humanly defeated?—no, just a big House-of-God odor.

Should I barricade myself in a confessional and divulge my many sins? No, bad idea. I pretended to look at the artwork and framed informational tags. I glanced back, and both the Donovan-looking man and the man in black were gone. I was just being paranoid. I could relax.

No. I saw the man in black again, coming from behind a column, still watching, and now plainly following me. He wore a tailored pinstriped coat. Was he really limping? He was holding something large. A weapon? It was only his hat. This was too freaky. I spotted a side door and swung it open and scurried through a murky storage area. I jumped at a figure in the room. I blurted, "What do you people want?"

With relief I saw that it was merely a robe hanging on a rack. I spied an emergency exit, and just as I bolted to the bright sunlight of the church's side parking lot, the unknown suited man's grim face appeared in the first doorway.

I ran swiftly out of the lot and into the playground of Washington Square Park where I sat down hidden on a shrub-surrounded bench. I raked the surroundings making sure no one had followed. Wow. My heralded return to the fold was not encouraging. I watched Chinese women push their little ones on chain swings. Children played in the sand. No kids, no playgrounds for me any time soon. I looked at the children in a new light—like little people.

I looked around, not seeing the men from the church. There were a couple of new characters sitting on a park bench in flannel shirts. One reminded me of one of the sidekicks I got in a fight with in Nevada City. I bee-lined to my bike. I watched the man out of the corner of my eye while I quickly examined my brake cables, axle nuts and other parts, to make sure no one had screwed with them. Sabotaging a motorcycle is very easy. A thought rose in my mind like Rover, the security balloon in the TV masterpiece of paranoia, *The Prisoner*. I was right, Duzinella hired those three hillbillies in Nevada City to fuck me up. And it was not over. I jumped on my bike and took off fast, weaving through Columbus Avenue traffic.

CHAPTER 19

Speeding my motorcycle through rush hour traffic and illegally splitting lanes at red lights took the edge off and made me feel in control again. When I slowed for a police car near the Greyhound Station, I finally remembered the odd name of the book the officer had returned—Harington's *Some Other Place. The Right Place.*

At Townsend Street Yellow Cab lot, bright yellow cars rolled in and out. I spotted Monty near the dispatch kiosk. He leaned sullenly against a short brick wall, his sleeves rolled up, beret pushed back. He was smoking a Kool and looked cool. I pulled up in front of him and hit my engine kill switch. "Hey, Professor. Or should I call you Marlboro Man?" I noticed something else. He had a tattoo on his bicep.

Monty languidly looked at his Kool and shrugged. I guess he tried to keep up his clean image around Bretta and the entourage. He seemed different, more relaxed.

"How you doing?"

"All things considered, all right," he answered.

"What? What happened?"

"Cabbie was killed last night. Not one of ours, but an indy I'd seen around."

"Sorry. What happened?"

"Black guy gets in, rides out to Sunnydale and Hahn projects, robs him, and shoots him in the head with a .357."

"Whoa."   "Tragic. But he fucked up. The general rule among cabbies—don't pick up black dudes."

"That sounds racist."

"I'm sure it's a comfort to the men's families that they were shot in the head while not racist."

"Yeah, but..."

"Tell you what, call my black cabbie friends racist—there's one there." He pointed and the tall bony, black man nodded. "Go on.

He'll tell you the same thing. They maybe pick a brother up, if a woman's with them."

"All the brothers in my dojo are good guys."

"Yeah, the good ones are learning self-defense against the violent ones, too. They're living next door to the motherfuckers. Anyway, we're not talking what's right and wrong politically, we're talking street survival. Different thing. Second shooting recently. Everybody's freaking. More cabbies started carrying now. On the night shift, some of us always have."

I knew he was right, but I didn't want to make his righteousness easy for him. I pretended to look him over for a gun, which I believed he was packing, but was really getting a look at his tattoo. He rolled his sleeves down, but not before I figured out what it was. In a red design that looked like Bretta's artwork was a blue script-like signature. I only saw the that the first letters were "Br."

I just came out with it. "You heard? About Bretta."

"I figured as much."

"She got an abortion today without even talking to me, and I don't know what I'm supposed to do."

"She all right?"

I shrugged and nodded.

He sighed out Kool in a big puff. "Women always seem to make the man the bad guy. I know if I were the one who could get knocked up and have something growing in me the size of a watermelon, I would be the one who took responsibility to made sure it didn't happen, if I didn't want it to happen. Sometimes, they want it, subconsciously. Sometimes, intentionally."

I was still uncertain. "I don't get why Duzinella excluded me. It's my baby, too."

"Is it?"

The air left me like I was hit in the stomach. Monty hurried, "Sorry, just teasing. I know she was smitten with you. Look, Bretta's mother is a control freak. She doesn't want Bretta to get serious with a musician, a writer, another artist, certainly not a mere clerk like you…"

"I'm a manager."

"Of clerks. Or a lowly cab driver like me. Jack, don't you get it? Duzinella loved Winston when he was the darling Sonoma winery executive and heir apparent. Not as a druggie, though. Now

Duzinella is loath to trust Bretta's choice of a boyfriend, let alone The Boyfriend. None of us are good enough."

I watched more yellow cars humming out of the lot like bees off to gather green nectar. I finally spoke, "I heard you and Winston were friends."

"Used to be best friends."

"What went down?"

"He did. What went down is the shit that you're doing right now. Winston would fit in better with the hardcore gay scene. Who the hell knows? Maybe he does when he disappears." This image was difficult for me. Monty continued, "The rest of what went down? The name begins with a B, you figure it out."

Monty ground his Kool into the asphalt. "Jack. Listen, Jack. You people are so frustrating. You're a good guy, a brainy guy. Just because you came of age in the seventies, you're not required to destroy your brain. The seventies are over. California is over. The hippie peace, love and drug movement is done. Drugs are a serious business now, or maybe occasional recreation— not a lifestyle. Make a decision—become a drunken druggie, become a coke dealer just one dropped dime away from a free room at San Quentin. Or you can start a real life in the real world."

"Now you sound more like a preacher than a professor. Come on, Monty, I'm just having a good time!"

Monty came up to my face and stared me in the eyes. He looked disgusted. "Yes, you're a barrel of laughs right now. Hanging out with Winston is not just a good time. He's a destructive influence. He'll suck you in."

"Winston's just had some rough luck, like me."

Monty raised his voice. "Don't kid yourself, Jack. He was a privileged elite and he threw it away. Winston sees the world through the eye of a needle, man." Monty let me absorb this, lighting another Kool. "I bet Z.Z. could get you a job in the Financial District. My executive clients tell me there's going to be some real money made in the stock market. And in technology, like home electronics and computers."

"Monty, now you sound like the man in *The Graduate* who advised, 'Plastics.' I couldn't stand it with all those suits. I'd rather be a rock star."

Monty rolled his eyes. "Music's a tough business. If you aren't in the tiny percentage that make it, you will definitely hit the skids."

"Gee, thanks."

Monty sucked on his cigarette. "You know of course, Winston was not in Scotland, but in rehab? Back east."

This surprised me, so I lied, "Yes." I was putting up with this lesson because I wanted more information.

Monty added, "The first two times were in Hawaii."

"Right," I lied again. "Monty, what really happened at the Sir Francis Drake?"

He looked at me, reluctant, judging how high I was. "You're only young once. Don't screw it up. You know, drugs don't really let you get away."

"What?"

"Wherever you go, there you fucking are."

"Monty, you're right."

Satisfied, Monty confided, "Some questions remained if it was really an accident. Winston hinted to me that he could have been drugged and pushed. Blood was found on the windowsill."

"Wait a minute, blood before he fell? That means, fuck, Monty, you think that really happened?" Monty shrugged. I asked, "You think something like that could happen to me?"

He answered the question with a question. "You mean who, the cabbie killer, Zodiac Killer, maybe the Zebra Killer?"

"No. Isn't it apparent? Winston and I know prostitutes, we're musicians, we do drugs, we both wanted—I mean, we were seriously involved with Bretta. And I just got her pregnant. Her family hates Winston and now me." I glanced around and murmured, "Now I think her brother is following me with a knife. I'm afraid someone wants a piece of me."

"Donovan? Jack, Jack, you're freaking out, man. If you are going to do too many drugs you should get Winston to give you paranoia-management lessons."

"I'm not paranoid. Just before I came here, these two men, maybe Donovan, were chasing me inside the cathedral in North Beach."

"In the church? If you were acting as weird as you are now they were probably security, worried you that were about to shoot up with their holy water."

"Very funny." But I mulled this over. "It's possible, I guess."

"Winston's mutilation was probably more like a drug deal or kinky sex with some whore gone wrong." Monty flicked his cigarette and walked away. "I'm going home. Who knows, Jack. That shit he's got you on makes people sexually perverse and paranoid, and that can for sure happen to you. Speed's the snows of kill'em 'n jar'em."

Monty paced into the office building. Most of the time my policy was to ask no questions. Often you can get into more trouble knowing the answers. It may be better not to know the truth. If you don't know the truth, you don't have to lie—to yourself, or to others. Like about Winston. Like about Bretta and Finn's and Bretta and Monty's history. But the questions plagued me. Did somebody do that to Winston, and could I be next? Just because you're paranoid, it doesn't mean they're not after you.

I didn't feel like going home. Since I was on the east side of town I decided to go to Mission Rock bar and grill. I rode past the Caltrain station and thought of Bretta and our train ride together. I tried again to keep Bretta out of my thoughts. Some commuters looked blankly out of the train windows, while others just looked down—I assume at their boring *Wall Street Journals.* Maybe they should write in their journal rather than reading the *Journal.* There should be a blank page in newspapers with the headline: "Write Your Own News!" Like KFOG's "Scoop" Nisker's byline, "If you don't like the news, go out and make some of your own."

They were as zombie-like as the San Francisco "pod people" from that new *Body Snatchers* remake. I expected Donald Sutherland to run out in front of my motorcycle, chased by Spock. What was wrong with everybody today? They reminded me of people in L.A. waiting under bus stop shelters instead of enjoying the sun, or driving by palm trees and ocean views while staring straight ahead through their windshields. Some just seem so unaware, the oblivious ones. They should do a study of the personality types of lookers and looker-downers. Maybe the ones on the sidelines of life were happier? No, probably not. Maybe I was too keenly aware. Aren't creative types supposed to be more sensitive? Maybe my father was the same way—just too sensitive? I tried to remember if my father had some creative outlet. I almost hit a pothole, and dropped the interior monologue to focus on the road.

My bike rumbled across the old Third Street drawbridge designed by the same man who took questionable credit for the Golden Gate Bridge. I wondered if it began to open, could I jump the drawbridge of this giant Erector Set? I sped up just in case.

Mission Rock Resort was not a resort by any stretch, except for some who dubbed it the "Last Resort." I walked up the weather-beaten gangplank and entered the funky nautical bar. Mission Rock was San Francisco's only large waterfront restaurant that was not up-scale or touristy like Fisherman's Wharf. I sat at a hatch cover table on the deck and ordered a draft Bud from the jeans-clad waitress. The place was quiet with only a handful of ship builder types and a middle-aged couple.

The waitress reappeared with my beer and asked her few pa-trons, "You all heard? Our helicopters attempted to rescue the Iran hostages. They crashed in the desert; a bunch of our soldiers killed. It was a total nightmare."

The woman asked, "So the hostages were not rescued?"

"Not a one."

Two of the blue collar men swore. One cursed, "Jimmy Carter's a fucking peanut."

The woman cried into her husband's shoulder. I was stunned. That was why everyone seemed so zombie-like at the Train Station. For five long months, the hostage crisis had eaten away at America like maggots on unhealed wounds. Would the embassy hostages be tortured, mutilated, raped and killed in retribution? I moved into the bar to watch the breaking news of "Operation Eagle Claw" on the small black-and-white TV. A haggard male hostage was talking slowly, saying they were being well treated. I looked into his eyes, and was certain he had already been tortured and was being forced to lie. He knew no one could help him and would probably kill himself if he had the chance.

I wandered back to the deck. On the City side were the dry docks and the enormous ships floating serenely at the piers. I looked across to the rays of the late afternoon sun glinting on the windows of the Oakland Hills. The giant steel shipping cranes at, I supposed, Alameda, towered menacingly like the Darth Vader's Imperial walk-ers. I had just seen the preview for the latest *Star Wars* called *The Empire Strikes Back*. Were we falling to the Iran's Evil Empire?

I watched one of the men's ongoing flirtatious engagements with the waitress. I was killing time, when really it is time that kills us. Or sometimes it is love. The memory of my mother and father re-gurgitated. My mother had been a waitress. My father didn't like it but we needed the money. Always the money. My uncle was the one who ended up getting the money. And my mother. I felt even more vulnerable and disturbed. On my way out, I took another look at the TV. A military commander was speaking. He made me think of Finn. I drained my Bud.

It was late and foggy that same Friday night when I cruised my motorcycle South of Market. In Jack London's day, this area was termed South of the Slot, referring to the old underground cable slot of Market Street's cable car line. London fog, I punned to myself. South of Market, the city could become less savory very quickly, yesteryear and now. The newer real-estate-friendly term, SoMa, slanted it to a SoHosy art optimism. Sure.

Under the concrete pillars of the mammoth Bay Bridge, near unsigned crossroads, I jumped the curb. Finn was waiting for me. He motioned me deeper in. When I killed the engine, he had me keep my headlight on. He looked over my bike. I knew what he was thinking. Not a Harley. We walked through the dinge with the muffled sound of traffic overhead.

Suddenly, Finn pulled out a black steely revolver. A Ruger Speed Six, snub nose .38 DA with a sawed-off hammer for quick draw.

Finn dragged on his Camel straight and warned me, "Now, I may have made it sound like no big deal, but killing somebody for the first time is. Once that lead leaves the barrel, you can't take it back, and what's done is done. Right?"

"Got it," I assured him.

"All right, just three things, man."

"What?"

"Don't shoot anybody by mistake, don't get busted with it, and don't get shot with your own gun."

"Good rules," I agreed.

"It's loaded." Finn palmed me the gun, sideways. I looked it over, checked the action, handed him a hundred-dollar bill. He handed me a box of ammo in a plastic bag. He said, "I already wiped off any prints." He stuffed the money in his Army jacket. "I didn't want to say no to you, so I wanted to wait 'til you had it, so it wouldn't seem a judgment by me. Now that it's yours, if you don't mind me asking, who you afraid of?"

"That's the problem; I'm not sure who the enemy is."

Finn snorted. "That was the fuckin' problem in 'Nam, too, man. That's what got to us. Friend, foe—all look alike. At least the damn Iranians have hanky-heads."

"If this goes wrong, I may need to disappear."

Finn looked away as he answered. "After I was discharged, I did. I just said so long, farewell. Farewell to the whole shootin' match, ya know. I took off, slummed around Mexico, lived on a commune up in Oregon for a while." Finn swiftly changed the subject. "You been drinking?"

I didn't know what he was getting at. "Of course."

"You high?"

I made my confession. "Yeah, I'm high."

He surprised me by saying, "Good. You're probably going to be under those conditions when you need this. So, time to practice."

"Here?"

"Why not? You've shot before?"

"Plenty. Mostly long guns. I won a stuffed lion at the shooting gallery."

"All right, Sundance." He set up some empty beer bottles about fifteen feet away.

"That's pretty close."

"If you have to shoot somebody, they're going to be closer than that. If they weren't, you probably wouldn't have to shoot them."

He had me load, pull, and practice-fire a couple of loud, echoing, bullet-skidding shots. A couple more, and then the last couple before he said, "Not bad, not bad. So, like that *Streets of San Francisco* guy, Karl Malden, says, 'Don't leave home without it.' Reload and let's split."

We disappeared our separate ways into the inky SoMa streets of San Francisco. I wondered if Finn had sold me the gun of V. Garrone, but I didn't care. I took off on my bike and, all of a sudden, had a flash of paranoia about Finn. After what he had done, the kills, could he have had anything to do with Winston?

I drove into an alley and pulled out my new piece. At first it felt reassuring in my hand. I leaned over the handlebars and held it in the headlight beam. Looking for what? A pin to fall out of the hammer so it would backfire in my eyes? Ballistics of a murder weapon that now had my prints? Were Finn and Winston vying for Bretta at the same time? Did I just make a deal with the devil? No, that was crazy. But what about Monty? He had a poker face. It could be like the G.K. Chesterton short story. No one gives the professional people a second thought. Like a mailman. Like a cab driver at the Drake hotel.

Monty admitted Winston and he were both Bretta's suitors. He still hated Winston.

My thoughts turned dark. Maybe I should do everybody a favor and just end it right here. As a dare, I held the barrel to my temple. One squeeze, just like my ole' man.

"Jesus Christ," I spoke out loud, "Heigh-Ho, Heigh-Ho, down the rabbit hole I go." I stuck the gun away and calmed myself by looking at the life and heart lines in my palm. I rode on. I had business to take care of.

When I had phoned Nick again, he gave me the scoop on the Scarlet Pimpernel. This was the city's latest phenomenon—large-scale afterhours parties in the South of Market industrial area. Put on by some millionaire playboy known as Scarlet Pimpernel, Nick promised that it would be more kick-ass than any members-only dance club, even the Trocadero Transfer. I cruised by and parked my bike down the street, chaining it to a signpost. A couple smoking a joint against the wall slurred, "Hi, uh, Jack. It's Mason."

With my hand on my gun in my leather jacket pocket I answered, "Yeah, hi, how's the party?" to the couple I kinda' recognized from State. While I toked the proffered joint, the man told me, "Wild, man! Like, supercharged. But it's eight whole bucks to get in." His tipsy, foxy date offered, "You wanna' mirror my hand-stamp?" I liberally licked the back of my hand. The girl held my cold hand in the warmth of hers, and pressed hard to her other hand's stamp. I avoided her flirty eyes as she got close. The red flower, or a reasonable facsimile thereof, transferred, and I said, "Nice one." I took a last toke, holding it in, nodded thanks and walked to the entry.

Cool, I flashed my hand to the pair of leather-coated heavies at the door playing with their head-cracking five-D-cell, Maglite flashlights, and entered the dim, crowded space. I had felt spacey from the coke crash but the pot and this vibrant scene revived me. Techno-disco-electro music boomed. Strobe and colored lights flashed. Blacklights exposed glowing art and psychedelic Day-Glo paint highlighted floors, walls, and ceilings. Hundreds of young people of all persuasions and dress and undress, leather, Deadheads, dread-heads, punks, urban professionals, gays, straights, sumptuous-look-ing chicks, danced, gyrated, twirled, and freestyled crazily in the var-ious rooms. Numerous plywood-hewn bars were fully operational and folding chairs lined the sides. Dilated pupils, blacklight-bright stoned grins, and the smell of sweat, the good kind—of sex, a masking scent of musk, and underlying hint of something industrial, like detergent. This was an industrial-strength disco. Except disco clubs were dying and this was happening. And this was a trip.

Rick and Ruby, the comedy music duo, hung out with Danny Elfman, red-headed leader of Oingo Boingo band. A group of single chicks, draped around one of the few tables, checked me out making me practically bump into Bill Graham. He was called in print, "the music impresario," although no one knew what that meant. Yet everyone knew who he was and what he did. I blurted out, "Hey, Bill, you going to get the Stones back anytime soon?"

Graham glared at me, his bodyguard wingman glaring, too. The Rolling Stones had not toured the U.S. since Ariel took me to the concert at Oakland Coliseum's "Day on the Green." He didn't say a word. I guess it was a sore subject. I stared back. He eventually shook his head no.

I said, "Damn, that's a drag." Bill moved on. Many thought he was a big asshole, but I had run into him before and disagreed with that assessment. Bill Graham was just a regular asshole, amplified with power and money. Maybe Bill *was* Scarlet? No, but Bill was probably doing business with him. I tried to spot the host, who I imagined as a flamboyant, scarlet-plumed playboy in a cape, with a drag queen on each arm. Like Hugh Hefner crossed-dressed with *Rocky Horror's* Frank-N-Furter.

New wave music now enveloped the club with a resultant energy shift. Kinetic colored lights shimmied over the dancers. Revelers wore necklaces of plastic-straw tubing with dyed florescent liquid, like synthetic fireflies from my childhood's Lantern of Summer. I touched a necklace on a lithe tube-topped and silver-shorts-clad chick to see if it was warm. Totally zonked, she kissed me before she was dragged away by two other similarly cute creatures. I spotted Nick bartending. Like the other workers he wore a black tee with centered white-filled circle—a scarlet pimpernel imprinted in the circle. Nick looked good and he shook my hand in the thumbs-first shake. He poured a couple of tequila grapes for us and snapped his fists apart to his partner in the "taking a break" sign. Pointing to his ear, he led us up stairs to the third story's flat roof where only the sound of the heavy sub-woofers woofed through. Other than the party noise, the whole area was quiet as a graveyard. Fresh from the zoo below, the ever-mellow Nick lit a cigarette and proffered, "Sorry about the whole Bretta thing. You all right?"

"Yeah, I'm cool now."

Nick grunted and casually pointed out, "A little cloudy tonight."

I looked up breathing in fresh night air. I said, "Smells like rain. You know what gets me? It's amazing that people want to party after the hostage debacle."

"Yeah, those poor fucks over there. But what are we supposed to do? Enjoy it while you can. If Ray-gun gets in we may be drafted to invade Iran."

I reflected on this as Nick pulled out a joint. "You want a hit?"

"Sure." I toked. "Hey, what's Bill Graham doing here?"

"Don't know." Nick shrugged.

"Maybe he's going to try to take over like he did the whole live music scene."

"Doubt that," Nick replied, "considering our situation here. Probably just getting ideas."

"You mean stealing. He stole all of his ideas from the Diggers and Ken Kesey's Trips events."

"Bill's all right. He brought takin' care of business to San Francisco's chaotic music scene, making a lot of people rich and famous."

"True," I said. "This space is huge. Scarlet Pimpernel must be one cool guy. Renting this place, throwing these parties. Who is he, anyway?"

Nick chuckled. "This is between you and me, right? Most people think Pimpernel's parties are invitation-only events. Actually, these are totally underground, illegal from start to finish. Some call them acid house parties for obvious reasons. The owner of this building has no idea what's going on—a B&E job—the gear was just set up a few hours ago."

"Are you kidding? I don't get it."

"Exactly. Scarlet Pimpernel is not some rich eccentric. He's a ghost. The Pimpernel is really a group of bar owners and partners. They were sick of the regulations, taxes, ridiculous two a.m. closing time and all the other BS. There's a ton of money in the booze biz and they hate handing it over to the man. They pick out a closed-down or no-security building in an industrial area and bring in makeshift bars, DJ booths, staff and security. Their promo team hits the cool dance scenes like the I-Beam, the Stud, Earl's, just before closing time, and invite the hottest-looking clubbers, 'Psst, I hear there's a party at 666 De Haro,' or whatever."

"Wild. So everybody clears out in the morning?"

"Used to. At first the 'house parties' went just overnight. Once the pieces were in play, the organizers saw how easy and lucrative it was to keep the party going. The parties have become more elaborate and usually run all weekend long. We only have to be out before the street opens for business Monday morning. Next time, the party pops up someplace else."

"Right. I get it. 'That damn elusive Pimpernel!' That's so crafty, I love it. Living like Robin Hood. But, what happens if the cops come?"

"These areas are as good as closed down for the weekends. The cops don't even patrol here. Even if someone might complain, and the police swing by, they're told it's a private party for the employees. Last month the cops got a wild hair up their ass and did raid us. Everyone just scattered, as we were trained. We pulled off these identifying black tees and dropped them. We have different tops on hand. No one can be pinned down as "in charge." The Pimpernel makes so much money—the cover charge, the drinks, their cut of the drugs sold—all cash, that abandoning the watered-down booze and the equipment is an acceptable loss. Since then, we've been left alone. I bet those cops are paid off now."

This was a modern gypsy speakeasy, ballsy and brilliant, and they avoided the damn Revenuers. I did a quick calculation—say four hundred people times eight, plus twelve hundred drinks times two-three bucks' profit—and smiled. No wonder they can afford to open the fancy new legit clubs and bistros that were springing up.

I grunted, "We're in the wrong business, man." I was re-energized. I darted over and jumped on the roof riser's narrow edge, and stood with a joint in one hand, a drink in the other, and my gun in my pocket. I looked down to the bouncers and the swarm of new arrivals fifty feet below. I called, "I feel like Superman!"

Nick asked with concern, "Uh, Superman, what're you doing?"

"It's great to be this high. I used to check the cables for the tight rope act."

"I believe you. Get down and I'll show you the ticket back to Bretta. I got a guy I'll introduce you to." I pirouetted on the ledge and jumped back to the roof. Nick led us down the dark stairs to the second floor, which was now filling up. Nick said, "The "Love Drug." We jammed our way through the wild, swelling throng. The music had switched to a medley of Motown dance hits.

Nick introduced me to a shirtless man clad in leather chaps and vest. "Candy, this is Jack. Jack is good people. He's having trouble with his old lady. I have to get back to the bar." Nick left and Candy grinned with a gold-capped tooth and led me away. He had no jeans under the chaps and his entire bare ass was showing. I assumed Candy was gay or bi or even tri, whatever that was. At a frosted-glass-topped door we entered a small office, empty save for a "three-card Monte" style cardboard box and a flicker-humm, flicker-humm fluorescent fixture. Candy went over and stood behind the box. I wondered if he had a gun in the box, or if it was just filled with drugs. He looked me up and down, mostly down. Candy sounded as hoarse as Wolfman Jack. "I have just the ticket for your Love Boat. MDMA *is* Love Potion # 9. This will put the *more* in your amour." He winked. "Twenty-five caps to a bag, fifty bucks a bag, sell for four a cap, good markup. How many can you handle?"

"I'm not big time, I only need a couple."

He sing-songed, "'Have you ever been experienced?'"

"Oh, that way? No."

"Oh man! You gotta' get some L to go with it. For Candyflip-ping."

"I never heard of that."

"Named after me. I came up with it. Gets you ravin' man."

"What is it?"

"You drop LSD, which takes about an hour to get off, and a half hour in you take the MDMA, so you get off on both at the same time. You simul-trip, dig it."

"That sounds really intense."

Candy nodded and said, "Yeah, it's for professional partiers—best in a supportive cocoon environment like this. Just don't drive, or go eat at that Kawasaki-green, fluorescent-lit Chinese restaurant on Broadway, or anything stupid like that." I laughed. He continued, "Honey, you look like you could handle it. You'll know you've gone too far when you've lost syntax."

"You what?"

"Lost syntax—you talk like this, 'Mine learly up uffked no-oww. Drink you go—want?'"

"Some time other. After practice I this with."

He grinned maniacally. "Speed?"

"No thanks, I'm trying to quit."

"Coke?"

"Mmm. Good for now."

Candy made hand signals like a catcher to a pitcher. This confused me until I realized they were to somebody outside the door. I mentally rehearsed pulling my gun and firing twice. In a moment a generic, skinny Castro clone in a dark baseball cap, unidentifiable in a police line-up, rabbited in, tossed two entire baggies of capsules on the box, and back out. The caps' powder was white with brown flecks. Shit. I had meant only two caps, not two bags. I was too embarrassed to re-neg and counted out all the money I had left after paying Finn—ninety-eight fifty. I handed it over, but he pointed down to the box. I laid it there.

"Close enough, pretty-boy. You come back and get your Candy anytime, you hear?"

I split, feeling tingly like I had already dropped. With my baggies and my new gun, I wasn't Superman, I was Super Fuckin' Fly.

CHAPTER 20

A lion's low rumbling growl sounded from the animal tent. Inside, a group of teenagers surrounded the younger boy. A lanky, loudmouthed boy, maybe sixteen, belted the younger boy in the nose. It gushed blood. He shoved the kid to the straw-strewn ground. The teen stood above, unzipped his pants, and made motions to piss on the boy. Instead, he grabbed a shovel from his friend and plunged it into the ground next to the boy's face.

"New kid, from now on your little puny ass is going to scoop the shit for me. Otherwise," he glanced to his pals, and back to the kid, "your ass is grass."

The group laughed. The lions, from their rolling cage, feigned disinterest, the flick of tails the only warning sign. From the ground, the boy looked up at the lions. If only... The lions' yellow eyes looked at him.

"Sure, sure, OK." The boy, with surprising speed, sprang to his feet. He slugged the bully in the face. Whiff. He completely missed. The teen walloped the boy in the gut, hard, knocking the wind entirely from him. The boy fell to his knees, not able to gasp air. He wondered if he was dying.

The teen grabbed the boy's jacket, lifted him dangling toward the bars of the lion cage.

"Got it?" he snarled.

A shadow covered them. The boy's eyes widened. He smiled through bloody lips. The teen's feet rose high above the ground. The clutched boy rose with him. They spun around together and dropped, stumbling on the ground. The giant stood, massive above them. The bully looked around for help. His pals were gone.

"I got it," the man said. "Here, everyvone carry their own veights." Dark eyes under darker brows, leaned in until an inche away from the teen's. "Unless you vant that I carry yours?"

The teen sputtered. He pissed his pants.

That afternoon, Rollo began teaching me to fight as if my life depended on it. A number of times it would.

#

Bretta called me a few long days later. She apologized for being under the weather and out of touch. She lamented, that she had missed me desperately. To come over right away.

When I arrived, she was sitting on the steps to her building. No hugs. No kisses. Bretta pretended that nothing had happened. I sat down.

"I went through the wringer over you. I was so worried," I said.

"Why? Here I am."

"For God's sake, Bretta. You have to get in touch with your emotions."

She looked up the street and down the street before she looked at me and answered. "My emotions go into the canvas."

I shook my head in despair.

"Jack, I am truly, deeply fascinated by you. Isn't that enough?" She kissed me for a long time. She stood up and said in Mae West's voice, "Come on up big boy and have a drink."

I did. Of course, I did.

#

Our recent physical and psychological ordeal was officially a *verboten* subject. Her entourage closed ranks around Bretta with the same vow of silence as they had done regarding the Winston affair. The honeymoon with Bretta was over and we were in a deep relationship. The question was, what were we going to do with it?

We resumed drinking with fervor. We resumed to the good times and bar games. One night at the Sav, Bretta, Francine and Robin had all somehow worn brown-colored outfits. I considered Robin as Winston had described her, as a slender freckled girl of my age. I remarked to Robert, Benjamin and George the barman, "They look like Brownies."

Robert joked, "Good enough to eat."   "No, I meant like Girl Scout Brownies."   Robert eyed them appraisingly, "Oh, still…"

Francine pretended to be offended. From down the bar, a familiar slurred voice called out from the Peanut Gallery, "You still look like an Earthly delight, blondie."

Robin boasted, "I was a Girl Scout. We made hot cocoa around the campfire. A chocolaty drink would be—"

"I've got it." Francine exclaimed, stepping in front of Robin. "We should order chocolate drinks."

"Fabulous idea, Francine," Bretta and everyone agreed. "George, what can you make for us?"

"Um, how about a Chocolatini?" George suggested.   "Yumm. What's that?"

"I don't know, Bretta, I'm improvising." George pulled some bottles out. "Say, Bailey's, chocolate liqueur, vodka, cocoa sprinkles?"   Francine liked it. "Let's do it."   Robin nodded. Bretta ordered, "Three Chocolatinis."

George mixed and garnished with dollops of fresh whipped cream. Robin proffered a half-eaten chocolate bar, which George grated over the cocktails. Bretta huddled the girls together, whispering and elevating their Chocolatinis. They put hair strands under their noses like mustaches. Bretta announced in a French accent, "Attention." The trio chorused Frenchily together, "We are the Three Chocolatiers! One for all, and all for one, and none for you."

The bar cheered and the girls drank. And we drank and we drank. And somehow ended up in the old Saloon down Grant Avenue. I vaguely remember cabbing, no, getting a ride, maybe cabbing, back to Bretta's. We made it back and stood swaying in her tiled Victorian bathroom with the porcelain claw-foot tub and large porcelain pedestal basin with the faucets a foot apart. I sat on the rim of the tub and watched porcelain-naked Bretta as she held onto the basin, leaning over, using her Bass boar bristle brush on her feathery blonde locks in extended strokes. There were two Brettas.

"You *are* a Gemini," I said. "Twins. And you have four tits."

I stared at the two Dr. Bronner's Magic Soap bottles. There was two of everything. I remember closing one eye and then the other, seeing one bottle, then trying to make sense of the three thousand tiny blue-and-white words on the big bottle. I twisted my head one way and the other as I rotated and spun the bottle—"More good is caused by evil than by good, do what's right!" What!? Do evil? "All-One or None"—with only the panorama of her gorgeous moon of an ass as a backdrop. I remember standing behind her with my hardness pressed against her rear and squirting the pepperminty soap on her hands while she was trying to wash her face, and Bretta complaining with aggravated humor, "What the hell? To wash, you have to keep moving your hands back and forth, from HOT ouch to COLD brr."

I said, "Com'on Mama Bear, I'll make your porridge just right; WARM." I wanted porcelain girl. I was going to have her right then and there...

...I...

... I yi yi woke up at nine thirty. It was Saturday. I felt terrible. Ohhhh noooo. My mouth was sooo dry. I tried to utter something and only croaked. I drank a stale glass of beer from the nightstand. I nudged Bretta awake and grouchily complained, "I missed my sparring class for the first time since recycling. We should not have stayed up so late. We're drinking too much."

She became upset and scolded, "You're complaining about spending time with me? That sounds like you don't love me." She turned her back.

I tried to reason with her. I told her, "Missing my class is a problem."

"I may have problems. *At least I* have fascinating problems." She pulled a pillow over her head.

I dressed quickly, leaned under and drank thirstily from the same bathroom sink faucet, which looked less romantic, dirty really, in the harsh light of day. I unzipped my leather Dopp kit for my trusty double-edged razor but decided against attempting with my shaky hands. Another risky item was now in my bag. Since Jack's Lost Day, my private parts had thankfully stayed intact. I had laid off the coke and I upped my Valiums. Love Potion # 9 remained for a rainy day. My gun, I also stashed in my Dopp kit. When I wasn't packing it, that is. My new friend only came out at night. But his potency was always there. I stroked his sleek black snub-nose. A gun was the only thing a man could truly count on. Well, besides his dog. The gun was reassuring. Yet unsettling. My family had a history.

On the chilly sidewalk, I could not even remember who had been in the Saloon with us. I had a strong coffee at Tassajara, and did a couple of stretches in the warming sun.

I felt like shit. I probably would have gotten that beat out of me anyway this morning. I tried to comfort myself, thinking, You're just hungover again, you should be in your comfort zone this way, like Finn, I'm a pro, no big deal.

Missing the class was considered bad form. I enjoyed sparring—donning the protective gear and fighting full-bore rounds, one right after another. Sensei was always encouraging me to represent Karate Do in tournament competition. Sensei told me, "Jackie, you fast, plenty fast. You fight good. You go, you win big, big trophies like mine up there." I was in it for the challenge of fighting and fitness, not to win prizes like in a circus midway.

I jogged raggedly to the Panhandle—the eight-block strip of green thrusting east from Golden Gate Park, shaded by pine, maple and eucs. A dozen years earlier, residents had barely saved it from being bulldozed into a freeway, and bulldozed is what my head felt like. Here, I would do my own practice in penance. The group of black youths playing basketball, gave me dirty looks. I glared back, almost hoping they would mess with me. I kicked the crap out of the nearby tree limbs and bushes with some front kicks and roundhouses. I wondered if any of the street toughs would take the bait, but they were too busy jiving each other. "You can call me the professor, 'cause I be teaching you a lesson." "Sheet!" After a spinning back kick, I leaned over and threw up alcohol and coffee. Now they were watching me and laughing. The smell made me heave again. I was still spinning. I punched some branches. I threw up and gagged and coughed only in dry heaves like my chi was going to tear loose by its fingernails from the very essence of my gut. If I lost my chi I would just die on the spot but it might be for the best, because I've had a good life. I dropped down on the cold earth in a heap. I needed to literally get grounded.

I heard my heartbeat in my temples. A couple of the youths came over. One poked my leg with his red Reebok. "Shit, man, you all right?"

"I think the mutha'fucka's dead!"

"Hope so."

"I'm just..." I groaned, "resting."

"You look kinda' pale, man." They all laughed.

I said, "Ha, fucking ha."

The first kid said, "Leave whitey the fuck alone. He's a crazy motherfucker."

#

Bretta became increasingly anxious as she and Robin prepared for the gallery opening. Robin matched Bretta with her own off-kilter energy. With all their contagious anxiety no one needed drugs, or so I thought. After getting so sick and weird, I had quit, at least for a while. Bretta complained, "My lines have to be perfect, otherwise the entire piece is trashed."

The opening added more stress to our relationship, which if I dared to mention, would start an argument. But, I never wholly understood what it was about this gallery show that got her so edgy. I asked, "I don't get it. You've had openings before, right?"

Bretta moaned, "Yes. I'm nervous at every opening. I'm expected to be 'on' the whole time."

"You're already on all the time, Bretta. You're a performer at home and in bars, but not at your own opening?"

"I'm a free spirit. I cannot perform on demand. My parents were the damned performers."

Monty and Winston must have gone through this before and stayed clear of the scene. I braved a brilliant idea. "I have an idea. Let's have the opening at a bar. The Sav."

She gave me an appalled look, as if I'd proposed a coal mine or a poorhouse. Bretta informed me that she would be working, for hours. Non-stop. Starting now. I took the hint, split, and went for a run through the Park's Band Concourse and museum area and returned through the tunnel by the Prince-Edwardian-era-exquisite Conservatory of Flowers.

The next night, I returned to Bretta's flat and discovered that she had not been alone. Monsieurs Courvoisier and Remy Martin had paid a visit. Her creativity had not. A white smear and a straw remained on a work stand. I let that go, but indicated the bottles.

Bretta declared, "I'm so glad I'm not an alcoholic."

"W-what?" I stuttered.

"Because, I would have to stop drinking."

I laughed. "Then, what is your definition of an alcoholic?'

She thought before replying. "An alcoholic is anybody that drinks more than I do." I thought that was perfectly funny. Until Bretta announced, "I hope you don't mind I'm going out with the girls tonight." This was something she had done maybe once during our relationship. She saw my dismay and explained, "They are helping me cope with my opening."

As Bretta bathed, I fretted if it was really "the girls." When she emerged, yummy fresh and pinky-squeaky clean, I made my move. Right in the hallway, amidst the myriad of paintings, I pounced like a Tom-cat. As her breasts swung against her monkey painting, I made love to her. She enjoyed my spontaneity but protested, I'm running late. Soon, from my tongue test, I knew that Bretta had not orgasmed.

In her bedroom, with me lying back, watching in increasing interest, she slithered into white panties, bra, garter and stockings. She put on a flowing skirt and modeled it for me. I approved. Bretta bent over to pick out some pumps. As soon as she slipped them on, the milk train came back. I pulled her back on the bed despite protestations, You're mussing my outfit, to screw her once more for as long as I could hold out. I was successful this time—she passed the tongue test.

"Jack," she gasped. "Where did that come from?"

"Honestly? Bretta. I don't want you going out horny, without me."

#

The night of Bretta's opening finally arrived, thank God. She and I stood in a doorway across from the gallery and I smoked some pot with her in hopes it would calm her down. Unfortunately, I had no Valiums with me. My shrink had finally cut me off. The Galleria Di Belle Arti was a brick-faced storefront, and Bretta's largest *Shogun* piece was showcased in the window. The gallery sat on Hayes Street between the striking Beaux-Arts dome of City Hall and the Vorpal Gallery. Vorpal specialized in the inside-out, upside-down art of the late Escher.

I told her, "Escher claimed 'I don't use drugs, my dreams are frightening enough,' but I think he ate too many mobius strips."

She laughed. "Too late for us. He captured the reflections between the dark and the light, and the fifth dimension in between. How far should one go for art before one touches crazy?"

I put my arm around her. "I know. This show has driven us both crazy. I have worries, too, but I just want to get you through this opening, Bretta. Then we can get back to normal; just have fun again."

She looked at me, then across to the gallery. "I never know what to say."

Although perhaps a double entendre, I went the safer direction, suggesting, "Just have some prepared lines for answers. Let's rehearse. I have a notepad and pencil. I'll write them down for you, all right?"

"All right, fine." "If someone asks you, oh, 'What does your art represent,' no maybe, 'Tell me what are you saying to society with your art,' you would say…"

She thought. "I want to move people…"   "Bigger words," I suggested.

"I—desire to—divert my audience into a place, no, into a mind state of joyful distraction."

"Yes, yes, what else?" I scribbled rapidly.

"I want people to—experience the strange…"   I finished, "…to be transported?"

"Hmm. I want the viewer to be transported into a childlike curiosity of the strange and fanciful. My purpose—is to let their imagination freely fill in what they desire to see."

"That's perfect, you'll do fine. Is all that true?"

"I don't know. I just do my art."

"It's true now. Keep thinking of fancy answers to inane questions. Now, put some of this Visine in your eyes."

Robin let us in, assessed Bretta's nervous face, gave reassurances in her gallery-manager tone of voice, "It will be fine. It will be just fine, just fine, just fine." She reminded me of Tie-dye. She flitted off to assist the always unobtrusive owner, a middle-aged society matron, in last minute preparations. Bretta was still in casual dress, as she would change there. I was suited up, no tie, with a long London Fog over.

I had been to this gallery with Bretta for another artist's opening. There were long bone-white hanging panels displaying the artwork, which acted as room dividers. Bretta's larger bold pieces were along the matching walls. Some of her older pieces were displayed on the far brick wall. I averted my eyes from focusing on the new art as I wanted to EXPERIENCE the full effect of the anticipated life-changing, hallowed, trumpets-blaring, OHH-Pening.

I assisted Robin by O-pen-ing bottles of wine while Bretta changed. When I went upstairs to the office, Bretta looked striking in a strapless, long white dress and pearls. She was pacing, adjusting her apparel. I pulled off my coat and hugged her. Robin rejoined us. "The pair of you look fabulous, darlings. Jack—so-o handsome in your dark suit, and Bretta in your white dress." She smoothed my wayward curls. "You two are perfectly minimalist together!" She skittered off.

Bretta flounced into the rolling office chair. "I don't know if I can do this." She spun herself around.

In my best Monty-authoritative voice, I said, "This is the life you have chosen, Bretta. Or it has chosen you. It's like being a musician; a gallery opening is your time to hit the stage. Only your work is done, you can just lip synch."

She shook her head, so I asked, "Your mother is still coming, right?"

"I told her you were still upset. She didn't want a scene, so we thought it best that she not attend."

"Shit. I'm not upset now. That's a terrible idea. Now I'm upset. She's going to hate me even more. How about your father?"

"Jack, I have to tell you, my father never did care for my artistic life."

"I bet he did. I mean does. I thought I saw one of your drawings in his home." I lied.

"Really? He has never, ever attended any of my openings."

I wanted to say, Maybe he'll come tonight. I was glad I didn't. I wanted to say, You picked the wrong dude to deal with Daddy issues. Instead I said, "He probably doesn't come to these because he knows it would then be about him. He would be the star in the room, when he knows this has to be about you. Baby, you are the star." I didn't know if what I said was true, but it sounded good.

"Oh. Still, he's a big baboon."

"Bretta, your Dad is an artist, too, an actor. He's had to suffer and deal with his emotions and talent, just like you have."

"My mother and father were *performers*. They wanted me to be an actress or a dancer. I was forced to take performing arts classes all my life. All I wanted to do was stay home and draw and paint." Bretta started crying for the first time I had seen. She sobbed, "I've been a disappointment to them." She screamed, "I'm not a performer!"

Francine strutted in, stiletto heels clicking, appearing head-turning enough for a Hollywood gala. I held Bretta. "It's not about them anymore. It's your life."

Francine gave me a dirty look and groused, "Jack, you don't have to fix Bretta! Why do men always think they have to fix women?"

Bretta accepted a hug from Francine and mouthed, "Thanks" to me behind Francine's back. Francine ordered, "But I am going to fix your makeup, honey. You're a mess."

I still didn't get it. Bretta was such an outgoing, uninhibited person, but she was a mess. Robin returned and massaged Bretta's neck and shoulders.

Francine handed Bretta a tube of lipstick with a wink. "This will help." She wheeled to me. "Jack, you have to stay away from her. Bretta, you'll sell more artwork without a fucking boyfriend."

"Jack, I need you. Don't leave me."

"Bretta, I'll be with you, just further away."

"I'm whoring myself out again. It's like I'm hanging up there on the wall, with a price tag."

"Yes, buying a pretty piece of your artwork is like getting a piece of you. That's the way it works. And you are a pretty piece. They want to take you home with them. Francine's right, more so, if I am not glommed onto you."

Francine agreed, of course. "Jack's right. Sexist but right."

Robin said, "Hysteria is a way of life for an artist at openings. Bretta, Francine, it's showtime." The girls pulled Bretta away, trailing hands with me, with her clutching my notebook. I felt bad, but...

The young urban professionals arrived. The BMWs arrived. The press, the art aficionados, faux-cionados, and the freeloaders arrived. Aging fart-tistes, past their creative expiration dates, arrived, in passé Andy Warhol-pop attire which they could only wear to gallery openings and rock concerts.

Robin impressed me with her zest as she greeted, directed, described, defined and, if necessary, schmoozed. I strolled through the exhibit. Bretta *had* captured the *Shogun* look. Her work was bold minimalism with few brush strokes, red and black on white; or black and white on red backgrounds; imagery of swords, sails, *sake* barrels, robes, chopsticks, symbol-like writing, fans, martial-arts hands. Her art stirred within me all the emotional ups and downs and passionate intimacies of our whirlwind affair. I realized that pretty pieces of me also hung on these walls.

Bretta's entourage showed up in force, having wisely avoided the pre-show drama. Z.Z. and assorted Macys' fashionistas, Robert in a tux, a quiescent Winston, Edith, in short, fringed flapper dress and long pearls, trailed Francine and Bretta alternately. Monty appeared with a well-heeled executive in tow, a passenger on his way to the St. Francis Hotel.

Bretta's friends, wannabe friends, followers and strangers arrived. I swear as many attended for free wine and cheese as for art. Some appeared to be re-enacting the stealing free food party scene from *Midnight Cowboy*. Robert Mondavi flowed with Almedens and Inglenooks. Fume blanc, merlot, pinot noir flowed. A fair measure of wine flowed into Bretta. Just as the opening really kicked in, there was a slight hiccup. Bretta disappeared. A franticly-restrained search ensued.

At last, Edith located the artiste up in the office. On the stairs, as Robin and I went to retrieve her, I asked, "Bretta's crazed. So, how many openings has she done?"

"Let's see. In San Francisco—about one every nine months. So, you've made her fifth opening. She's doing much better this time. With you." In the office, we were stunned at the sight in front of us. Robin finished, "Or not."

Bretta sat at the desk, doing lines of coke on the framed photo of the gallery owner's family. Robin and I cried, "No, no, no. What the hell?"

Francine's "lipstick" tube sitting on the desk was a coke vial. "Francine said it could help." She spun around madly in the chair.

"Yeah, help her sabotage you." I seized the paraphernalia from Bretta.

Bretta whined, "They're not going to like my work."

"Yes they do, Bretta they will. But it's more important they like you. Though, they might lose confidence if you are shaking like a leaf."

I looked around the room. "I have an idea." I took Robin's big-brimmed hat and my long coat from the standing coat rack, attiring Bretta. I place my shades on her wide eyes. She evoked a femininized Sam Spade from *Maltese Falcon*. I escorted her downstairs, secreting her behind a broad panel, so she could eavesdrop comments. The rave reviews boosted her confidence. We discarded her disguise and Bretta did Take 2 of her grand entrance.

Z.Z. snagged me to smoke a fat number out back. I was ready.

"Jack, you clean up good, but where's your tie? Oh, you ever find that tie I lost at your party?"

"No. I'm allergic to ties."

"Sometimes, one must suffer for fashion."

"If you only knew. No thanks."

Z.Z. looked perplexed. "Speaking of which, see that hot man in the Oscar de la Renta? He may invest in my men's couturier boutique. It won't quite be Wilkes Bashford, but still, men's designer dress and casual."

"Excellent. Get me a backstage pass to the grand opening. It won't be like this, right? Question: Why does Bretta act like she 'suffers' through these openings?"

"I know. She can be so-o insufferable."

"Is it the chicken or egg? Do artists suffer because they do art, or must they do art because they suffer?"

Z.Z. exhaled a doughnut of smoke. "Ultimately—the artist's friends are the ones who suffer."

"Tell me about it." I took a toke. "But do you think they drink and do drugs to numb their senses from their sensitivity and suffering?"

"Who, the friends?" We snickered, tossed down the roach and re-entered the gallery.

We looked at a Samurai piece and Z.Z. commented, "You know, you're her only male muse she couldn't capture..." he paused, suddenly uncomfortable, "...in her art." I looked at him. He covered by saying, "Oh, just teasing."

Robert walked up in his tux and skinny tie. "You see Edith lately? No? Wish me luck, I'm auditioning for *A Life in the Theatre* at Berkeley Rep Monday."

As Robert left, Z.Z. stage-whispered, "A tux? Seriously? Poor Robert. The extent of his stage career consists of auditions."

Edith breezed by with a little Great Gatsby-esque Charleston dance-step, and fluttered her fingers at us. Z.Z. remarked, "Poor Edith. I don't think she's ever going to have much success with her art. She just goes through the motions."

"Maybe we need to make her suffer more. Go be mean to her, Z.Z. You seem in fine form tonight."

"Jack, do you consider Edith sexy?"

"Truthfully?" Z.Z. leaned in for my pearl of wisdom. "I think everybody is sexy. Under the right conditions."

"Oh." Z.Z. spoke in a funny voice. I knew he was dying to ask me if he qualified. "Edith does look quite good tonight."

"Maybe you should take her upstairs, taste her to see if she is good, and report back."

Z.Z. turned red, and then were distracted by Monty's fare tooting up in front of everybody, enraptured by Bretta's *The Red Geisha* piece.

I told Z.Z., "Sure seems that coke is becoming more causally used."

"I know, right? It's almost like the word is out—hard drugs are OK, as long as they are expensive," Z.Z. replied.

"Ha. Right. Deo told me that on a lot of Hollywood movie sets, 'everybody take five' means 'let's go toot some blow.'"

"Even my straight corporate friend said he tooted up with his boss in his Embarcadero Center office. On his Salesman of the Year plaque."

As we both reflexively rubbed our noses, we listened to Bretta's conversation with an older flamboyant man in a bright white suit. Z.Z. whispered, "Like he is Tom Wolfe!" We repressed giggles as I retorted, "And like Tom Wolfe stole Mark Twain's wardrobe!!" "That would be trippy if he is Tom Wolfe!!! He seems to have the right stuff!!!!" "He is so bright I wished I'd worn my shades!!!!!" "Here, take mine." Z.Z. put them on. I continued, "Maybe Wolfe and Ken Kesey have returned to San Francisco for one more acid test." We wound down our stoned giggling fit but couldn't resist looking around to see if the real Merry Prankster was there.

"Wolfeman" asked Bretta, "This piece is unpretentious save for ingenious contrary underlying complexities. How protracted was the creative process for this accomplishment?"

"My purpose," she responded, "is to let one's imagination— freely fill in that which—one desires to see."

"Ohh, I see. Very good, my dear. I must have this piece." He patted her bare shoulder with a lingering touch. No wonder she had been nervous. After she won over Wolfeman, Bretta shined. Bretta made the rounds like the social firefly she was, followed by admirers and male groupies. As I had encouraged her to work the room, I kept my jealousy in check. I did glare at Francine when our eyes met.

Robin declared this opening "Best in show." I declared to Bretta, "You're a star, baby." Red dot stickers were everywhere. An acquisition of the most expensive piece came in by phone to the owner. I secretly hoped the buyer was Bretta's father. Wolfeman ne- gotiated a three-piece buy from Robin. Monty's executive passenger offered Bretta some lines, which she declined. He persisted, making a not-so-veiled cash offer for a "private showing," which she less po- litely declined. He settled for a piece of her artwork and left with Francine. Still hopeful, he slipped Bretta his card.

I gained new respect for Robin. She had really pulled it off. The gallery owner and Robin wanted us to celebrate at the new Hayes Street Grill. I disappointed them by whisking my pretty piece of faded star home. There we partied by ourselves with the bottle of Moet I pilfered out of Frigidaire de Galleria Di Belle Arti.

CHAPTER 21

I wake before dawn to the sound of rain. Something is not right. I reach for her but she is gone. I love her. More than love, I desire her—more than desire, I crave her—the most extraordinary indescribable craving. Love is **the** drug.

In a moment of anxiety, I click on the lamp. I spot her Little Blue Journal with silver stars, on her end table. Unlocked, the book sits silent yet speaks volumes. I reach, rub my fingertips across the leather cover. I hesitate. Open it for the first time, and read the inscription:

"To Bretta. You are my love, Benjamin." I thumb through the pages of calligraphic verse and drawings searching for my name and see Ws.

I read: Poor W. Why did it have to happen? A terrible, terrible night. I must confess It was all my fault. If only I had not gone.

I wonder: Gone? Gone—left? Gone—where? Gone—there!?

I read: Did W deserve this?

I skip ahead: I am so lonely. Benjy is there for me. He loves me I know, but...I met the most fascinating young man in the oddest place. J.

My breath stops at my name.

I skip ahead:...J. I want him. He inspires me.

I skip ahead: J oh my J.

I raise the book: I am so crazy about J it frightens me.

I read: I am too happy with J. I cannot work. I feel smothered. Must I make J leave me? Perhaps I should return to W just for a while?

I listen to the rain for a few moments, almost afraid to continue. I close my eyes.

Realization comes to me like a flash of white light, white heat. Five art openings in San Francisco. I do the math. I must be mistaken. I count on my fingers. Finn, Monty, Winston, Benjamin, and me, Jack. Five boyfriends.

I precipitously hate her. I hear a man's voice murmuring. Who the hell is she with? I reach under the bed for my bag. I yank out my Dopp kit. Pull out the revolver. My finger tests the trigger tension before the spring engages. I flip open the cylinder, spin it. The bullets whirl 'round like six diminutive pinballs of lead death. One ball starts the game and one ball ends it.

Naked, I walk through the shadowed living room. I carry my Dopp kit, where my cocked gun nestles next to my double-edged razor, spare blades, and empty Valium bottle.

Light slants from the cracked open door to her studio. Soft, muted classical guitar music plays dreamily, blending with the rain. The crack of light strikes me in the face. I peer through to her linseed-oil-scented studio. A new rag paper picture hangs from the wall. Her painting —cattails wave above dark water. An alligator floats, half in dark river water, half exposed. On the primordial shore, doll parts are partially buried—arms, legs, heads. A child's eyes innocently peek from the peacock-feathered reeds. Across the top hangs a tattered theatrical curtain with a metallic sharp edge bottom. Yet, from under the guillotined curtain, a sliver of morning sunlight shines on the child's face.

I think back to Bretta's story—burying her Barbie and Kens. I am hit with a jolt of déjà vu—the morning I ran away from home. The morning I took the hatchet into Uncle's bedroom.

Have I told Bretta about this? No, I have told no one. Not even my ex-therapist. Still, was Bretta fucking with my mind? Or was it only about her? And her father, the actor.

I hear Winston murmuring to her again. I tingle with hot passion that runs cold as ice. My hand caresses the smooth steel of my friend. Noiselessly I stick my head in and cock my eyes for a further view of her studio. I feel like I am watching the opening scene of her play.

Act I, Scene I. Raindrops tap against the bay window glass. Bretta sits on the hardwood floor above a large sketchpad. Her legs are crossed under her; so childlike, yet a woman in full bloom. She wears only a short, color-splattered artist smock. She looks exquisite, her hair up, held by one chopstick and one slender paintbrush stuck crosswise through the woven bun of blonde. She concentrates with artistic focus, a brush poised surgically in her fingers.

For a moment, I stand silently in the doorway, unable to resist admiring the artist as a work of art, unto herself.

Bretta strokes lines. A line drawing—a minimalist impression, hooves, horns, a circus ring? No, Spanish. Bullfighting. A bullfight ring. A matador.

Winston's music and occasional voice emanates from the little cassette player I have given for Bretta's birthday. Winston is not there. I push open the door, swinging in to startle her. I ask softly, What are you doing, Bretta?

Oh. You frightened me.

I couldn't sleep, either.

Of course, the coke.

The rain must be inspiration for you.

Blank rag paper on the walls, crumpled paper everywhere, two easels with blank canvas, paints, brushes, charcoal, pastels, pencils. Three cardboard boxes stacked on the floor. The labels are from Nevada City. From her Mother.

I say, You never stop, do you?

My inspiration is coming faster, she says.

I move to her, You look sexy in your artist costume.

She gives me a distracted look.

Come back to bed.

Bretta pulls herself up, her hand accidentally oozing yellow paint from a tube onto the little table. She frowns, Eveready, I must work.

I am entranced by the surreal colors on her palette—mood indigo, verdigris, smalt, vermillion, titian, bittersweet. I take a brush. I say, Let me try.

She says, A number four filbert brush, a fine choice. She lets me dip it in the yellow paint and touch it to the blank canvas on one of the easels. I do it wrong. She stands behind me and guides. She holds my hand, makes the brush strokes with me. We struggle for control. I want to do it my way—the wrong way.

She says, No like this. One cannot be in charge the whole time. Yin and the yang.

We try again. We paint a circle. She splits the circle with a partial S. We draw two dots.

I say, That's like my martial arts symbol.

Bretta whispers, *A continual movement of two energies in perfect balance. Contrary, yet complementary. Yin is left, feminine dark moon. Yang is right, masculine light sun.*

I give into her, and we paint the symbol. She paints masculine with blue, I paint feminine with yellow. We kiss delicately. We kiss again. She runs her fingers in my hair, turning curls into ringlets. I grab a tube of blue paint and with my brush ready, reach to paint her. She says, *No.* She dabs a brush, applies to my chest. I protest.

She goes, *Shhh, you'll see.* She paints a blue yin yang around my chest, painting my nipples as the dots. They are very sensitive and I become aroused. She opens her smock. She squeezes yellow on her engorging nipples and rubs her breasts against my wet blue paint. I kiss her neck. I squeeze a tube of vermillion paint onto the palette.

I pull up the back of her smock and make a vermillion handprint on her butt cheek. She squeezes a bittersweet tube. Before she can reach it, I put my hand into her smock and clamp onto a breast, leaving a blue handprint, like a Berserker. We are giggling and breathing fast. The windows fog up.

I squeeze yellow to paint a sunflower around her navel. We drop to the floor, roll in the paint in ecstasy. She looks down. I am hard now. She pulls at it. She says, *Maybe we should paint it blue-grey like the Moby Dick it is.* She strokes me and reconsiders. *No, I have a better idea.* She dips a brush into the vermillion, and taking me by the balls, paints a spiral on my erection like a barber pole. She teases, *Where's your razor? Maybe I should shave you first.*

She reaches for my Dopp kit, filled with very dangerous things. I pull her back. Bretta shivers. She has goose bumps. Even her goose bumps are sexy. The rain becomes more intense against the steamy windows. We both pause and listen. She goes down on my barber pole and sucks me. Clutching a tube of white I squeeze it all over the canvas as I orgasm.

I brush my fingertips across her face, leaving a blue streak of paint. I blurt out, *Couldn't we just live together? At my place, Bretta? Get away from all these people?*

She looks at me, placing a hand on my knee. But she looks at the rain.

I thought, *At least she thought about it.*

Bretta, you know, the baby and all that. I would have gone through with it, if that was what you wanted.

I know. Oh, Jack, it really would have been such a handsome baby. But, none of it would really work for us. Not right now.

Why didn't you just talk to me?

That's why. I didn't want you to agonize with the decision.

I protest, But...

Jack, our child would have been artistic, too sensitive. We would just have made it suffer as we suffered under our parents. Jack, you know this better than I...

Bretta...

Life is art. An illusion. We want it to be a beautiful illusion yet we create a distorted interpretation of reality.

I ask, Interpretation by the artist or the beholder?

Both. Nothing I create is real. The beholder makes it real to their eye.

No, our love is real. Our baby was real.

How do you know, Jack? Did you see it?

Bretta, no, no.

My Jack, you love beautiful illusions. She kisses me, whispering, Shhh,shh, shh. I'm sorry, lover, I need to finish <u>my</u> illusion. She turned away to her work. Raindrops tap harder against the windows.

I whisper a song, I am just a dreamer, but you are just a dream...

I jar awake shivering in her bed in the dark. I realize that I have been naked and all alone. Bretta heals me and opens a wound at the same time. My sun and my shadow. This has long been my fear.

CHAPTER 22

People are very much like dogs. Men sensed my leash to Bretta slipping and began hounding her scent. Bretta's allure radiated like she was in heat. I found my tongue test too often outside acceptable limits of tolerance, or failing completely. Who was walking whom? I was about to find out.

One night at Bretta's flat, after a few drinks and a blast of coke, hoping to reignite our relationship, I convinced Bretta to go out dancing. While she showered, I quickly undressed and searched everywhere for my boots. Dashing into her studio, I found them in the corner next to the cardboard boxes that Duzinella had delivered months ago. I sat down on the boxes and pulled on my worn boots to test their dancibility. Something poked me in my naked ass. I opened a tucked flap, marveling on the engineered strength of corrugated cardboard, and there, sticking out among old art supplies and Magic Markers, bundled with a deteriorating red rubber band, was a slim object rolled in yellowed silk. Curious, I unfurled the handkerchief. Out rolled a blonde naked Barbie doll into my hand. Over Barbie's perfect boobies, Scarlett O'Hara waist, impossibly long thighs, and Mattel-stamped butt—an "outfit" in yellow and blue had been colored on her skin.

Excited, I scrambled through the box looking for the Kens and yanked out a clear plastic bag of Barbie outfits and accessories. I poked my hand between the flaps of the other boxes feeling around to discover a similar bag of Ken clothes. However, no Kens were to be found. I was about to call out to Bretta that Duzinella had found her long-lost buried Barbie. Huh? Wait. Something was not right with this. I sniffed the Barbie, 1960s—storage musty, but absolutely no smell of earth. And no Kens. Sweet Bretta's brushstrokes were darkening.

A squeal startled me, the old water pipes, and the shower went dead with an eerie silence. A disturbing realization descended with a prickly heat. I wrapped Barbie up and hurriedly replaced everything as it had been. I scooted over on the floor. Bretta glided in naked, wild blonde hair dripping, holding up a large pair of silver scissors. A creepy tingler crawled up my naked spine.

"What are you doing, Jack?"

I looked up at Bretta from my knees. "Admiring your craft."

Her eyes narrowed. I pointed to the wall. Her eyes panned to her newest artwork, over to the boxes, and down to my exposed body. She thrust the scissors at me. "Jack, will you please cut it off? It's really starting to bother me."

I placed a hand over my genitals and stared in shock at my own gorgeous, but now scary, Barbie doll.

"I'm tired of it, Jack. Time for change."

Bretta lifted up a stray tuft of her hair. She had cut her waist-long hair to shoulder-length.

"What the hell are *you* doing?" I asked. "Don't most women go to a hairdresser?"

"I will. I couldn't wait to get rid of it. I'm still adorable, don't ya think?" She pirouetted her lusciousness, scissors flashing.

I stood and took the scissors from her while her back was turned. I didn't know what else to say, so I told her the truth. "You could shave your head bald and still be the sexiest woman in San Francisco." I carefully cut the tuft. She disappeared and returned after a blow dry and gel—her impromptu hacking looked surprisingly good.

I tried to put Barbie and Kens out of my mind as we headed to a revamped Haight-Fillmore club. I had heard that more whites were venturing to the Fillmore for entertainment. The all-black Fillmore—whose bony, red-eyed men, street-corner-talkin' in front of the liquor stores, drinking out of paper bags, jiving and panhandling, were no longer considered deterrents to upscale fun-seekers. They were just "local color" and the area was "safer now." Ready or not, the gays had started gentrifying the 'hood.

The Buck Fifty Club was still mostly black and in 1980, the 70's pastel sports jackets, bell-bottoms and pimp hats remained en vogue. A few white "safety-in-numbers" group were there. The joint was jumping with a live bluesy jazz band. Bretta swore she would dance with me after a couple of drinks. After that couple of drinks, Bretta flirted with some black dudes, and I tried to call her back, but instead she smiled and ignored me. I felt the cords rise in my neck and told the Kessler-Smooth-as Black-Silk bartender, "Sometimes a great notion, Hank!" who gave me a deserved annoyed look. I ordered a shot of tequila and downed it to loosen up. Next thing I knew Bretta was standing between this one spade's spread knees as he sat on the barstool in his hip rectangular shades, her pale luminescence contrasting to the dark men around her. She felt his cornrows and told him, "I really like your hair." I felt like smacking her. Instead, I ordered, "One more shot of tequila." One more would make me just right, just enough to take the edge off and bolster my confidence, but not so much as to lose my coordination.

She, fortunately, excused herself and went to the lady's room. I told cornrow spade, as lightly as I could, "Hey man, ease up, she's my lady." As in Nevada City, I smelled trouble, and not just as in the old saying. I really did. The pungent testosterones, pheromones, and sexual animal swelter threatened like a thundercloud in the Rocky Mountains. The dude looked around to make sure his two buddies were still nearby, whom I had already noticed casually lurking. Why did it always have to be three of them?

Cornrow got all spade-heavy and racist on me, and "white boy this" and "honky white ass that," and "I'm gonna' make that pussy mine." Before I began the confrontation, I had sized Cornrow up as a gangly, medium-muscled, semi-drugged, untrained fighter, right-handed, with long arms and no weapons.

I asked Cornrow to step outside and he gave me a steel-hard look. When I didn't flinch, he grinned and nodded toward the door. His two friends followed, one saying with a disarming smile, "We're staying' outta this, man. We cool." As soon as we got out the door, Cornrow sucker-swung at me, as expected, underestimating me, but nervous enough to rush it, and I blocked his signaled right haymaker punch with my left and kept reaching in with that left to grab his shoulder sleeve, and back fisted him to his right cheek with my right, stepping in closer, and forearming him in the face with my right. The "we're cool" friend rushed me from behind, and over my shoulder, I back-fisted him in the bridge of the nose, and he backed away with his head bent over, gushing blood. The other friend saw this and hesitated just long enough to fumble for his blade, which gave me a clear side-kick to his gut, and he bent over, too. Cornrow settled into a defiant come-get-me stance. I knew that proximity freaked some out because I was one of them, but not wrestlers, judos, or homos. I gritted my aversion and darted up between his arms, and as he tried to back up for a clearer swing, I got inside his now ineffective long reach and holding onto his collar, forearmed him and reversed my arm back again to elbow his face. He dropped to his ass on the pavement.

I made one mistake. I felt a jarring slam into my ear, and with my head ringing, a big fist with big gold rings came out of nowhere and into my right cheekbone and eye. I felt my cheekbone fragment and the blood in my ring-cut eye, blinding me. With my good eye, I saw the blur of the green-jacketed, square-shouldered, bulging-neck, crocodile-of-a-man with the big jaw and long, crooked nose, and recognized his dark mass from back in the bar. I had not realized Croc was part of the group. He surely was an amateur heavyweight boxer, and not only a mean fighter, but a dirty fighter. My only chance was to step back out of his fists so I could use my feet. Cornrow reached up and held me fast around my knees. As I tripped, the boxer's uppercut busted out a top front tooth with a snap, and, as I fell, he shoved my face grinding on the sidewalk, knocking out the other front tooth and breaking my nose.

That was the first fight I lost since my beating at the lion cage. It was a dangerously bad one to lose.

Fortunately, it didn't happen. I had changed my mind. My instinct had spooked me. I merely got in close to Cornrow on his barstool and told him most of the above, leaving out the last part where I got the shit beat out of me. I said, "This is what is going to go down."

"You crazy mother," he said. "You just told me your game plan?"

I said, "Or did I?" He looked confused, which is just what I wanted. I learned from Rollo's best friend, that it is better if you can take someone's brain out and play with it, undermining their confidence, before a possible physical confrontation. I spoke rapidly and in a low voice, getting closer and closer to him. "You look like you've been doing smack which slows you down, and I've been doing coke which speeds me up, and I already have lightening reflexes, so my plan could still work, and I could be all over you, even right here. Remember, once I get you to think that's my plan, I can still do something else, right?"

His over-confidence began failing, so he nodded, eyes completely crossed, and looked around for his partners. I smelled locker-room sweat and canvas and smelling salts and athlete's foot powder and leather. My stomach tightened. From the dim back-end of the bar, I saw big, white teeth coming fast. The teeth were part of the dusky, muscular mass that became the too-tight-green-jacketed, Nu-Niled-hair-glistening, boxer parting the drinking bodies like a bull crocodile charging through rotting cattails, up from the muddy-dark-dank depths of a watery hell, with "yo' my next unsuspecting meal" dead slit-eyes intent on me. The two friends sensed him coming and gave him space. I timed it for Croc to reach us and quickly continued, "Now, this is my real plan."

I stepped back, lifted up my leather jacket, holding my paw by my belt, millimeters over the .38, waiting snug but longing for bang-bang action. I said with a four-shot tequila voice, "White-boy this, motherfuckers."

Cornrow froze along with his two partners. Croc the Boxer retreated backwards as if snapped by a bungee cord, melding into the dark crowd and disappearing. I grabbed Bretta, who showed back, and who once again had no idea what had just happened. I pushed her out the door.

We jumped in a cab, and I coldly sat, replaying the incident in my mind, making sure what I did was the best plan. Surely, the Judge would appreciate that I refrained from the violence of a fist-fight. I blocked out Bretta's questions, as I convinced myself that I was not chicken, that I still had my nerve to fight. I didn't like what I was becoming.

I had the cabbie stop at her place and we got out. I stood there for a moment, watching the cab's taillights disappear into the fog.

I grasped Bretta's shoulders. "I'm done. It's over with us."

I walked away. She followed me to my apartment. On my landing, for an unreal moment—with Mr. Boots crying forlornly behind my apartment manager's door, and Bretta crying and apologizing, I trembled and forgave her.

"I'm afraid...I can't go on like this." Almost. I shut my door and locked her out. My affair with Bretta was over. My sun had eclipsed. What else could possibly happen after all that I had been through?

The End

BOOK III

CHAPTER 23

I was relieved that I had made a decision, and that it was done. I filled a beer mug with Scotch and slumped on the sofa, looking out my bay window to the lights of the neighborhood. I replayed the night's near-bar-fight and what the whole Black and White Thing was about. The blacks I had worked and lived with, and made friends with, were the most real and frank and caring of anyone I have known. But the bad ones were the most dangerous—as the ring imprint on my eyebrow and the knife scar on my arm testified. When and where I grew up, there certainly was mistrust and fear of blacks. And vice-versa. But here, in 1980, in cultured and progressive California?

I woke up chilled at 3:30 and reached for Bretta. It is easy to be a hard guy about things in the daytime, but in the middle of the night it is another thing.

I remembered back to Rollo's advice. Rollo the Strongman. A few years after I had left my Circus life, I heard he was sick. I visited him in Tuscaloosa in 1977. We sat in his little circus trailer, a frosty, quiet afternoon, in front of the built-in cook stove, with its burners and the oven lit, oven door open. The stove's gas flames were his combination cooking, heating, and entertainment source. Rollo watched the flames like TV. He had lost weight, his muscles sagged, and he suffered from arthritic pain.

He looked through the slatted window at the fall sky, leaves tumbling from the trees, and gave an exaggerated shiver. He spoke in his slow, deliberate, resonant Hungarian-Southern voice that was working-class poetry— Karo syrup pouring over goulash.

"Yes, Jackie, getting about zat time to shack up for ze winter. Nothing like a nice soft, varm voman in bed vith you, when ze vind picks up, ze frost gets on the vindows, and ze snows coming. Umm-umm. Varmer than sleeping with un dog. Hell, it is varmer than sleeping vith two dogs. You have good voman, Jackie?'"

Even in temperate California, each winter I thought of that advice. Some are not suited to sleeping alone.

Now, he was losing his job. I offered him money, which he refused. "Rollo, please, let me help you out." This was the man who saved my life. My tears welled up.

"Jackie. No. I had good life. I vas *performer*. People loved me. And I vas something, vasn't I? I vas *somebody*. Now, I am old. No shame. No regret. This es vhat happens. A man does the best one can, and then he cannot."

Rollo really was something. Soon after my first run-in with the boys, he surprised me saying that some men liked to pick fights with him. Why? "So zey brag zey tangle vith the biggest man in ze place."

Occasionally I witnessed this. I had seen him just bear hug men until they passed out. Sometimes, lift and toss foolhardy men into the air and let them drop, like gunnysacks of animal feed. My gentle giant did not like to fight, but he always won.

"Now I know, I may not vin such fights," he lamented. He labored to breathe and winced. Rollo had taken up smoking since I last saw him. I had never seen him insecure.

"Look, new trick." He dragged on a Viceroy and laid it on his stiffened palm. I now saw fully how knotted with the arthritis were his fingers and hands, from a lifetime of bending and lifting. He smacked the back of his hand, which popped the cigarette up into his mouth. He looked at the February calendar on the wall three feet away, and puffed, "Pick date."

"The twentieth. My uncle's birthday."

Rollo puffed his cheeks and the cigarette shot out of his mouth, hitting the twentieth square, leaving a charred mark. He caught it after the bounce and the bent Viceroy was back in his lips. "That could hit a man right in his eyeball." He bent down over the burner to relight it, and looked up into my eyeballs. "A colored friend once told me..."

Rollo had seemed most comfortable with the hard-knock-life-looking black roustabouts who did our rigging and such. He hung out with them, so I followed suit. Rollo and his black companions were the first to teach me the not-so-artistic art of self-defense.

I had heard this story before. In fact, I had heard the advice first hand from old Jarvis. Jarvis was a former prize-fighter, having ruined his career by drink, who turned to street fighting for money, before being hired by the circus as security. I still loved the way Rollo retold it with his surprisingly good black dialect, with Cajun flavoring his accent.

"'You get down for some ass kickin', you jus' best be ready. There be fo' ways t'beat a man. You 'member, don't matter much, it mebbe any size ass, mebbe any color ass, that ass still be full of jus' four tings. Blood—still red on de' inside, full of air, full o'shit, full of jism. You take any of dem tings away, you can take de' man. You know what I'm talkin' about? You make 'em bleed, you cut off de'air, you call der' bluff, you make'm lose d'manly confidence— de' be givin' up—o' dying, one o' the other.'"

I nodded solemnly to Rollo. Then, I tried to cheer the mood by impersonating him in a story he had told me long ago: "Circus boss, he bill me 'Rollo ze Romanian Strongman.' What is funny? Ha. I am Hungarian."

Rollo slapped me tenderly on the back and laughed. Which turned into a suspicious cough. "Now, Jackie, vat you say, we celebrate vith oatmeal vith fisheyes?"

Before we said farewells, I secretly placed my baggie of a thousand dollars inside his Quaker Oats box. After Los Angeles, I lost touch with him. Sadly, I never knew what became of Rollo, my real-life superhero.

I glided back to a sleep redolent with circus imagery. The tantalizing, jet-black-haired knife-throwing lady was my first crush at age thirteen. I had been hopeful for a kiss when she had invited me to her trailer but all she gave me was a throwing knife, which I still cherished.

There were so many circus characters—the aloof trapeze couple that always ate meals by themselves, the eccentric elephant trainer, the emotional roller-coaster-of-a-ringmaster who was father to us all. They segued into a cartoon-like dream, where everything was off-kilter. Bretta's mother Duzinella was the garishly-clad and made-up ringmaster, who pirouetted and danced around the ring between her announcements. I was Rollo, in a Scottish kilt, holding a large barbell. Calliope circus music played with a fusion of discordant jazz notes. Bretta's father was the tamer with matching gold pith helmet and boots in the lion cage. His encircling whip was made of celluloid frames, which showed Bretta as a girl, spinning on a swing, Barbie's head peaking up from her blouse. The big cats had jabbering monkey faces. The audience appreciatively tossed gold coins into the cage. The music changed, with the audience singing, "All around the mulberry bush the monkey chased the Liesl." Bretta, the alluring knife thrower, in knee socks and blouse-less, leather mini-dirndl, threw kitchen knives at a naked Winston who spun asymmetrically, on a rickety boardwalk platform.

The tent sucked and bellowed like an asthmatic breathing creature, while high above, Monty sailed on the circus trapezes with Francine. Barefoot Robin stood atop a circling dusky horse. Finn, with a strapped tray, called, "Bee-eeR. Pea-NUTS." Edith and Robert, as twin clowns, tumbled around the rings.

I was balancing on the high wire at the peak of the big top, far above everyone, still holding the barbell. I looked through the tent's vents, saw the bright sun, which obscured over in a blood-red eclipse. The barbell shifted and when I looked down, Bretta was dangling from one end and Winston from the other.

"Jackie. Jackie." I heard the familiar voice from the stands. I peered through the faces to see... my foot slipped, I almost fell, the barbell tilted, slid through my hands, and horribly, I could only save one.

As I left my apartment the next morning, Mr. Boots meowed through his mistress's door reminding me that she was gone. I let myself in with her extra key, overfed the cat to make up for his missed dinner, and emptied the stinky litter box out the rear window, which an unknown peeping neighbor observed. Purring contentedly Mr. Boots ran into the spare bedroom that the manager used as an office. Mr. Boots jumped on the desk, showing me the latest competition for his mistress's affection. A new toy was now taking up half the desk. Next to the only answering machine I'd encountered, and a cooler cordless phone than Bretta's, was another first for me—a walnut wood, humming, North Star Horizon computer with a little tube screen. It pissed me off for some reason.

I thought, The rise of the machines. My manager's really gone professional businesswoman on me. Next, she'll be driving a BMW. The box's glowing green "READY" was followed by a square, blinking at me. Ready for what? Ready to take over the world? Ready to tell us what to think? Can't Big Brother wait 'til 1984? I said outloud, "HAL, play "Daisy." I half expected the thing to answer, like in the *2001* movie. What a crazy thought.

My hangover and I jumped on a streetcar and transferred to the diesel-perfumed Muni bus. My stomach and I lurched at every damn stop: Shriner's Hospital, Conservatory of Music, real F-8 fighter jet cum children's playground equipment, campus, the gun in my backpack. The annoying yammering students disappeared into the foggy campus grounds. I paused at the bus exit. I was in no hurry to carry out my plan. Gazing at this place for perhaps the last time, I knew the fog would soon burn off, but my fog would not. In my dream, after hearing my uncle's voice, I had let Winston plummet down, down, to the ground.

Graduation day had been foggy last spring. I hadn't cared about my graduation ceremony. Why go through pomp and circumstance without Ariel's smile? I stopped now, realizing I stood right in the middle, between two departments. On my right—Business, and on my left—Art. Were these valid choices? Was I fated to slowly climb the managerial ladder, or to start my own business? Bretta's art and her creative entourage also enthralled me. I felt creative, but where was my fourth dimension? Even Bretta could not find it. Let alone a fifth dimension. As I entered the Student Union, Martin Luther King seemed to looked down unfavorably on me. The huge mural portrayed the purpose, loss, frustration and triumph of a generation. My purpose this morning was feeling more frustrated than triumphant.

I punched in and accepted the greetings from Bookstore coworkers. Montesha welcomed me with her usual toothy grin, "Mornin' there, Play'ah." She was a gem, and her no-BS attitude reminded me of Ariel. Montesha seemed to sense my heart was no longer in my work. In fact, my heart was no longer anywhere. "A little under the weather again?" she inquired.

"Yeah. My girlfriend. It shows?"

"I know you have your reputation and all to keep up, but you might want to consider stayin' home and readin' a book sometime." She pointed at the bookshelves, and then lowered her voice. "Bossman has been noticin' you, Play'ah."

I nodded to her in deferment. Montesha was right as usual. I was tired of this place—it was boring. The crazy scene of the SOMA party and Nick's description of the Pimpernels operating outside the bounds and rules of society resonated deep within me. Caught up in the circus-like atmosphere, I was hooked into buying all that stuff from the Candy man. I had only intended to buy a couple of hits of the love drug to take with Bretta. The thrill of becoming an outlaw had taken away the pain—of the whole child thing. I had stashed the pills for a rainy day.

Between going out all the time with Bretta and paying rent alone, I need better income. Selling drugs couldn't be that hard of a business and I was a hard worker. Deo was rich. And Rockstar—he just took a few art and film classes, played Frisbee, publicly brushed his beautiful long hair, and sold drugs. Now I was ready. Easy seed money for my next enterprise. Maybe Nick and I could host our own Pimpernel party and make some quick bread. On lunch break I withdrew most of my dough from the BofA at Stonestown Shopping Center. On the quad's green lawn, Rockstar slid from his backpack, into mine, the pound of popular Columbian, a lid of Maui Wowie, and some hash along with a dozen 714 Quaaludes. Rock Star gave me some friendly business advice, "Man, you have two choices—the rep to *always* have some kind of pot, or the rep that you might not always have some, but when you do, it will only be *choice, quality* stuff. Like this. Dig?"

I dug it. I returned to the Bookstore and kissed Montesha goodbye. I told my boss, thanks for everything, and that I was taking the plunge and becoming a professional pinball player. His smile turned into a big "O" and his eyes popped out like a squozen Obie doll.

It didn't take long for my business to light up. Ha-ha. I sold a lot of quality pot and sundries in the Haight. Where so many people smoked a fat one before breakfast, business was brisk. I even took example from the local liquor stores and accepted food stamps.

#

One other time, a couple of years back, dealing as a supplemental income was a consideration. Ariel was visiting home in Southern California and one of those magic days was unfurling. Under a park bench in the Rose Garden, I found a Sucrets box. Inside were three pre-rolled joints. I wasn't much of a smoker but I figured it was meant to be. I strolled over to the more discrete Rhododendron Dell to light up and ran into a slight, super-nice man. I shared a joint with him.

Dennis inhaled in sips, paused, and said, "Not bad." He handed me a little baggie with an exotic bud. "You want variety, come see me at The Island tonight."

On the corner of 16th and Sanchez, The Island restaurant was opened-floored with the interior and counters covered in unfinished wood slats, like a funkier Hamburger Mary's, only without the humorous signs and nippled, baby bottle creamers. Filled with standing potted plants and Tiffany-knockoff hanging lamps, the place was bustling. I scanned for Dennis and finally asked one of the gay, and happy, waiters if he was working. He looked me over, smiled, and indicated up, with his eyes and head. I made my way to the upstairs flat and knocked. Dennis welcomed me up to the living room, which he called "the Big Top." I chuckled. Inside was indeed a circus—an emporium of exotic grass and drugs for sale—which blew my mind. Stoned patrons lounged about while Sylvester played on a Marantz system.

Turned out my new friend actually owned The Island and he got me really zonked. Everything was very casual, almost like he ran a licensed drug store. I don't know how he got away with it. The hiding in plain sight theory? Dennis told me he was making marijuana available to "The People," no matter what happened to him. Apparently, he was, like, on a mission. While hanging out on a frayed sofa, chatting, it became clear who Dennis was: Dennis Peron, the biggest dealer in the Castro, close friend and financial supporter of Supervisor Harvey Milk. I wasn't comfortable at all with this exposure. Feeling more oblige than desire, I bought a half-o.z. of Oaxacan, seedless on sticks, and never returned.

A short time later, Dennis made the headlines. His Big Top was busted big time with a quarter of a million dollars, a hundred keys of grass, four pounds of mushrooms and 3,000 hits of acid. Sweet Dennis was shot and almost killed by a homo-hating cop pal of Dan White. This went down just *before* Dan White went psycho and murdered Milk and Moscone.

#

The important thing for me at this point, was to stay busy. To keep moving. To keep my mind from wandering... I read, I went to movies, I went for exhausting runs in the Park. In my ju-jitsu and tae-kwon-do classes, I surprised sparring opponents with my aggression, until most declined. I worked out until I was drenched with sweat and could barely lift my limbs. Days passed like weeks. I practiced my guitar and singing. I almost called her. Every day.

Instead, I bought a journal at Mendel's Far Out Fabrics and jotted some thoughts. That night, I awoke at three a.m. From my Ariel moment in the Shakespeare Garden, I recollected the song my mother had sang to me: "When the one who left us here, returns for us at last. We are but a moment's sunlight, fading on the grass..." The chorus would prove foretelling. I was inspired and composed some verses:

One Thousand Doves
Your rose-like kiss
and gold embrace
The secret garden of your grace
beckons to your special place
The spiraling aura
of heat and light
play a melody
on lute and lyre
A scent of Shalimar
in the night
After all is said then done
you and only you
are the only one.

CHAPTER 24

"Jack, it's been too long. We've all missed you so much. We're having an entourage reunion at the Sav Saturday." Z.Z. had called.

"No, thanks."

"Please, please, pretty please?"

"I'm too busy."

"All right. I suppose I'll cancel the whole affair."

"I just don't think she…"

"She? She wants you there."

"Oh? All right. I guess I'll swing by."

"Fantasico. Ciao." He hung up.

Saturday night, I stepped from the cab and I looked up at the goldenrod Sav. It looked different now. This was no longer our place, this was again her place. I walked in, and like the very first night, she was at her place at the bar, looking fantastic and surrounded by the entourage. Something was different—Bretta sported a new even-shorter hairstyle. Z.Z. saw me hesitate and he rushed over. As soon as he moved, I saw the young, dark, and handsome man holding Bretta's waist.

Z.Z. greeted me. "Jack. You came."

"I'm just stopping by to say hi." I stared.

"Oh, the new kid—she's rebounding. I'm sure he's just a fling thing," Z.Z. said without conviction. "Lo-ve the lid, so jaunty." He referred to my new charcoal salt-and-pepper Irish tweed cap. We approached the entourage where Bretta saw me, but loudly spoke to Edith, "Alejandro is from Spain. He is the son of Romero the famous matador, and is a *novillo,* training to be a bullfighter himself."

Alejandro was not tall, yet stood very erect in his white button-down shirt and too-tight black trousers. Alejandro did seem an appropriate next choice for her, since she loved Spanish guitar. He spoke almost no English, so Bretta spoke Spanish to him, which I comprendo'ed some-o although I pretendo'ed not, in order to eavesdrop. She told him, "You are exciting to me." And he told her, "Estás muy emocionante para mi, yo no puedo esperar para esta noche."

I must have let slip a glum look, because Baskin' Robin hugged me and whispered, "Bretta almost called you every day, almost." She surprised me by kissing my cheek.

Bretta wore a low-cut, fitted black stretch top with a red shawl, and a long, ruffled red-and-black skirt. Her hair was brushed back, and she looked so good it would start a style in North Beach. Seeing Bretta with him knocked the scab off my heart. Did she really want to see me? Or really see me jealous? If Bretta was trying for that, it worked, but also backfired, because I was trying to act like I didn't care anymore, so she would want me again, which I guess made her try harder to make me jealous, fucking et cetera.

I could see that everyone was a little uncomfortable, as Bretta and I still retained smoldering chemistry, mixed with a test tube of smoldering resentment. We kept glancing at each other, yet she remained on the Spaniard's arm, while Robin kept maneuvering around me. Fingering the Spaniard's dark hair, she proclaimed to Francine, Robin and Edith, "My god, Alejandro's a lovely boy!"

With which they enthusiastically agreed. I had to admit, outside of L.A. Alejandro was one of the best-looking boys I had seen. Benjamin orbited at the perimeter of the entourage, talking geo-global politics as usual.

Edith went over to him. "Benjamin, I have an idea for a political art project. We should talk."

Alejandro bothered me, so I focused on everybody else. Benjamin looked over Edith's head at the Spaniard, also appearing to be bothered by the newcomer. Winston, whom I had never seen with a woman, was with my friend Georgia, which slightly bothered me. Alejandro's presence also bothered Winston, and Winston gave me a sympathetic look. Winston was bothered by Benjamin's hovering, but Benjamin stayed away from Winston. Winston, belying his fun Hawaiian shirt, was apparently already in a rare surly mood, which probably meant that he was crashing. Plus, I saw that Winston was drinking again, which seemed to bother everybody.

Winston kept complimenting, "Bretta, how good you look," while pretending Alejandro wasn't there. Bretta counteracted Winston by over-emphasizing the sexy breathiness of "hand" while she sing-songed, "Ale-jand-ro, Ale-Ale-jand-ro. Isn't that a sexy name?"

Bretta sure bothered me the way she said it. Good thing I came with two plans. I thought if I could pretend hard enough that I was not hurt, I could believe it myself. And, because I wanted to impress her I had a little of everything with me that night. I was a real Rexall—hash, pot, cocaine, MDMA, in a Sucrets box. Even some coke, as the Boston Boys had turned me on to their coke dealer. My plan was to get everybody high and make it all fun like it used to be.

I ordered two tequila shots in tumblers from George and noticed the new lights. The translucent deco fixtures above the bar glowed subtly with a pastel rainbow of colored bulbs. George saw me staring and said, "The owner just did that today. What do you think?"

"Trippy." He nodded in agreement as he situated the drinks in front of me.

I murmured to Winston and Georgia, "You primed for some party favors?" They nodded enthusiastically, so I took them down the No EXIT corridor. We all ate a cap and I hoped it would level Winston out. Winston and Georgia helped me mix in the MDMA powder from four of my capsules into the two shots. We all took a toke of hash. I told Winston, "Robin's really hanging close to me."

"She always has. You've never noticed?" I shrugged. I felt a little badly as I hadn't really given Robin much consideration.

Winston led us out and Georgia hung back to tell me, "Jack, just so you know, I am on duty." She pointed at Winston.

Feeling more confident from the high, I returned and whispered to Bretta, "You like the new lights?"

"Yes, it was my suggestion. The owner consulted with me on the colors. I like what he did."

"Very cool. You want to enhance the colors with some MDMA?"

Her eyes widened and I gave her a shot to share with Alejandro. I gave the other to Edith saying, "Split with one." I found it interesting that Edith immediately shared hers with Z.Z. and not Robert or Benjamin. I gave Robert two caps to share with Benjamin. Robert and Benjamin took them as Robert said, "I'm auditioning for the Rhubarb Revue!" "Never heard of it," Benjamin said. Robert looked hurt. "It's community theatre. In Mill Valley. I think."

Taking Francine aside I asked her, "You want to join in some extra-curricular activities?" She licked her lips close to me. She took my hand as I led her back to the spot, but she diverted us into the ladies room. Francine remained predictably unpredictable as she kept up a stream of chatting as she squatted over an open stall and shame-lessly streamed in front of me. At the mirror, more shamelessly, she brushed her hair back like Bretta's. I gave her a cap. We clinked glasses toasted, she said, Chin chin, as we swallowed and drank. She seemed to expect something more. Despite her appeal, it felt wrong to have sex with my ex's girlfriend. I smiled, unbolted the door, and we headed back to the bar.

Z.Z. became uncharacteristically loaded. "I'm so distraught. My investor for my men's boutique fell through. I probably shouldn't have slept with him."

I pansied, "The little bitch."

He sighed. "You know Alejandro is only nineteen—practically jailbait." Z.Z. surprised me, saying, "He is very cute, but I still think you're hotter."

This was to be a night of surprises. Not the good kind. Finn sauntered in. He nodded to everyone, hugged Bretta, threw back a shot, winked at Georgia. When Bretta choked at introducing Alejandro, Finn gave me an empathetic look, left, and most certainly went back to his stool at the Lost and Found. Just like that.

I hoped the MDMA all worked out with the approximate shar-ing. All this attention from being "the man" gave me a confidence boost. My idea was if everybody had fun in the Sav, I would invite the entourage next weekend to a Pimpernel Party. I didn't feel any-thing yet so I palmed a half-capsule out of my pocket, and washed it down with my tequila grapefruit. Even though the drug had no real taste I did an involuntary head shake and shiver. I felt warm and tin-gly. The lights and colors did seem more vibrant. Oops. I was al-ready coming on. People looked interesting. Baskin' Robin was building an impressive three-story house of cards with red bar coast-ers. In my chemically enhanced state, Bretta's fluid movements oozed sensuality.

Monty, on duty, in a bright red beret stopped by. I said, "You look like one of those Guardian Angels, out crime-patrolling." A Kool dangled from his thin lips. Apparently, he had given up hiding his smoking. Our crazy crew probably drove him to smoke.

"Yeah? Is there a crime in progress?"

"You could say that. I'm glad you're here. We need a straight man for our jokes." Robin's construction site distracted me and I pointed for Monty. "Check Robin out. Hey, I always thought you and Robin might make a good couple. She's like you. She doesn't do drugs either, thank god." I laughed. "With her loveable giddiness, she's high naturally."

Monty looked at me, then her. Robin gave a timid smile. I said, "Giddyup, Robin."

Monty said, "Really? Jesus, Jack." He went to the jukebox. After making a quick round of the entourage, Monty tapped me on the shoulder. "Listen, I'm playing your song. 'Bewitched, Bothered and Bewildered.'"

"Perfect," I said. He motioned me out to the street. At his Yellow cab, he reached a long arm in to turn on the radio. Jazz music filtered out and I dug the idiosyncratic rhythm as I visualized black quarter notes floating in the air. Joni Mitchell's crystalline voice mixed with—howling?

"Nice tune; so strange."

"Mingus. 'The Wolf in the Library.'" Monty lit up another Kool and scowled at me.

I ignored that and moving my head to the beat, told him, "What a cool job, go everywhere, park anywhere, listen to your jazz, get paid, get laid."

He turned on me, "Jack, you're wasted, you're all wasted and you're wasting your lives. Winston corrupted you, now you're corrupting that kid, Alejandro."

He walked away. I retorted, "'All work and no play makes Jack a dull boy.'"

He turned. "What?"

"*The Shining*. The movie? Monty, you have to see it, man. It just opened at the Coronet. Jack Nicholson is the crazy writer." I didn't tell him that Nick and I saw it on MDMA. "Wow, really intense."

"You're the one who's crazy. Go to hell, Jack."

"Monty, take that back!" I stepped toward him, and he said nothing. "You wouldn't be so uptight if you got high once in a while. Why are you afraid to get high? Afraid you might actually enjoy yourself for once and start living? Or afraid you might lose control?"

He rushed at me, his red Guardian Angel-like beret intimidating me into taking a retreating step. I figured he still carried a gun on the job, but he wouldn't know that I was carrying, too. We stood there, facing off, with hard secrets in our pants. He spoke firmly, "Jack, you're the one who's making our friends lose control." He turned his head toward the sky. "Look. It's a full moon. People go weird on a full moon anyway. This is not going to end well tonight."

I looked up. He was right. A beautiful moon glowed. "Relax, Professor. Everything's cool." A tipsy couple came out of the Sav, pointed at the cab. He motioned them to get in.

"Jack, for a cocky know-it-all, you are so damn naive. I've tried to look out for you, but I give up."

"Monty, why the hell do you have so much anger? You have no idea what I've gone through."

Monty wasn't finished. "One more thing. Regarding Winston's blood on the windowsill?" Monty held his cigarette straight up in front of my face, tore it in half, and tossed it into the gutter. "He was a mess. Consider if he did it to himself."

"What?" I stumbled back and could only shake my head no. Monty got in, grabbed the red meter flag, and with significance yanked the flag down, and cut into traffic.

I slipped back into the Sav, shocked. An engaging woman put her hand on my arm. "Are you all right, Jack?"

She wiped my tears away with both of her soft hands. I hadn't realized I was crying. She smelled of cinnamon. I mumbled, "It's a full moon, Cinnamon Girl." She reluctantly let me slip away. I had absolutely no idea who she was.

I went up to Georgia to ask her about Winston, but I knew she maintained professional-client privilege. I fake slurred, "Hiiighh," and went around her to Winston. I tried to see into Winston's eyes, except it was no good—he was too wasted. But, maybe this was the best time. I nudged Winston to come in the back. Under the absinthe-green No EXIT sign, I pulled out my pipe and put in hash. I told him, "You're right, when we're this buzzed on chemicals, smoking really mellows things out." I started, "I been talking to Monty."

"Yeah?"

"He seems to know a lot."

"He acts like he does."

"That's why I call him The Professor. You guys were good friends?"

"Yes. Until Bretta wanted me more."

"That's kind of what I thought."

We smoked. Winston said, "You know, I never wanted to sell wine. I wanted to play my guitar. My folks rejected that part of me.

Why?" He kicked the wall. "I hope they're happy. I haven't seen them in years."

"We have a lot in common, Winston. That's what scares me." I blurted, "I'm worried, man. I was afraid after I got Bretta pregnant, the same thing would happen to me. You know, like happened to you at the Drake."

"What!? Nothing is going to happen to you that you don't do to yourself. You're going to be OK."

"You sure?"

Winston laughed. "Yeah. I'm the fucking expert on personal responsibility and safety. Jack, just cool out. And I don't want to talk about the shit that happened."

He walked away, turned. "I tell you what, my friend, I will sometime."

I felt the touch of apprehension and my mood pivoted and reeled to dark. I knocked the ash from the pipe and hurried back to the bar. I stared, as if for the first time. at the Sav's Persian archways and the deco light fixtures shimmering colorfully, hookah-mystically, HIGH above the bar bathing the bar area patrons in a new otherworldly light. It was evocative of a psychedelic opium-den.

George looked at me and remarked, "It is trippy, huh?"

Bretta's laughter circulated across the bar like a prima ballerina across the grandest stage. My mood swung as high as a trapeze. I felt like I owned the place. This was my bar, Bretta's and my bar, and my friends' bar. No wonder Finn stuck to his regular barstool. That was the way it was. I thought, I love this place! Some people turned around, so I guess I said it out loud.

Alejandro seemed like an OK kid, and I hoped he knew what he was in for. I convinced myself that I was happy that Bretta was happy. Almost. A heightened sensitivity washed over me. I felt soothed, like a hot towel from a Japantown sushi bar was covering my entire body. I stared at the new colors of the lamps. I thought of my nights working the circus's cotton candy concession and how the air-blown, spun, pink strands were now covering my brain with sugar. Confection concession. Our group, my friends, the en-tour-age, the en-tou-rage, the ent-our-age, all seemed so amazing and filled with this—vitality. A rush of sexuality coursed through me. I felt tingly feelers from everyone; mating signals? Francine looked charged with sexual energy and was acting sexier than ever.

I heard the signature laugh-snort, and witnessed Baskin' Robin performing card tricks, somehow, with the cardboard coasters. Others gathered around her and she was her own center of attention. Or maybe she was a center and I never noticed before. Z.Z. announced Robin's coaster tricks like an emcee. She looked especially attractive tonight, so sugary and silly, her earth-toned dress reminiscent of butterscotch and pistachio. I visualized her as a 31 Flavors ice cream cone. Filled with chocolate. I thought, if I was candy-flipping on L, I probably would lick her to make sure. Winston explained to Georgia the different properties between green, red leaf, butter and Romaine lettuces. So many thoughts of food. Maybe I was hungry?

I looked to the bar mirror and reflected that my normally hyper mind was now reflecting like Playland's funhouse mirrors in *The Lady from Shanghai*. Georgia winked at me. I pointed to George and back again to Georgia. "George, Georgia—Georgia, George." They smiled at one another. The Love Drug was taking over. Bretta glowed with a galactic radiance that moved everyone. This radiance, or aura, I experienced my first night at Bretta's flat, Robin had described on boy's night out. I should talk to Robin about that. Strange thing was—I got no reading from the Spanish kid.

"Bret-taaa. Brettaaa." She looked at me with laughing eyes. "Have I told you how much I love your name? It's a beautiful name. It's true what you said our first night here."

With a stoned look she asked, "Whaa-at?"

"It seems so long ago, but what was it, seven months? You said, 'we're in a Garden of Earthly Delights.'"

"Ah, I remember." Her succulent lips with her sexy mole pulled me in.

Francine's intense energy invaded our space and she gave Bretta and me an annoyed look. She announced, "I'm doing modeling now."

Our group looked up in slow motion. "Modeling what? Modeling clay?" Z.Z. joked.

"I have been doing NUDE modeling for artists." That got everyone's attention. She struck a pose, draping herself back toward the bar and Alejandro. Her audience primed, she revealed, "One client I posed for, his work is very abstract. This artist, posed me," she lifted her chin, "and tied a paintbrush to his cock." Gasps and snickers sounded. "As he painted, his hard-on raised up and down, and up and all around, the canvas that is. I was paid extra for that."

"I bet." The voice from down the bar slurred. "Miss, could I get your card?" In a moment Francine was surrounded by men. The sexual tension in the Sav was substantial.

About midnight, the spring was pulled back a little too far, the ball careened, and the flippers really hit the group. Francine had a bare thigh hiked up to her cocktail-glass-shaped breasts, with a high heel resting on another barstool. Benjamin, heavy with a flirtatious monologue, came on to her with some success, until her claws came out. He shrank. Francine was Francine. She reveled in being a world-class cock tease.

A drunken Winston took his new antipathy toward Alejandro, out on Benjamin, and told him, "Why don't you just go away, *Benja-minnie*? Don't you know when you've worn out your welcome, Benjaminnie?"

Georgia said, "Hush, Winston."

Others shushed her, because they were glad someone was finally telling Benjamin off. Winston continued with, "You're fucking obnoxious. Do you think Francine, or Bretta, or any of us want you around all the time with your depressing political commentary? Why don't you go stalk and somewhere else?"

Benjamin pretended to smile, stating the obvious, "Come on, Winston, you're drunk."

Robin spoke up. "Hey now, don't forget our friendships."

Winston said with sarcasm, "Well, thank god, at least I still have that."

I motioned my head to Bretta and Alejandro and then to the back. We moved fast. At the absinthe-green No EXIT, I stopped. The two regarded my pockets expectantly. Winston's voice boomed through the wall: "What do you add to the party, Benjie? Not a goddamn thing."

I swallowed. I finally did it. I pushed the bar on the forbidden door. I swept us through No EXIT.

CHAPTER 25

The three of us russh-hed out, quickly feeling the body ruuussh of the MDMA in the changed street environment, and down Grant Avenue. I held up at the large Sherwin-Williams Paints red-and-blue neon sign hanging above the sidewalk. I had seen it numerous times. Now, the blue paint can seemed to hover and spill intense-neon red paint over the earth. As we gazed I told Bretta, "Your art will soon be covering the earth."

She laughed, and they followed me, scurrying around the corner. I told Bretta, "Let's show AlejandrO, the flamencO…" She continued my thought, "…at the Old Spaghetti-O, Factory that is." We giggled. We were still in tune. Striding up the hill, I pointed out the full moon. "No wonder there's such weird energy."

We charged into the restaurant's big iron-gated walkway. The live music drew us in with the irresistible suction of a Star-Trek-like aural tractor beam. The Old Spaghetti Factory was a large, open-beam space with broken-string guitars and worn wooden chairs hung from ceiling rafters. Odors of pasta and garlic and tomato aromas aroused my hunger. Both Bretta and I said simultaneously, "This is perfect." Bullfight posters adorned the brick walls, and Alejandro exclaimed, "¡Conozco estos hombres!"

In a few steps, we were cocooned in the smaller brick-walled front annex amid the excitement of a Flamenco performance. The music filled me, as if my entire body were an auditory organ. A spot at the bar parted as if we were charmed. We melded into the bar, saw sangria fruit floating, and I ordered a pitcher of sangria in what felt like slow motion. We watched the flamenco as Bretta moved with the sensuousness that first attracted me to her. The main dancer was middle-aged, strong and striking with a proud carriage in her flowing, frilly red dress, tightly-pulled-back hair, large hoop earrings. Her fan movements were crisp yet flirtatious. A young dancer handclapped, awaiting her turn. Alejandro was delighted and said with reverence, "El baile flamenco!"

Being this high, in the less-familiar location, away from our friends, felt different. I liked it. It gave a perfect spin to my stone. Bretta and I gave each other the conspiratorial eyes and knowing grins that people give one another when they have just gotten really high together, and are trying to mix with normal people. "And you may see me tonight with an illegal smile..." as the song goes.

Bretta came close and explained to me, "The *toque* is the guitar, the *cante* is the singing, and *palmas* are the handclaps. The dancers are considered best over age thirty, mature and with more *duende*, or soul." She was about to say something else, but heard Robin's chirpy voice, "Hey, there you are."

Feeling expansive, I spontaneously asked Robin, "You're a Sagittarius, aren't you?" Robin perked at my interest, and replied, "Yes, Jack, how did you know?" She wasn't the classic Sag like my late Sag, but Robin was blunt, gullible, optimistic, and far-out, for sure.

Unfortunately, the rest of entourage had managed to stalk us, and Z.Z. and Francine and everybody carried on, like we hadn't tried to escape. Benjamin trailed in, beaten down but still around. He didn't seem very comfortable with the high and ignored the performance. I didn't see Winston.

I told him, "Benjamin, just go with the flow and watch the show. Don't fight it." I felt sorry for him and poured him a glass of sangria. Even though he made more money than I did writing for the paper, he never bought when it was time for his round. I asked him loudly over the music, "Why is your neck so red?" and he rubbed it and shrugged. I asked him, "Where's Winston?"

"Winston?" Benjamin looked at me angrily. "Winston's a dick."

I only uncovered later what had transpired between them. I wanted to talk to Bretta about the flamenco, but Benjamin kept whining to me. I tried to ignore him, until he said, "I was right, you were not meant to be the man to tame her."

He pointed to Alejandro and walked away without thanking me for the drink. Benjamin was the dick. I had thought Edith was kind of checking out Benjamin, but when he walked away, she still looked in my direction. Robert was eyeing Edith. Edith headed over to stand uncomfortably close to me. I scanned the crowd, yearning that Jan Kerouac ("like her dad, only cuter") might have returned, to be my new soul mate. Jack and Jan, together again. The applause clued me that the song had ended. The younger dancer took her position and a new tune began. It was about that time that our mood elevators must have hit the top floor. I was physically and emotionally drawn into the flamenco. This truly was the blues of the Gypsies and I wished Winston were here to enjoy it.

Flamenco blues filled with flaming passion—opera, ballet and symphony all at once. Clicking, ticking, tapping. Stomping, stamping, handclapping. The anguished cries and urgent pleas of the singer—of passions, lost and won—the vocal pitch descending from high to low in lamentations, a shouting, quivering voice. By God they could play and dance. Polyrhythmic clapping, spicy caliente, hot fast, but faster, faster, FASTER...slow, slower, SLOW, and fast again, guitar toques plucking, singer vibrato wavering, voice cracking, hearts aching, strings breaking, dance shoes flying.

The wrenching sounds, the interplay between the singer, dancers and guitarists—the strumming, picking, polyrhythmic clapping, the long dresses lifting and revealing of tight calves, the dancers' serpentine hands and staccato whirlwind of footwork. I was getting turned on. Flamenco was like sex standing up.

We all watched the brightly dressed dancers twirl and prance to peaks and valleys, and build up before the big finish. I noticed that Francine was not watching the dancers. She stared, entranced at Bretta like she wanted to be her, or—it flashed on me—even be with her. She had not been looking at Alejandro earlier—she was winkling eyes at Bretta. Francine always attracted, then rejected, men in the bars, like earlier tonight. Francine had been the one who said, Hey, let's go to that dyke bar. That's right, Francine was very curious about the porno girls—Are they nymphos? Well. Maybe Monty was right. I am naïve, sometimes. I looked around, expecting the rest of the entourage to realize Francine's secret at the same time, too. But they didn't.

I looked at Francine in a new light. In fact, she was literally standing in a glowing ring of an overhead light, bringing attention to herself. It was working. A shorthaired platinum blonde, Annie-Lennox-toughly-pleasing, in leather jacket and skirt, with revealed red-lace bra, swayed next to Francine and spoke in her ear.

Bretta came over to me, edging out Edith, and stood alluringly close. She touched me, the touch that only true lovers can give, of intimate knowledge. She was feeling it, too. She exclaimed, "I have to talk to that dancer. She's so good. I need to meet her."

Behind Bretta, Francine and her new friend still distracted me. Leather-Lennox kissed Francine's ear. Francine pulled back and I thought, Uh oh, somebody is going to get punched, but next thing I knew, they were kissing.

Bretta intentionally dance-rubbed against me, and we connected with a warm, tingly, body-rushing sensation. Her breasts trembled against me. I wanted to wrap my arms around her delicacy and melt into her bosom once more. She said loudly, "Jack. Jack, I want to tell you something."

The music and performance had ended just as she said, still a little loudly, over the now momentarily quiet room, "Jack, my darling, I love you, you know."

The sun came from behind a cloud. I melted. Applause and yells filled the air. I felt others looking at us—a movie moment. The moment was actually the performers taking a break. Applause. Taped flamenco music squealed on. With the opening of the romantic classic "Malaguena." Bretta and I locked eyes, I floated into her and we were dancing. Almost.

Alejandro called, "Vamos a bailar!" and grabbed Bretta. With her look lingering at me he promenaded my love to the middle of the floor. I was insulted. Bretta had yet to dance publicly with me and here she was center ring with the newcomer. I noticed Robin watching my expressions.

Bretta used her red shawl in her flowing-and-posing Isadora Duncan movements, juxtaposed with rhythmic foot stamping. Soon the two worked up to flamenco point-and-counter-point moves and the room tuned in with hands clapping, knuckles rapping and wine glasses banging on tables, while some sway-danced along. When the pair partnered their moves, they looked magnetic, with the Spaniard in his white shirt, and she with red shawl flowing, with her hair and her skirt flying. Alejandro, striking and virile, with all the women's eyes on him, grasped Bretta's red shawl and used it as a cape as they performed a mock bullfight. His moves made me believe he *was* a bullfighter and that Bretta was a better dancer than the women on stage. Bretta made eye contact with me briefly, enough for me to feel better about her show.

A rapt audience packed a semicircle around the dancers. Bretta would occasionally undulate in a provocative belly-dance move that was an obvious hit with the gasping men. Francine and leather girl were keeping the rhythm with co-joined dance moves. Alejandro wrapped the red shawl around Bretta as they built up to their climax. People chanted "¡Olé!," including the returning performers who joined in, clicking castanets, the guitarist playing along for them, the singer vocalizing, until the room's passionate urgency intensified to another level.

"Bretta moves so beautifully," Robin enthused.

Her remark made me momentarily intensely jealous, and consequently completely depressed. Robin shot me a concerned look. My brain seemed to bounce around like a pinball. I thought, Why couldn't Bretta do what she wanted? It's not like we were married. If women were all over me the way men were her, I'd probably fuck around, too. I knew I was really high and I felt unexpectedly happy despite the past lows of the high.

I suddenly felt relieved. Relieved that I didn't have to be in the main show with Bretta, that I didn't have to perform, that I didn't have to guard her from other men any longer, and other men from her. What a night of revelations. What a night! I was relieved to be in the secondary ring. Except for Robin politely hovering at my side, and Z.Z. holding on Edith for support and Edith holding onto me for support, I could just relax and enjoy myself and have a quiet drink. Francine and Leather-Lennox were now performing a suggestive mirror dance under the light. The sizzling pair matched each other's thrusting and grinding moves in their third ring of turned-on spectators to this sensual bullfight. The crowd still chanting, "Ole! OLE! O-LE!!"

That's when all hell broke loose.

Damned Benjamin launched his comeback in our little circus's center ring. He charged up to Alejandro and Bretta and yelled, "Chinga tu madre!" to Alejandro and expertly front-kicked him in the gut. Alejandro toppled over the tables and curved-back chairs to the sawdust floor as wine glasses spilled and broke, dripping dark wine, splattering Alejandro's white shirt, making him look gored and bloody. Gasps, then everyone paralyzed.

Several thoughts raced through my fevered brow: Not my problem. I am free to stay out of it. I should do something. I can't get into *another* bar fight. Fighting on MDMA is probably not a great idea. My gun will probably fall out of my pants. The Professor is right, tonight is not going to end well. Yet, I moved through the seemingly freeze-tagged bodies.

Benjamin, himself stunned that not a creature was stirring, grinned and moved in. The Spanish kid raised his head. Benjamin pulled his left back to finger-spear the downed kid in the throat, potentially killing him. I leapt between them. Benjamin made a Bruce Lee warning sound.

"Benjamin, you big baboon!" Bretta yelled.

"No, don't hurt her!" Z.Z. shrilled. I wondered who Z.Z. actually meant?

Benjamin now focused on Bretta. Benjamin moved to her, his hands ready to hug or hurt? She dramatically spread her shawl-draped arms high.

"You, the s-sorceress-s." Benjamin stuttered. "No, a Siren. A S-siren! You drive men mad and lure them to sh-shipwreck shores!"

Benjamin was being absurd, although I had to admit, he was right on. I had to end this without hurting him. "Come on, that's enough." I murmured, holding his arm.

He struck upwards to my nose with a claw-formed hand, in a palm-strike. In theory, this strike would break my nose, driving the cartilage shards into my brain, killing me. I barely managed to tilt my head down and as the ball of his palm smacked my forehead, a snap cracked. I saw stars and dropped to my knees. He winced in pain, holding his hand, so I knew he had broken his wrist, not my head. I was totally vulnerable so I made a risky move. As Benjamin shifted his feet to kick me in the face, I grabbed the fronts of his pants cuffs with each hand and yanked up as I bounded up.

In slow motion Benjamin's legs went into the air and he went down hard WHAM flat on his back and head. He lay still as death, not breathing.

Suddenly he gasped, sobbed, pleaded, "Bretta, b-but I love you. I LOVE YOU!" Bretta backed away. Everything hyped up now. Everybody was yelling. Z.Z. was still shrieking. A big Italian leg-breaker bouncer pulled Benjamin up by his collar and the owner yelled, "If you punks wanna' fight, go over to the Mabuhay!"

In the excitement I rushed Bretta and Alejandro away from the entourage and outside the big iron gate to the sidewalk. Alejandro was breathing hard and bleeding a bit from some cuts, but otherwise OK. Bretta looked at me close in the face and she sighed, "Thank God for you, Jack."

Alejandro and I both rubbed our cabezas, both with headache from our head bangers. We needed to get further away from everybody. "Broadway," I said.

We hurried from the dark comfortable familiarity of Grant Avenue for the tawdry touristy end of North Beach on a late Saturday night. As it turned out, it was more—Go ahead, Bambi, cut right across the meadow.

CHAPTER 26

The Condor club displayed the gigantic marquee cartoon of Carol Doda with her own Twin Peaks—44Ds in flashing lights. The Condor, at the crossroads of Broadway and Columbus, was the gateway to the rest—Big Als, Roaring 20s, the new Hungry I, and more. Barkers and strippers stood in doorways, hawking their performers—techniques derived from the circus sideshows. The Broadway strip clubs' garish lights and neon made the Cover the Earth sign look like a toy. If little Italian Pinocchio aspired to turn his Woody into a real toy, North Beach's Broadway was certainly Pleasure Island.

Bretta bought Alejandro an "I Left My (heart symbol) in SF" tee shirt at a tourist shop and he trash-binned his stained and bloody one. The new shirt was bright yellow-gold and tight enough to reveal his physique. We continued down Columbus Avenue. As the street's namesake Christopher Columbus, we too, were bravely exploring. Bretta and I had individually navigated here before, but not this mind-altered. We ducked in the tiny alcove alley to the dimly lit Specs bar with its Bohemian-eccentric clientele and boxy walls covered in travel mementos and faded signs. I waved off both the ever-wandering handwriting-analysis crone and the pesky rose-peddler lady. I wanted to check out something Monty had told me. By the men's room, I led them up the secret back narrow stairway, through a curtained door and lo and behold—there were naked women and tits onstage before us. We were in the Hungry I strip club. Even though there was the typical club two-drink minimum per person, I negotiated with the waitress. "Look, we're just going to be here five minutes, to show our friend. Just bring one margarita, all right?"

We shared the weak, sugary drink, but it was still such a rip off that I ripped off them. I concealed the stemware when we left through the front door. We were back in the lights on Broadway. On the marquee sign across the street was an enormous green snake and a bright-red apple. It was in the Garden of Eden club, advertising "Live, nude, erotic Hot Adam & Eve Action."

"There's that Garden again," I said. "I'm starving. Maybe we can get something to eat at Enrico's."

"Ooh, yes, I used to be a hostess these. I bet I can get a complimentary cocktail."

A peculiar alteration comes over me. I am still really high but I have adjusted and am really flowing now. Something. I sense—danger? but can't put my finger on. Fuck it. I feel bullet-proof. Bretta is looking at me, "Jack?"

"Come on." I lead them down Broadway again. "Afterward, we should get White Nun nightcaps at Tosca Café."

"Alejandro, vas a amar la Monja Blanca."

We stop at the Kearny intersection to watch the latest generation of lost souls—the Troll-Dolled, safety-pinned, purple-haired punks and their attitudes—tromping in their Doc Martens, heading to The Mabuhay Gardens, the notorious punk live music hall. As we cross to Enrico's, I say, "So many bars, so little brain cells."

Bretta declares, "We simply must go to El Matador club. Georgia told Winston and me that one of the only American bullfighters, Barnaby Conrad, who wrote the novel *Matador* opened the club. It's perfect for Alejandro."

I protest, "I'm not sure I feel like bullfighting tonight. Let's stick with the plan." After putting Alejandro in his briar patch for the flamenco I do not want to compete with that machismo again. Alejandro becomes excited at the Matador name and that settles it for Bretta. We approach El Matador and look in the windows. It does look perfect—for them. Spanish music drifted through the open door.

Alejandro moans, "Tengo delor me cabeza," so I say, "I bet, poor guy—yo consego, momento." I am so stoned I am forgetting I am pretending to not knowing much espanol. Whoa, really stoned syntax. Just a ways down is a liquor store. I suggest, "Let's get Alejandro some aspirin first." I usher them along as I don't want them to get a head start on me at El Matador. Bretta and Alejandro wait out in front of the store.

The tired clerk at the counter looks like all other tired clerks I've ever seen at counters across America. Resigned to being a tired clerk, resigned that some night some asshole will come in with a gun. I startle, realizing that I am some asshole with a gun. The fluorescent lights make my mind flicker. I see my pinkish visage in a mirror. Jesus, I look high. Is this only through my kaleidoscope eyes, or everyone's eyes?

I see why Monty called the place, "the dirty liquor store," with
its porno, dildos, booze, and milk of course. Back in the racks are
dirty magazines. I don't like them although I feel compelled to peek.
My uncle used to make me look at them with him. On the cover of
one of the Dominatrix mags, a man in handcuffs kneels while a
leather-clad bitch with a cop cap and baton stands above him. I give
a snort that it's supposed to turn me on. A drink in my hand feels so
normal I don't think much about my margarita glass until the clerk
eyes it askance but doesn't say anything. I figure I'll ditch it at El
Matador. I buy the Anacin tin and return to my friends.

We step through the open door and into another world. El Matador looks and feels like we traveled back in time and space to old
Spain. El Matador is filled with Spanish and bullfighter regalia—
framed black-and-white bullfight photos, a long red *muleta* or cape,
posters, wine skins, swords, lances, barbed *banderillas*, the odd
shaped black *montera* hats. Deo has described all this to me. And unbelievably, there it is. On a blue-velvet-faced wooden plaque,
mounted on the wall is an immense and very real, pitch-black stuffed
bull head, with broad skull, intimidating hooked horns and giant
shiny-black eyes. A man would have to be a real stud to face that animal alone in a dusty ring. Alejandro gives a cry of, "Toro, huhuh,
huhuh!" and performs a little bowing faux-pass to the bull.

The anachronisms are the dozen and a half, semi-seedy patrons
and the two active pool tables. I step up to the dark polished bar on
the right, about to order drinks for the aspirin. The bartender looks
vaguely familiar. Bretta and Alejandro stand near the door, taking it
all in. Bretta glows, the kid looking uneasy, perhaps his cabeza, perhaps because he is underage. Whatever, I feel great, really in charge,
totally comfortable now with just being myself. A lovely dark-
haired, Hispanic beauty sits alone at the bar and makes eye contact
with me. I'm tantalized and think, Three's a crowd, but four... I'm
pleased that Bretta is observing my interaction with the *senorita
bonita*. Within this setting, I imagine that I am a dashing literary figure in Pamplona. The bartender looks my way. I'm now the center of
attention. The stage is set for sweeping this Iberian beauty off her
feet, and showing Bretta that I, Romeo—no, Don Juan—loves on.

I close in on my romantic conquest when she is blotted out by a
dark blue-suited figure. Her soon to be cuckolded lover? No, a big,
ugly bull cop looms in front of me. The fuzz says, "Evening, Wilson," to the bartender, but for some reason the cop stares right at me

with big, dark, animal eyes above his bushy mustached snout. I realize I still have my pilfered margarita glass in my hand, and that my touted instinct has gone limp. I nonchalantly set the glass on the bar. The bull's snout zeroes in on the glass, which I now notice is clearly labeled, "Garden of Eden."

The bull cop heads a charge straight for me. I figure he'll just have me dump what little cheap-boozed Margarita foam remains and leave it with Wilson. Instead he declares, "I saw you walk in with that drink. You're under arrest for open container and theft."

What? Open container was street legal in this town in a paper bag, but I was in a bar for chrisakes. I didn't think it was a federal case here. I wonder if the Garden of Eden had called the cops or what? The bull snatches my glass and grabs the back of my arm with his right hand and shoves me toward the door. This causes a commotion in the crowd with some pool players heckling, "That's not right, you pig" and "What a bullshit bust."

This is very bad. I feel so stupid. This is now my third lame arrest. Maybe fourth. I can't remember. I see my friends' wide-eyed faces, they see me and the cop, and we all know I'm fucked because I'm high as a kite and holding all sorts of drugs. What they don't know is that I am still packing a piece.

The bull cop holds onto my elbow very tight and is just way too close to me and he stinks of pork and doughnuts and sweat and smoke like my fucking uncle and the handcuff case on his belt is smashing into me, and his dangling billy club is poking my ass and I feel like the pig is on me suffocating me forcing me...

This moment is one of those slow-motion, oh-shit moments.

The bull is stupidly holding my margarita glass in his other hand, for evidence I guess, which renders him one armed. Just before we hit the door, I look to the bartender. Wilson. That's who he is, the gambler on the train! I say, "Wilson Harris, tell your wife to take your gambling money and come bail me out," which distracts the bull for a second. I do a ju-jitsu move, arm straight up and round over his beefy arm to break his hold, and, instead of capturing his arm, with one smooth motion I back-fist him in his ugly mustached snout. If he wasn't a pig, I would've roundhouse kicked him in his left elbow to disable his gun hand, and maybe more, although what I did was so easy—I just bolt.

I race by my stunned friends, Alejandro looks terrified and jumps behind Bretta, who waves her red scarf, I assume to distract the cop. I give them the *shhh*-sign to my lips and I'm out the door with the bull stomping after me. A cheer erupts from the pool players and an "¡Olé!" from my senorita at the bar. I have a moment of elation before I hear stemware break on the sidewalk, so I know he's dropped "Exhibit A" and is going for his gun. He yells through his bleeding lips, "Stop! Halt! Or I'll shoot!" which is the signal for fleeing criminals to start weaving erratically, so I do, feeling that I had a bull's eye on my back, but also concerned that the shot would drop some innocent bystander. I consider darting up the steep alley steps toward Telegraph Hill, easily winding the cop, but figure a squad car could beat me. I race around past the strip clubs and barkers, diagonally cutting across the four lanes of Columbus Avenue traffic, brakes squealing in near misses. Thinking I hear stampeding footsteps behind me, I cut left. I head toward Club Fugazi's *Beach Blanket Babylon* to maybe mix with the crowd, but there is nobody on the sidewalk. Surreally, I hear live jazz saxophone riffs gliding toward me and I hope this is just a bad dream. The notes come from Monty's favorite club, Keystone Corner, and I attempt to materialize him in his red Guardian Angel beret and Yellow getaway car. I finally notice three parked cop cars, and seeing one moving, I totally freak out, thinking they have me. I realize I fucked up and have run right to the fucking Central Police Station. The Keystone Cops themselves.

I already have this assault and battery rap, so I could do some real time for assault on an officer, resisting arrest, multiple possession and multiple "intent to distribute" charges, and sundry weapons charges. I wonder how many are felonies and how many are just misdemeanors. Whatever it is equals serious time for me. I know now the cop cars are there, independent of me, so I slow to a fast walk. I pull stuff out of my pockets and start tossing shit under parked cars. Lighter, pipe, baggie, box. Stuff is flying. I duck into the alley to double back on the dingy, red-walled, cobblestoned, narrow lane past toppled trashcans. I glance over my shoulder and see some dark shapes lurch toward me and my heart pounds and I glance again and I see horns, and I flash on the running of the bulls, and I feel like I'm about to be trampled. I yank the gun from my waistband, stop and turn in the dinge, hold the gun up in both hands, and fire. BOOM. Sparks fly from the muzzle. There is a yelp. With horror, I see it is just a couple of huge stray dogs with restaurant-size rib bones in their muzzles, staring at a very frightened and half-crazed man. They drop their bones and run the other way with yelps and whimpers.

Jesus. I realize how high I must be. I have gotten away and I shoot off my gun to attract attention? I feel as dumb as Lee Harvey Oswald. I stick the piece under a dumpster, strip off my shirt and stuff it in after, walk out back to Broadway in my tee shirt, hail a cab, jump in, duck down and tell the cabbie to, "Drive, because there's some asshole running after me!" which was true. We shoot right into the Broadway Tunnel, swerving, with the cabbie's eyes too often in the rearview mirror.

I have the driver drop me off a few blocks from my house, just in case. He was probably suspicious, but cabbies are cool, they don't want any trouble. I run to my house, and see no surveillance, so I go up and bag my drug collection, hide it in places I had already figured out: behind a loose board on the roof—recollecting that time when Bretta was not yet my lover and we almost had sex up here—and in the back-garbage area, hoping my apartment manager doesn't wake up. I am hoping to God my friends haven't squealed. The thought gives me needed comedic relief, thinking that Alejandro, the brave bullfighter, when he was charged, absurdly hid behind a woman's red cape.

Grabbing a sweater, peanut butter jar, bread, a beer and the cash, I go across Frederick Street to Kezar Stadium lot. I stash the cash and sit down on a curb stop next to a big truck to watch my residence. My home may not be Houdini's fake mansion, but it is better than "850," the County lockup. This could be the last time I see it for a while. I pop the beer.

And I wait. I hope that the Boston Boys aren't holding, in case the search spreads. After nearly an hour, I figure I am in the clear. I walk to Nick's shared flat on Central. I spend the night on the couch next to the yellow-painted upright piano. It is torture. I am wired and I am tired. I am still hungry. All I wanted was for everyone to have a good time. And it had all gone to hell.

#

I couldn't sleep, so at 5:30 in the morning I walked up the steep hill of Buena Vista East in the street-lit dark. The full moon was down, the orb's ebb and flow of unpredictable sorcery complete. Monty had been right. Or had jinxed us. I looked up at the imposing former Sanatorium, now used as apartments, where Hitchcock's lovesick Scottie was treated. Did the current residents know of the madness once circling within their walls?

On my right, rose the dark knob of the park, that during the day, swarmed with dozens of men in the bushes having random anonymous quick drug-like jolts of jism-filled meaningless emotionless sex. Why? Because they could—as easily as taking a piss.

I trekked up to Corona Heights. Breathing hard and using a lighter's light, I clambered up the terra cotta rock cliff, which was dangerous in daylight, and even more so under my stressful circumstances and the state of a drug hangover mind. I didn't give a damn. I wanted to watch the sunrise. If this cop thing went bad, it could go very, very bad. The heavy bass beat of Led Zeppelin's "Dazed and Confused" rolled through my mind. With only the lights from the City and East Bay below, I sat in the cold damp air and tried not to think of Bretta in bed, snuggled warm and cozy with Alejandro. This was the bed I helped her move, into the room I chose, with the Pendleton blanket I gave her, the two making love—high on the love drug I gave them. The thought of all this was killing me. *Wanted a woman, never bargained for you…*

On the cliff. My mind was racing. I squinted over the blackness of the right side. I knew from previous visits it was a sheer drop of maybe thirty feet. I dropped a stone and counted to three before it skittered at the bottom, but I couldn't remember what the formula was. I wondered if it was an adequate distance if one wanted to do it. It would be better if one landed headfirst like a dive, to be sure. *Soul of a woman was created below.* I shivered. I wished I had my gun with me. I felt naked without it now.

The sky lit up. Gradually as dawn came, a false start of blue appeared far across the Bay in Oakland. Stripes of red paint. Yellow light. Creamy orange. The girl. The girl at the church cemetery. Once again, I regretted not speaking to her. I should have. I have done weirder things. Like last night, and well, climbing here. Seeing the forlorn girl—was not only reminiscent of Ariel's service, but was like seeing me—at my daddy's funeral, at the same church where he had pulled the trigger with my shotgun. The sad Carlotta of *Vertigo*. I thought about the lovely, sad girl when the bells tolled at the unknown funeral and now I allowed myself to realize why it was such a haunting image. Not only did she look similar to my Ariel, and remind me of *her* service, but…

I thought of the John Lennon song that begins with the bells tolling. It was about his parents. My mind wandered in circles. I wished now I would have stopped and comforted the girl. Why not,

I've done weirder things. Maybe *she* was my soul mate. I wondered whom she had lost. I reconsidered. It is not so much who, but what— the love, the experiences, the memories that you would have had with that person. Would I prefer my senses be dulled? My heart hardened? My emotions stifled?

My sadness. My betrayal. My abandonment. My father. How I imagined he must have felt. How I felt when I saw Bretta with Alejandro last night. *Sweet little baby, I want you again.* I didn't have to imagine. I knew.

#

The Phillips 66 owner, for whom Mother ruined my life, turned out to be a friend of Uncle. He stayed a safe distance away from Mother for a time. Even though most folks learned of the affair, they still would feign distant civility, to keep up appearances in the small town and all.

After my mother and I moved into the mansion, Uncle was very nice to me. Publicly, he gave me Snickers bars, Hardy Boy mysteries, an Aurora HO racecar set, and a Zebco rod and reel. In private, he asked me, "You get something from someone you're supposed to give something back. That makes sense, right, Jackie? Didn't your old man teach you anything? You have no money so you can't buy me a present. I've opened my home to you and given you so much. Don't you want to give me something? You can only give what you have. I'll come up to your room tonight and we'll talk about it."

I soon wished Daddy had at least shot my uncle. I don't know. My uncle told me, "Relax, Jackie, and you will enjoy it."

I didn't enjoy it. He tied me to my bedposts with his belts. He made me suck him and he stuck a hard, green apple in my mouth to stifle the sounds while he took me. Later he'd threaten, "I could be making your Mama pay me back like this, or worse. Would you have your Mama bent over paying me back? No, I didn't think so. Screaming or telling anyone about this is very dangerous. Your poor Auntie fell bang, bang, bang all the way down those stairs, breaking bone after bone, bang, bang, bang."

I couldn't relax. I still struggled. So, he experimented, using props that were so commonplace that I could have proved nothing, even if I dared. The Hustler magazines, the mousetraps, the necktie he slip knotted around my... all so I would get excited, get aroused— to start wanting the release—the sick, sick fuck. Once I was hard, he knew he had me. I wouldn't struggle as much when he bent me over.

He made me repeat phrases like, "I'm a dirty boy, and, I deserve what you do to me." He did reach-arounds. Sometimes for variety, he would put women's underwear on me. I tried to distract myself. I tried counting backwards from one hundred. I tried counting backwards from one thousand. I tried counting forward from one hundred and backwards from one thousand simultaneously. I tried not to get hard, I tried not to cum, I tried not to—take any pleasure from it, not to enjoy any of it, but he was right. I quit fighting. If I resisted and tightened my muscles, it would hurt worse. Don't you understand I had to let him in? I had to relax and give in. That was the worst. I gave in. I was not strong enough. I felt guilty. It's the thoughts that count.

Until that one dark night, after our circus trip, I found out the truth. I heard the chopping sound, I crept to eavesdrop at the dining room sliding doors. I heard his hard laugh. I crawled on my belly to look through the crack between the doors. My uncle stood in front of the fireplace, chopping kindling with a hatchet. Mother sat in a chair at the long table. With a gentle voice Uncle instructed Mother to do something. She was agitated yet stayed quiet. He wiped the hatchet on his pants and dipped his knife into a little plastic bag on the mantel. He put a line of brown powder on the side of the sharp blade. He raised the hatchet to the front of her beautiful face. He taunted her in his fake British accent, "Right between the eyes, where your beauty…lies." He leaned in. "My sister, tell me again what our arrangement is."

She stared at the powder more than the blade inches from her nose. She answered, "Jack and I can live for free in your mansion. And you take care of us."

"Like I always have."

"Like you always have."

"And?" Mother doesn't speak. "And?" Still nothing. Uncle lifted a lock of a lustrous hair from mother's head and held it in front of her eyes. He sliced it with the hatchet. "You do like Jackie's boy bits intact, don't you?"

"Yes. Yes. And, and, Jack is yours. To do what you want."

Uncle leaned in close and kissed my mother on the mouth as she shivered. I must have made a noise, because Uncle looked right at the doors. He looked at eye level and did not see me. I tried to unbend the big bent nail. I thought I could stab him in the heart. But my weak hands bent and bled. Uncle relaxed. "Right. We are now clear.

You will now say goodbye to Jack, and tell him you're leaving for a few days."

She held a nostril and bravely sniffed the powder from the proffered blade. I was so frightened I considered hiding, or running, but I just sneaked back up to my room. Shortly, Mother came up. She acted dazed and seemed to be putting on a happy face. She looked at me with the prettiest but saddest hazel eyes I have ever seen.

"I'm so sorry, sweetie," she told me. "I have to go on a little trip with my friend." Meaning the Phillips 66 man. "We're driving down to the Ozarks." She whispered, conspiratorial and intimate, "You be strong for me, just a little longer. I'll get us away from here soon. You have to buy me a little more time, my Jack."

She tried to kiss me, but I pulled away. I did not give her the stuffed lion. When she left, my bedroom door rattled and locked from the outside. To me, that sound was like a snake ready to strike. I heard Mother's Bug putt away.

In the middle of that dark night, my door banged open. A man entered, followed by a woman. Mother and her boyfriend were coming to rescue me! The man lit two candles. The light flickered. The man was my uncle. He wore a top hat and tails like the circus ringmaster. He held a whip. The woman was a young, big-haired floozy. She stumbled toward me. She had aging hooker heavy makeup and over-applied clown-red lipstick. The floozy reeked of "Evening in Paris," which I recognized because Mother occasionally dabbled it. Uncle must have brought home the floozy from the tavern. They were both very drunk.

"The circus got me all hot and bothered, Jack," Uncle said. "How about you? What did you think about that knife-throwing gal? Great legs, huh?" He looked at the floozy's legs. "Not as nice as these, though." Beneath the mini-skirt she wore fishnet stockings. "Jackie, you're a big girl now. Drink some Rum and Cherry Coke with us." We all had drinks. I could barely taste any Coke. When he put down his cigar, I knew it was coming. "Let's have some fun, what do you say?" The floozy stripped down to bra, panties and gartered fishnets. They dressed me in her skirt and wig and applied makeup up to my face. They stood me on a short stool and tied my hands to the footposts with me facing the bed. I jumped as Uncle made a trial crack with his whip. I yelped when the whip slashed my rear.

"That's a nice stripe. I'm pretty good with this thing." Uncle fingered the stripe. "Jacqueline" is very sexy. I may just take her with me on my next trip to the Orient—keep her dressed this way as my young bride. No one would guess. Unless they notice that big hot dog, hanging out from Jacqueline's mini-skirt." He yanked it. "Hmm. It's kind of in the way. Where's my…"

"No, no!" The floozy cried.

"You better see what you can do with that thing, then."

The floozy quickly flounced on the bed in front of me and reapplied her clown lipstick and smacked her lips. My stuffed animal Leo watched, paralyzed. The floozy sucked me before he took me from the rear. I guess he thought I would get turned on and participate more this way, with a woman. And I did. I became the hardest I had ever been. Uncle was the one who sounded like an animal, roaring and snarling and trumpeting as he kept thrusting and thrusting until he finally finished in a satisfied loud groan. Yet she kept at it, she hungrily sucked me hard, she sucked me 'til I came, she sucked me 'til it was uncomfortable, she sucked me 'til it hurt, she sucked me until I couldn't stand it, she sucked me until she sucked everything— my childhood, my manhood, my love, out of me.

I looked at my bent-nail on the nightstand. If only I was the Strongman, I could have stopped them. But I was weak. Leo fell to the floor. Uncle stepped on him, saw what it was, and stomped on my Leo. That was it. If I continued, I could never live with myself or forgive myself.

Very early the next morning, before light, I crept into my uncle's huge master bedroom on the second floor. In his canopied and draped bed, he was laying there naked, dead to the world. In my hand was his hatchet. I raised the hatchet over his stumped-leg body. I wanted to make him lose more parts. I wanted to make him really dead to the world. Just before I brought the hatchet down, the pile of satin sheets moved and the floozy slid away from him. Her eyes fluttered wide. She nodded, and silently mouthed, urging, Yes, yes.

Wham! I went springing angrily out of the back gate, hanging poised for a second, unsure which way to go, barely in control. My senses launched into overdrive, speeding around the lane's curve, banging against the fence rail, and into the cornfield, once dropping the trash bag with the damn thing, half expecting sirens with red lights flashing after me, keeping in motion, bumping against corn stalks with split-second, instinctual decisions. I had postponed the inevitable long enough, and now free, yet spent with all my frantic efforts, relentlessly I lost momentum. My organs were raw and battered, and despite frantic efforts—I plummeted down to my knees. By that same cat-tailed dark pond where my friend had drowned.

I peered into the peaceful murky water. I jumped when a bluegill jumped. After what my Dad had done, I now wondered if my young classmate had my same problems and lulled himself into a premature sleep. I hurt; the water looked soothing. It seemed so inviting, so easy. I could be with my Daddy. A tune played in my head—"Don't hang around and let your problems surround you. Go down, down."

I opened the trash bag, knotted the pillowcase inside, and filled it with rocks. I swung the pillowcase around my head and threw the whole nasty business out into the water and watched it sink. After what had happened to me that night, I thought I had seen it all and was ready for anything. Tragically, I was mistaken. That morning, I had chickened out. I had backed out of Uncle's bedroom in revulsion. I had run. But that small act of defiance made me feel better, that I had enacted some small revenge. The sunken bag held only my uncle's artificial leg. I hurried across the fields to the circus and never went back home.

My mother? I had wondered how much did she really know. She was clearly afraid of him—under Uncle's spell. My innocence was just the cost of doing business. Me paying her rent. Damage of a collateral nature. I thought she had turned her back— better her son offered up to her brother than herself. A sacrificial lamb. That was an illusion. Mother did know everything. The floozy who violated me, and had remained in Uncle's bed, was my mother.

CHAPTER 27

Giving me up was Mother's way of getting back at her dead husband—whom she apparently hated, and of whom I was a constant reminder. She could look down to the Catholic's Hell for Suicides, with a special cellar for renounced ones, and smirk to him a Fuck you, every time I bent over for her brother. At least, that's what had I thought for a long time. Later, I wasn't sure. Since my Ariel died, I suffered for my parallel betrayals: my Ariel, my mother. I didn't want to leave her. But I had to. She gave me no choice. Her final request to me, I refused. Would she feel better knowing that it haunts me still?

Months after I ran away, I heard about my uncle. My uncle had put up big billboards in the cornfields and got himself elected Mayor of my hometown. Even as a Southerner and an outsider. He was that smooth. I struggled to forget the details of the whole uncle thing. You forgot it before, forget it again, don't think about it now. Think of…

#

No, think of something else. My lovely Ariel, with the life draining from her eyes, in front of me? No. If we had not been drinking that day, would it have happened? Who knows? Finn's Army buddy Bobby. Yes. Finn could never forgive himself, either. Maybe that's what he saw in me. Stultifying our senses. Isn't drug addiction or alcoholism or compulsive Russian-Roulette-strange-sex a slow suicide? Is there a difference?

I waited for the sunrise. One must time the watching to protect one's eyes. It is hard to watch a sunrise on a clear morning, staring into the sun. I thought of the old, worn *Ripley's Believe It or Not* my father would read with me. A cult of fakirs living in India called the Sun Gazers, gazed into the sun so long they burnt out their retinas. They continued staring. Jesus. I must have gotten higher last night than I thought.

The sun rose. The sun always rises. First, a hint of the bright glow, followed by wispy pink strands, then the light blue, before the dawn's sliver of red. When the yellow orb appeared and turned gold, with the promise of a new day and chance to begin again, I was renewed. I would be all right. The sunrise is like God giving his children a new ball to play with every morning. Every day begins and ends with a show. I laughed; the shows were like something Deo would arrange if he were God. I gazed over the Maxfield Parish-lit city neighborhoods, and watched until the sunrise was too intense to enjoy. I wished I had a cigarette. A few headlights appeared on dark streets below like beads—or white musical notes on blackboard. Music of the cityscape. A chill came over me—not from the cold—a mystic, goose-bump chill. Words danced in my head. My guitar. I was filled with an urge to play music.

I tentatively sang my bluesy-jazzy lyrics to "Boulevard of Broken Dreams." Morning traffic just started below. I came down. I clambered down the slippery cliff. By morning light, I could see how precarious my position had been. In a parallel life gone wrong, I could have fallen.

A phone booth stood on the street outside the Randall Museum. I called Bretta. It was too early and she sounded hoarse. "Oh, Jack. Jack, my God." She rambled, "The cop was so pissed and almost rousted me and Alejandro, and I gave him my adorable young girl act, as you call it, and told him we had just met, and didn't know who you were. Alejandro just pretended he spoke even less English than he does. We didn't give you up."

"Hey, sorry about all that. And thanks, you guys."

"It was insane. The cops all descended in a stampede and searched half of North Beach for you."

I made a joke. "Especially the strip club's dressing rooms."

"Haha. You want to hear something funnier? The cop said you ran like a Jack-rabbit! I laughed and laughed, and he thought I was nuts, and he moved on. Jack, you are a Jackrabbit." She went on, "And in all the excitement we were able to slip away, and watched it from the hot dog counter across the street. To save face, the cop arrested the first tourist he saw who looked a little like you and had had too much to drink, and threw him in the back of the patrol car, intentionally bumping his head, and afterwards, telling him to watch his head. It's all Benjamin's fault, the big baboon. What a bunch of bullshit." Her trilling laughter was medicine.

"Yeah. But it's all right, Bretta. My luck's still good. I played my Get Out of Jail Free card. Maybe even won the free game."

I felt much better. Alive. Purposeful. After another check of my building for surveillance, I ran in and picked up a guitar. I strapped the case over my back and jumped on my Honda. Taking a gamble, I cruised back into North Beach that early Sunday morning, which meant many parked cars stayed put. I left my helmet on to disguise my face and retraced the last part of my getaway. Under cars and in the gutter, I recovered most of my goodies. Except the pipe and the gun. There were drops of blood on the pavement. I must have grazed a dog with a bullet. So stupid. I flashed on Beagle Boy at the Recycling Center. Inspired, I got on my knees and looked under a dumpster. To my relief, my piece was under the dumpster, along with a bonus.

Incredibly, as a stop block for a dumpster wheel, as if someone placed it there for my return, was a paperback. *The Magus.* This novel was such a mind-blower I wished I'd never read it so I could read it again for the first time. This was the revised version, and nobody revises novels. I wondered if indeed I was being watched. I held the dumpster with my knee and opened the novel to the Ezra Pound quote, "...First must thou go the road—to hell And to the bower of Ceres' daughter Proserpine...knowing less than the drugged beasts." Heavy, I thought. I looked at my handful of drugs and flashed on what Monty told me last night. I opened the dumpster lid with an elbow. *I flung it all in.* I tucked the book under my arm and walked away as the dumpster careened into the sloping alley.

I grabbed a couple of muffins and OJ at the Coffee Gallery and wound my way up Telegraph Hill. Behind Coit Tower, overlooking the City rather than the Bay, had been a refuge of *The Frisco Kid*, twenty years back. Now I, a kindred spirit, sat under the bushes. I played the living shit out of my guitar, banging out a Lou Reed song—"Ooohhh, her life was saved by rock 'n' roll. Hey baby, rock 'n' roll." I sang like there was no tomorrow. Last night there almost had not been. I let it all out—the frustration, pain, my uncle, the deaths, Bretta—and felt better than I had in a very long while.

I smoked a joint. I have a confession. I lied. I faked throwing the drugs away. They were still in my pockets. And the gun. My fingers just wouldn't—couldn't—let go of the flipper buttons.

Is the truth more important than what one believes? Is it more important than what one needs to believe? Maybe I have lied about some other things, too. I have said before, It is funny, how life works. I would soon discover other lies—that my entire life was an illusion.

#

I became more cautious after that escapade and sadly, didn't go back to the Sav or North Beach for some time. Ironically, I misplaced my gun and spent hours combing my apartment. It was a mystery, which along with mysteries that I didn't even know were mysteries, would be solved at the same time, by dancing with a gorilla.

I did not see Bretta. Z.Z. called to tell me that Monty had apologized for his remarks in front of the Sav. Z.Z. had more. Bretta and Alejandro were going to Pamplona to run with the bulls and experience the legendary bullfights. Perhaps they would stay for a while at Alejandro's family's vast cattle ranch. Robin and Francine organized a bon voyage for Bretta. I did not attend.

My near bust cooled my jets for the glamorous lifestyle of a drug dealer. I put a quarter in a new game. Music so consumed me now that I took a sales job at the largest music store in San Francisco, Guitar Center. Technology was rocking the music world with an array of goodies. The revolutionary Sony "Walkman" hit in June. The pocket-sized, cassette-playing Walkman became a craze as everyone plugged into their personal tunes, "creating private worlds," as I told my new co-worker, "So Near, Yet so Far from the Madding Crowd." I was excited to have mixed media of Griffith with Hardy in one sentence, but like much of my literary humor, it went unappreciated.

I was also excited that Bretta called me from New York. "Jack, Robin told me you were working at Guitar Center." She laughed.

"What's so funny?"

"From Recycling Center to Guitar Center."

"Something about centers, I guess..."

"And, you once told me, 'I don't like being the center of attention.'"

"Maybe I do have a secret craving for attention."

She laughed again before crying and telling me with the real reason for her call—Alejandro. She was broken-up about her breakup. New York was as far as she and Alejandro had made it. I was not in much of a consoling mood.

"Darling, meet me in New York and you and I will go to Spain," she asked.

"I just got a new job."

"If it's only the money, Jack, I'll pay."

Sunday morning, a disheveled and emotional Bretta showed up at my door. A truly attractive person can be desirable even under duress. She flung herself at me and held me tight, crying, "Oh, Jack, Jack, what am I to do?"

I led her into the living room. Close to me on the sofa, she explained what happened in New York. "We were at LaGuardia, leaving for Spain, and these federal agents appeared and forced us to a back office. We were separated and interrogated. The whole thing was terrifying!"

"What was going on?"

"Alejandro was arrested for forged papers. He was deported."

"What happened?"

"He is not Spaniard after all. He's Mexican." She continued, "And the kid is not a kid, he's twenty-five. He totally conned me."

I laughed at the absurdity. Bretta scolded, "It's not funny. Well, it is funny. I'm glad he's not nineteen. At least I won't be one of those bitches who ruin children."

We both laughed. I found myself being drawn in. She added, "Perhaps his only truth was that he wanted to be a famous bullfighter in Spain." We were quiet for a few moments. "Oh, something else, Jack. I didn't think much about it at the time, but Alejandro did say something to that cop in North Beach—in English."

"I thought he couldn't speak English."

"He actually does."

"I thought he didn't say anything to the pigs?"

She said, "I mean, he said something to that cop *before* you were arrested. While we were waiting in front of the dirty liquor store."

"Before? That little bastard. The little shit. He squealed on me about the drink. Or the drugs, or maybe both. We were so nice to him. And he made a fool out of all of us. If I see him again…"

"Well, it's all over now. I made a mistake. With him, and especially you." She rubbed against me and lilted, "Jack, I'm so sorry. I want to make it all up to you."

All this was unexpected. Bretta lifted her leg over mine. "I became caught up in allure of the bullfight, and the bullfighter. He did seem to love me. I need that. You understand, Jack." She reached for my belt buckle. I protested. I was strong. I pushed her away. I told her firmly, "No."

Bretta raped me there on the sofa. Twice. Bretta gave me a hungry, panting, steamy, full-throttle, un-un-un-unbelievable half a blowjob. I managed to pull on a condom before she jumped on me. With love or comfort? Desire or horniness? As make up sex? No, sex was what we were best at. Now it felt so wrong and so very bad. In other words, it was damned good.

As we looked for missing apparel, she asked melodically, "Dónde está la fiesta?"

"There's the Haight Street Fair today."

The third annual Haight Street Fair was a big one, and took over the several blocks from Masonic to Stanyan Street. Arts-and-crafts booths covered the middle of the street and a stage was set up at each end. Blues music filled the air from the dark, cheap-suited band impersonating the recent movie, *The Blues Brothers* with John Belushi clearly coked to the gills. Two towering stilt walkers in costumes strode by. Face painters gave the crowd a psychedelic appearance. Balloons floated, banners waved, and all was festive.

"This must be reminiscent of your circus days."

Yes, it was. I steered us toward a corndog and lemonade stand; my old favorites. I noticed a couple of Berkeley-looking and Berkeley-smelling guys. Even in the Haight, some looked down on the self-righteous Berkeley radicals. The pair was thrusting flyers into the faces of fairgoers. We saw the flyer: "Reagan = War," a cartoon Reagan with a Hitler mustache holding a monkey, labeled "U.S." Benjamin had been right to worry; global politics were very tense.

Bretta became upset, asking me, "Is Reagan really going to get us into a war?"

While we walked by, one of the guys nudged his friend to look at Bretta's breasts. Giving a quiet wolf-whistle he jammed another flyer in Bretta's face—an obscene "Boycott Moscow Olympics, Let Them Play with Themselves," with a Russian jacking off his tiny penis. She turned away. I took it and dropped it to the ground. I smiled and said, "Oops. Can I have another?" He stupidly gave me one and wadded and it up and threw it down. "Dang, I'm clumsy today. One more." I reached for his whole stack. "In fact, let me help you pass these out."

"Hey man, that's not cool," he protested, backing up.

"You're freaking out my girlfriend and raining on the parade. Drop the political bad vibes and go have some fun."

His friend rushed up, and the guys sized me up and walked off, muttering, "Crazy asshole."

"Thanks Jack, but I thought you were trying to be less confrontational?"

I had changed, yet I realized there was something about this woman that brought out my protective belligerence.

"Am I still really your girlfriend?"

I pulled a good one out of a "no right answer" scenario; "Baby, no matter what happens or how we end up, I will always love you." She kissed me.

"But, Bretta, you know, I love you too much to only like you."

She looked askance and said, "I'm moving to L.A."

I had broken away from Bretta's gravitational pull once again. I needed to be in my own galaxy, away from the circus of her sun. I didn't hear from Bretta, and her number was disconnected. Some of the entourage stayed in touch with me, so I heard that Bretta had indeed moved down to L.A. and was going out with a movie director. She was "having a ball."

Fortunately, there was a new distraction in the city. Beautiful young blondes with exotic accents had appeared everywhere overnight. They sported out-of-fashion micro-mini-skirts to the delight of the straight male population. Scandinavian nannies were now in vogue in San Francisco.

The entourage rolled around like pinballs in Bretta's absence. Sprung here and there with seen and unseen flippers, some lit up, and some, no longer orbiting around Bretta's sun, seemed to lose their shine. Winston needed a new crash pad. I let him hang out at my place like he had with Bretta, and although unspoken, we formed a Bretta survivor support group. He did confess, that stored in an Oakland warehouse, were dozens of her art pieces which he had purchased anonymously to support her gallery openings.

We joked about, "Alejandro, the Bullfighter." which initiated ongoing repartee, in Spanish accents, "Ola! I present Ale-Handro, the Bull-fight-tare" and the other would respond, "You mean Ale-Handro, the Bull-shit-tare." The first go-round, I added, "Ale-Handro, he will dance the Fandango, with his fan in one hand, and his dango in the other." Considering Winston's "circum(cision)stance," gone wrong, I refrained from that joke again.

It was cool working at Guitar Center where I could practice guitar *and* talk to local musicians like Translator, Tower of Power, Romeo Void, Santana, Sammy Hagar, The Avengers, and the Tubes.

After standing at work all day I decided that I needed exercise to earn a drink. I sprinted up Van Ness Avenue to Henry Africa's, the original fern bar, where Ariel had been a waitress for a time and we often met. I filled with melancholy. I gazed through the window to our preferred loveseat. A bobbed brunette in a dark blazer lounged in our loveseat with another woman. My heart skipped a beat. She looked like Ariel. Her friend pointed and she twisted to return my wide-eyed look with emboldening bemusement. When the Italian girl raised her glass and motioned me in, I blushed and scurried up the hill.

On Polk Street was the literary-titled Lord Jim's, the "classier" competing fern bar. Of course, Polk Street was where Norris's turn-of-the-century *McTeague*, plied his unlicensed dentist trade. I fought the urge to stop and down a quick toast, for purely literary purposes, of course. No, sir, I resist. I continued into the smoggy-tiled Broadway Tunnel. One night on my motorcycle, I hit one hundred and eight miles per hour through that tunnel. I was a fast walker and still, it seemed long on foot; me, the solitary pedestrian.

At bustling Stockton Street, hundreds of tiny Chinese, many of them elderly, trudged like members of an ant colony for the collective purpose of food gathering. Faces oddly intent and downward, looking to their black Kung-Fu slippers, some had freakishly bent-over necks. Despite their reputation for fighting "fast as light-niiing," they moved slowly. I strode by them with my long legs—seemingly unnoticed.

I passed the deep-fried-eggroll-and-algae-laden "fresh" fish-tank-smelling restaurants, Candy man's Kawasaki-green restaurant, the exceedingly omnivorian little markets—with whiffs of hanging ducks, chickens, unidentifiable meats, and what the hell is that?—intermingling with strangely compelling shops, wafting exotic herbs, sawed-off horns, mysterious powders and under-the-counter fireworks.

Soon I was immersed in the reassuring aromas of the Italian restaurants of North Beach—garlic, sausage, basil, and fresh tomatoes. I resisted the urge to go *there*—to our old bar. At the odd triangular-shaped Mario's Bohemian Cigar Store, I sat down at the stool closest to the side door. Mario's was really a café but still stocked a few cigars. North Beach, with its relaxing old-world warmth was appealing, despite all I had been through. I thirsted for the advertised Moretti but held strong. Ever-smiling, old Mario himself served me one of their finest, a double cap, along with cannoli he had personally baked that morning. I savored that slice of heaven, and told Mario, "Someday, I'm going to get out of the Haight, and move here to North Beach."

Mario encouraged, "Thatsa good." I watched a carefree foursome play on the worn foosball table, despite the broken "man." As my mood caffeinated, I swiveled on the barstool and looked out the open side door across Washington Square to Saints Peter and Paul cathedral. I watched the sunlight fade on the twin spires. Like Bretta and I. The moment surged with symbolic portent and from phantoms of that day—the abortion. An ache formed deep in my belly.

I wandered down Columbus and under the big neon Gold Spike sign; I looked in through the open door. The Gold Spike was an authentic San Francisco Italian family dining saloon—a yellowed ceiling, papered with yellower currency, and worn red-leather bar stools seemingly calling to me to sit. This was not Bretta's style. I thought of Bretta and the things we had done, but more the things we had not. Not once had we strolled through the San Francisco State campus and visited the bookstore where I had worked. We never flew a kite at Stinson Beach. We never hiked Mount Tam. She never heard me play my guitar. We had never gone dancing. What had we *done* the whole time? Aside from the drinking and the sex? Admittedly, both of which were unbelievably good. If so, how can the most passionate relationship of my life, and perhaps my future life, be filled with such regret? What was wrong with me? I'd made a mistake. My mistake had been expecting my relationship with Bretta would transform into the one I'd had with Ariel. I lost my resistance. I needed a drink. I stood at the bar, desultorily ordered a shot of tequila, and threw it back.

Still restless, I left. There was a big yeasty-homey-smelling bakery on Grant Avenue. I inhaled the aroma as if I could absorb it for food, but what I needed was a fix from the Sav. Our friendly barman George was now at the classy Palace Hotel on Market Street, serving fine cocktails under Maxfield Parish's glowing *The Pied Piper*. How appropriate. One of these lonely nights, I would have to follow him and his enticing lyrical liquors.

I grasped the handle of the Sav's familiar worn door and saw an attractive young couple, palpably mad with love, sitting on our old stools at the bar. I stalled, lingering half-in-hope, half-in-fear, as if— as if *She* and her entire entourage would be there, forever suspended in time, drinking, joking, laughing—waiting for me—like waxen animatronics at a hybrid-from-hell Madame Tussaudesyland. Ha-ha. But would I buy a ticket? Pathetically, the answer was yes. I would even buy a season pass.

#

I wandered on into the evening and eventually took the N streetcar back to the Haight. Going through the bleak tunnel, the tunnel of love, as I had called it, seemed sadly ironic.

At Bretta's periwinkle Victorian I stared with melancholy up at her bay windows. We had some good times there. We really did. The new tenant had put up some hideous off-white roll-up shades. The kind that my Midwestern mother had relished. Sickened by the memories, I headed to Haight Street.

In front of Mendel's I stopped in my tracks. There was Bretta. My emotions rebounded. Her blonde hair was up in a fringed gold scarf and she pushed a cart. No, it was a blue baby stroller. A flood of betrayal washed over me. She had the baby! She had my child, our child, after all. How could she do this to me? She was a liar. A fury filled my heart. I rushed up to Bretta and seized her arm.

CHAPTER 28

I twirled Bretta around, ready to scream at her. It was not Bretta. I was relieved, but not glad. I don't know who was more shocked. The only thing that came out of my lips was, "Is this your baby?"

The pale, pretty woman looked at me quizzically, and up and down the sidewalk, bouncing tight curls. She peered into the baby's face and replied in a European accent. "Thankfully, no. Is it yours?"

"Uh, I don't think so. Let me look." I too, peered down at the infant. "Uh, no. It's cute, bu...Sorry." We kept walking. "I thought you were someone else."

"Then you were right, American crazy man. I am someone else."

This stunning blonde was Anneka, a Dutch nanny. She gave me her number, teasing, "In case you do find your baby."

#

The hyperkinetic energy and intermittent waves of customers at Guitar Center matched my hyper personality. Like a car dealership, all the prices at Guitar Centers were negotiable, making sales more entertaining for me, and for savvy shoppers. Utilizing techniques from drug wheeling and dealing I became a top salesman. During slow moments and after hours I practiced on high-end gear, with other aspiring rock gods.

The early Saturday morning meetings insured that I would not party hearty the night before. The meetings also killed my karate classes. I reluctantly quit my dojo. It seemed everything in my life was changing.

Party invites and passes were laid on me for shows at clubs like the Stone and On Broadway. One day a Belgian man came in to look at our pre-release, Roland Drumatix drum synthesizer box. He shouted, "*Il Giro*! There they are." A group of pro bicycle racers flew by the store in matching colored jerseys on their shiny road bikes. We ran to the door. The man said, "Look, there is your Greg LeMond. He is a fine rider, for an American. He was the winner of this race last year and should win yet again. This is a training race for le Tour de France. Two years ago, they went down the dangerous bricks of Lombard Street."

I gave him a knowing grin. He continued with animation. "Of course, LeMond has no chance, no chance at all, to win Le Tour de France."

His enthusiasm was infectious. He introduced himself. "I once was a racer for Belgium."

"I prefer an engine on my bike."

"Oh, a motorcyclist? You should try the racing bicycle." He pointed to the large wall of hanging acoustic and shiny-colored, beautiful Strats, Gibsons, Rickenbacker electric guitars—the wall of musical art for which Guitar Center was famous. The Belgian continued. "Imagine on this wall, not guitars, but sleek bicycles. The difference of the motorcycle and a race bike compares to strapping a heavy electric guitar around your neck, versus fondling a handcrafted classical guitar on your lap. The electric does much of the work for you. The acoustic you must caress, coax, extract the music. You would love road biking as you love music—if you would but try."

His Belgian-accented metaphors and passion for gear had me spellbound. "Bicycle road racing is the only sport in the world. The Tour—the greatest sporting event in the galaxy. Up, down, pain, suffering, little triumphs and defeats along the way, riding *piano*—gently, soon to up cadence, riding *tempo*, the whispering quiet, swishing rhythm of the ride, anticipating the breakaway."

"Sounds like my last relationship."

"You've seen *Breaking Away*? It won your Oscar for screenplay this year. You must see it. A young man, a bicyclist, in trying to find his identity, deludes others, and worse, himself, to believe he is something that he is not." The friendly bicycle nut insisted that I attend his big party that night.

I asked Winston to come with me, as I knew he would find the former racer interesting. He did. It turned out my new acquaintance worked with the Brewmeister at the Anchor Brewing Company, which had recently moved into an old Mariposa Street coffee roastery on Potrero Hill, aka Pot Hill. Around the top of the tall structure, the owner had installed permanent festive-colored lighting which quickly became regarded as the City's modern landmark. The lighting, along with the seventy-foot, welcoming neon Coca-Cola billboard above Bryant Street, were especially visible when crossing the Bay Bridge.

The brewery was celebrating a new batch of its signature steam beer with an all-out bash. The revelers were a diverse mix of people. We all partied amongst the huge copper brewing tanks.

"Jack London drank steam beer," my new Belgian friend said. He pointed out the bespectacled owner. "That is Fritz Maytag, as in THE Maytag washer family."

"I thought these big tanks looked like the tubs of washing machines," I joked.

"Fritz and this microbrewery are going to revolutionize the beer business. You'll see."

After drinking copious amounts of the new batch of delicious amber, creamy beer, I felt like having a revolution myself. There was no music, so I convinced Winston to fetch his stealth Martin from his wagon. I was fascinated with the beautiful empty copper brewing tanks. I asked Winston, "Remember the Palace of Fine Arts? The acoustics?" I pointed at the largest tanks. "Let's have some fun."

Winston stood on the metal steps and leaned in the hatch to play the intro of a classical tune, which echoed, rich and resonant. Partiers gathered around, eager for a show. Winston built up into a fast song. I had no idea what he was playing or if he was improvising. I scat-sang Spanish phrases into the tank to accompany Winston's glorious guitar. The sound was otherworldly and the crowd applauded and called for more. Fritz and the Belgian peered in and said, "Bravo" and "Nice vocal highlights, Jack."

Emboldened and "hoppy," I spontaneously leapt down into the empty tank and called to Winston, "Come on in, the beer's fine!" Inside the copper tank he performed another intricate song as I improvised some phrasings. At the finish, the partiers cheered.

The Belgian raved to Winston, "Masterful! Joaquin Rodrigo's *Concierto de Aranjuez, 2 adagio* à la John Williams, segueing to allegro, with flamenco stylings and creative original riffs."

I told Winston, "I want to do one of my songs." He was surprised but pleased. I asked, "Anybody have a guitar I can borrow?"

"A moment, Jack," my Belgian friend called, "I shall give you mine."

Winston and I climbed onto the top of the big copper tank. The Belgian handed me his sweet Guild Westerly F40 acoustic and I did a quick tune. I opened my pocket journal to a song and conferred

with Winston. With a wad of gum, Winston stuck my sheet on top of
his guitar. I said, "Slow and moody. If I screw up, just take over." I
told the crowd, "This is my original and we're winging it. Called
'Boulevard of Broken Dreams.'"

>Bottle is empty, last cigarette gone (acapella, crumple and
>throw "pack")
>Pen is dry; damn near dawn   (first guitar begins soft)
>Living alone is dying a dream
>in Heartbreak Hotel on Dead End Street
>Off the Boulevard of Broken Dreams   (second guitar begins)

>Miss your sharp smile,
>your slooow red kiisss
>Afraid I can't go on like this
>Torn apart at the seams
>on Boulevard of Broken Dreams   (walk stage left, look out
>"window")

>My window's cracked, neon sign still glows
>Morning traffic just started below
>I love you more than I can fake,
>Love you more than life it seems
>The Boulevard
>The Boulevard of Broken Dreams

>Saw you on the street today
>choked the words I meant to say
>You feared the prayer that I gave
>The wind just swept my song away
>Down The Boulevard of Broken Dreams

>Needed you so, but our love
>turned down a dark alleyway
>that vacant lonely night upon
>The Boulevard of Broken Dreams
>Boulevard of Broken Dreams

>My good fortune's lost
>to a poor beggar's soul

And now, I shall have my cup of 'jo
with Elvis, Dean, and Monroe

My heart is beatin' on the pavement.
My heart is bleedin' on my sleeve!
The Boulevard, the Boulevard,
Boulevard of Broken Dreams
How can you disregard, just discard me
Our Boulevard of Broken Dreams?

Winston's lead guitar chops gave confidence to my playing, and I was surprised at the range and emotion in my vocals. The partiers went wild. We played one more song, this one upbeat, and called it a night. Encouraged by my accolades at the Anchor party, I tried to convince Winston to start a rock band with me. He declined. "No bands for me. I like rock, but I'm not really a rock-and-roll animal."

"You're so damn good. How come you never play gigs?"

"Used to. Some managers are still pissed at me." He looked away. "I'm not very dependable."

I was stoked about making music and called Nick the next day. Perfect timing. Nick's job with the Pimpernel Parties had come to an unforeseen termination. Nick told it this way: "The way it went down was a total fluke. A limo pulls up at four A.M. in front of the party building. An old Chinese man jumps out wearing a silk suit, and starts gesticulating and jabbering in Mandarin. The doorman accepts his yen for the cover charge. The guy runs all over the place checking out the women, somehow got dosed, and becomes the life of the party. Unfortunately, he didn't let his limo driver know he was staying. So, the driver became increasingly concerned, finally barges in at six. He spots his boss all Day-Glo, dressed in only his silk undershorts, socks, garters and erection, having the time of his life. The driver freaks, calls the cops, and the party gets raided like a four-alarm fire. Turned out the Chinese dude had just landed at SFO from Hong Kong, was owner of pretty much the whole block, and decided to tour his properties in the middle of the night. The Pimpernel operators had to seriously cool it. They consoled themselves by using their ill-gotten gains to buy out a couple of South of Market dive bars, which they converted to more-lucrative dive 'clubs'."

Nick was a fine keyboardist and enthusiastic to start up a band. Besides the yellow piano he owned a Fender Rhodes, and could easily play leads that I couldn't master. I was relieved to be a rhythm guitarist so I could focus on vocals and performance. I purchased discounted gear at Guitar Center including a Fender Strat with Deluxe amp, a Peavy PA system and a couple of Shure SM58s. A young drummer from Haight Street Music joined us. We agreed that a start-up band needed a catchy name, a hot chick and a gimmick. We held auditions and a henna-haired petite dynamo with a sultry voice was our pick. The fact that Rocky was a decent bass player with a distractingly firm body was a bonus. We used my songs and wrote originals together and a week later we were The Café Razors. The name was a play on "Café Racers," originally a term for English sports-bikers who zipped from café to café, fueled on caffeine and American rock 'n roll; aka "rockers."

From Haight Ashbury Vintage shop we bought Italian suits and leather jackets. We rehearsed constantly in my egg-carton-and-blanket-insulated garage until the neighbors raised hell, then rented a dank studio, only to return shortly to my garage, to save money, until complaints began again. Wash, rinse, repeat. Our punk flavored songs, like "Dancing with Bella Donna," "Ciao Ciao Now!" and "Lipstick and Perfume," we mixed in with covers like "Tainted Love." I attached a bullet fairing to my Honda and the bassist painted flames on the tank. Terrain and logistics willing, I would ride or push the bike up to the stage as a prop, as I had seen The Tubes do in a performance of "White Punks on Dope" at Bimbos. We played at storefront parties and some minor bar gigs for exposure, and all we could drink. One wild gig was with Redd Kross and Bad Brains at The Farm, a very alternative community center\animal farm\gallery\party space out on Army Street. The new indy record label, Subterranean Music, was also part of the mix but the owner, Fox, snubbed our hopes of an audition calling us "medium core." He said, "Come see me when you're not just hard core, but rotten core."

One night I gave Rocky, clutching her bass case, a ride home on my bike and she, her bass and I ended up in bed. However, she said that, "Your rebounding emotions are not happening." As I feared, it got weird in our group and she soon left. Café Razors acquired another bassist, a tall, skinny young man, a boy, really. He was not nearly as good as our last and was a complainer to boot. "God, I have to play the same riff, over and over."

Nick and I shook our heads and Nick teased, "Stick with it and learn our playlist, and tell you what, we'll eventually get another

bass player for the boring bassline, and then you can play lead bass."
The kid brightened, "Can't wait."

Meanwhile, Z.Z. unveiled the big news to me. Benjamin won
the high score, meaning his novel was finally published. I guess his
broken hand had delayed his writing. He received a huge advance in
a three-book deal. The book title—*The Sun in Our Eyes*. The dust
cover trumpeted: "The sexy saga of a stunning artist and her bohemian entourage." According to reviews the novel was "a good story
poorly told." Z.Z. related that when Benjamin had asked Bretta to
read a draft for her opinion, she declared, "I can render an opinion
without reading it—leave my part out." Z.Z. further reported that,
"He may have a tough time coming up with books two and three, as
no one is speaking to him." He was wrong. One person, who knew
absolutely everything, was speaking to him. Guess who?

When I reported the book to Winston, he shoplifted two copies
from Stacy's Bookstore. He grumbled, "That fucking Benjamin portrays me as a dissolute bankrupt eunuch." I browsed through the
copy Winston gave me and I couldn't believe that he used Winston
as the detached narrator, which made for damn slow reading, especially with the no sex and all. Poor Bretta was portrayed as a narcis-
sistic alcoholic nympho. Worse, he made me out to be a drug-dealing
violent psycho, alternatively full of self-loathing and braggadocio,
and the one who attacks the "bullfighter."

None of us liked the way we were depicted while the "poet"
Benjamin appeared as the brilliant, sophisticated, and misunderstood,
leading man—with well-defined pectorals. Winston and I criticized
Benjamin and nit-picked his novel. Winston confessed, "I started
strangling Benjamin that night at the Sav and now I wished I had finished the job."

"Right, only after Benjamin had finished Ale-Handro, the Bull-
fight-tare."

The book, or the advance check, did impress Francine suffi-
ciently to accept Benjamin's marriage proposal. I considered that
sadly appropriate. Of course, it wouldn't last.

#

The bass-player one-night stand primed my pump for the comfort of a woman. I called Anneka, the baby pusher. We met at the
café on the corner of Haight and Masonic for coffee where she
flaunted her European superiority. Along with her bare thighs and
centerfold curves. We rented skates and rolled around Golden Gate

Park—Stow Lake to the buffalo paddock, where I sadly discovered half the buffalo herd missing, "relocated due to bovine TB." Then on through the archery field, and out to the ocean-side, where I presented to Anneka the antiquated windmills and tulip garden. Anneka's Dutch beauty was irresistible against the backdrop of the multi-hued tulips and one thing led to another.

We became quickly involved and I invited the buxom Anneka to move in. Winston was more on than off at my place and Anneka soon made us a tightknit threesome. With a woman in the house, Winston's floral arrangements once again made their appearances. I was busy at Guitar Center and with band rehearsals, so to keep Anneka occupied on her off days, I bought her a painting kit at Mendel's. My hope was that she would take up painting instead of magnetizing men at cafés. After her initial enthusiasm and some very-still-lifes of Winston's florals, Anneka's interest waned.

In the dead of the night, I would leave Anneka slumbering, so I could sit at my window and write romantically melancholic lyrics in my journal. This was one:

Peaches and Dream
I dream of you when I'm asleep
I dream of you while I'm awake
I sleep with you while I dream,
I awaken next to you in my dream
If I were a sorcerer, I'd creep softly into yours
and you would dream that I'm your horse,
 as I nuzzle your delicate neck with my warm fuzzy nose.
You would dream, that you are the perfect peach
as I take little nibbles, and let your
sweet sticky juices, flow slowly, slowly, into my kiss

One evening, walking to Tommy's Joint after work, a woman stopped me on Van Ness. Her chestnut hair was styled with a long ponytail pulled to the front and she looked very attractive in a bright-orange dress, red jacket and heels. It took me a moment to recognize her.

"You look really good, Robin."

Robin had shed several pounds, as well as her large dark-framed glasses, revealing the luminosity of her warm horse-brown eyes. "So do you, Jack, but you always look good to me."

We stood awkwardly so she blurted, "The gallery owner has been on me about improving my image, umm, for the business that is, and exercising, you know, working out. She's friends with Jane Fonda."

"The actress? I just saw her in the preview for *9 to 5* and she's a working secretary, not working out."

Baskin' Robin giggled. "Yes. Jane has her *Workout Book* that's going to be published next year and my boss told me a few workouts from it. So, I've been, well, working out." She spun around for me.

"Wow. Good for you. I bet you feel good, too. I mean, you know, feel better."

"Yes. And you won't believe this, I gave up chocolate. That was the hardest part."

"Ha, I bet. You were a chocoholic."

"Gave up, well not counting, you know, special occasions." She smiled before casting her eyes down. "Winston told me that your new girlfriend is gorgeous."

"Yeah. She's nice. Well, except for she's actually kind of a bitch." We laughed.

"Oh, speaking of which..." she said, "That Benjamin and his book. He bitched to me, 'I wanted to portray my literary self accurately, but my agent insisted that my character be 'more likable.'"

"That must have been such a challenge."

She chuckled. "On the other hand..." From her large bag, Robin tugged a book that looked like a giant Camel cigarette pack, with a flying red-headed woodpecker carrying a match. The book was *Still Life with Woodpecker*. "This crazy 'Sort of a Love Story' is so much better. You have to read it, Jack. 'Yum!'"

"Oh cool. *Another Roadside Attraction*—Tom Robbins is great. And the red, red Robin is reading the Woodpecker."

She hugged me and we parted with her suggestion, "Let's get together some time."

I knew what that meant in California. Nothing.

CHAPTER 29

Some Irish lads called U2 released their first U.S. album, *Boy,* and knocked everyone's socks off. Rock reborn with a post-punk attitude by real musicians. U2 spoke to Nick and I more than the X and their album, *Los Angeles*. During Café Razors' next practice in my garage, I put on U2's single "I Will Follow," cranking up the flange-filled guitar opening radiating into the vocals. The "titular" young boy on the cover made our bass player think it was a gay band. I played more cuts. "Twilight...In the shadow, boy meets man." "In my sleep I discover the one, but she ran with the morning sun." His voice, Bono's voice! I wanted to sound like him. I determined to emulate his ringing, plaintive tones.

We took a vote for our ongoing Hamletian dilemma—to punk or not to punk. We decided to take arms against the start of this decade's sea of trouble and stick with punk, hoping for a better chance at gigs. Nick and I scrambled to find a following for the band. Influenced by The Cars *Candy-O*, we knew that Nick, our best musician, could better fill out our sound with a synth. I got Nick a deal on a Prophet-5 synthesizer from a Guitar Center connection, eager to upgrade to the upcoming Roland Jupiter-8. We changed the band's name to simply the Razors and we played faster with a rougher edge. Nick already had short hair, but I was not willing to give up my long curls, so just spiked some and jelled the rest back for gigs. I rehearsed my bad attitude and my snarling.

One of Nick's ex-roommates was dating singer Jello Biafra, whom Nick persuaded to get us a gig as one of the groups opening for Jello's well-known local punk band, The Dead Kennedys. Jello had prank-run for mayor last year on a wild platform which included requiring businessmen to wear clown suits. He came in fourth. The gig was at the Mabuhay Gardens which was a big deal for our band's exposure. I was disappointed that Winston declined to come, stating he couldn't handle the scene. I was more disappointed that Anneka declined as well, apologizing that she had some Dutch friends

visiting. The dearth of Anneka's passion for music, and for art, as her
painting had shown, matched her dispassionate lovemaking.
Anneka's flippant air, facetious zest and sexual charms, contradicted
her being, what a more insensitive man such as Wild Bill would call,
"a cold fish." I dismissed this—compared to Bretta, Raquel Welch
could probably seem a cold fish—as I was quite infatuated with
Anneka.

Broadway's Mabuhay Gardens, aka the Fab Mab was San Francisco's premier punk palace, hosting both coasts punk bands du jour,
but one would never know from the facade. The only advertising was
the tacky, yellow plastic palm-tree sign from the defunct Filipino restaurant. The building's exterior looked like a cross between Masonic
Hall and the Alamo.

Fortunately, they also allowed a few no-name bands like ours to
warm up the disorderly, anarchistic crowd. At least the entourage
turned out to support me. Z.Z. and Monty and Edith, who appeared
to be together, showed up at the grungy Mab to check us out.

"You know I'm a jazz cat, but I'm here for you, man," Monty
said.

Z.Z. saw that I was nervous and encouraged me. "Play your as-
sets."

"What?"

"Take off your pants. No, just kidding. At least take off your
shirt, though."

"No way."

"It worked for Iggy Pop."

To bring out my punk, I purposely did not eat before the gig, to
make myself mean and hungry. In the trash-strewn backstage, some
of the other warm-up band's skinhead, leather-and-chain-attired
members jeered us as "fresh meat." Nick and I affected Sex Pistols
Brit accents and Nick told them, "Go bugger yourselves." I snarled,
"Piss off, ya' bloody wankers." To our surprise, they did piss off.

We were first bill for the still-arriving, unsettled and lukewarm,
safety-pin-pierced, dark-makeup crowd. Too quickly, there was a
mic squealing and M.C. Dirk Dirkson's trademark jibing, "To start
things off, here's a band you never heard of—'Remember, no re-
funds.' Ha-ha, no, seriously. The band's real name is...the Ray-zors!"

Only a smattering of applause sounded from our friends and a
pair of Cal-Trans-orange-haired girls with raccoon eyes. I realized
with loathing, Dirk's split pronunciation incorporated Uncle's

name—Ray. Was there no escape? Only this stage. I strapped on my Strat. We kicked in with our opener and sang in Devo style with a Rocky Horror antici-pa---shun flourish "...and I try, and I try, and I try t-t-try, try...but I can't get me no...satis-fac—shun."

The vampy-campy song fell a little flat because of our nerves. The second song was Nick's nightmare-inducing, synthesizer-heavy, minor-chord rocker, "Lipstick and Perfume," with my all-too-close-to-home lyrics. "She lives for the night, afraid of daylight. No Suuun. No Fuuun. The smell of stale perfume. Lipstick scrawl on the mirror. Or is it only blood?"

We cheated by smash-segueing that tune unevenly into another original song because we were only allotted three. The mosh audience perked up. For our last-chance song, I called for my new tune, "Romeo Void." I explained, "Romeo is the asshole, or bitch, your love loves more than you."

"Who cares?" somebody heckled. I screamed back, "I fuckin' care, asshole! I fuckin' care." I tore off my shirt and threw it toward the voice, a dangerous move because Jello warned us the crowd was known to lob shit at the stage—like crushed ice which looked like glass shards when it flew at you, and worse. But I tensed my abs and pretended to go for my pants button. I heard a few girls go, "ooh." The room quieted. I had their attention. I yelled to my mates, "Let's stick it to 'em fast and hard, boys." The bass player and drummer kicked it in. I varied my faux Brit accent between moaning and screaming, lathering up an anger that scared even my "mates."

> If only I were Romeo, Don't you understand?
> If only I were Romeo, I'd be a happy man
> I wish that I were Romeo, Then you'd love only me
> How I wish that I were Romeo, Legendary lover 'cross the land.
> Forget Don Juan, Casanova, greatest lovers of them all.
> Just let me be your Ro-me-o, I'd have your heart 'n soul.
> To me you would devote yourself, call my name in reverie.
> You'd give me all your passion, you'd think of only Romeo me.
>   (Instrumental with Nick playing hot harpsichord on synth)
> O I wish that I were Romeo, if only I were he
> He'd be yearning for you, for I s'pose, *he'd* have to be me!
> Never mind gifts and roses, Never mind the ring.
> You would love me as I *am,* love me 'cause *I'm* your man.
> If only I were Romeo that would be the best.

I could just be Romeo, And you should do the rest.
If only I could be Romeo, I could die a happy man.
If only I were Romeo, I'd die a happy-fuckin' man!

We thrashed to a raucous ending where I impulsively picked up
the mic stand, bent it over my knee, strongman-style, and tossed it
down on the stage with a clatter. I stalked off, followed by the rest of
the somewhat dumbfounded Razors. The hardcore crowd screamed
appreciation. One of the musicians backstage yelled to me, "Fuckin'
A, man!" Others nodded in approval.

On the floor, I reintroduced Nick to my impressed friends. Even
Professor Monty gave me an A. My grade was negated by the fact
that not only was he drinking, but he was drunk. Z.Z. teased, "Wow,
Jack, you do have some issues. I love it." He had a tequila grapefruit
waiting for me. Edith, a little culture shocked, raved a laughably in-
accurate musical review, and declared me, "a sexy singer," while she
counted my abs with her fingers. Monty looked on, disgruntled by
this intimacy. Was he jealous of Edith?

I looked around at the Mab's misfits, freaks, performers, costumed weekend punkers, "civilian" observers, clowns and cultural
oddities. This was really an urban circus. Had I returned to the fold?
With born-again fervor I spouted to Nick, "We can do this. I can be a
punk. Fuck that, I am a punk!"

The follow-up band that had given us attitude stomped onstage,
and after a couple of spastic songs, the slam-dancing moshers threw
some beer cans and ice onstage until a tussle ensued and the performers kicked at the assholes faces. Nick indicated the Mad Max
scene and admitted, "I don't know about this shit." After the last
warm-up band, merely a formulaic poseur punk group, I remained
cocky—until ringmaster Dirk announced, "Now, in the center ring,
The Dead Kennedys!" The band stormed the stage and Jello com-
mandeered a kick-ass set with the trippy "Holiday in Cambodia."
They made The Razors look and sound like the amateurs we were.

Toward the end of the band's loud set, it became apparent that
Monty and Edith were not together, as Edith was holding onto a
now-happier Nick, who winked, nodding to the door, indicating that
they were leaving together. Z.Z. got moody and bolted. I wended
through the crowd and recognized the sexy, red-haired Filipina
singer, Pearl Harbor, surrounded by her own entourage. She yelled
over the din, "You looked good up there." I yelled back, "Thanks,

but how'd I fuckin' sound?" She gave me a come-hither look. I spotted the Professor slumping against a dark wall, so stupidly, I kept moving to check on him.

Monty was next to several couples lip-locking and groping under each other's clothes. How they avoided pulling the safety pins out of each other's faces, I did not know. Next to Monty was an older straight-looking dude I immediately disliked. He smelled like Porsche, and money, coke sweat, cigars and Rodeo Drive salon hair gel—in other words, a record exec. He had an arm draped around a bruised-looking underage chick wearing an insignificant leather skirt and a dog collar. She eyed me but I eyed him, until he gave me a wolfish grin. That's when I saw another frail girl on her knees going down on him right in front of everybody. I tensed; I felt like busting the asshole in the teeth, right in his grin, but not in front of Monty. Monty grasped my arm, I assumed to restrain me. No, he was drunk and holding me for support. No. He pulled me closer, and I leaned in but couldn't hear his words over the deafening decibels from the stage. "California, uber alles! uh-uh-uh-uh... Now it is 1984 Knock-knock at your front door"—the song Jello had refused to play as the token punks at this year's Bammy Awards, denigrated by punks as "Bambi Awards."

Monty reached into his shirt pocket to retrieve a cigarette and a clear Bic pen dropped to the floor. I picked it up and almost dropped it again. It was not a pen; it was a capped syringe. "What the hell, Monty?"

"Whoopsie." Monty took it and fumbled it into a jacket pocket. He slurred, "You metmyjuunkiemonkey. Now you know, so shhh."

"You? Are you kidding me?"

He placed a hand behind my neck and looked me in the eyes, "And ya'know what else, Jack? Edith is right for a change."

I was getting a warning vibe now. "How so?"

He put a hand on my chest. "Jack, you...are a sexy...singer."

I jolted like I was hit with a current, but managed to stay put long enough to protest, "This is not right, man." I slipped away.

I forged straight out into the city night, slamming some punks sending them spinning. Uncaring, my mind was like a book flipping through dog-eared pages—Monty's a little bitchy, overly concerned with my wellbeing, I've never seen him with a chick. He preaches against drugs but he hangs in jazz clubs, acts too cool... Worse, the only solid person in our entourage was a fuck-up, too.

#

Winston, Anneka, and I were great friends and roommates. Nick and his dates would sometimes join us in outings. I was forming my own entourage. At Guitar Center, with my new Mab "rep," I was invited to a private punk party. Anneka wanted to go, but Winston needed convincing. Anneka finally batted her lashes and asked, "Please?" For the occasion, I presented Anneka a bottle of Shalimar. Winston drove us to the party in his green, metal-flake Chevy wagon, Anneka poised between us.

"You hear about Z.Z. and Edith?" Winston asked.

"What?"

"They've been kind of seeing each other."

"No way. He's a total fruit." I was improbably defending Z.Z.'s gayness.

Anneka smirked in my face. "How do *you* know?"

Winston continued, "Well, Robert's pissed. He was at the Ultasheen show at the I-Beam the other night and saw them going at each other."

"They were probably just dancing," I insisted.

"As they went into the ladies room?"

I flashed back on some of the recent scenes with them. Not a lot of clues. "You know, at Bretta's opening, I kind of encouraged him to taste her."

Anneka snarled at Bretta's name. She switched to her Dutch accented, Wicked-Witch-of-The-West voice, "Oh, the almighty artist Bret-ta. Hee-he-he-he-he-hee!" Winston and I looked at this creature between us. We always marveled that she was the only person we knew who hated Bretta.

Anneka asked, "So what if Z.Z. is bi-bi with E.D." We laughed as she continued, "What's the no big deal? Americans think they are so liberated sexually. Tsch, come to my Amsterdam."

Anneka yanked the rearview mirror down to reapply her red lipstick and powder her face. She remained concerned about being so pale in California, even though Winston and I assured her she had a model's porcelain complexion. She smelled deliciously of the Shalimar as she rearranged her long silk scarf—another gift from me—around her short, curly blonde hair. I said, "I'd love it if you grew your hair out."

She stared out the car window for a moment and asked, "Why? You do not think I am gorgeous now?"

"No, I mean, of course you are, Anneka, it would just be a nice change…"

Winston unexpectedly turned on me. "I think her hair is perfect. Leave her alone." We drove on in silence through the Mission District until Winston stuck in a classical guitar cassette.

"Crankypants. You must be crashing," I said.

"If you didn't like drugs, you sure picked wrong neighborhoods not to like them in."

"See what I mean, cranky. Anyway, you're the one who manipulated me into that shit."

"You sound like Monty." He turned the rearview mirror toward me. "Look in the mirror. You can manipulate people with the best of them."

"Hey, did you force drugs on Doc, too? He flipped out awfully quick after you came back."

Winston made a sharp turn. "You and Bretta drove him fucking crazy. Literally, fucking crazy."

"Watch it. Not in front of the lady."

"Your nice guy, naïve-farm-boy act is a little old hat. You've not been in Kansas anymore for quite some time, Dorothy." He spat out the window. "You don't know, do you?"

I had a bad feeling. "Know what?"

"Doc. Doc was in treatment in Dallas. He escaped again. He broke into some garage or something. Bretta didn't tell you, huh?"

I looked at him. "So, jail now?"

"The cops shot him. He's dead."

"What? Jesus. Why didn't… I didn't… Fuck you."

Anneka said, "Stop, you little boys. Fuck both of you both. There, that must be the party. Relax or you'll ruin our *grande entrée*."

We cruised by the band's grungy, graffitied storefront on Shotwell, spotted a battered car pulling out, squeezed into the parking space, and headed in. Winston gave me a final shot, "Remember what Mark Twain said about humans, they 'can resist everything…but temptation.'"

"That was Oscar Wilde, and he was as bitchy as you," I retorted. Anneka glared at me like the argument was my fault.

The look was drainpipe jeans, Doc Martens, partially shaved heads, tees and tattoos. These guys were the real deal, the hardcore punk band Red Assfault, and the party was equally hardcore. I introduced my friends to Bruce, the ripped-tee-shirt, skinny, muscular lead singer who had invited me. He hurried to the stage and I made my way across the floor of peeling linoleum over concrete slab to fill up a couple of plastic cups, gypsy-blue for him, tulip-yellow for her, from the keg in the filthy freestanding-and-inoperable bathtub. I brought them back for Winston and Anneka. The party was raucous fun and an extreme contrast to the brewery party.

A few drum bashes, an "Allrightallrightallright!" and Red Assfault jumped into a set of original harsh, screaming punk songs, while partiers danced by jumping up and down, and banging into each other. The band was loud, of course—fast, loud, tight, loud, and Bruce was a compelling, animated performer. I wondered how Bretta would handle this scene.

Anneka came over to me in her barely-there mini-skirt, which only European women still fearlessly sported, and gave me her sultry model look, with her hands motioning to dance. Lost in Bretta-thought, I insanely remarked, "Cool party, but I don't think Bretta would like it." Anneka froze as if I had shot her with my missing gun. I saw her pink palm rising, but let it go. Her palm hit my face hard with the *SLAP* for which it was named. It was my turn. I held up my palm to her as she cringed and I gave her a fierce glare. Instead of slapping her, I slapped my own face even harder. Anneka gave me a surprised look and I did it again. She grabbed my hand and cried, "Crazy Americans!" and stamped away. I tasted the salt of blood, and there in that place with that music, it tasted perfect. Maybe THIS was what it was all about. I felt like sticking safety pins through *my* face. Pain and punk and fuck it. I screamed, "Fuck it all!"

The band segued into a cover of "Down By the River." The intense-eyed guitarist led off in normal time, and the band kicked in at double-time, and at mid-song to triple time. Bruce stretched or repeated phrasing, keeping with the furious rhythm for an even louder, hardcore, bass thumping, drum banging and guitar grinding. "This much maaaadness, is too much sorrow, too much, too much, too much."

I thought of poor Doc. Too much.

For the climax, the band stopped for the guitarist to screech his sliding pick in a full guitar-neck-distortion buildup as Bruce climbed onto the Ampeg bass cab, wrapped the mic cord around his upper arm, and screamed a cappella, "I shot my! I shot my! I shot my ....
... ... fuckin' baa-beeeee!" while pantomiming shooting up, to

complete the double entendre, emulating Lou Reed's live *Heroin.*
The drummer struck a rim-shot on his tom with a final BANG and
Bruce fell off the amp into some waiting moshers. Everyone yowled
and yelled.

It was an impressive triple-decibel near-pain-threshold set. I
despaired; I should shoot myself. Red Assfault was even more hardcore than the Dead Kennedys. This is what The Razors have to compete with? Nonetheless, I bolted over to congratulate Red Assfault
and the singer on the rousing last song, a Neil Young cover. As the
group stowed their gear, I spoke to Bruce. His rough, pierced, tattooed look belied his open, hyper-friendliness. I told him, "You guys
are gnarly. How is the gigging going?"

He was rank with sweat and responded in an already hoarse
voice, "We're gigging so much but there's still no money. I mean
look at this dump!" He motioned around. He lifted a booted foot.
"See these Doc Martens. Not! These are the cheap-ass work boots I
bought from the Mexican shoe store and dyed black because I can't
afford the real ones. Those big Altecs? Fell off a truck, if you know
what I mean."

"So what are we supposed to do?"

"I'm going to do what I do no matter what happens with the
money or the band, man. I used to not give a shit about most things.
Now I don't give a shit about anything." He slurped from a beer bottle, and nonchalantly spit out a cigarette butt. "Except for that." He
laughed, and grabbed a cup from the hand of a passing partier.

"Look," I said, "I'm maybe not a real punker but my band, The
Razors, is trying to make the local music scene with original songs.
What do you think?"

Still buzzed from his performance, he spoke rapid-fire, "Punk is
definitely where it's at right now. Don't worry, a lot of the acts are
just that, acts. Playing poseur punk is all right, because it does lead to
harder stuff, you know. Everyone is just tired of the corporate and label rip-off bullshit, you know, and just have a good time. Besides,
you're not a poseur. I can tell you're a scrapper. I say you're as much
street punk as any fuckin' body here." He splashed his cup of beer in
all directions for emphasis.

"But Dirk Dirksen acted like a dick to us at the Mab."

"Look at the fuckups he's dealing with. Dirk acts like a dick on
stage, but that's mostly showbiz, cuz he knows, a lot of the audience
are just *Rocky Horror* 'let's dress up like punks for the night' types.

He's anointed as the 'Pope of Punk' so he plays the part, too." He lowered his voice. "I bet you didn't know that his uncle was Senate Minority Leader Everett Dirksen. Republican. So, he came out of that background."

"You're kidding." Late Senator Dirksen was from Illinois, so I knew about him. He had been very pro-Vietnam War.

"Anyway, I could talk to Dirk, if you wanted to play there again. Just for, you know, the experience, until you can get your own thing going." He glanced at the entry. "You want punks? Here comes the real fuckin' deal."

A latecomer group of mean-looking punks and two fishnet-leggy, spiked-dyed-haired, raccoon-eyed, nose-pierced, weirdly-sexy girls walked in and yelled at him. One guy chest-banged him and I thought a fight was imminent. The lithesome teenage girl with the riveted leather skirt and exposed vinyl garter's holding torn stockings, kept staring at me and slipped a pierced tongue out. Her pouty lips grinned teeth like she wanted to bite my neck, or something else. I spotted her dog collar; she had recognized me first, the girl from the Mab. The lead punk wrapped an arm around Bruce's head, and I was about to intervene when the punk merely whispered to him, and they all headed to the back together. The girl stomped away with them, looking back at me. I asked a saucer-eyed partier about the newcomers.

"They're from Flippur, and a couple of dudes from The Mute Ants, and some groupies, I guess. Something about a chick in a dog collar—I about creamed my jeans. She sure checked you out. They just gigged down the street at The Deaf Club. You've played there, right?"

The party intensified. The huge Altec Lansing speakers were cranked up with a mix of local punk music. I went looking for Winston and Anneka who had disappeared. In the back was a group surrounding a big box that was making weird noises. The box was a scuffed-up Pac-Man console with the coin box hanging open. Since the thing had just been released, it had unquestionably been ripped off. Pac-Man was like a yellow sun, with a missing piece. It spent the entire game chasing and being chased around the maze. I muttered, "We're all fucking Pac-Man."

I noticed some steep plywood stairs and climbed up to the little loft above, still looking for Anneka. An odor of burnt matches hung in the air. Cloistered in the rank, cluttered candlelit room were

Bruce, his bassist, some of the other bands' members who had come, and the two skinny groupies, all sitting on two double stacks of bare, worn mattresses. No Anneka. Dog collar girl gave me no recognition. Some saw me come in but didn't care. No coitus interruptus for a sacrament that far along.

It was a type of ritual. I saw six arms strapped up at once using skinny ties or surgical tubing, some hand spanking of the veins, the syringes being tapped or slid in, and heard muttered swear words. They "registered," the plungers being pulled back slightly so the little droplet of red blood crept into the syringes, straps off, and they slowly injected it all home. Two of the figures jacked off the injected needle's plunger, drug-and-blood mixture repeatedly clouding and swirling in and out, prolonging the act, until the syringe was almost all blood. The ultimate substitute masturbation. I felt like a voyeur to a profane, yet sacred, sexual encounter. The process—foreplay to the climax before the entire body's orgasm. For the group—a kind of orgy.

They emitted little moans and "ahhhs." I assumed it was smack, or maybe speed and smack mixed into a speedball, coke being too pricey for the mix. Probably they had already been up earlier, and now were going completely the other direction. Bruce raised his hand and motioned me in. He mumbled, "Hey, Jack, you want to get down?" The others paid no attention as they fiddled with their works, leaned back, or stared vacantly.

Yes, it was junk, horse, H—the high of musicians for fifty years. Hell, even Monty was doing it. This was my chance to join the big leagues of hard-core punk rock. I was being welcomed into the eye of the storm, to the eye of the needle, the veritable lions' den of iniquity.

Fascinated, I said, "Why not." I had done everything else. It might be just what I needed right now. I stepped forward.

I stiffened. "No, man, you know, I'm good, I'm already trippin'. Enjoy." I backed away. I was lying. Enjoy? Jesus. What a lame thing to say.

Guys and these sexy young chicks on the mattress, and they would rather do drugs than have sex? It made me wonder if the musical lifestyle was worth it. I realized that it was not in me to be a punk rocker, even for musical success. If I did that, it would be worse than selling out to the Financial District. It would be undoubtedly worse for my health. Maybe I should have said "Give my regards to Sid

Vicious," since he just had ODed last year. And the girl, the teenage girl—what was I supposed to do? Carry her away like I was a fireman rescuing her from a burning building? Suck the smack out of her vein like poison from a snake bite? I ran away. Do I always run when a woman needs me? Is that what Duzinella sensed when she "interviewed" me? I reluctantly admitted to myself that I was more comfortable and happier with the normal crowd at the brewery party. In San Francisco there were numerous choices of lifestyle. If one desired anarchistic and anything goes, hard-core punk was the road. Or, at least a back alley.

I found Winston and Anneka very relaxed and a little too close on a broken wing back chair in the corner. Anneka was sweeping back her hair, and Winston fitted a beret to her head. Both had glazed eyes. I wondered if they had been upstairs. When I approached they turned serious-faced. Anneka poked Winston and he slowly said, "Jack. Jack, I'm afraid I have some bad news for you."

I just stood there. Winston was clearly uncomfortable as he continued, "Anneka and I are in...involved. Sorry, man."

Anneka slurred, "We're in love, you mean. We are sorry, Jack, but Winston and I must move out and start a life together."

This was conspicuously pre-planned. It hit me harder that her slap to my face. I flung my cup of beer on them, then stormed out to the street. Stunned, I wandered past the partiers and up the dark sidewalk. It was a heartbreaking double betrayal. I muttered a paraphrase from the *Airplane!* movie Anneka and I had seen. "It looks like I picked the wrong day to give up heroin."

"Hold up, Jack." Winston followed me.

I stepped up to him, in a defensive-yet-offensive-ready position, arms crossed protecting my solar plexus and chin, yet able to snap a disabling chop with either hand. He backed away, stumbled. "Whoa, Jack, don't hit me. I just want to talk."

"Talk what, backstabber?"

"I told you I'd tell you, so I'm going to tell you."

"You just did. Oh, NOW, the hotel thing?"

"Yes. How I lost it? You heard that I might have done it, or...?"

Winston's green eyes stared into me. I retorted, "Yeah, that's bullshit, right? Who did it Winston, who would do such a thing to you? That's crazy."

He put up his palms, and made an inch sign with one. "I was this close—this close—to marrying the elusive Bretta, Jack. Closer than any man, and you know how many have wanted to— all of them. I was a few hourglasses away from having the woman of my dreams, my Cowgirl in the Sand."

My eyes acknowledged Winston's meaning. I recited, "'When so many love you, is it the same?' And?"

"And then it was all gone. Gone like a beautiful dream that you can't remember, though you try and try. Bretta dumped me, it all went south. I did too many drugs that night—speedballs, opium, mescaline. You know, the usual." Winston laughed and went on in a TV commercial's voice, "But wait. There's more. I even got a black-market bottle of absinthe from the dirty liquor store."

"Isn't that shit supposed to make you go crazy?"

"I did go crazy. I was crazy. I was supposed to have died. Not live this way. Live with this—this grotesque embarrassment."

"What the fuck, Winston, what did you do?'

Winston whipped out his large folding knife, quickly opened by the holster. He held it up in front of my face. It was my turn to step back. "I missed Bretta so much. You know how she gets into you. She's so fucking good, she's addictive. She is sugary candy and smack and sex and magic and music and love and..."

I continued, "...and pinball and motorcycling and a fairy angel all mixed into one gorgeous..."

Winston put on the capper, "...devil in disguise of fucking Eve."

"I know. Winston, I know."

"I was planning on jumping, you know. I had the room, I had the window open. I was straddling the sill. But I was a pussy. I couldn't do it. I just couldn't. And then I didn't want to. I wanted to try to get her back. I started thinking about Bretta and I started whacking off—and I thought if I wasn't man enough to kill myself, then I wasn't really a man, and I didn't deserve to be a man. And—I pulled out my knife, the same as this one, in fact, and I just—I whacked off my whole fucking hard-on."

He jammed the knife into the wall. He left it there. I felt nauseated and gasped, "Oh, fuck."

"Yeah, well, it's really gone. It's Hell on earth." I couldn't think of a thing to say. He spoke earnestly, "At least I didn't wrap my cock in cloth and present it to her as a gift." He tugged on his ear. I took a breath and half turned away as Winston continued. "I was actually going to do that, you know? But I bled so much I went unconscious. And I fell."

"That is really sick, Winston. It's too weird. It's too much like my own father..."

"Jack, it's fine. See, I'm fine. It is what it is. Now I have to take the woman that will have Frankenstein's fucking monster. Sorry, Jack. Even if I have to take her from you." He limped away, with the knife jutting out of the wall at an obscene angle.

I tried to collect myself and leaned back against the brick wall. I had wanted to know; now I fucking knew. It was horrible, but that was that. I could move on. I thought back to Winston and our tour of San Francisco and sitting outside the real fake Houdini mansion. Winston had pulled a Houdini on everyone. His whole macabre mutilation saga was classic misdirection.

#

Winston and I were now best ex-friends. After the breakup with Bretta and the whole Winston thing, I hit a new low. Nick consoled me with, "Look, I know you had the hots for Anneka, but it was plain you were not in love. I saw what you were like in love. You do know how much Anneka looks like Bretta, right? No wonder Winston wanted to poach her."

"Was I that much in denial? Was Anneka really our doppelganger for Bretta?'

Nick continued. "Don't hate her. Thank her. Anneka did you a favor by getting him out of your life. He would have turned you into a goddamn drug addict."

It was like a déjà vu revelation from my pinball episode. Perhaps that's how life works— that you have to get a bad in order to get a good. And if you have too much good, you get a bad to wake your ass up. I became more depressed. Soon, Winston performed the big disappearing act—with his lovely assistant Anneka, he went springing and spinning to Amsterdam—land of the truly lost. I had a bad feeling about their whole sordid affair.

CHAPTER 30

My life was resuming, meaning I almost had Bretta out of my mind, and I was over the worst aches about Anneka, and the betrayal by my buddy, my pal, my good friend Winston.

I bounded on the streetcar, inside that is, and went to the Café Flore for a bite to eat. Seeing the great visage of Kar-mi, after what Monty had told me, made me more unsettled now than thrilled. Was everything an illusion? Did humans need illusion to survive? I didn't. After all I'd been through, I had a very realistic and disillusioned view of the world.

It was an off time at the café, and I had a choice of tables. To prove the betrayal didn't bother me, or perhaps because I was a mas-ochist, I sat at the same corner patio table Winston and I had sat on boy's night out. I thought of that crazy-wild night and how my jeal-ousy of Winston had changed to friendship. Now the jealousy was back. My gut feeling about him had been right after all. I also flashed on my paranoia that night, how I wondered if my uncle would show up. The paranoia had amounted to just that. On Noe Street, a car alarm abruptly pulsed, a new disturbance to city life.

I settled into my eggs Florentine when someone said, "They make pretty good Florentine here. Mind if I join you?"

I looked up to see Uncle, and almost choked on the spinach. I jumped up as he stiffly sat across the table with hands up. "Relax, Jack, relax. Nothin's gonna' happen. I know you're good with your feet, so I'm sitting down before you use them."

He was in the same dark, pin-striped-suit I had seen at the cathe-dral. His nose had been broken once, flattened really. He placed a North Beach shopping bag on a chair. He kept his broad hat on. "U-uncle?" I stuttered.

He chuckled gruffly as he smoothed his large mustache. "Now, that would be a good trick. No, we spent a lot of time together, so you know… I've heard I look like him. Raymond had a lot of style. He gave me my moniker, 'The Joker.'"

"What—what do you want?"

"Sit down, kid, and maybe I'll tell you."

Examining him more closely, I saw he had the similar Italian looks and was of the same age as Uncle, now ten-years aged. But this man was more than aged; he'd worn down, like a spring that could snap at any time. I warily sat. He smelled of garlic and stale sweat and something else; his suit needed dry-cleaning.

"I am here on behalf of your Uncle. But don't karate-chop me, I'm just the messenger." The Joker's laugh turned into a cough.

"That's why you're carrying a piece?"

"Nah, can't carry anymore after the 'hard time.' That'd be breaking the law. Just mechanic's tools—a sharpened screwdriver, pliers of course, and a coil of wire."

A garotte wire. "You were in with Unc…Ray?"

The Joker looked annoyed, and ordered, "Espresso with lemon peel," from a passing waitress. "Interrogations give me heartburn, kid. You want to hear what I have to say, or what?"

"I'm not sure."

"Finish your Florentine."

"I lost my appetite."

He scrutinized my food, before locking hard eyes on me until I looked away. The Joker gave me a sly smile. "You are a good-looking young man. I didn't mind tailing you around, I tell you that."

I realized the man's mysterious odor—fear. Not his, others' fear.

He coughed and continued, "I loved Raymond. All he asked of me, at first, was to come out to Frisco, and kinda keep an eye on you. Report back to him how you're doing."

"What did you tell him?"

"I told him your life was a real circus." The Joker laughed. "But, jeez, I thought you were really going to lose it at Saints Peter's & Paul. So, why was that other muscle head following you around there?"

"So, I was right. I don't know."

"I asked the mug, and he got real smart with me. I told him if I caught him following you again, it would be the last time he followed anybody. He asked me why, and I told him, because I would pull his fuckin' eyes out." The Joker grinned. "Ray was more worried about what you were going to do with the pistola. That's why he had me boost it from your pad. You know, the whole 'suicide runs in the family' myth.'"

This sinister eyeball-popping man had been in my apartment. In my bedroom. I shivered. I raised my voice. "God damn you, it about drove me crazy looking for it." A few scattered patrons glanced over at us, and the man gave them a big, reassuring, crooked, stay-the-fuck-out-of-this smile.

The Joker lowered his voice to the prison-yard whisper that is not really a whisper. "Anyways, he had this whole plan, a good plan, to break out of Leavenworth. He knew you wouldn't come to him. He talked about you a lot, Jack. He only wanted to see you one last time. That's all he wanted. Then, whatever happened to him, happened. But the staff doctor turned chicken and pulled the plug on the escape."

He strangled the lemon peel over his demitasse cup with gnarled hands. "Now. Three things, I'm gonna' tell you. I tell you, they're real beauties. So, I'm sorry in advance. You are only going to like one, kind of."

I said nothing.

"Ready?" He stirred his espresso, coughed. "Good thing you're sitting down."

I didn't know if he was trying to be kind or cruel. He was a professional—having cruel fun while befuddling the victim.

"Here's the thing, I'm sorry about your father."

"That was a long time ago."

"There's the rub, Jackie. I mean your *father. Raymond.* He just died recently."

First, I was dumbfounded. Then acid tore through my guts. "No. Wait. You're lying. No way."

The demon seed once planted, grows quickly. Years of repression and of dark fears were being revealed in flickering flashes. Step right up! Come into the booth and peek behind the tattered curtain. See the Freak Show with me, the star freak of Ray's perversions— The Two-Headed Baby.

"No, no, no. Not Ray," I said.

I pushed away from the table and jerked up. He reached under his jacket. I stumbled out to the sidewalk and walked away. I gagged and coughed, almost choked. A crazy notion came to me, to run up to the garaged Camaro and just take off. When The Joker followed me, I would run him over. I would.

He was finishing my Florentine when I sat back down. The Joker smiled, "I wasn't about to chase you down. I've already seen you're a hard one to keep up with. I knew you'd be back."

He had not seen me palm and pocket something from an un-cleared table on the way in. "How?"

"Because you have to know. I ordered you a double Punt e Mes." The icy dark-brown drink was already on my side. I looked at it suspiciously. He moved his bag on the table. The bag was from North Beach's Biordi Art Imports. "This dough is for you. From Raymond, your father that is, if you just sit through this."

I looked at the bag. From watching old movies, I figured twenty-five grand. "I don't want his money."

"Money or morals, the age-old dilemma. Hard to have both. Look, Raymond may have hurt you. And his sister—that is your mother—and well, a lot of other people." The Joker chuckled. "But he was still your father. Consider that he put on that whole 'Uncle' charade to protect you. Imagine you growing up knowing the truth, and not to mention what your hick town would have thought of you."

He laid a hand on a passing waiter's arm to signal for another espresso. "Why is it so forbidden? Why is it wrong to love one's sis-ter? Is it more wrong than what they do around here?" He circled his finger to point toward the Castro. "And Ray was truly in love with her. Within every beauty, lurks a monster. Within every monster—the sublime. Remember your Uncle's artwork collection? He loved his art. But he loved you the best, Jack." He pointed a gun-barrel-of a-finger to my face. "Don't you ever forget that."

Disgusted, I shook my head. First no. But then slowly, almost as if hypnotized, my head moved up and down in agreement. I felt some emotion for the sick bastard. My father. What would cause a man to be this way? Such a sexual drive. Is that what I had inherited from him? But he'd had a mental illness. If I had reported him back then, perhaps he could have gotten help. Maybe some drugs or ther-apy would have brought him back. He did have a good side. I was so confused. Maybe I should have talked to the shrink. Maybe I still should. I absentmindedly took a swig of the Punt e Mes. My tongue curled. Sweet and bitter. I finally said, "But I'm nothing like him. He's a criminal."

The Joker chuckled. "You sure drink like him." He leaned across the table to me, now serious. "Remember, unlike your friends, we know who you really are, what you've done." He enumerated on his fingers. "You started out on B&E of libraries, of all places. You were in the porn business, fucked anything with a hole and a heartbeat, you were in jail, and you kick the shit out of people. Did I miss anything? Oh yeah, I need more fingers. You're a drug dealer, packed some heat, before you, uh, "misplaced" it, you assaulted an officer, and ran from the law. So, drop the choirboy act."

I was silent as I digested his heartwarming grasp of reality.

"I'll take that as an understanding that your nuts don't fall far from the tree. He-he. You know, your Uncle started out as a pusher, too? His gang was the forerunner to the Dixie Mafia. Memphis, Nashville, later East St. Louis were his territories." He picked lint from his lapel. "Anyway, out here in *Sin* Francisco, it was all peace and love. Ha. Hardly. Didn't last, did it? Man has a propensity for violence. I have had a lot of time to think about this, where I've been. See Jack, that's the way a man's made. If a man doesn't hurt something, he'll only end up hurting himself. Even pussified men, like you see around here." He circled his finger again. "They're hurting themselves, right? It's all physics. Physics of testosterone, or something. For example, soldiering was once a highly respectable career. Hunting and killing, that's how men fed their families, expanded their tribe's land. Now, society's trying to castrate us."

I shrugged.

"I know you have it, Jack. You like to hurt people, Jack."

"I do not. I like people."

The Joker lifted and lowered my fork. "Consider this, Jack: you confuse people liking you, for you liking people. You hurt your mother. You beat the shit out of people all the time. You killed your poor girlfriend when you ran into that tree."

"Bullshit. That was a fucking accident."

"Maybe you couldn't help it. Maybe you couldn't help yourself. You do have a propensity for risky behavior." He held up his trigger finger. "You can't deny you tried to kill your own kin in his bed when you were thirteen." He had me there. "And, putting aside the fact that you'd like to hurt me right now, which would be a risky move, I bet you are considering ways to, well, get rid of me."

I tried to hold his eyes, but couldn't, and looked out to the street.

"You're a man, Jack, a real man. So, I know you know what I'm talking about. Your father, your father is, was, very proud of you. About most things, that is." He looked around the nearly empty café to make sure no was listening. "Stay with me now, Jack, cuz' it's going to get more complicated All right? I'm going to lay all my cards on the table."

The Joker rolling up his sleeves with a flourish, and reached, this time slowly, into his jacket pocket. To my surprise, he pulled out a red deck of Bicycle playing cards. Expertly, he cut open the wrapper with a thumbnail, shuffled the cards with capable hands, and fanned them in front of me. Like this was some kind of game. It was. He indicated and I reluctantly picked. It was the Joker.

"My business card." He grinned.

I spun the card onto the table. Joker shot out four more cards face down. He looked at me, as he flipped them over one at a time. "Jack, you, of course. Queen, your mother. The King?"

"Ray." "Right. Who's left?" "My supposed father."

"Here's the card that will really blow your mind." He turned over, not the Ace, but the Tarot's "Hanged Man." With the Bicycle logo back—a trick deck. "The man you thought was your father—his suicide? Remember that? A work of art really. A perfect suicide? Not so much."

My brow furrowed. He cleared a cough and continued, "That's good news, right? Well, mostly. To put it delicately, Raymond gave him a lot of guidance up in that church."

With the King, he flipped the Hanged Man card cartwheeling off the table. I made a grab for it and caught it just above the floor.

I cried, "What the fuck, man." With that card, I had just dropped from the flying trapeze, with no net below, only the ground rushing up, up, up. Like I was still, and the earth was coming to get me. The earth of a grave.

"Impressive reflexes. Look, after seeing your mother's new affair with the Phillips 66 man, your 'father' was going to spill the beans about her and Raymond and you. Maybe more, because there was more. But Raymond said to make sure you understand, even though your 'Daddy' knew all along that he wasn't your real daddy, he still accepted you."

I sat there with my mouth open, stunned. My mind spun like the *Vertigo* spiral. I fingered the handle of the dirty steak knife in my pocket. The one I filched from the un-cleared table.

"Take a drink, kid. Take it easy. I know you don't want to believe it, but I'm here to help. I don't think anybody else around here is going to help you."

I thought I knew what he meant, but I glanced around. He was right, figuratively and literally. Everyone seemed to have vanished. Couldn't blame them, considering our bad vibes.

"You've been running your whole life, but once we're finished here, you can quit running."

Could I do it in one move? It had to be two; I needed to stand to reach his neck. Down into the little triangle under his Adam's apple. No. Wait. Another odor was emanating from The Joker now. A long-forgotten odor. I would have to play *my* cards very carefully from here out. I picked up the drink and downed it. I almost hoped it *was* a Mickey Finn.

"After Ray became Mayor, he got put away for the embezzling, which was no big deal. The tax evasion, different story. We were cellmates. But then, they pulled out the murder rap on the old lady."

"No. Not my mother?"

"No, that was later with her. Oh, you mean? No, no, she's still around. She's like you, you know—family. Raymond had a lot of love for family. Your mother thinks she's hiding out in Florida. Ha. I'm talking 'bout the rich dame, you called your Aunt. He got the death penalty for that one."

"So, he was executed?"

The Joker's face turned into a full grin. "Hell no, Ray wouldn't go for the man putting him down like a dog! Don't you read the papers? A lot of good information in those papers. That's how we found you, even though you changed your name after you got popped in L.A. That tree falling on your girlfriend, and then the funeral—that was what the press calls 'a human-interest story.'"

"OK, OK. How did he die?"

"Raymond figured out a way to give himself a heart attack."

Joker unfolded a news clipping. There "Uncle" was. An older photo of Ray, mayoral looking in top hat: "Heiress Killer, Days before Execution, Suffers Heart Attack." I tried to visualize Ray gasping and dying on his knees in a bare cell, repentant for his crimes, scared and alone.

"Yeah, your pop had it figured right. The screws got him to medical and got him ticking again. And you know? What he did the next day? Even with one wrist handcuffed to the bed, he was able to rape that chicken-shit doctor before he offed his self."

Joker's face filled with admiration. He pushed over the Biordi bag. "Can you imagine?"

Yes, I could.

CHAPTER 31

Thank God for the Niners. The San Francisco Forty Niners invigorated San Francisco like nothing the city had seen. After the maelstrom of murder and havoc of the previous years, football was bringing San Francisco back to life and our City was giddy. And football was bringing me back. Even as a non-sports fan, I caught 49er Fever helping lose my worried mind. The Joker? His revelations? What was a boy to do? I refused to keep dwelling on it. Perhaps "the truth" had set me free.

One evening, I watched the game at my apartment, excited about pro-football for the first time in my life. The Niners were back on a winning streak. This second season with Bill Walsh and Joe Montana looked promising. We had just beaten the Patriots the week before. Tonight's *Monday Night Football* was between the Patriots, and the Dolphins who had beaten us. My ex-apartment manager interrupted the game to phone and tell me, "You have to buy apple stock, right now."

"Where, Cala's Grocery? Petrini's Market?" I asked.

She laughed. "No, Jack, you sweet idiot. Apple Computer. They're going public December twelfth."

I got a second interruption. The doorbell rang. Bretta. I forgot all about buying Apple, which was my first mistake. Bretta radiated desirability and it was almost like seeing her for the first time again in that Kezar parking lot. She hugged me and gave me a tentative kiss. I thought, Jack, don't be a fool. "What are you doing back in town?"

"Oh my, Jack, my movie director friend and I went to the 'Friday Night in San Francisco' concert at the Warfield. I wish Winston could have been there. John McLaughlin, Al Di Meola, Paco de Lucia together—on stage. Monty got us tickets in second row center." I led her into my living room. "The performance was so emotional, I wept. I've missed you terribly, Jack. You've never seen me cry, right?"

I had. A few times. The image of her shimmering pool-chalked golden eyes in tears, hurt me. I said, "No."

"I heard that you've been playing music yourself. Monty says you're a zealous performer. And that you've developed a following."

"Well, I'm not playing the Warfield—but I've found my fourth dimension we were looking for."

"That's marvelous, Jack. Oh, after the show, I split up from my director friend." She looked at me closely for an indication. "He didn't even like the music."

It all felt so good, except Bretta provoked feelings I didn't want. I didn't know what to think or feel, or what I wanted. My mind knotted and my guts churned as my face remained passive. I formed a non-committal, "Oh? You all right?"

"Fine. Those directors are zanier than me." My eyes rolled before they wandered back to the football game. Bretta surprised me by plopping onto the couch to watch. When I looked at her askew, she huffed, "I do have a brother and a dad, you know. Viva Patriots."

As we relaxed together, Howard Cosell's reassuring staccato voice announced the plays. It was a little after eight. She asked for a drink. I said, let's not drink tonight, and offered Earl Grey tea instead. I just had the kettle on the boil and was pulling out cups when we heard...

(**Cosell**:) ...but (the game)'s suddenly been placed in total perspective for us; I'll finish this, they're in the hurry-up offense. (**Gifford**:) Third down, four. Foreman...it'll be fourth down. Cavanaugh will let it run down for one final attempt, he'll let the seconds tick off to give Miami no opportunity whatsoever. (whistle blows) Timeout is called with three seconds remaining; John Smith is on the line. And I don't care what's on the line, Howard—you have got to say what we know in the booth. (**Cosell**:) Yes, we have to say it. Remember this is just a football game, no matter who wins or loses. An unspeakable tragedy confirmed to us by ABC News in New York City: John Lennon, outside of his apartment building on the West Side of New York City. The most famous perhaps, of all of The Beatles, shot twice in the back, rushed to Roosevelt Hospital, dead on arrival.

The whistle of the kettle. I ignored it. Bretta, called, "Jack!" I ran into the living room to stare at the TV.

(**Cosell**:) Hard to go back to the game after that news flash, which, in duty bound, we have to take.

"Oh, no, no, no, no, no!" I wailed. Bretta's face fell.

(**Cosell:**) John Lennon had just been shot in New York. He was just outside his apartment —coming home.

I felt like I'd been shot. I dropped to my knees. Why? He was one of the most creative musical forces on Earth. He was only forty. We were stunned. How could this happen? It was an end to our time. Now I needed a drink. I slammed a beer in the kitchen. I felt closed in on, claustrophobic. I took a swig from my gin bottle. I needed to get out of there, get Bretta away from my apartment so I would not be tempted. I wanted Bretta although I did not want to go down that road again. I already had a bad feeling about all of this. I took a longer swig from the bottle. About Lennon getting murdered in front of his own home. About tonight. About Bretta.

I recalled my promise to take Bretta to Persian Aub Zam Zam. I impressed her by oiling and brushing my hair back behind my ears, and donning a sweater with raw-silk sports jacket over. Bretta and I walked up the increasingly littered and dingy-looking Haight Street. As we passed an opened door of Park Bowl bowling alley, the cacophony of pinball machines called to me like a symphony. Again, at Murio's Trophy Room corner bar the urgent bells, flanged hums and alien voices beckoned from "Fireball" and I glimpsed its bright-red Demon cum Superhero graphics. My pulse raced and I felt on edge, sensing that something was about to happen. I continued on with Bretta on my arm.

I warned her. "The owner, Bruno, runs a tight ship. More so than, you know that Chinatown restaurant, where you get chop suey with a side of steaming abuse?"

"Sam Wo's."

"Right. The attitude is part of the appeal. Bruno is particular about his patrons. The game is to not only get into his little oasis, but not get kicked out. Hence, the blazer is a disguise. Bruno believes that I'm respectable."

Out front, I paused at the Islamic arched entry, incongruently Christmas-color tiled, with diminutive minarets above the overhang.

"My ex-neighbor Bino, the one I told you taught me cocktail skills? He was one of the privileged regulars here, who Bruno calls his "Senior Staff Officers." They all have nicknames that Bruno gave them. Bino coached me on protocol, gave me this jacket, and brought me as a guest. Otherwise, the chances that I would have been accepted into this club were slim to none, with Slim being out of town."

"I'd like to meet Bino. Maybe we'll see him?"

"That'd be nice, but he's a family man with a baby girl and a little house in Noe Valley now. His Haight outings are less frequent."

"Well, take me to zeh Cazbah."

I swung a door for Bretta. In the calm, orderly, Moroccan-like interior a few non-regulars, men, sat reverently on the stools before the curving bar as if infidels in a Martini mosque cum library. The Senior Staff Officers, also men, sat at their favored end and were more relaxed. I scanned the group hoping to see Bino, but no luck. Two, I most familiar with, and I exchanged friendly nods. We sat on the other side of the bar, Bretta receiving her usual ogles.

Bruno "greeted" me with a non-curmudgeonly look on his aged, broad, swarthy face, which was, for me, his equivalent to a big, friendly hello. Bruno reigned—white-shirted, black-tied, and vested—as if the maître de of a swanky dinner club.

I gave a low-key introduction of Bretta to the squat and sturdy Bruno. Accomplished at recognizing class, Bruno gave an approving nod to her. Bruno was a treasure. He was "real," confident, frank, and alas, an anachronism—he owned a bar on Haight Street, nevertheless was very conservative, didn't like hippie types, and made instant calls on walk-ins like a tennis judge. "Fault!"

A muscular longhair wandered in behind us, whom I had noted on the sidewalk, possibly to take another look at Bretta's statuesque form. Sure enough, Bruno professionally erected his force field before the hapless man, advising him, "You should try the Trophy Room." The man jolted as if he had hit a wall of ice. Came the coup de gras: "You'll like it *there*."

After the man had floundered backwards out the double doors, the Senior Staff Officers chanted, "And stay out." I waved my hand and whispered, "This is not the bar you are looking for." Bretta suppressed a giggle.

Bretta noted the Moorish arches over the doorways and murmured to me, "This place is like a miniature Sav. Perfect."

"Bookend bars, except this one is owned by a strict librarian."

Some were speaking softly of Lennon's shooting. One of the regulars said, "A friend in New York said after the guy shot him, he just sat there reading *Catcher in the Rye*."

"What a nut," another said.

"Hmm. Rye to die. Two Manhattans, please." I placed my fiver down. Bruno preferred cash on the barrelhead.

Within his large nickeled shaker, his cufflinks flashing, Bruno crafted our artisan Manhattans and poured so fully that the frosted glasses appeared convex, and we had to lip-sip them as they stood—she on the precisely placed, for-ladies-only napkin, as men were served only on the polished bar—before we could raise them.

Bretta elevated her cocktail glass to the bar, "To John." The regulars and I hesitated, looking to Bruno's reaction. Not wanting to leave her hanging, I chimed in, "To John." Bruno lifted his shot glass and the bar toasted.

Bruno followed with, "An early New Year's resolution: Smoke more, drink more, and eat more animal fat. For tomorrow..."

Bruno astonished us all by speaking to Bretta—a lady with a gentleman—and more so by confessing, with his thick Persian accent, "I enjoyed some of the early Beatles songs." Bretta shined, and a murmur of agreement spread. "On the other hand, that Lennon," Bruno continued, "he became...too radical."

The cold whiskey warmth lightened my mood. Not quite an appropriate enough time later I said, "Bruno please, another round." Emboldened I added, as I had heard Bino say, "And perhaps one for yourself?"

He gave an almost imperceptible nod. After mixing ours, Bruno filled his personal shot glass with Jim Beam, we three raised glasses and drank. Bruno threw his back and refilled it from his squat, black deco pitcher for a water chaser. Bretta and I spoke of some things, which I forget. I do remember that Bretta put her cold, sweet and bitter-flavored lips to mine. I was a little afraid of what the no-nonsense Bruno would think, but he seemed to be in an unusually affable mood this evening. Shortly, I said: "Bruno is also the master of Martinis. Bretta, you must try one. May we, Bruno?"

Bruno huffed but acquiesced, reaching for the Boord's gin. He was bending his arcane rule of X (particular patron) divided by Y (behavior) plus or minus Z (Bruno's mood) = number of drinks. He kept serving, with the occasional proffered "one for yourself." With Lennon's death, really the bandied "Beatles Reunion" death, so heavy upon the group, Bruno appeared uncharacteristically empathetic.

Bretta regarded the lush landscape mural behind the bar—a Persian fairytale princess in a yellow dress and her Princely suitor on horseback, possibly a Scheherazade tale. I didn't see a fairytale castle

but the Princess had a red lap. The horses similarly appeared bloody
red on their lowers. Odd. I fixated on the two large hares, which
were not red. Yet. In my mind I blasted them with my childhood
shotgun. I felt a weird chemical tingle and jonesed for my medica-
tion. I elevated my arms in shotgun position to aim at the Prince.

"Jack..."

I thought Bretta was about to critically comment on the mural
from an artist's perspective. Instead, she sprang this upon me: "You
are..." her golden eyes looked deeply into mine "...the only man who
ever left me."

"Besides your father."

She dropped her eyes. "Besides my father."

Oh. I hadn't meant to be so cruel. I tried to add humor. "And
your Ken dolls."

That must have stung more because her eyes flashed. "Jack, can
you just... Let's move to one of the little tables in back."

"He doesn't like it," I prison-whispered. "He calls it 'the horrible
back room.'"

Bretta pulled me away to the back anyway, past the classic
Wurlitzer with only pre-war tunes, where I guided her to a table for
two, not four, attempting at least to follow some of the inexplicable
house rules. She immediately kissed me, which I desultorily returned. She took a Martini sip, found my lips again and stunned me
with an olive secreted in her mouth. With her tongue she pushed the
olive forward as I pushed back, playing olive ball and tongue wres-
tling. With half of the olive in each of our mouths we squeezed and
sucked dirty Martini juice. French-kissing through the olive, she
poked the pimento through to my tongue and I poked back, jacking
off the olive in the most erotic fashion. It was the best damn olive I
ever had. Bretta finally sucked the pimento out and we bit the olive
in half, chewing lips to lips to ellipsis... Bruno eyeballed us, but
Bretta gave him her little-girl-innocent smile, and he surprised me
again, forgiving the breach of decorum by diverting his icy glower to
his vintage brass cash register. Snake-charming Bretta.

I swallowed and told her, "I should not take more than a swallow. I no longer care about being able to read Hemingway and relax
in the evening." I continued misquoting to her, "All the things I enjoyed and have forgotten come back to me when I taste your tongue-
numbing, brain-warming, stomach-pleasing, idea-changing alchemy."

A feeling settled into me, the feeling that Bruno was as familiar with untimely death as I. Deaths of those perhaps he knew under the deposed Shah of Iran. Or just maybe! he was former SAVAK, the Shah's U.S. trained secret police torturers. I felt Bruno's judgmental eyes on me.

Bretta placed her hand on my lap and suggested, "Jack, we should go." My Bruno paranoia parted and I chuckled. I vaguely remember stupidly   trying to order the   absinthe and Bruno shaking his head   "You know the green fairy is illegal."

Just like that   we were on the street and   at the Trophy Room and, "Jack, why are you so thirsty," and   She tried to bring me back to our conversation, which must have been a not a very good one, or perchance stated as a natural progression of the conversation.   "A   G&T for me, and"   she shook her head she quit drinking, said, "Jack, don't get drunk"   and "another Martini, I mean gin and tonic ifyouplease"

Her: "Jack, don't get drunk"   Me: "I want some god damn absinthe"

Bartender considered: his hand drip-dripped water over the sugar cube and the drink became all milky radiation glowing yellow my eyes blurred and flashed on a green No Exit or maybe Exit sign   and I draaank it   and my tongue   tasted all licoricey

Her: "It's Pernod, Jack.   why are you   getting drunk   ?"   "Because this is the day the music died."
          I tried   to order another absinthe, and Bretta led me toward the door   but I stopped   and somehow I was playing "Fireball"   my only   pinball   since Lost and Found …. while Bretta watched me   and the pool players
          The silver ball was like a fix   Red demon red rye   red-rum   I got multi-ball game talking to me   taunting   a burly asshole rubbed himself across Bretta   it was the same damn longhair from earlier   Burly Asshole: "was an accident" so I body-shoved him bang into Fireball   TILT   and he held up a fist   told me "GET out and stay out of the Haight, suit"   I forgot I was wearing my nice jacket and Somebody warned me   "Careful, he's with the

White Panthers" Bretta pushed me outside   and I felt a
punch against my ear and a "ya' better run away, 'suit'"
and   I kicked panther in the chest just as a warning
                and we both stumbled back   off-bal-
ance   and   so drunk   we both backed away
and looked like it was over
        bunch people came out of the bar to watch "Give
peace a chance" but   "Fight! Fight!" won   so asshole grabbed a longneck bottle from his buddy I guess
and broke the bottom against the wall and
        I tore off my jacket and wrapped it around my left
hand like in movies for knife-fight protection
                but faked it cause it would have been useless
                instead snapped a big buttons sleeve
into his eyes   panther yelped   jerked his hand to
his face   panther forgot about the broken bottle
scream   bleeding Bretta screaming   and yelling and
        "Pigs!" a siren whoop-whooped scattering
Bretta pulling me   stumbling away   and
then we did run away, better run run run AWAY Yi yi
yi   And next thing we were   back at
my apartment   she said, Jack, you really hurt
him andI remember putting on John Lennon's "All
You Need is Love"   scraping the needle against the
record into   the French anthem intro   Bretta **calling**
from the bedroom **Jackie stay away from the stereo,**
you'll break it, you big baboon ***but I didn't care***
and I sang **wagh - wagh, wagh, wagh, wagh**   Come
to bed JACK and Bretta pulled me down   I said
STOP   I want to put on a rubber   she sucked me
and I cried OW   you bit me
        she climbed on top I said NO wait   she held my
arms down   NO BRETTA and she gave me a fero-
cious fucking
        I rolled us over and fucked her
        she said   Jack you're hurting me you're too
deep,   I wanted to hurt her because sex was a
weapon and she should know that since she hurt me
        JACK PLEASE she STRUGGLED   I

pulled out   and I rolled her over I reached under
the bed
          for the   necktie   Z.Z.'s "lost" tie from my
party   I   tied   her   wrists tight.   I gripped the
bitch's elbows   like motorcycle bars   or a pinball
game
          I stuck it in like a writhing serpent
          I yelled, Instant karma's going to get you!   We all
shine on!   like the moon and the stars and the
fucking sun
          Mother   Sister   Uncle   Father
               Not my Father
          Not My Father who aren't in Heaven
          I fucked her in the ass   she struggled
          she yelled JACK! FUCK!   You're too
BIG and I said FUCK YOU BRETTA
          he hurt me she hurt me he hurt me she hurt me he
hurt me she hurt me
          Jack SLOW DOWN
          FUCK you fuck YOU fuck you FUCK YOU
          he hurt me she hurt me he hurt me she hurt me
he hurt me she hurt me
          Jack, Easy, easy, that's IT   Yes   YES
               and I probably said something vicious   be-
cause   YOU ASSHOLE
          because   waking up
          I woke UP that   morning and FELT LIKE
SHIT
          because Bretta   had already   left
          All that remained were blood   spots and
               a sickly once-familiar
          brown-red stain on my sheets
          I was headachy   hot   shallow breathing like I
had   sunstroke.
          Because I felt empty.   It was seven oh four
I wrote this down.

          The next day was a fog. My nicest jacket was ruined. If the cops
had caught me...

John was still dead. Maybe the panther asshole from the Trophy Room was dead. Maybe Bretta was dead. Romance was dead. Everyone was dead.

I wished I was dead.

CHAPTER 32

Rocky, the band's ex-bass player, was alive. And lively. She called me to go with her to the Lennon memorial on the Marina Green. I met her there with a group of hollow-eyed mourners with flowers and we all lit candles, sang Lennon songs, trying to fill the emptiness inside. We were filmed for the KRON news, singing, "Give Peace a Chance." A distraught man compared Lennon's murder to the JFK assassination. Rocky and I watched us on the ten o'clock news that night at my pad. She wanted to go to bed with me. I told her, "I just hurt my ex-girlfriend. In bed. I don't trust myself. You shouldn't trust me."

"What'd I fuckin' tell you." She walked out, banging the door.

The next day, a neighbor across the street happened to mention that he had gone to the old Polytechnic High just down the street. With Bruno. So much for my "Ayatollah paranoiah." A few nights later I entered Bruno's to apologize. One step in, he held up a palm and coldly advised me, "You should try the Trophy Room. You'll like it there."

The Boston Boys moved back home to Southie. Too soon after, my apartment manager made a bushel basket of money in Apple stock, bought a black BMW, a golden retriever, and a condo in Sausalito with a hot tub on the dock.

"You are really on a spending spree," I marveled.

"He who dies with the most toys wins," she said with only a half-smile.

She handed me a gold embossed, satin business card from one of her boyfriends, who worked in the Pyramid Building as a headhunter. He was "really bringing home the K." 120K a year. She told me to call him to arrange an interview and if I got a position there, she would invite me over to her new place to celebrate in her hot-tub. She gave me a lingering goodbye kiss and shocked me by offering me her pussy.

I accepted Mr. Boots as my new roommate. The changes and shockers in my life were not over. Apparently Anneka felt remorse, because she phoned one morning from Amsterdam. Through the hum and scratch on her long distance, she said, "I'm sorry Jack. He needed me. He needs me."

"Sorry about the way I—you know, Anneka, the whole Bretta thing, but…"

Anneka shouted, "Bretta, Bretta, Bretta!"

"Ok, Ok, it's over," I said.

"It is never over with her. That fucking bitch! I am sick, sick of her. And you two *boys*. She did it to him, you know?"

I grunted at the obvious, "I know."

"No, I mean she did it. She was at the hotel that night."

"No, they had broken up."

"Ha. Not so easy you find, right? They were both fucked up. It is her fault."

Now I was confused.

"She sat him there on the sill of the window."

I shook my head furiously. "Anneka, what the fuck are you talking about?"

"Something…something went wrong."

"No, no, don't tell me this bullshit! Winston told me what happened. Why would he lie to me?"

"Why do you think?"

I didn't answer, I wouldn't answer.

"Wake up, Jack!" she screamed. "Why you don't want to believe your beautiful butterfly has teeth?"

I slammed the receiver down. What an absurd notion. Complete and utter jealous bullshit. Winston lied to Anneka or Anneka was lying to me. Why? Suddenly, I flashed on that night or day she patted her hand on the kitchen counter and me hopping up, with my pants around my ankles like a trained dog. I imagined Bretta on her knees, Winston falling, falling backwards, Bretta's mouth filled with everything, and then everything but nothing, with so much red everywhere.

#

On my Monday off after a busy Clearance Sale weekend at Guitar Center, I impulsively called up Baskin' Robin at the Gallery. "Hey, let's get together. Go for a motorcycle ride."

She gave a little gasp. "I've never been on a motorcycle."

At her Larkin Street apartment, I sat at the curb and beeped my horn. She came out and looked at my motorcycle. "Oh my, you have a new one. It's so pretty. I mean, ruggedly attractive."

The bent-nail keychain was all that remained of my old Honda. Yes, I had taken the money. I bought a nice used gold-flecked Harley Sportster. This had been the Joker's compelling argument:

"So your father's 'filthy lucre'—you have three choices." Joker held up fingers. "The money. Your moral indignation. Or both, the money and your morals, which you rationalize away, like most people. Don't be a dummy; after all this bullshit you went through, you might as well. And for Chrissakes get a haircut. Buy some nice clothes, maybe a suit."

I rolled my eyes. He continued, "Otherwise, you want it to go to me? And the racetrack, of course."

San Francisco ends and Marin County begins mid-span of the chilly Golden Gate Bridge. We roared across on my motorcycle with Robin's arms wrapped around me awkwardly tight. Robin loved riding my steel horse for the first time and was one exhilarated Sagittarian.

"I can't wait to introduce you to Bosco," she yelled behind my shoulder.

I took the Vista Point exit and climbed the steep grade to stop next to the abandoned artillery bunkers that once guarded the Gate. We were windblown as we drank in the magnificent fog-wafted view of the orange Bridge against San Francisco's white skyline. To the North, beckoned the intoxicating magic of the valleys and mountain of Marin. We were perched between two worlds and I felt naturally high.

Back down the roller coaster hill, we soon turned off at the Mt. Tamalpais exit, to ride out Tennessee Valley's country road, past farms and oak trees. Tennessee—my parents' home state. I surprised Robin by impulsively riding past the stables, around the steel gate, and along the fire road out to the small beach. Vehicles were prohibited, but only a couple of hikers were there to admonish us. For a few moments we just sat on my Harley below the arched red cliff, watching the ocean wave to us, retreat shyly as a child, and rush eagerly, waving to us again.

I doubled back. At the rustic, clapboard Miwok livery stable across from the aging barn and riding ring, Robin led beautiful brown Bosco out of a row of stalls. She literally introduced us and as

I stared at his large Robinesque eyes she saddled up. Flashing back to my circus animal days I suddenly felt like a wild stallion myself, happy and free, and I told her in a Texas drawl, "Boy, howdy, this would be a good ole spot for a hoedown." I hooked her elbow and spun us around in a square dance, kicking up dust while now, Bosco stared. Realizing that I was dancing with my ex-girlfriend's best friend, I dropped her arm.

"Well, ready to mount up?" Robin switched our "driver" roles and took me on a two-up trail ride on her Bosco. The trail ascended, sharply zig-zagging past manzanita and fennel, and soon across a couple of muddy creeks.

"You know, I'm thinking about finally finishing up to get my teaching certificate. I'd like to teach art."

Before I could respond, a guy on an old paperboy bicycle breezed down toward us, fishtailed to a slower pace, gave a grin, and went wide around our horse.

"What the... That looks like fun. He's riding it enduro style, like a dirt bike without a motor," I said in wonder.

"That's one of the Charlie's, Cunningham or Kelly, I get them mixed up, on what they call a mountain bike. They've made it a big thing now."

"Cool. I want one." I said. The scent of freshly washed hair swathed me and I nuzzled into Robin's chocolaty sweetness, innocence and purity. I sang across the valley, "De do do do, de da da da, is all I want to say to you. De do do do, de da da da..." Robin harmonized with me in a crystal voice. "...Their innocence will pull me through. De do do do, de da da da, is all I want to say to you."

Robin's spontaneity and musicality resonated within me. Something else happened I never saw coming. Crammed against her bouncing rear, my involuntary hardness rose against Robin. She shivered making Bosco startle. Robin laughed, saying, "We'd better get Bosco back to the old barn."

The barn with straw, alfalfa and ammonia odors stirred memories of my teenage circus days. There, on a horse blanket in the hay-filed loft, she pulled me down, stroked my face, and gave me a ride. She smelled almost like a child. I was brought back. Back to my own short childhood. Back to my beagle, Mootsie; my "father" tucking me into my own little bed with chocolaty ponies on my flannel sheets, and so many many things. Memories I had lost and thought I would never find again. And there they were. My eyes teared up and

I held her tight. Robin's tenderness enveloped me and I could not help feel stirrings of emotion for this woman I had long neglected. As we lay there, Robin chewed on a piece of hay and kept looking into my eyes. I asked her, "What are you looking for?"

"Oh Jack," she whispered, "if you only knew what I can see." She tossed the hay and asked, "Jack, would you like to see—my poetry, sometime?"

"I think I just did." I felt bad; I didn't even know she was a writer. There were apparently a lot of things I didn't know about this woman.

Robin sighed. "Wouldn't it be marvelous to get out of the City and away from everything and everybody, maybe just live here in Mill Valley?"

#

Back in the City, I dropped Robin off at the Galleria Di Belle Arti. In the storefront window, next to one of Bretta's largest pieces, which the owner purchased, hung a new piece. It was a modern collage of alternative varying reds and other opulent colors in semi-geometric contours. Occasionally rising to the surface were thicker vague forms, reminiscent of shapes one might imagine in shifting clouds, which gave the collage more of a 3D effect.

"Wow. That's beautiful."

"Thank you. It's one of mine."

"What? Really? Robin, I love it."

The sun, just retired, reflected the silvery magic-hour sheen of Maxfield Parrish onto our faces. Robin recited her poetry, "Opiate my senses from obsession and desire, through your smile-swirled day, and on to shadowed dusk."

I kissed Robin a lingering goodbye. This moment, tinted in the diffused two-tone light, seemed to embody the magic and spirit of boundless possibility; no need for the dazzling sun to perceive what is essential.

I returned to my Haight Ashbury apartment in an exhilarated mood. Robin, who we all thought so delightfully different, was turning out to be the most stable out of the entourage. Chuckling at my inadvertent pun I opened my apartment's brass mailbox. Amidst the bills, a postcard. On it, the artist Kolar's collage of a woman's lovely dark eye circled by a ring of musical notes and surrounded by a spiraling vortex of probably Czech words. Stickers and stamps marked "luchtpost par avion" and "Klantenservice" told me that it was a card from Anneka and Winston. I sat down on my front steps. I read, "Dearest love, again with deepest apology—please do forgive me my leaving you. I was swept up." I felt somewhat better and a smile came to my face. I read further, "Winston just told me he considers you his best friend and asks forgiveness, also. He has been gigging at cafés and told me how much he now loves life here with me."

The ink changed and her writing became more cramped. I read her real news: "Winston left two days ago to hock his guitar for rent money. He used our money to buy one last hit. Winston was found in Needle Park this morning. He's gone."

I dropped the card as if shocked with its current. This is the end, my only friend, the end. Winston had rolleddownthedrain. Game Over.

Nick had been right about Winston. Monty had been right. Which made me wrong. I looked up at the weird wispy fingers of clouds overhead. Was God's hand reaching out? I thought back to Z.Z. and our conversations about suffering artists. Was it a fair trade for someone so brilliant, so talented as Winston, to be so demonized? To be inexorably sucked into the creative vortex, swirling into the black hole? The sunlight clouded over. I never replied to Anneka to thank her for her sacrifice, but I did thank God.

I thought of Doc for the first time in a while. It came to me like a flash. Oh, man. I thought about this crazy life we were living in this crazy, whatever-turns-you-on time. How far is too far? How much is too much? How fast is too fast? How much can one love before they go past the point of no return? When someone gets badly hurt or dies. You never know the edge until you fall.

I walked slowly upstairs to my green-pastel-tiled bath and looked into the beveled mirror. I appeared older. I thought back to what Winston had said about sniffing glue. Through the looking glass I could see Winston, walking dreamily through a green park, stepping up to the dark gauzy veil and pulling it aside. He smiled, reaching, reaching, stretching his fingertips, only to fall forward in slow motion. I thought, I guess you've finally found it, buddy. I opened the cabinet and examined the razor and blades. I kneeled and pulled out my wooden stash box hidden under the tub. Pills, pow-ders, and buds. I filled a glass with water. So many choices—mostly bad ones. I poured some pills into my palm.

I dumped them into the toilet. I took my last emergency bottle of Valium and slowly dumped it, too. Followed by the contents of my stash box. I flushed and I flushed and I flushed. The drugs went spiraling reluctantly down, down into the toilet's dark-eyed vortex. I slid down the bathroom wall to the tiled floor, where I sat holding my face. I thought of my mother. Was she a drug addict like Winston? My "uncle" had probably addicted Mother to control her. At that moment, I forgave her. I forgave my mother. It felt like ten years of emotional acid was released.

#

The Joker knew many things that I did not know. I knew something the Joker did not know. I too, had a Joker up my sleeve. I knew that there was no such person as the Joker. The Joker was an alias, an alter ego, a Dr. Jekyll, The Joker was really Ray, my uncle. The smell, the smell. I figured it out before I downed the drink. Ray knew his confessions through the Joker would be more palatable to me. And less confrontational. The Ten-Year Reunion of Father from Hell and The Two-Headed Baby was a smash success.

I had less to worry about now. I knew Ray wouldn't stick around San Francisco. He couldn't know for sure whether I would drop a dime on "the Joker." I took Ray's suggestion and researched the newspapers in the Main Library. The older papers were on microfiche. Uncle had been put away in Stateville, up in Joliet. Ray was not one of the Blues Brothers. *Chicago Tribune*: "Suicidal Convict Kills Doctor." He had not killed himself. Again. He had escaped. "Murderer at Large." *Reno Gazette*: "Escaped Convict Reported in Kentucky." A body matching Ray's description was found. "Head, Hands Missing from New Jersey Corpse." "Decapitated Corpse Suspected to be Escaped Convict." "Underworld Suspected of Taking Care of Their Own." "Escaped Convict Presumed Dead." Perhaps the authorities pretended that he was "Presumed Dead" to see if Ray become careless, slip up. The fact remained: Ray was not dead. Ray was X Ray; X Ray was the Joker; the Joker had made me an offer that I could not refuse.

#

Bretta called the next Sunday morning to let me know she was coming over. The doorbell rang. I went downstairs to meet her on the steps. Bretta looked pale and tired, her glow diminished. Her jacket was missing a button. She stared. "You cut off your curls." I had cut my hair to a short length. "You look handsome. Very professional."

"I'm still getting used to it." I acted nonchalant, but after ten years of having long hair, it was a big deal.

"Jack, Z.Z. told me you heard about Winston."

We hugged for a while and she said, "Winston lived so passionately. But he was a tragic soul."

I thought back. "He reminded me of a sad clown in the circus. He kept pulling flowers for you out of sleeve."

"Yes. Poor Winston. I believe he did have a gypsy curse. I tried to help him, but..." She sighed. "Once, I let him stay at my flat while I was away for a week, to 'clean up.' I came back early and looked up at my windows...he had blacked out every window. Every window."

"What the hell?"

"Winston and his *friend,* whom he called "the man who knows all there is to know about drugs," just stayed in my place the whole-time, doing drugs. They had painted my art paper black and taped to over the bays, and every window. They were like animals...living in a cave. Literally on the floor. The place was an utter mess. That's when I trundled him off to rehab."

"Jesus." I shook my head. "Speaking of which, I'm sorry about, you know, getting so drunk, and...did I hurt you?"

"I'm all right, my drunken angel. I've been fucked before." She stared me down.

"Yeah?" I didn't blink. "So have I."

Bretta clutched my hand. "Look. I'm sorry about everything, Jack...everything getting so...complicated."

Now she's sorry? "Our complications... have been fascinating."

"It's the drinking, Jack." She held me. "I'm trying to stop. I'm really trying."

"That's good, my drunken Princess. After Winston...I flushed down all my drugs."

We searched one another's eyes as if looking for lies. Bretta broke the silence. "One day at a time, right? But what are we going to do, Jack?"

"I don't know." I knew she meant the capital "What," but I responded in the lowercase. I suggested, "Let's go do something normal."

"What do you mean?"

"Let's do something real. Like real people, like real friends. Like no drinking."

"Let's go to the Park."

We strolled past Golden Gate Park's Conservatory of Flowers and reminisced about our *Shogun* watching days. So, we continued to the Japanese Tea Garden. There we climbed up the severely vertical, arched wooden footbridge and paused at the pinnacle. We watched the salmon-sized coy, orange and white in their little ponds, drifting with the illusion of freedom.

On the tea deck, we savored little pots of green tea and almond cookies and spoke fractured Japanese. From a new Moroccan shoulder bag, Bretta showed me some brushes and drawing pens she had just purchased at Mendel's. She glowed and I felt happy. Like the old magic was coming back.

I suggested we go next door to the imposing Asian Art Museum, to continue our old theme. Bretta preferred to go across the Concourse to the Academy of Science. We entered the African Diorama Hall and looked at still life with water buffalo. The dead stuffed animals and dead plants were impressively lifelike. In front of the wildebeest, Bretta kissed me slowly and spoke using her lilting, child-like voice, "Let's hide under Kilimanjaro and make love."

A couple and their excited young son passed by. The boy clasped a stuffed lion to his heart. My voice cracked, "Hi there, buddy." He gave a dimpled grin. Bretta didn't seem to notice. I said to her, perhaps roughly, "It's too soon."

Bretta appeared upset. I should have told her the truth. Then, maybe I never really had.

She stepped back and intently contemplated the diorama. "A sculptor friend—his pieces are very dynamic—has asked me to do an opening with him this summer in Manhattan," she said. "I need to work out my theme."

A tall black man wandered by. Bretta followed his handsome reflection in the glass. His appearance was authentic enough for him to be mounted in the diorama, under Mount Kilimanjaro.

"Jack, remember... "Bretta spoke softly "...when we first got together and played house? I wondered from the start if we could be good together."

I restlessly glanced on to the next display. Bretta slipped an artist's brush from her bag and idly fingered the fine dark camel hair bristles. I looked deep into Bretta's golden eyes.

"We were. Damn good together."

THE END

ACKNOWLEDGMENTS

I gratefully acknowledge the following people for their early literary support, suggestions, and corrections of recollections of times gone by: Perry King, muse, fine-tuner, and Perry-White-tough editor. Louis B. Jones, for early draft praise and encouraging the backstory brought more to the fore; Catherine Coulter, "your hero needs more likeability;" Lisa Kent, fellow North Beach aficionado, "Lost and Found" from back in the day; Jane Miller for suggesting Pat Conroy seasoning; Caroline Pierce; Carolyn Adams; fellow Literary Salonist Christie Nelson; Amory Willis; Ken Shabino—Bruno's "Senior Staff Officer;" Jeb Harrison, and others. Of course, to the Man himself, wellspring in some fashion to aspiring literary writers everywhere.

Hemingway, Harold Loeb, Lady Duff Twysden
Hadley Hemingway, Donald Ogden, Pat Guthrie,
Pamplona 1925.

Discography of Music Credits

We are grateful for the musicians' lyrics, melodies, memories, moods, and inspirations essential to the writing of this novel. This is not necessarily a complete list, and a few Easter Eggs are nested.

Boogie Woogie Bugle Boy	Andrew Sisters
Brass in Pocket	Pretenders
London Calling	The Clash
Al Di Meola	Mediterranean Sundance
Le Vie en Rose	Piaf
She Belongs to Me	Bob Dylan
Evil Ways	Santana
Won't Get Fooled Again	The Who
I Feel Like I'm Fixin' to Die Rag	Country Joe and the Fish
The End	Doors
Longer Boats	Cat Stevens
Money, Money	Ebb, Kandor from Cabaret
Friday on My Mind	David Bowie's cover/Easybeats)
Sunshine Superman	Donovan
Get Together	The Youngbloods/Chet Powers
Rock n' Roll	Lou Reed
Downtown	Petula Clark
(I Can't Get No) Satisfaction	Devo's cover/Rolling Stones
California, uber alles!	Dead Kennedys
Down by the River	Neil Young
Boulevard of Broken Dreams	J. Macon King original
I Will Follow	U2
California, uber alles	Dead Kennedys
Heroin	Lou Reed
De Do Do Do, De Da Da Da	Police

Played or referred to:

	Ten Years After
Season of the Witch	Donovan
Break on Through…	The Doors
Somebody to Love	Jefferson Airplane
Bad Girls	Donna Summer

Hotel California	The Eagles
Black Magic Woman	Santâna
Take Me to the River	Talking Heads cover/Al Green
Those Were the Days	Mary Hopkin

Musicians: Devo, Elvis Costello, Talking Heads, Lene Lovich, Romeo Void, Peter Tosh, Bob Marley, Pretenders, Beautiful Day

One Step Beyond	Madness
Lust for Life	Iggy Pop
Take Five	Dave Brubeck
George Harrison	While My Guitar Gently Weeps
George Harrison	Here Comes the Sun
Layla	Eric Clapton
Freebird	Lennard Skynnard

If You Got the Money, I Got the Time - Willie Nelson

Pinball Wizard	The Who
Georgia on My Mind	Ray Charles
Fooled Around and Fell in Love	Elvin Bishop
Hellbound Train	Savoy Brown
Behind Blue Eyes	The Who

Sometimes I Feel Like a Motherless Child-R. Havens

Don't Let the Stars Get in Your Eyes- Ray Price

Can't you Hear Me Knockin'?	Rolling Stones
Sunshine Superman	Donovan
Are You Experienced?	Jimi Hendrix
Love is the Drug	Bryan Ferry
Down by the River	Neil Young
Like a Hurricane	Neil Young

Bewitched, Bothered and Bewildered -Joni Mitchell

Illegal Smile	John Prine
Dazed and Confused	Led Zeppelin
Concierto de Aranjuez, 2 adagio	Joaquin Rodrigo
Give Peace a Chance	John Lennon

Howard Cosell's Lennon death announcement courtesy of ABC News.

v 7.96

Made in the USA
Las Vegas, NV
27 December 2020

14780169R00208